Chasing Down
The Night

Book Three – Crater Lake Series

Also by Francis Guenette

Disappearing in Plain Sight – Book One of the Crater Lake Series
(2013)

The Light Never Lies – Book Two of the Crater Lake Series
(2014)

Strands of Sorrow, Threads of Hope: A Book of Short Stories
(2014)

Chasing Down
The Night

Book Three – Crater Lake Series

FRANCIS L. GUENETTE

HUCKLEBERRY
HAVEN
PUBLISHING

Author's note: This book is a work of fiction. Names, characters, places and incidents either are the product of the author's imagination or are used fictitiously and any resemblance to actual persons living or dead, events, or locales is entirely coincidental.

ISBN
978-0-9920770-8-2 (Softcover)
978-0-9920770-9-9 (Kindle)
978-0-9940664-0-4 (epub)

Cover Photos: Fr. Charles Brandt & Bruce Witzel
Cover Design: Bruce Witzel

Huckleberry Haven Publishing
Box 309
Port Alice, BC
V0N 2N0
disappearinginplainsight.com

For my brother: Tony Leo Guenette. 1959-1993
You left us far too soon.
It is that simple and that sad.

ONE

T he minivan turned onto the gravel road and bumped along until it came to a large sign that showed a map of Crater Lake. This has to be good enough, the man told himself. The drive had been a nerve-wracking three hours of hoping he wouldn't get stopped for any reason and enduring the sounds that came from the back of the vehicle. He had done most of the trip with the windows wide open to the rain and wind because of the unbelievable stench. He doubted he'd ever get the stink out of the vehicle or his nose.

Leaving the engine idling, he got out. The force of the wind knocked him back for a moment. He flipped on the large flashlight in his hand and headed around the van. Swinging open the door, he shone the light on the plywood cage that filled the entire back of the vehicle. The animal leapt towards him, pushing the heavy cage forward a few inches. An eye glowed against a wire-covered slit; a spine-chilling growl rumbled forth, magnified by the small space so it seemed to fill the night air and echo back from the evergreens that hovered over the road.

The man hurried around to the driver's door. The cage's locking mechanism had been designed carefully for this moment. Crawling between the front seats, he hoisted his body over the top of the plywood cage. The animal beneath him twisted and turned and slammed its huge paws against the wood. He fit the key into the lock, clicked it open and slid it out of the two metal clasps. The animal knew what that sound meant and hurled its one hundred and fifty pounds out into the freedom of the night.

Leaping from the cage, the cougar twisted a half-circle in mid-air to come to rest on all four paws; fierce eyes stared through the door of the van and up to where the human body lay spread-eagle atop the cage. In that split second of eye contact with the animal, the man panicked – what if the cougar launched its body into the space between the top of the cage and roof of the van?

He pushed frantically backwards. Sliding into the driver's seat, he slammed his foot on the gas and sprayed gravel out from under the spinning tires. Adrenalin pumping, he glanced into the rear-view mirror expecting to see the cougar wedged head and shoulders in the vehicle, grasping for purchase on the plywood cage and trying to slither forward.

The vehicle swerved and slewed in the gravel as the man sped up. Narrowly missing a deep ditch at the side of the road, he wrenched on the steering wheel to compensate as his eyes went again and again to the mirror. Visions of snarling lips drawn back over lethal canines filled his thoughts. The open backdoor of the van banged and the tires slammed into potholes as he took the corners too quickly.

Only when he reached the pavement again, a kilometer down the dark, deserted highway did he pull off the road to an overlook by a small lake. With nervous glances over his shoulder, he dragged the stinking crate across the gravel and pushed it over the edge of a steep drop-off. It rattled and slammed its way down the cliff side and landed with an insignificant splash in the water far below.

TWO

I zzy slowly spun herself around in the center of Micah Camp's empty Director's office. Not that the previous occupant had needed to do a lot of packing. He wasn't the type of man to adorn a work space with personal touches. To her eye, the surface of the large desk had always seemed overexposed.

She sat down and examined the small nameplate in her hand. A break in the clouds caused a slanting ray of April sunshine to stream in through the windows that overlooked the circular drive. The light glinted off the edge of the gold letters. *Izzy Montgomery - Director.* She'd get Jim to take Roland's name off the door as soon as possible.

The phone on the desk rang and the sound echoed off the empty walls. As she reached over to answer it, Izzy rubbed at her forehead. The office definitely needed bookshelves and pictures. "Hello -"

The voice of Micah Camp's local Board Member, Darlene Evans boomed into her ear, "Are you sitting down, Izzy? .... Good. I've got big news. The Camp has received a one-time-only, very generous donation and the Board wants the money allocated quickly. Expansion is on for us at Crater Lake ... finally. The word is out about the great work we're doing with young people and you wouldn't believe what some families are willing to pay to get their kids into our program. With government funding drying up the way it has been, these privately-funded kids will more than compensate for the others we want to help. But we need more spaces. We want you to contact the architect who designed the original buildings. We're going to need at least four more resident cabins and two staff cabins. Line up the local contractors ... I know they're in short supply but we can afford to be generous; they should be beating down your door once you get the word out. And we're going to revise the criteria for accepting residents. The Board feels the existing rules might be leaving out kids who could really use our help and you know that has always been something I've harped on –"

"For the love of God, Darlene, slow down." With each bombshell announcement, Izzy had felt her jaw drop further. "I haven't even moved into Roland's office yet. How could all of this have come up so quickly? We met with the Board not even a month ago and none of this was discussed."

"The money fell into our laps; that's how."

"But why such a quick decision on how to allocate the funds?" Her hand continued to massage her forehead, "Did none of you think it might be useful to consult me? I've been saying forever we need a full-time career counsellor before we even consider expansion."

"The Board sees it differently. What can I say?"

Izzy switched gears, "Having more privately-funded clients is going to mean an overhaul of a bunch of things. Those kids come with different profiles and expectations."

"That's the type of thing you can lead the way on. When is your replacement ... what's his name ... supposed to arrive?" Before Izzy could answer, Darlene spoke again. "I know you're probably not going to be thrilled with this news. The Board has decided that you need to supervise a selection of his sessions for the first few months."

Izzy's stomach tightened. "Nick, his name is Nick Anderson. He's a qualified trauma counsellor. We wouldn't have hired him otherwise. How am I supposed to create a team atmosphere when I have to poke my nose into his sessions like I don't trust him?"

"The Board has every confidence in you, Izzy. I've got to run. The Mayor will have my head on the chopping block if I'm not home in time to get ready for polka night at the Legion. For five bucks you can get a great dinner. You and Liam should come out and join us. I think they're having cabbage rolls tonight."

Izzy hung up the phone as an image popped into her head – Roland, the Camp's previous director, and his new-found love, Jillian, flying off on their travelling adventure. If she were to discover that Roland had known about the expansion plans when he suggested she fill in for him, she'd kill him with her bare hands.

Why had she agreed to set aside her job as Micah Camp's trauma counsellor to step into the Director's role? Before her thoughts could drift down a road she felt contained its fair share of dangerous curves, Izzy looked up from the empty desk to see Dylan; his white apron was flapping as he rounded the corner and skidded up against the glass doors to her office. He pushed through, gesturing back toward the kitchen as he said, "Cook slipped on the wet floor. I think she's broken her ankle. I left Arianna with her." Izzy jumped up from her chair and followed Dylan as he ran back to the kitchen.

Cook lay on the shining tiles of the floor near the walk-in fridge. Arianna had bunched her sweat shirt under the woman's head and was sitting cross-legged on the floor, holding her hand.

Attempting a smile that quickly turned to a grimace of pain, Cook looked up at Izzy, "Don't go blaming this on Dylan. I'm a stupid old woman who should have retired years ago. The wet floor sign was there clear as day; I just didn't notice it until I was down here beside it."

Dylan waved the residents back to the dining room, "Clear out. Go finish eating. Cook's going to be okay." He turned to tell Izzy, "The ambulance is on the way but it's going to be at least half an hour. They said not to move her or give her anything to eat or drink."

Cook let out a long breath as she closed her eyes, "And here was me wanting my dinner."

Later, with Cook strapped to a stretcher and waving goodbye, Izzy accompanied the paramedics out to the waiting ambulance. Still busy in the kitchen with clean-up and preparing to get the dessert out to the dining room, Dylan glanced over at Arianna, "I'm glad you were here when she fell. I would have made a mess of things on my own."

"Wasn't much anyone could have done. Poor Cook." Arianna pointed to the trays of cupcakes on the counter, "Do you want me to start taking these out."

"Ya, and bring back the bins of dirty dishes as you go, okay?"

As Dylan scrubbed pots and Arianna loaded the commercial dishwasher, he asked, "Have you told anyone about the letter?"

Her dark eyes filled with a look of confusion as she shook her head. "I'm not sure what to say. I don't want to let anyone down."

Dylan bit back his first response – *Stop worrying about what everyone else wants. Think about yourself.* She deserved more from him. Arianna had liked him from the moment they had arrived the previous year to start their time as residents at Micah Camp. If he had been able to fall for a girl, it certainly would have been Arianna, with her toned body and long, midnight-black hair. Though he wasn't able to be what she wanted, they had remained friends and their relationship mattered to him.

He wiped his wet hands on his apron and stood with his back to the sink.

"Getting accepted to university with a full scholarship is good news. You aren't going to be letting anyone down."

"It isn't what my Band has planned for me and they've been so supportive ... it might seem like I don't appreciate what they're offering me."

"Oh for frig sakes Ari ... maybe if they knew you had it in you to go to university they wouldn't have offered to groom you for some hotel management job. Did you ever think of that?" Accepting her silent shrug, he changed the subject. "Have you heard from Mark since he got to Vancouver?"

"He phoned me this morning. He's doing okay, all settled in. I wish he hadn't gone before the summer. I miss him."

"He's lucky to have gotten into a pre-apprenticeship program so quickly. He'll get all tuned up with the schooling and when he comes back to Dearborn in the fall, there will be a full-time job waiting for him." Dylan paused to laugh. "In four years, he'll be an electrician making more money than we can dream of."

"We'll be gone by the time he comes back. I'll probably never see him again. And who knows if anyone is going to understand how quirky Mark is without us around?"

"People get by. You don't have to hold everyone's hand." He glanced around the kitchen and smiled over at her, "But could you hold mine for a while? I'm on my own for the foreseeable future and I've got a ton of prep to do for tomorrow."

⚜ ⚜ ⚜ ⚜

Liam hunched on the ground between the coffee table and the comfortably-worn, leather sofa and held out his arms, "Come on, Sophie. You can do it. Walk to me." The child banged her hands down on the table, making her shiny black curls dance around her face. Her bright pink T-shirt set off the brown of her skin to a perfect glow. She turned away from the lean man whose dark hair hung past his collar and took one step towards the sofa. Throwing herself forward, she gripped the arm and smiled back triumphantly. "Chicken," Liam laughed.

He got up, grabbed a chunk of firewood and moved aside the wrought iron grating that enclosed the stove. He threw the log on the fire and stood warming himself in front of the glass door. A noise drew his eyes up the length of the burnished, copper-coloured stovepipe that disappeared into the cedar ceiling far above. His gaze stopped at the railing that enclosed the upper floor. He watched as his young brother, Robbie, made his way along the hallway.

6

Soon enough, the sound of feet slamming down the staircase had Sophie smiling and clapping her hands. The boy wandered into the living room and tossed a book on the table. He knelt down beside Sophie and began to tickle her. The baby's eyes sparkled as she laughed in delight. She placed her small hands on Robbie's cheeks and squeezed while she gurgled out a number of unintelligible, word-like sounds. Robbie made wet fish noises at her and laughed when she tried to do the same back at him.

"Don't laugh when she does stuff like that. Izzy will have a fit if Sophie starts spitting at everyone." Liam sat down in the recliner and watched as Robbie stacked Sophie's brightly coloured blocks in a tower on the table so the baby could send them flying all over the room. He wasn't sure Izzy would approve of that lesson either.

The sound of Robbie's voice mingled with Sophie's giggles lulled Liam into a rare moment of relaxation. He was the stay-at-home member of the family, with an eleven-month-old child to care for, a nine-year-old brother to home school, chickens to tend, gardens to look after, laundry to fold, meals to prepare and a million other tasks to fill his days. And he had never been happier in his forty-seven years of life.

He smiled at the thought of the small package he had picked up in town and hidden in the bottom drawer of the workshop desk. Two silver wedding rings nestled together inside the velvet box; an intricate killer-whale design was etched around the shining surfaces. Izzy had been more than happy to leave all the wedding preparations to Liam and he had thrown himself into the planning with an enthusiasm that he knew not only surprised her but made her nervous.

As Sophie's block pitching reached danger levels, Liam gestured for Robbie to put the toys away. He pulled Sophie's favourite bunny from the corner of the chair and tossed it to her before her pouting lip could morph into a howl. Liam pointed to the discarded book, "How did you like, *Owls in the Family?*"

"It's good. I just finished it. I like any book with animals. I want to read *Call of the Wild* next." Robbie threw the last of the blocks into the toy box and glanced up at the clock, "I'm starving. When's dinner? How come Izzy's not home yet?"

Liam shrugged and said, "I'm thinking the new job is holding her up. Looks like we'll have to go ahead and have supper without her."

"I could walk over to the Camp to get her." Robbie's face wore a look of concern.

"Best not. She's probably got her hands full. I'll call and make sure everything's alright, though."

The boy suddenly scrunched up his nose and whistled, "Whew, Sophie, what is that smell?"

Liam clunked down the footrest of the recliner as he sat forward. "What's your pick – change a dirty diaper or start heating up the leftover lasagna?"

Robbie headed for the three stairs to the kitchen without needing to be asked twice. Liam scooped Sophie up and told his daughter, "Just you and me kid when it comes to dirty diapers."

❧❧❧❧

Holding a peanut butter sandwich in one hand and a glass of milk in the other, Izzy walked into Robbie's bedroom. The boy had his back to her. The legs of his Spiderman pajamas were too short and the sleeves rode up his arms; he had grown like the proverbial beanstalk over the last few months. Dante, her aging Irish setter, raised his head from a comfortable position in the middle of the bed. He acknowledged Izzy's presence with a slow wag of his tail and directed a low whine at the sandwich she was carrying.

"Robbie," Izzy waited for the boy to turn but he seemed unaware of her presence. She set the food down and walked over to stand beside him. The window reflected back their images as she put an arm around his shoulder and squeezed him close. She studied the boy's face in the glass. His distant expression made her shiver. "What is it? Are you okay?"

"Something is angry," Robbie pointed toward the black night beyond the window, "out there."

Izzy was well aware of Robbie's ability to see patterns of light and colour around people. She knew that what he saw told him things about the feelings of those individuals. But he'd never before told her that he sensed an emotion without being in the presence of a person.

"Something or someone?" Izzy stared out the window.

"It isn't anyone I know. It feels different."

Izzy followed him as he moved over to the bed and sat down. She stroked his dark hair. "Let it go for now, okay? Whatever you need to understand will come to you when you're ready."

Robbie nodded slowly before asking, "Is Cook going to be alright? Liam says she broke her ankle."

Izzy smiled. "She'll be fine. I'm not sure how we're going to manage at the Camp without her though." She reached over for the worn copy of *Lord of the Rings* on the shelf above the bed. "Should we read a chapter or two?"

The boy scooted under his covers. He pushed Dante up against the far wall and made room for Izzy.

❧❧❧❧

Justin felt like a total asshole. Despite Lauren's sexy pout, he could hardly change his mind now about leaving, after carefully explaining that he had two exams coming up in the next four days and a final paper to finish. He had to pack up his dorm room and be ready to leave at the end of the week. Obviously, he wasn't going to start studying after midnight but if he didn't make a move now, he'd miss the last bus. Of course, Lauren would offer to drive him back the next day. That would mean staying in bed for most of the morning, going out for a leisurely breakfast and not arriving back at his dorm until well into the afternoon. He couldn't risk it; things were down to the wire as it was.

He sat on the side of the bed buttoning his shirt as he looked over his shoulder. "You know I would stay if I could, right?"

Lauren stretched her naked body, clearly visible in the moonlight glinting off the silvery high-rise buildings that peered through the bedroom window of her Yale Town apartment. "If you have to go, then go. I understand."

She smiled the smile that had first caught Justin's attention way back on New Year's Eve. One of the guys in his dorm had insisted he come to a party downtown. He had not been in the crowded apartment for more than a few minutes before he began to feel claustrophobic and wanted to get the hell out of there. At that moment, he had spotted a young woman wearing a strapless dress that seemed to defy gravity by staying in place. She had glanced over at him through a cloud of golden hair and smiled. He had actually looked over his shoulder to see if she was smiling at someone else but no one stood behind him. Grabbing two glasses from a tray, she had walked over to him. After introducing herself, she had asked if he wanted to get some air. They had taken the elevator up to the roof, sipped champagne and strolled through a small garden to enjoy the spectacle of the city lights spread out below. He learned that Lauren had come from Ottawa to study architecture at the University of British Columbia.

She had reached up a slim arm to encircle his neck and had kissed him lightly on the lips as the fireworks signalling the advent of the New Year splashed colour around them. He had only discovered a week later that the party apartment belonged to her, a gift from her parents.

She had called him to get together for a day of wandering the frosty downtown streets, dipping in and out of Starbuck locations to warm up and enjoy the caffeine jolts. Later that night, following dinner and a couple of stops at clubs on the way back to her place, he had seen the surprise on her face when he refused her invitation to stay. He told her he would take a rain check, wait until they knew each other better. Lauren had shrugged and given him a look that obviously meant it was his loss. But the next weekend when he called her, she had agreed to go out with him.

They dated for almost two months. He knew she was seeing other guys. Then one night, as they were leaving an Italian restaurant down the street from her building, she had hooked her arm through his and said, "We know each other better now and, if you're ready, I'd like to make this relationship exclusive." He had spent that night at her apartment. The last two months had gone by in a whirl of weekends with Lauren and weekdays trying to catch up as the last semester of his second year at UBC wound down with assignments due, one after another.

The bus rounded the corner. Bright lights flickered off the wet pavement as Justin came out of Lauren's building. He managed to sprint across the street, yank out his wallet and skid to a stop at the bus shelter in time to catch the driver's eye. The door cranked open and the man behind the wheel spoke gruffly, "Last run of the night. I don't stop if no one's around. You're lucky I saw you."

Justin stepped up the three stairs. He smiled tiredly, swiped his pass and lurched down the aisle as the bus pulled away from the curb. He slouched into a seat and raked his hand through his hair, dislodging several rain drops. Closing his eyes, he leaned his head against the window, hopeful he might catch some sleep before the deserted bus pulled into the UBC exchange. But a nagging concern that had been gnawing at the edge of his awareness for days kept sleep at bay. In a week he would be back at Crater Lake. How would he feel when he saw Lisa-Marie again?

❧❧❧❧

Liam brushed his fingers in a slow caress along the side of Izzy's face. Tucking a strand of dark hair behind her ear, he let his touch drift down her neck before he stroked his palm over her full breast and rested his hand against her stomach. As she moved from her side of the bed to wrap her body around his, her sudden intake of breath satisfied him. Her hands gripped his back to pull him close. He groaned as the length of her body made contact with his and the slow dance of their lovemaking continued.

Later she cuddled close to him and said, "I don't get it. Roland always made the job look like a breeze. I never thought I'd be coming home late.

Did Sophie go to sleep okay?"

"I think we had fewer rounds than last night. She's so tired she can hardly keep her eyes open but she fights it." Liam shook his head in wonder at Sophie's ability to assert her will.

"She's got a good dose of her mom's stubbornness, hey?" Liam could almost feel Izzy's smile in the dark of the bedroom they had shared for well over a year.

"Wish she had my easy-going nature when it comes to going to bed," he joked. Returning to the subject of Izzy's new job, he asked, "What are you going to do about Cook?"

"Dylan can fill in for now. Did I tell you he's been accepted to a culinary school in Montreal? But I'll have to find someone else, and fast. Dylan will be leaving in August and I'd like him to be able to show a new person the ropes. And talk about bad luck ... out of the blue, I'm landed with the responsibility for all this expansion crap ... contacting the architect, contractors and maybe a butcher, a baker and a candlestick maker, for all I know. I can't imagine what tomorrow might bring."

Liam chuckled. After a few moments of silence, he changed the subject to ask, "Did you know that Caleb kept journals?"

Izzy pushed her pillow into a more comfortable position under her head. "I can't imagine Caleb keeping a journal. He wasn't the type. Strange notes and odd bits of paper maybe, but not a journal."

"I found a whole bunch of them in the bottom of a drawer out in the workshop. Would you like to see them?"

She pushed the question aside quickly, "No. Since I know nothing about any journals, he obviously wanted them to be private. I respect that."

In the silence that followed that remark, Liam carefully considered his request before he asked, "Do you mind if I go through them? Or would you rather I get rid of them?"

Izzy's voice held an edge of impatience as she said, "Do whatever makes you feel comfortable. I only know what's best for me."

As the bedroom filled with the sound of the wind splattering rain against the skylight, Liam thought about how he'd found the journals. When he had hidden the rings earlier that day, he had reached to the far back of the lower desk drawer, shoved his hand under a pile of old newspapers and discovered a thick sheaf of notebooks tied together with string. Smiling at the sudden remembrance of high school supplies – bright coloured exercise books, three-hole punched to fit in a binder – he had slowly untied the string and flipped through the pile. Every cover was marked with a year extending forward from

1971 until the year of Caleb's death. There were thirty-five in all, each one divided into monthly sections by tabs stapled to the pages.

He had sat for a long time with his hands flat on the pile of books in front of him. Memories of Caleb and the friendship they had shared washed over him until his grief and longing felt as fresh as they had ever been. He accepted that he would never get over missing Caleb. As he stowed the black velvet box away, Liam considered the odd coincidence of having found Caleb's journals at the very time he was hiding away the rings with which he planned to wed his best friend's wife.

THREE

B eulah reached out to take the dessert plate from Bethany's hand. She didn't miss a beat in her conversation with Craig who lounged on the sofa in the A-Frame's living room. "My truck still has more than a few good years left in her."

Craig took a bite of his cake and waved his fork in the air as he chewed. "You have to know when to pull the plug. Too many repairs on an older vehicle ... it's like flushing money down the toilet. You've got to take a page from Liam's book. I saw him driving a brand new GM in town the other day. That Dodge he used to drive was way overdue for retirement."

"But when he has to drive that truck, you won't find an unhappier guy than Liam." Beulah sipped her coffee. "A new truck doesn't come cheap. I don't have that kind of money to throw around. I could do a lot more repairs before I came close to spending what it would take to buy a new truck."

"You'd still have to dish out the cost and all that repair money would be wasted. I haven't spent the last thirty years being my own mechanic without learning a thing or two." Craig smiled over at Bethany and added, "This cake is great." His compliment came around a large bite.

Bethany returned the smile as she settled into a chair and drew her legs up under her flowing dress. Helen pushed Craig's teetering cup further onto the table and laughed as he swatted at her hand and told her not to fuss around him.

Bethany had met Helen when the two of them arrived at Dearborn's local college to write exams for distant education courses they were taking. After the tests were completed, they had gone for coffee together. Their educational pursuits gave them a lot to chat about and before long they had agreed to meet in town a couple of afternoons a week to study together. Soon after that, Helen had invited Bethany and Beulah for dinner at the family's home in Dearborn.

Beulah recalled the conversation she'd had with Bethany during a drive back to Crater Lake after making their bread deliveries. She had been well aware that Bethany was working her way around to saying something. She hadn't lived with the woman for over seventeen years without learning a thing or two about her body language.

"You know my friend, Helen?" Beulah nodded and Bethany continued, "She'd like you and me to come to her house for supper this Saturday. Her husband, Craig, will be there."

"Where else would he be? He does live there, right?"

"Don't make fun of me, Beulah. Just say if you want to go or not."

Beulah had tapped her open palm on the steering wheel. She'd met a lot of people in Dearborn over the years. Five days a week, she delivered organic bread, the product of the home-based bakery she and Bethany ran, to local stores and a couple of restaurants. She'd seen Craig a few times at the Building Supply Store he managed and Helen was famous for walking everywhere she went. Small town life dictated that most people were well versed in their neighbours' business but you never could tell for sure. Beulah shifted her eyes from the gravel road to ask, "How much does Helen know about me?"

Bethany exhaled loudly as she tipped her head back to gaze at the roof of the truck, "She knows you're female, if that's what you mean."

That was exactly what she had meant. Beulah made up her mind quickly, "It's about time we found some new people to hang out with. Doesn't Craig have his own mechanic shop in his garage? I wouldn't mind getting to know a guy who can strip down an engine. It sounds good to me."

Craig and Beulah got along great and that first dinner was soon followed by a reciprocal invitation out to Crater Lake where Beulah proudly showed off the bakery and got Craig to help her light the wood-burning oven – the heart of the operation. Sometimes the four of them passed an enjoyable evening playing Whist, a game at which Bethany and Helen were as hopeless as any two people could be. Instead of paying attention to the cards, they preferred to chat and enjoy themselves. This resulted in games in which Craig and Beulah went for each other's jugular, doing everything they could to work around the choices made by their respective partners. Bethany and Helen's indifference added an element of challenge juxtaposed with constant frustration and Beulah and Craig seemed to thrive on the combination.

Helen smiled and her eyes twinkled as she set aside her dessert plate. "Liam came to see me the other day about decorating the cake for the wedding."

Beulah raised her eyebrows, "I can imagine what that was like. I have never known a guy to get so particular about the details of a wedding. He came over last week to ask me if I could make sure my socks matched the tuxedo he had rented for me. When I told him I had my heart set on bright red and yellow argyles, he looked like he might faint."

"I think it's kind of sweet." Helen glanced at Beulah and Bethany before asking, "Which one of you did the planning for your wedding?"

Bethany flashed her hand as she said, "There wasn't that much to plan – a few friends, a nice ring and a winter honeymoon in Palm Springs." She smiled at Beulah and added, "Our wedding was a good excuse for the first vacation we've ever taken together."

Bethany looked beautiful when she smiled and the transformation always slammed Beulah in the gut. It reminded her of why she had fallen in love with this woman. She had come close to losing the life she and Bethany had built together – all because of her bullheaded way of crashing around in the world. The depth of her own stupidity was a thing of wonder to her. This last year had been a time of making up for past mistakes and the Christmas wedding was only the first step.

Beulah's eyes lingered on Bethany's long, blonde hair. She saw the way her dress accentuated her curves and brought out the blue of her eyes. She cleared her throat and asked, "Have you told Helen about the new job?"

Bethany straightened in her chair and her face lit up. "Jillian, the researcher I worked with at Micah Camp last year, asked if I'd do a bunch of follow-up interviews with the residents and staff, transcribe the tapes and have everything ready so she can analyze the new data when she and Roland come back. I'll start at the beginning of next month."

Helen clapped her hands, "Beth, that's great. Good for you."

Craig bounded up from the couch and leaned over to give Bethany a quick kiss on the cheek. "There is nothing like being offered a job to bolster the ego, hey?"

Beulah watched Bethany deal with her discomfort at Craig's friendly enthusiasm. No one else noticed her tensing muscles or darting eyes. But deal with it, Bethany did. Her ability to move beyond a past that had made her seriously distrust men, totally captured Beulah's admiration.

"How are the kids?" Bethany smoothed the dress down over her legs and turned to Helen with a question that would certainly divert all attention from herself. Helen and Craig had three children they loved to talk about.

"Is Mike working full-time at the sawmill, now?" Beulah asked. "I thought I saw his beater of a truck there most of last week." She pointed a finger at Craig, "Maybe you should buy your son a new truck."

Craig's face wore a comical look of disbelief. "No way ... he'll earn the money on his own. He has a full-time job now. It was bound to happen. He's worked summers up there since he was sixteen. Geez, it was Caleb that hired him." Craig studied Beulah's face for a moment. "A lot of people in Dearborn wondered if Izzy would keep the woodlot and sawmill going after Caleb died. Liam was an okay guy to fill in but the business had slipped before they got Reg to run things."

Beulah only shrugged, so Craig returned to the discussion of his oldest son. "Reg is training Mike to be his head sawyer." Ignoring the sudden frown on Helen's face, he went on, "Mike had nothing but good things to say about the way Reg showed that university kid, Justin, how a real logging and sawmill operation works. Mike says Justin will be back again this summer. It's a good thing for university kids to see what real work is like."

Helen patted at her hair as she said, "I did hope Mike would follow Zach's example and consider college or a trade school but the two of them have been out of school for a year and Mike really isn't interested."

Craig gave his wife a warning stare. "Nothing wrong with working at a sawmill. I manage a lumber yard and that's always been good enough for us. A guy doesn't need a university degree or a trade to make good money in a resource-based community like Dearborn. Too many kids from around here go off to school and never come back."

Bethany circled the room with the coffee pot. "Did Mike and Zach graduate the same year?"

Helen waved a hand over her cup, "Not for me, thanks. They did, but Mike's almost a year older – Irish twins those boys." She smiled before going on, "We decided to keep Mike back so the boys could start school together. Mike was so young with his birthday in December and Zach would have been devastated without having him around every day." She sat forward on the couch to push Craig's teetering cake fork back onto his plate. "Now that Mike is working full-time and training for the half marathon in August, there are days I can hardly get him to sit down long enough to eat."

"I guess Zach will be home from school soon." Bethany knew Helen had a soft spot for her second son. The woman's smile proved the point.

"He's already got a job lined up with the local satellite internet people. He'll be doing remote installations and working in the store." A quick frown crossed Helen's face. "I'm sure neither of the boys ever gave me the trouble that Hannah does. I suppose she's your typical sixteen year old but she's driving me crazy with wanting to get her driver's license, staying out late and talking like a little potty mouth all the time."

"There you go, again." Craig pointed his finger at his wife, "You think Hannah is going to be some sort of a china doll on a shelf or something. She's her own person."

"Well, you would say that. You spoil her rotten and think you can treat her like the boys. Someone's got to make sure she doesn't run wild." Helen dropped the subject of their youngest child to ask, "When is Lisa-Marie due home?"

Bethany smiled, "She'll be up in time for Sophie's first birthday."

"And she'll be staying with you?"

"Oh, she'll be back and forth between here and next door at Izzy and Liam's."

Beulah noted how Bethany neatly dodged offering any more information about her niece's living arrangements. Obviously, she had not trusted Helen with a large piece of their collective history. Helen was curious but she was also a good enough friend to keep her curiosity from turning the corner to nosiness.

Beulah waded into the conversation, "This half marathon Mike's training for ... it's one of the events at Dipsy-Doodle Days, right?" She caught Bethany's relieved look at the change of subject.

Helen's mouth pulled down as she said, "Why on earth that horrible name has stuck around all these years, is beyond me. But there you have it ... life in a small town. I'm sure the whole Island laughs at us for having an annual celebration with such a ridiculous name but no one around here seems to care. It's always been the Dearborn Dipsy-Doodle Days and it always will be." Helen got up and began to gather the empty cake plates. "The whole time is taken up with silly races in which the true meaning of dipsy-doodle comes into play. But the half marathon is serious. We have runners registering from all over; I just received an email from a guy in Germany."

Bethany picked up the coffee tray and followed Helen to the kitchen. "Dipsy-Doodle actually means something?"

"It certainly does." Helen put the plates down and directed her words to the ceiling as if she were giving a speech, "Most often a hockey evasion move where the defending team uses feints, dekes, or swerving motions and stickhandling finesse."

Bethany laughed, "Seriously?"

Craig got up to demonstrate, skating across the floor between the living room and the kitchen of the A-Frame with an imaginary hockey stick in hand. "See the way I deke around this guy. He shoots, he scores." He held his arms up in the air triumphantly. "Of course, a dipsy-doodle can be any evasive movement used deliberately to outwit an opponent during competition. That's why most of the races are a riot. Everyone takes dipsy-doodle to the limit."

From the pile by the sink, Craig grabbed Helen's plate which still contained a good-sized bite of cake. "No need to waste food." Helen gave him a frown which he pointedly ignored.

Beulah came into the kitchen and stood by Bethany. She smiled over at Helen. "I've come up with an idea I want to run by you, since you're heading up the organizing committee for Dipsy-Doodle Days this year." Paying no attention to the quizzical expression on Bethany's face, Beulah threw out the words, "*The First Annual Caleb Jenkins Memorial Ball Tournament.*"

Craig smacked Beulah on the back and whistled. "Great idea. Ball tournaments bring the cash into town, for sure. And remembering Caleb out on the ball field is something he would have loved."

"My thoughts exactly," Beulah said, looking to Helen and Bethany for their reactions.

"I can't see why not," Helen said. "There are going to be some kids' races held on the ball field and some people want to set up vending booths. We can easily push the booths out to the edge of the playground and the races can be held between games. A ball tournament would certainly help swell the numbers for the dance on the Saturday night."

Bethany stared at Beulah for a moment before asking, "Have you talked this over with Izzy?"

Beulah shrugged off the question with a wave of her hand, "Izzy's going to the love the idea."

FOUR

Nick Anderson studied the woman standing behind the desk as she turned away to grab the phone and hold it to her ear. The way she had thrown her hands up in exasperation and apologized for having to take the call was comical. He motioned to the door to indicate he could wait outside but she shook her head and told him she'd only be a moment.

Izzy Montgomery was an attractive woman. In the close confines of her office, he guessed her age to be more than a few years beyond his thirty-six, but he would not have thought so from a distance.

When he had knocked on the open door a few minutes before, she had stood up from the desk and walked over to shake his hand. He'd had a moment to cast a quick glance over her as she moved across the room. Her feet were clad in attractive sandals and her toe-nails flashed a deep red polish. Her shapely legs disappeared into an above-the-knee dress that accentuated her curves; the V at the top hinted at other attractions. A necklace of overlapping silver medallions highlighted the slight hollows near her collarbones. Glossy, dark hair with the occasional strand of silver fell around her face and a pair of red-framed glasses pushed into the curls at the top of her head. A warm smile that crinkled the corners of her brown eyes drew him closer. Nick felt sure that his initial reaction to meeting Micah Camp's Director was typical of any man who might find himself in her presence for the first time.

As Izzy continued her phone conversation, Nick wandered over to the bookshelf that ran the length of the far wall. He picked up a framed photo and studied it. The setting was obviously a hospital room. A native man with shoulder-length hair sat in a chair with a newborn baby in his arms. Izzy stood behind him with her hand on his shoulder. Her other arm was wrapped around a teenage girl who was looking up at the tall guy standing next to her. A young boy hunched down beside the chair. Apparently, the birth of a baby had gathered a family together and his new boss seemed to be a central figure in that family. Nick glanced at the photo again. It was odd that the teenage girl wore a hospital gown.

Further down the shelf sat a more recent picture of the baby. Round, dark eyes flashed from a heart-shaped face. Another frame held a close-up of the young boy sitting out on a deck with a view of Crater Lake in the background – a view similar to the one Nick had seen from his office windows. The final frame held a photo of two men standing beside an old Dodge truck. He recognized one as the native guy. The second was a tall, blonde man who laughed heartily as he rubbed one hand along his beard-covered jaw and draped the other around the man beside him.

Izzy hung up the phone and turned towards him. He placed the picture frame back on the shelf. "Your family?" he asked.

She raised one eyebrow slightly, "In a manner of speaking,"

Nick was more than willing to drop the subject based on the ambiguity of her response. With the number of societal permutations these days, family wasn't always an easy topic.

Izzy surprised him when she said, "My family life is somewhat unusual but it's only a matter of time until you've met everyone coming and going between the Camp and our place. We live a ten-minute walk away. My partner Liam and I," she pointed to the man holding the baby in the photo, "are getting married in July and you'll be more than welcome to join the celebration. You probably won't be able to miss it since the dinner and reception are being held here at the Camp. We also have a book-club potluck once a month. If you like reading, you should come out."

Nick relaxed. Working with an attractive woman who was clearly attached amounted to the best-case scenario for him. He wanted no temptations to any sort of entanglements.

As if one of the photos on the shelf had come to life, a dark-haired boy peered in through the glass door of the office. Izzy's face lit up with a smile. "What did I tell you?" She waved the boy into the room. "Robbie, I'd like you to meet Nick Anderson. He's going to be our new counsellor while I fill in for Roland." Looking over at Nick, Izzy explained, "Robbie is Liam's brother."

The boy tipped his head to one side and narrowed his eyes slightly as he looked up. After a moment, he seemed satisfied. He said a quiet hello before turning to Izzy and talking quickly, "Can I go to the swimming pool in Cedar Falls with Bethany and Helen this afternoon? Liam says to ask you because I won't get home till five-thirty; but we probably won't have dinner before then, anyway, right?"

"If it's okay with Bethany." Looking at her watch, Izzy asked, "Aren't you supposed to be with Gordon right now for your math lesson?"

Robbie nodded. "Liam says he has no cash. Can I have some money?"

"Come back after you've finished math and we'll talk about it then."

"Enough for the pool and two hotdogs and a pop and a new comic book, okay?"

Izzy pointed to the door as Robbie grinned and strolled out. She looked at Nick and gestured toward the two chairs. "He's home schooled. That's mostly Liam's responsibility but Robbie gets some tutoring here, as well. Okay, I promise no more interruptions. So, what have you seen of the Camp so far?"

Nick settled into the chair as he spoke, "I got here at about seven last night. It's a longer trip than I anticipated. That last part," he let out a low whistle, "I never knew there were that many trees in the whole province let alone along one, two-hour stretch of highway. The map you emailed me was great. My cabin is as comfortable as the Board promised it would be." In offering Nick a year-long contract, the Board had sweetened the pot by including his accommodations at the Camp. They had assured him that he would not be disappointed because they had arranged for him to use the director's cabin.

"I got out early this morning and ran into the young guy who works in the kitchen. I had breakfast in the dining room, so I've met a few of the residents. I've checked out my office," Nick smiled. "Your old office. The view is something else."

Izzy glanced at the circular drive and flower beds that were outside her window. "I will miss my view of the lake, for sure. Feel free to move things around or make any changes necessary so the space works for you." She gestured back to the phone on her desk, "That call I had to take was from Darlene Evans, our local Board Member. She let me know that the Board has lined up a new cook for us and the woman will be living in the smaller cabin down the way from yours. She should be arriving soon and part of her job will be to spell you off when it comes to keeping a lid on things around here at night."

"I gathered from one of the emails I got, that the overnight supervision consists mostly of locking up the main building and being available in case anything goes wrong."

"You can translate that to mean everything goes along fine until it doesn't. A facility with two dozen eighteen to twenty-year-olds in residence obviously has an occasional overnight issue or two."

"I did a stint, living in the dorms at university. I can imagine." He laughed.

"There are strict rules about no alcohol or drug use on the premises and, for the most part, the kids are really good about that. I'd be lying if I said it was always a smooth go, though." Izzy shrugged before switching to a new subject, "I'd like to talk about the team approach we take here. All members of the staff take the time to coordinate their work with the residents so that every young person who comes here can benefit from the opportunities that a place like Micah Camp has to offer."

"While I was on the ferry from Vancouver yesterday, I read one of the papers you emailed me – the one by the researcher who did her PhD work here. Her conclusions really make sense. Educational upgrading, counselling and work experience combined with the extended length of the program and the wilderness setting appear to produce some great results."

"That would be Jillian Matthews' work ... the same Jillian who swept our director off his feet and is now travelling with him for a year. I doubt I'd be sitting here talking to you right now if it weren't for Jillian turning Roland's life upside down." Izzy laughed, "In a good way. Her research into what we do at Micah Camp and her journal articles have really put us on the radar of more than a few funders. I wouldn't be surprised if the recent influx of money we've received could be traced back to her work. She has obtained a sizable grant to do a second round of interviews here at the Camp and she's hired someone to get started on that task." Izzy took a deep breath, "And that brings me back to what I'm talking about when it comes to team work. Every adult on site works with residents in one capacity or another and everyone has something of value to impart. I've seen Jim, our maintenance man, make progress with a client during work supervision while I got nowhere in trying to counsel the same kid. The team approach goes for the teachers, or a researcher like Jillian, or her assistant or our cleaning woman, Penny. We all work together."

Nick nodded thoughtfully. "Sounds like a solid approach. I'm looking forward to the first staff meeting so I can put some faces to all the names and positions."

"There is one other thing I need to discuss with you and the sooner, the better, I suppose." Izzy's eyebrows came together in a slight frown. "The Board is insisting that I make myself available to supervise some of your sessions during the first couple of months. I didn't expect anything like this,

Nick. The Board believes that because your past work was not done specifically with young adults, we would be wise to err on the side of caution."

Nick took a moment to digest the information. He hadn't worked under supervision for years. At the same time, he recognized the value in discussing cases with a supervisor and he'd never been particularly threatened by other people's ideas. He stared steadily at the woman across from him. "If that's what they want, I don't have a problem with supervision. Actually, I'm a big fan of your approach to trauma work, Izzy. I've read your articles and I sat in on a presentation you gave at a conference in Vancouver a few years ago. I'm not the kind of counsellor who thinks he's got everything figured out." He paused for a moment and added, "Can we make the supervision based on video-taped sessions? That really looks good on a resume these days."

"Good grief, Nick ... that was the next bombshell I thought I'd have to drop on you." Izzy stared wide-eyed at him. "The Board asked for video-taped sessions and they've sent up all this fancy equipment that I hope to God you know how to operate." She visibly relaxed into her chair and smiled, "You're taking all of this way better than I would have." Changing the subject, she said, "I'm impressed by the number of recent articles you've had published in peer-reviewed journals. It's a huge accomplishment for someone working full-time in the field and not attached to a university. How did you become focused on school shootings as a research topic?"

Nick weighed his options. Why not put his cards on the table? He knew he'd end up doing it eventually. Something about Izzy invited self-disclosure and her tone suggested more than a simple chat about his research. "You'll have to bear with some history. The topic has been a personal one for me."

Izzy held his gaze while she said, "No problem."

"I married my high-school sweetheart and we went to university together to get teaching degrees. We both got hired to work at W.J. Myers High School in Tabor, Alberta. It was the fall of 1998. In April of the next year, eight days after the shootings in Columbine, a fourteen-year-old kid with a history of being brutally bullied walked into WJ Myers and started shooting. There were three kids in the hallway. He killed one, wounded another and missed the third. He was wrestled to the ground by a gym teacher and that ended the incident."

Nick made eye contact with Izzy for a moment and caught the intensity of her stare. He went on, "I didn't see anything but I certainly felt the repercussions. Several colleagues struggled with post-traumatic stress over the incident, including my wife. I went through my own version of it. I became obsessed with school shootings; I read everything I could get my hands on."

He gave a half-hearted shrug, "Because my behavior was keeping my wife from moving on, she presented me with an ultimatum – stop obsessing about the shooting. I couldn't. She left me." He glanced up at the ceiling for a moment before adding, "She always was a woman of her word. Anyway, that was my wake-up call. I got into counselling to deal with things. I was lucky to work with a guy who really knew his stuff. Then I applied for a graduate program at the University of Alberta where I trained to be a trauma counsellor and wrote my thesis on the topic of school shootings. In the end, that turned out to be the only way I could make sense of it all. Most of my recent articles have spun out from my thesis. Unfortunately, gun violence in school is a topic that keeps on having traction."

Izzy stared thoughtfully at him, "Why apply for a job like this, Nick? You obviously don't need the experience and your career trajectory seems aimed at PhD work."

"I'm coming out of a messy divorce ... my second." He frowned as he shook his head. "Can you believe that both of my wives were named Jennifer? What are the chances of that? If anyone ever introduces me to a woman named Jennifer again, I'll be running for the hills. I'm about as financially strapped as I ever want to be and Jennifer number two got all the friends in the settlement. It's a good time for me to get away from Vancouver. I've got a downtown apartment with a killer mortgage but I've managed to sublet it for the entire year at a ridiculous price because of the Winter Olympics." Nick sat forward to meet Izzy's eyes, "My plan is to work hard, save every cent I make and get my personal life in order."

"I hope this year gives you the space you need to meet those goals, Nick." Izzy glanced at her watch and seemed surprised at what she saw. "I've got a conference call in about twenty minutes. I need to pull up some documents on my laptop and read a few things before then." She got up and walked with Nick to the door. "I'll leave you to go over the stack of paperwork I put on your desk. Jim will bring that video equipment to your office. Take a couple of days to meet everyone then you and I can get together, go over the client files and set up your counselling calendar."

FIVE

R obbie groaned as he slipped deeper into his dream. He stood in the dark. Fear and confusion swirled in flashes of light around him. He felt a presence. It sniffed the wet, night air and Robbie moved off into the trees behind it. The creature sensed a force stronger than anything it had ever felt before and instinct drove it forward. The ground was uneven, littered with fallen trees and huge stumps. The glossy leaves of the salal bushes glistened in the stray splashes of moonlight that the scudding clouds allowed.

Rain fell steadily now and in an open space, Robbie saw the animal; the cougar's body quivered as its extraordinary night vision picked up movement below in an alder bottom interspersed with massive ferns. Now they were crouched and stalking, moving like shadows down the slope, picking their way through the trees, many of which had fallen like matchsticks one over the other in a mass of dying limbs.

The dream took him to another place. A man held out a shoe box that contained a small cub, golden brown with darker splotches spread over its body. It had black markings around its mouth and Groucho Marx slashes above its strange blue eyes. It looked like a stuffed animal. The man handed a bottle to a boy and told him it would be his job to make sure the cougar ate or it would starve to death.

Now the dream itself became a race across time. The boy held the cub close and scratched it behind the ear ... he ran with a ball of yarn and the playful cat chased after him ... he snuck into the utility room, lifted the soft animal from its box and brought it to his bed. Now the man and the boy laughed together as the growing cub swiped at their dog and laid claim to its food dish ... equal in size, the animals sprawled out together on the carpet ...

25

the submissive dog shared water from its bowl with the large cat.

The cougar was much bigger; strength and power coiled in its body. Robbie peered into a cage in a dark garage. He could feel the tight space and the cougar's longing for release into an outside pen. When the cat bounded into the pen, Robbie watched the boy push a large container filled with raw meat through a sliding door. The boy's voice, the ups and downs of it, were soothing to the animal. When the man disappeared into the garage to clean the cat's cage, the boy slid up close to the heavy wire that separated him from the cougar. Robbie understood the cat's pleasure as it stretched out on the ground by the edge of the cage so the boy could reach in and scratch behind its ear. A deep, satisfying purr rumbled forth and a tongue lolled out to lick the boy's hand.

Everything in the dream had suddenly changed and now anger spiked in splintering light everywhere. The cat paced a small cage in a strange house that smelled bad. Whenever people came into this place, they walked a large circle around the cage as they headed for the stairs to a basement. The sound of fans and machines whirred constantly. At night, everyone would leave and the man would stand by the outside door and crank a lever that opened the cage. Robbie felt the cat's frustration as it hurtled forward, night after night, trying to get to the man before he slammed the door that must lead outside of this prison and back to the boy. The food in its dish was never enough and Robbie's own stomach twisted and gnawed away inside his body.

The cougar prowled the main floor of the house; its large paws padded in total silence. He watched the cat scratch at the wood of the door frames and the floors. The tearing and rending felt good against sharp claws and Robbie took pleasure in the destruction. Morning after morning, the cougar sought out the familiarity of the cage and was sleeping there when the man returned and slammed the door to confine the animal for yet another day.

A great wave of rage at the injustice of the cat's situation caused Robbie to stand by the outer door of the stinking, dream house, the door the man came through every day, and call for the cougar to come out of its cage. He whispered encouragement.

That morning the cat's long tail swished to and fro in rapid movements as it kept vigil by the door and its possible triumph over the man felt like an explosion of light. Robbie shook his head sadly knowing the man was bound to look through the window before opening the door. That day no one entered the house and no food or water made its way to the dishes in the cage. Robbie's body jerked as the cat slammed against the door in fury. Then came what seemed like days and days of tortured thirst so that Robbie's mouth opened and he swallowed and licked at his lips. When the cat weakened from dehydration, men came with long poles that were sharp at the end. They cornered him and drove him into the cage where water was soon supplied. Emotions flooded through Robbie – relief for the animal's plight was followed quickly by bitter anger and the need for revenge.

A voice said, "I have a gun. If you want I'll shoot the thing for you. It's crazy to have an animal this dangerous around and downright cruel to keep it penned up this way."

The man shook his head – no. He remembered how the boy had fed and played with the cougar. The man said he would release it into the bush somewhere.

Still asleep, Robbie kicked off his blankets and sat up. He got out of bed and turned a blank stare to the window, breathing rapidly. Walking out of his loft, he moved silently along the short hall, down the stairs, across the living room and through the entryway. He opened the door and made his way into the night. The gravel of the driveway poked his bare feet but he didn't notice. His cougar was out there; he could feel it. The animal had gone back to the wild. It was chasing down the night toward what instinct recognized as food.

✻ ✻ ✻ ✻

Izzy smacked Dante's cold nose away from her face. The dog whined and nudged at her. She rolled over and shook Liam by the shoulder, "Something's wrong with the dog. Wake up."

Liam sat up and rubbed his eyes. Izzy got out of bed and moved across the bedroom as she whispered, "Dante, stop that damn barking before you wake Sophie ... the back door is wide open, Liam."

Izzy slipped her shoes on. Wrapping her arms around herself to ward off the night chill, she walked down the steps and stood outside the cabin near the edge of the large garden that stretched into the dark. A lopsided half-moon threw a weak light over the area. Dante trotted out to the driveway and stopped beside a thin figure in bare feet. The boy stared into the dark mass of trees that lined the edge of the road. Izzy called out, "Robbie, what are you doing out here?" He didn't turn around at the sound of her voice.

Liam came down the stairs behind her. She looked at him anxiously before they walked together out to the drive where Dante whined and nudged at Robbie's side. Izzy spoke Robbie's name again and put her hand on his arm. When he still did not respond, she moved in front of him and hunched down so she could get a look at his face.

She whispered over to Liam, "It doesn't seem like he's awake."

"If not, he's walking in his sleep."

Izzy touched Robbie's hand. "He's ice cold and he's got nothing on his feet."

Liam lifted the boy into his arms, carried him into the cabin and made him sit on the edge of the couch. Robbie's eyes were still blank and his dark hair hung over his face. Looking at Izzy, Liam asked, "What now?"

"Maybe we should get him back to bed." Izzy slipped her arm around Robbie, pulled him up and started walking him across the living room. His eyes fluttered. "Robbie, are you okay?" she asked.

The boy stared at her, "Ya ... I'm really thirsty and my stomach hurts." He walked up the stairs to the kitchen, got a glass from the cupboard, filled it with water and drank deeply before he headed toward his bedroom with Dante close behind.

"That was strange," Liam whispered.

Izzy waited for Robbie's door to close and heard a muffled thump when he got back into his bed. As she and Liam walked towards their bedroom, a plaintive cry came from the sun porch. Pearl, Liam's golden retriever, raised her head from where she lay on a mat by Sophie's crib and stared up at them. Her eyes in the glow of the nightlight admonished them to hurry up and do something.

Liam said, "Go back to bed; I'll take care of her."

"Give her half a bottle of milk if she won't settle down." Liam raised an eyebrow and Izzy shrugged, "I know, I know. We said we wouldn't give her any more middle-of-the-night bottles, but she was awake three times last night. Maybe she is hungry." As Sophie's cries ramped up, Izzy said, "Better hurry. I'm going to pull a bench against the back door, just in case. We'll have to think of something else in the morning."

SIX

Robbie grabbed a plate of pancakes out of Liam's hand as he passed by the stove. He plopped onto a chair at the kitchen table, poured syrup over the stack and crammed a large forkful into his mouth.

Izzy looked up, "Good morning to you, too, Robbie Robbie McBobbie.

A wide smile broke out on Robbie's face at the nickname Izzy had given him soon after they met. "I'm starving. I feel like I missed supper last night or something." He glanced back to Liam at the stove, "There's more, right?" When his question was confirmed with a nod, Robbie turned to Sophie who sat in her high chair greedily shoving chunks of banana into her mouth. "Hey, Sophie, want a bite?" He held up a piece of pancake on the end of his fork.

Sophie threw the lump of banana in her hand across the table where it landed next to Izzy. She leaned toward Robbie like a starving barracuda.

Izzy shook her head, "Not one dripping with syrup, Robbie." Too late, the piece of pancake was already in Sophie's mouth and a look of happiness plastered itself on the baby's face as she chewed.

Liam placed a cooled, plain pancake on Sophie's tray and dropped two more, fresh from the grill, onto Robbie's plate. Izzy sipped her coffee. She looked over at the boy and asked, "Did you sleep okay last night? I thought I heard you call out. Did you have a bad dream?"

"Can't remember anything. A big glass of milk would be perfect about now." He got up and went to the fridge.

Izzy met Liam's eyes for a moment. Sophie took a bite of her pancake, made a face and lobbed the offending food over her tray to Dante, who was lying on the floor by her chair.

Liam frowned. "She loved pancakes a few days ago. What gives?"

"Ask Robbie," Izzy rolled back her eyes and sighed. "I've given Penny the key to your old cabin so she can give it a good cleaning. Will you be here this morning to show her where the place is?" Penny was hired to do the cleaning at the Camp. Having driven all the way out from Dearborn, she was always happy to pick up a couple of extra hours of work. "Justin's getting here today," Izzy added.

The news momentarily stopped the steady flow of food into Robbie's mouth. "Cool."

Liam asked, "Are we planning anything special for dinner?"

"I've got a pork roast ready in the crock pot. You just have to turn it on. They're having the same thing over at the Camp tonight and Dylan's making corn bread. I'll get him to put in an extra pan for me and we can throw a salad together when I get home. Coleslaw would be good. I asked Beulah to pick up a cake in town."

Robbie drained his glass of milk. "Chocolate with lots of icing, right?"

"I know better than to order any other kind." Izzy glanced at Liam. "I got an email from Cynthia this morning. She and your Dad are leaving New Mexico today. She said they will be here in plenty of time for Sophie's birthday."

Robbie got up from the table and reached over to pull Sophie from her high chair. She giggled as he pretended to bite at her fingers. "Dad's bringing me a real native drum – a big one and a little one for you, too, Sophie." He poked at the baby's tummy and she chortled and smacked her hands in his hair.

"Oh joy," Izzy said, glancing at Liam who had finally sat down at the table with one small pancake and a cup of tea. She got up to take Sophie from Robbie. "Geez, her hands are covered in banana and now it's in your hair."

Robbie raked his fingers through his dark hair and laughed as he headed for the door.

"Don't go far," Liam called to the boy, "I want you to watch Sophie while I clean out the chicken coop."

Halfway out the kitchen door, Robbie said, "I'm going to check on my frogs." He had an elaborate experiment with tadpoles and frogs going on behind the cabin near the koi pond.

Izzy wiped at Sophie's face and hands with a washcloth as the child squirmed to get away. "He doesn't remember anything about last night." She put Sophie down on the floor. The baby immediately crawled over to Liam and held her arms up. Once in his lap, she grabbed his last bite of pancake and shoved it into her mouth.

"Why does food look better when it's on someone else's plate?" Liam balanced the little girl on one knee and sipped his tea. He examined the chunk of banana lying on the table before popping it into his mouth. "Should we make an appointment for Robbie to see Rosemary?"

"Not yet. I don't want to take him to the doctor and get him all worried. I'll read up on sleepwalking first. But let's see if we can install some sliding locks high on the inside of all the doors. It's a good idea anyway, with Sophie getting bigger." Izzy glanced at the clock, "I'm late. I've got a conference call with the architect first thing. The next two weeks are going to be crazy. The new cook arrives on Wednesday and two new residents are coming in next week. The place feels like Grand Central Station."

Liam set Sophie down on the floor near a pile of her toys. Dante sidled up to the baby and sniffed at her face, hopeful that Izzy's swiping might not have done a thorough job. Liam pushed the dog away with his foot as he walked over to Izzy. He tipped her chin up and kissed her parted lips before he stood back to look at her. "At least Micah Camp has a pretty station master."

Izzy made a face, "More like security guard, slash traffic director, slash building planner."

✦✦✦✦

"Your ass is really dragging this morning." Heading for the rising cabinet, Beulah shoved past Arianna. "We've got to pick up the pace."

Arianna hurried after with her full tray of dough loaves and thought about all the studying she still had to do. Her university acceptance was conditional on her final English and Math marks. She stifled a yawn as she followed Beulah outside to the wood burning oven to bring in the day's first loaves of cooked bread. She had been hitting the books until after two in the morning. She stacked the fragrant loaves of herb bread on the cooling racks and thought about the small flame of a dream that she had carried in her heart since she'd been a little girl. That flame had flared up bright and strong and she found she could hardly think of anything else.

Her mother used to drag all three of her kids to the doctor with her, having nowhere else to leave them. Arianna remembered the waiting room of the doctor's office – the smell of the place and the nurse all crisp and white and cold in her starched uniform. The woman's face had always looked stern and uncompromising as she waved them down the narrow hall to an examining room. The doctor was the opposite of his nurse. His white coat flapped around him when he walked and his eyes were kind despite his tired smile. He would give them each a hard candy and a tongue depressor to keep them occupied while he talked to their mom. Leaning forward, he would reach out a large hand to cover their mother's trembling fingers. She was so thin that she looked like a ragged, stuffed bird perched on the edge of her chair. Every time Arianna left that office, she smiled at the doctor and told him that someday she would be just like him. All she ever wanted to do was help people.

She finished up with the herb bread and started to clean the large butcher block table. Maybe she should tell Dylan about her desire to become a doctor. He'd be sure to encourage her. But the dream was too fragile yet to share, even with a good friend. She gave herself up to a moment of wallowing in self-pity because she and Dylan were only friends. It sucked, but it was just her kind of luck to fall for an unavailable guy.

Beulah rolled the large tub of cracked wheat dough from the rising cupboard in preparation for forming it into buns. With effort she slapped the large mound of dough down on the table and divided it into two sections, pushing one across the table. Stifling another yawn, Arianna got to work.

⁂⁂⁂⁂

Dylan leaned forward at the waist; his hands rested on the top of his thighs as he waited for his breath to slow. He figured he'd reached the five kilometer mark and he felt more than ready to turn and head back towards the Camp. He'd been running this stretch of logging road since the weather had improved a month ago and he was close to being back in shape, the way he'd been when he played hockey. The running and the workouts in the downstairs gym at the Camp took the edge off a lot of life's problems.

As he started moving again at a slow jog, his mind went back to the morning. He'd known his counselling time would soon come to an end but the last session was harder than he had imagined it would be. Izzy had encouraged him to recall how far they'd come together over the months of counselling work and only then, as he really thought about it, did he realize how much he'd changed. He had stopped being the victimized little boy who couldn't figure out whether or not he was gay and, more to the point, whether or not he was supposed to be gay. He understood that what mattered was who he was now, not what he might have been if his life had been different.

Izzy's last question had shaken him. What would it take for him to feel comfortable enough to be honest about who he was? He had stared at her and said, "Come out of the closet, right? That's what you're talking about."

Izzy had replied firmly, "I'm not talking about a grand announcement or anything like that. I'm not even talking about while you're here at the Camp. But when you move to Montreal, it will be a whole new start in a new place. You'll be meeting new people. It might be good to think about how you want to present yourself."

He hadn't wanted to get out of the chair when the session ended and he could tell Izzy knew it. She had reached out her hand and put it on his arm. "I always find these last sessions hard." As she stood up, so did he. She had put her arms out and said, "Can I hug you?" He'd let her pull him close and had rested his chin on the top of her black curls. Izzy's embrace meant a lot to him. She was the person who had helped him explore the painful moments of his past while pointing him in the direction of the doors to his future.

The skittering sound of sliding gravel brought Dylan to a skidding stop. He heard a thumping noise from around the next corner of the logging road; his heart pounded from more than exertion and memories. Visions of a bear lumbering out of the bush or a cougar leaping at him filled his mind. Instead he saw a slim guy walking towards him holding his left elbow and cursing to himself.

Dylan called out, "You okay?"

The guy looked up in surprise. "I slipped on some loose gravel on the hill and came down on my elbow. Hurts like hell." When he got close, he reached out his hand, "Mike Sampson. I work at the sawmill. I thought I was the only one crazy enough to jog on this road."

Dylan offered his hand for the shake. "I've been running up here for about a month. The noise you made there had me thinking I might end up as some animal's dinner."

"Well, you can't take the wildlife for granted but the most I've ever run into is a grouse." Mike sized Dylan up. "How far do you run?"

"I've been working up to ten kilometers. I'm almost there. I still walk bits of it and my time sucks but I'm making steady progress."

"I'm training for a half marathon in August. That's twenty-one K." Dylan whistled under his breath as Mike said, "I wouldn't mind a running partner, if you're up for it."

"I'm not in your league, man. I'd hold you back."

"I'm not up to the entire distance yet and you don't have to run the whole way with me. We could meet up for part of the run and maybe watch each other's back. We'd have safety in numbers in case we run into any of that wildlife."

"Are you headed back towards the sawmill now?"

"Ya, my truck's there and I'd better take it easy for a while and avoid swinging this elbow around."

The two guys began to run. Mike paced himself to Dylan's speed and Dylan pushed himself for Mike's benefit.

"This is where I turn off." Dylan pointed down the wide drive to Micah Camp.

Mike slowed to an on-the-spot jog. "You live down at the Camp? Hey, I thought I recognized you from somewhere. Aren't you the guy who cooked that dinner for the talent show last year?"

"Did you try the cheesecake?"

"Three slices."

Dylan chuckled as he waved and headed away. Mike seemed like an okay guy.

⛧⛧⛧⛧

Justin hopped out of the passenger side of Beulah's truck when it pulled into the sawmill yard. He walked forward to meet the boss. Sticking out his hand, he smiled broadly and said, "Reg, good to see you again."

The man jammed the ball cap on his head up and down a couple of times as he shook Justin's hand. "Great to have you back. The orders are piling up and I'm like a fuckin' one-armed paper hanger around here, running the show on my own. I've got the work lined up for you, boyo."

Beulah leaned out the driver's side window to shout, "I've got to get this cake down to Izzy's."

Justin spotted Mike cradling his elbow as he made his way towards his truck. He called back across the yard, "I'll walk down. You go ahead without me." Beulah waved and turned the truck in an arc to cross the gravel road and head down Izzy's twisting driveway.

Meeting Mike halfway, Justin said, "How's everything going, man? What happened to your arm?"

Reg joined them, scowling as he spoke, "This crazy running better not mean you're injured and can't work on that goddamn saw. We've got a huge order that has to be finished tomorrow."

Mike rubbed his arm and grinned, "It's nothing major. Don't have a coronary, Reg. Your face is so red you look like a tomato wearing a hat."

Digging a toothpick out of the top pocket of his shirt, Reg worked it frantically around his mouth. "Got every reason in the world to have a goddamn coronary the way the work is pouring in. Getting you trained on that saw has been the lighthouse beacon of hope that has kept my boat afloat." Reg grinned as he pointed over at Justin, "And having this guy back for the next four months is certainly going to bring my blood pressure down." He started to walk back towards the sawmill office, calling over his shoulder, "I'll see the pair of you bright and early tomorrow morning and you both better be good and ready to work your asses off."

Mike and Justin exchanged knowing smiles. Reg's colourful language and his obsession about keeping sawmill production booming was something they were both used to. Mike got into his truck. "I'm glad you're here to share the load. Reg isn't going to have as much time for chewing me out, now that you're back."

Justin leaned against the driver's side of the vehicle, "He'll probably delegate the job to me. I can see his list now ... right at the top ... chew Mike out once a day." They both laughed. "What's with the running?"

"I'm training for a half marathon. Hey, you should give it a go. Train with me. I just met up with a guy named Dylan, from down at the Camp. He's into running. We could all train together."

Justin backed up and held up his hands, "Running is not really my thing. I'm hoping to play some baseball this year. Beulah is talking about resurrecting the *Crater Lake Timber Wolves* for this big ball tournament she's planning. She needs people for a mixed softball team. Why don't you come out for the team? Or maybe for the girls."

"Sounds more like something for my brother, Zach. He's better at team sports and the guy thinks he's God's gift when it comes to girls. I'll let him know."

"Probably room for the both of you. Look, I'll make you a deal. I'll think about running if you think about the ball team."

"Deal," Mike said as he started his truck. "See you tomorrow, bright and early."

Justin watched Mike turn onto the gravel logging road towards Dearborn. He strolled over to Izzy and Liam's driveway and started the walk down. Stopping in the shade of the tall evergreens that arched over the road, he took a deep breath and stared up into the intricate pattern of branches. Trees had begun to fascinate him. These were second growth and he tried to estimate how old they were. A squirrel chattered angrily from the end of one of the branches, scolding Justin for having the nerve to interrupt its jump from one tree to the next. He smiled and called out, "Take it easy, little guy, or you'll fall right out of that tree." Walking again, he caught a glimpse of Crater Lake's sparkling water and he knew he was home.

Liam and Robbie met him in the driveway. Sophie was between them trying to take a few tentative steps while they each held one of her hands. Justin stopped dead in his tracks when he passed the brand new truck. He pointed back at it and gave a thumbs up to Liam who shook his head and said, "Don't ask."

Justin lifted the toddling child up into his arms and swung her around. "This can't be my little Sophie pie?" After about ten seconds of silent speculation, the baby patted his face and started a non-stop conversation of gibberish.

Inside the cabin, Izzy got up from one of the armchairs in the living room to greet him. She gave him a quick hug and pointed at Sophie in his arms, "She didn't make strange with you at all? She's been doing that lately with people she hasn't seen for a bit."

"Hey," he smiled back and turned to tickle the baby. "Sophie and I know how to get along, don't we kid?" Sniffing, Justin said, "Something sure smells good."

Izzy headed towards the kitchen, calling over her shoulder, "I get the hint. Dinner is on the way."

Later, when he pushed back from the table and refused Robbie's dare to eat yet another slice of cake, Justin handed his plate to Izzy. She asked, "So, the year at school was good?"

"Ya, things went well. I'm thinking of focusing my engineering major on forestry next year. The courses look interesting." Justin took a moment before adding, "I've got a girlfriend; her name is Lauren. I hope you guys don't mind but I invited her up for the weekend of your wedding."

There was the slightest pause before Izzy said, "Of course you are more than welcome to bring a guest to the wedding. We look forward to meeting her."

Robbie shoved the last bite of cake into his mouth and burped loudly. "Lisa-Marie won't like that." Liam gave him a pointed look but Robbie went on, unaware of the silence that had quite suddenly come over the people around the table, "I mean you bringing a girl named Lauren to the wedding. She won't like that at all."

Izzy took Robbie's plate and told him in a gentle tone, "How about deciding what you should be doing right now, okay? Come on; give me a hand with the dishes."

With the clean-up finished, Liam said, "I'll help you carry your stuff over to the cabin, Justin." He sat down in the entrance to shove his feet into his hiking boots.

Justin grabbed the large duffel and his pack, leaving Liam to carry the guitar case. As they went out he noticed the sliding bolt near the top of the entry door. "Crater Lake must have changed quite a bit if you have to double lock the doors now."

"We're trying to anticipate some of the issues we'll have with Sophie once she starts walking," Liam explained. "The last thing we'd want is for her to get outside on her own."

Justin pointed to the driveway, "That new truck is a beauty."

Liam shrugged, "I prefer the old Dodge. You can't haul much of anything in that short box. Take it for a spin anytime. The keys are hanging inside the workshop."

When they had almost reached the corner that led into the trees at the back of the garden, Liam said, "I meant what I said about the lock being great for Sophie but I put it up because of Robbie. We found him last night out in the driveway ... sleepwalking ... he didn't remember a thing about it this morning."

"That's weird."

"After the shooting he had more than a few bad dreams. He'd wake up really scared. But that passed and he hasn't had any problems for months. This sleepwalking thing came right out of the blue."

"He's not the only one that had a few bad dreams."

"I hear you, it was a terrible thing." The two men came out of the trees, walked past the guest cabin and carried on down a small hill. "A girlfriend, hey?" Liam's voice was quiet as they went in single file to cross the bridge.

"Ya, she's beautiful and smart. Sometimes I feel like I've been called up to the majors." When the silence had stretched out between them for as long as it took to climb the rise to his cabin, Justin added, "The first few months back at school in the fall were hard. I couldn't stop thinking about Lisa-Marie and I wasn't sure I'd done the right thing, letting her go. But then I met Lauren and things are good now."

Liam remained silent. Justin sounded like a guy who needed to convince himself more than anyone else, of the truth in what he was saying.

SEVEN

Izzy sat at one of the tables in the large, empty dining room at Micah Camp. She frowned down at a budget document on her laptop, gave up the effort to understand the columns of numbers and closed the lid. She watched Robbie finish his math homework. Sophie crawled around the room and pulled herself up to a standing position at every chair she encountered. Hoping to get away soon after lunch, Izzy had told Liam to drop the kids off with her when it was time for him to leave.

Liam drove up to the reserve outside of Cedar Falls once a week. He had told Izzy that while he was there, he mostly sat with guys who had problems. Sometimes they talked and sometimes they didn't. It was about being present more than anything else. Izzy certainly understood that from her own counselling work.

Robbie often went with his brother. The boy was accepted any day he showed up at the Band operated school on the reserve. He blended in, doing whatever the rest of the kids his age were doing. Sophie usually stayed with Bethany if she wasn't busy. Today, Robbie had a ton of math homework to finish and Bethany had an appointment in town, so Izzy took the kids.

She scanned the dining room to make sure Sophie was still in sight. Lately, the speed with which the little girl could get from place to place took Izzy by surprise. She checked her watch. Jim would be back any time.

Moments later, she caught sight of him coming through the door off the kitchen. He smiled broadly and chatted as he ushered in a woman and a child who hugged a small animal carrier to her chest. A confused frown flitted over Izzy's face as she got up and crossed the room.

Jim gestured towards Izzy, "Well, here she is ... the boss lady." He herded the woman and the child forward. "Our new cook, Brigit, and her daughter, Tabitha," he laughed when the little girl made a face at him. "Sorry. She prefers to be called, Tabby."

Izzy automatically reached forward to shake hands with the woman. Dark eyes met Izzy's from a face of chocolate black. Brigit's short, corkscrew curls were pulled back by a twisted, red hairband, revealing a broad forehead dominated by sweeping brows.

"Hello. I'm Izzy Montgomery. It's good to meet you, Brigit," Izzy's glanced at the girl by the woman's side. Before she could greet her, Robbie came across the room and crouched down to peer into the animal carrier.

"What's in there?" he asked. "Oh, a cat. What's its name?"

Tabby smiled shyly and leaned in against her mother's leg. "Mr. Jangles."

Robbie squinted at the girl for a moment before he said, "I'm nine. How old are you?"

Tabby drew herself up as tall as she could. Standing clear of her mother, she announced, "Almost nine."

Her mother shook her head, "Just-turned eight is not almost nine, Tabitha."

Tabby shrugged, "Well, it's more than eight, isn't it?"

Izzy watched Brigit drop an arm around her daughter's shoulder, squeeze her close and smile down at her. The mother's eyes shone with love. When the Board had informed Izzy that they'd hired a new cook, no one had said anything about the woman having a child. As far as Izzy was concerned, it was a reality worth mentioning.

Brigit glanced into the dining room. Her eyes widened to circles of concern as she pointed and rushed forward. Izzy spun around to see Sophie standing in the middle of a table, a look of delight on her face as she clapped her hands. In no time, Brigit had hold of the child and Izzy swept Sophie off the table and into her arms. The baby was still clapping as Izzy tucked her against her hip. "My goodness, this one is a handful at times." She frowned as she looked at Brigit, "Sorry for the drama. I don't usually have the baby here with me. Let me take care of her then we can meet in my office."

"Can Tabby and I go outside? I'll show her around." Robbie poked his finger inside the cage and rubbed the cat behind the ear as he spoke to Tabby, "Have you had him for long? I did a report on cats a while ago. Did you know cats are the only pets that never forget how to hunt? And they can see in the dark."

Tabby leaned close to the cage. "Mr. Jangles is a very smart cat. We put that bell on him so he can't hurt birds."

Robbie stood up and said, "He's way smaller than the other cat." He looked over at Izzy, "Can we go outside?"

"If her mom doesn't mind." Izzy glanced at Brigit, "Robbie knows his way around here and he'll keep a careful eye on Tabby." Izzy smiled at the girl who had glued herself to Robbie's side. She was adorable with her milk-chocolate skin a couple of shades lighter than her mom's and her shining, dark eyes.

Brigit pointed at the cat carrier, "Give Mr. Jangles to me. You listen to Robbie and don't wander off anywhere on your own."

Gesturing with her hand for Brigit to follow her, Izzy headed for the kitchen. She called over her shoulder as she went, "Don't go near the water, Robbie." When the boy waved back at her to acknowledge the warning, she thought about his words and wondered ... what other cat? He and Tabby were already chatting a mile a minute as they left the dining room, crossed the massive living room and made their way out the heavy doors of Micah Camp's main building.

Izzy grabbed Sophie's bottle out of the fridge and put it in the microwave to heat. Dylan stood at the kitchen counter grating a mountain of cheese for the baked pasta dish that was on the lunch menu. "Brigit, this is Dylan, one of our residents. He's almost finished his time with us and has been accepted to a prestigious culinary school in Montreal. Dylan has been running the kitchen on his own since our previous cook broke her ankle. I'm sure he is more than happy to meet you." Sophie started to fuss and squirm; Izzy glanced down at the baby and smoothed her hair away from her face, "Just a minute you little monkey. Diaper change and a bottle coming up."

Dylan said, "Hi ... I'd come over and shake your hand but I'd better keep at this. Izzy's right. It's going to be good to get back to being the cook's assistant and not the cook."

Brigit nodded as her gaze took in the spacious kitchen with its walk-in fridge, commercial stove, two wall ovens, massive counters and deep sinks – everything was polished and shining.

With the heated bottle in hand, Izzy turned to Dylan, "Brigit and I have a few things to go over. Then I'm sure she'll want to take the rest of today to get settled in and learn her way around the place." Glancing at Brigit she said, "Dylan will be staying on and working in the kitchen with you for the next couple of months. He'll be able to help you find everything and get used to our routines."

Again Brigit remained silent as she followed Izzy to her office.

"Have a seat; I'll be with you in a moment." Izzy laid Sophie in the playpen that stood in the corner of her office and changed the baby's diaper. She handed her the bottle and the pink bunny that Sophie couldn't be without.

The sound of Tabby's laugher floated in through the open window. The girl was chasing after Robbie who had the unfurling string of a kite in his hand. Izzy smiled over at Brigit. "Well, that game should end momentarily with yet another kite stuck in a tree." She gestured toward the baby who sucked avidly on her bottle, "She should settle down right away. It's past her nap time."

A knock drew both women's attention to the balding, portly man who stood outside the glass door. Izzy took a deep breath. *What now?* Then she remembered the time. She waved the man into the office, "Gordon, I'm sorry. Robbie's outside, I'll call him." She turned to Brigit, "This is our math instructor, Gordon." On her way to the window, she said "Brigit is our new cook."

Gordon shook Brigit's hand, "Welcome, welcome. Have you just arrived?"

"Yes, from Toronto."

"Oh gosh, the culture shock." Gordon's eyes widened dramatically as he shook his head. "Hope we'll be able to compete with the big city." Robbie and Tabby ran into the office. Gordon looked at the girl in surprise as he asked, "Who is this young lady?"

"That is my daughter, Tabitha," Brigit said.

The girl scowled at her mother, "Tabby." She glanced up at Gordon, "I like people to call me Tabby." Staring around the room, she said, "Where is Mr. Jangles."

"He's safe and sound right under my chair," Brigit pointed back at the carrier. "Please shake hands and say hello to Mr. -" she gave Gordon a quizzical look.

"McKenzie," Gordon said. He looked over at Izzy and added, "I hadn't heard about our new cook's daughter." He turned back to the little girl, leaned forward and said, "Please, call me Gordon."

"She'll call you Mr. McKenzie, thank you." Brigit nodded at Tabby.

"It is very nice to meet you, Mr. McKenzie."

Gordon smiled as he let go of the little girl's hand and glanced at Robbie, "Ready for your math lesson?"

Tabby hopped up and down with excitement. "I'm good at math, Mr. McKenzie. I know how to add and subtract and I can do most of the times tables by heart. I can count money, too."

Robbie whistled and asked, "Can Tabby come along to my lesson?"

Gordon nodded, "Of course. I think I need to assess the claim she has made about knowing the times tables." Tabby straightened her shoulders and waved goodbye to her mother as she followed Gordon and Robbie out of the room.

Brigit turned anxiously to Izzy, "I don't want her to be in the way."

"No worries. Gordon will keep her busy at something while he works with Robbie." Izzy settled into a chair, "At last. I'm not always so distracted and I don't often have an office full of kids."

Brigit stayed standing. "Your baby is beautiful. It's easy to forget that our children start out so small." She glanced away from Sophie, who was already asleep. "And your son is kind to show Tabby around."

"Robbie is my partner Liam's brother." Izzy would let the comment about Sophie slide for now.

Brigit cleared her throat, glanced toward the door and said, "I need to get a coffee before we talk. To be honest, I'm wiped out from the trip and I'm definitely feeling the effects of the three hour time difference."

Izzy got up quickly, "Brigit, I'm sorry. What am I thinking? My welcome is looking less and less considerate. I'll go straight to the kitchen and get coffee. If you want to freshen up a bit there's a washroom down the hall." She smiled apologetically and said, "I'll be back in a few minutes."

Later, after making small talk over coffee and raspberry scones, Izzy leaned forward and said, "Let's keep any work talk brief. You'll be anxious to settle in. Do you have any questions about the job that can't wait until tomorrow?"

Brigit set down her coffee cup and sat up ramrod straight in her chair. Her voice took on a clipped quality as she said, "I understood I would be the only cook. It's great that Dylan was able to step in and is willing to help out but I prefer to work on my own."

Izzy felt her eyebrow rise slightly. "Part of our program requires the residents to participate in work experience while they're here at the Camp. The kitchen has always been one of our primary sites. Dylan is different from the usual kitchen helper you might be asked to supervise. He came to us with a year of cooking school already under his belt and he has worked closely with our former cook for months." She paused, took a deep breath and went on, "Dylan will be working with you until he leaves in August." She didn't want to use a like-it-or-lump-it tone but she knew no other way to put it.

"If that's the way you do things," Brigit said. Izzy felt the other woman holding her gaze as if they were in a staring match. *Oh, this is ridiculous.* Izzy deliberately lowered her eyes. She heard Brigit say, "I wasn't aware I would be supervising residents in the kitchen as well as doing overnight duty."

Forcing her shoulders to relax, Izzy said, "All the adults at Micah Camp play a role in the residents' programs and progress. That is an integral part of what we do here. The kitchen is the heart of this place, as it is in many homes. The kids will gravitate to you."

"That makes sense." Brigit nodded with her brow furrowed in thought. "Thanks for setting me straight." She drained the last of her coffee and stood up. "I don't think there is anything else I need to know right now. I'd really like to collect Tabby, unpack and maybe even catch a short nap before I do any exploring."

Izzy stood and fumbled for the right words, "About Tabby –" A screeching howl came from the animal carrier under Brigit's chair. As the cat's protests continued, Izzy spoke faster, "Will Tabby stay here at the Camp with you?"

Izzy watched Brigit bristle as she pulled her body up even straighter. The woman's voice shook with anger, "Where else on earth would she go?" The question had obviously provoked a defensive reaction.

Izzy held up her hand, "No one told me that you had a daughter. I didn't mean to say anything to offend you and there isn't a problem with Tabby staying here. The cabin we were going to put you in is on the small size but I'll let you have a look at it and you can decide if you think it will be okay."

Brigit gave Izzy an incredulous stare, "No one told you that I was bringing my daughter with me?" When Izzy silently shook her head, Brigit's voice dripped with indignation, "How could something like that happen? I never tried to hide the fact that I have a child. Everyone I spoke with knew Tabby was coming with me."

"How it happened doesn't really matter," Izzy replied. "You and Tabby are here now." She paused for a moment to process a thought that had popped into her head. "What about school? Tabby can't have been finished the year when you left Toronto."

"I talked to her teacher and she told me some of the things I can do to make sure she'll be ready for grade four in the fall. To be honest, I didn't realize how isolated we'd be here at Micah Camp. I'll have to think about how Tabby is going to get to school."

"Dearborn is only twenty-five minutes away but it isn't an easy drive on the gravel road. People do come and go regularly but their schedules wouldn't always match up with school hours." Izzy decided that now was definitely the time to offer an olive branch. "Liam home schools Robbie, with the help of some people here at the Camp. Maybe he would be willing to teach the two kids together. It would be great for Robbie to have another child to study with.

Because he and Tabby are so close in age, I'm sure a lot of their work could overlap." In the face of Brigit's silence, Izzy backed off, "There's lots of time for you to think about that. You'll want to get to know us better and meet Liam before you decide."

"Thank you for the offer." Brigit retrieved the cat carrier from under her chair. "I'd better get this monster settled before he claws his way out of the cage."

"Right, I'll grab the keys and show you to your cabin." After checking that Sophie still slept, Izzy led the way out of her office.

EIGHT

B rigit stroked the hair from her sleeping daughter's face. At first Tabby had flat out refused to lie down and rest. She had insisted that she must go to Robbie's house to see his frogs. Only after a stern application of what Brigit called the look, a strategy used by her own mother, had Tabby gone to the bedroom. Within ten minutes she was fast asleep and Brigit prayed the child would stay that way for at least an hour.

She stretched out on the bed beside Tabby and tried to relax her body and her mind. The trip had exhausted her. They had flown into Vancouver from Toronto yesterday and had spent the night in a hotel by the airport. This morning, before six they had made their way to the smaller south terminal where they boarded a Pacific Coastal plane for the forty-five minute flight to the northern end of Vancouver Island and the small town of Cedar Falls. Met by Jim, they had piled into the Micah Camp van and an hour's drive later, they had arrived at their destination.

The view from the van had been an eye-opener. She and Tabitha had seen trees, trees and more trees and had caught glimpses of the vast Pacific Ocean. Jim had detoured into Dearborn so Tabby could use the restroom at the Petro-Canada station; then he had driven around the town to point out the various sites. Stunned, Brigit had realized that this rural town would be the place where she and Tabby might see a movie at the local theatre, go for a stroll on the boardwalk, share an order of fish and chips, or buy clothes at the Field's store.

What she had glimpsed of Micah Camp also amazed her. Expanses of grass ran down to the shores of the lake. A neat row of small cabins stretched out on one side of the chalet-style main building; on the other side, a covered

45

walkway led to a large workshop. Izzy had pointed out that building as they'd passed it on their way to the cabin that was to be Brigit and Tabby's new home. She'd made reference to the manufacture of paper and soap products but Brigit hadn't known what Izzy was talking about. By that time, she was so tired she wasn't taking in much of anything.

The cabin assigned to her and Tabby might be on the small side but it was certainly bigger than the bedroom in her parent's house that she and her daughter had shared for the last two years. Brigit had fallen in love with the place as soon as she saw it. The cedar panelling and wood floors, the small but perfectly-appointed bathroom and the comfy living room soothed her mind.

She closed her eyes and heard a bird warbling a one-note, two-note song somewhere in the trees. No sirens, no blasting horns or traffic noises, none of the steady thrumming hum of a city in constant motion. Life at Crater Lake promised to be very different than life in the Haitian neighbourhood in Toronto where she had been born and raised.

She glanced quickly at Tabby. The girl slept on, curled into a small ball with Mr. Jangles snuggled up to her. Brigit searched her daughter's face for any traces of what these last two years might have done to her. She saw nothing.

Lying back down, she pictured the guy who worked in the kitchen – Dylan. He was young, but imposing. His confidence, which was apparent even during their brief encounter, intimidated the hell out of her. The guy had way more cooking experience than she did. He was bound to notice that she wasn't as qualified as she pretended to be. Brigit would have to do something or Dylan would turn out to be another guy who screwed around with her plans.

What had she got herself into? So many things in her life had changed. It wasn't so long ago that she had been on top of the world – a strong woman who had brushed aside all the talk about how she was throwing her life away by raising a child on her own. She had received scholarships and finished college, working part-time all the way through so she could keep herself and Tabby in a clean, if not fancy apartment.

With a degree in criminology, she applied to become a Toronto City cop and off she went to the police academy. Everyone told her the job wouldn't be a breeze but she believed she had whatever it would take for her to become a good cop. At the academy, she saw the kind of crap the male officers could dish out and she had to admit, it shocked her. She came from a community and a culture that valued strong women. The adversity only strengthened her resolve to stand up to them. She wouldn't let any of it get to her – not the sexual innuendos, the covert and sometimes overt threats or the overwhelming sense that some of the men hated the uniformed women who stood beside them.

What Brigit couldn't take was the degree to which the daily attacks affected some of the other female cops with whom she worked. She had always been one to take up the cause of the underdog. When it came to sticking up for someone else, Brigit often let common sense go by the wayside. She started getting in the middle of disputes. She put herself forward; she made waves and got a reputation as a troublemaker. Things came to a head when she reported a ranking officer for sexual comments he made to one of the female recruits. Everyone told her to stay out of it – even the recruit – but Brigit wouldn't. The male officer denied everything; the recruit refused to make any accusations and applied for a transfer.

Things went downhill after that. Brigit was first in line for every shitty assignment. And a select group of male officers went after her with everything they had. More than once, she wakened in the middle of the night, reliving the harassment of the previous day. She lay there in a cold sweat, knowing that if the going got tough, no one would be there to cover her ass. But she wouldn't quit.

One day she got called into her captain's office. He informed her that he was putting her on disability leave until further notice. A series of complaints about her ability to perform her job had made their way to his desk. He suggested that perhaps she had some sort of a problem and told her outright that he had no interest in what that problem might be. Then he advised her to see the department shrink.

No way would she take that kind of set-up without hearing the complaints and challenging the captain's decision. She got a lawyer and fought back, but the deck was stacked against her and no one came forward to speak up for her. Two years of battling for reinstatement drained her savings and wore her out. She and Tabby had to move back home. Her parents finally convinced her to give up the fight, take the settlement her lawyer recommended – a slap-in-the-face pittance – and get on with her life. Their suggested course of action amounted to giving up and she had gone along with it.

But quitting dealt a heavy blow to her self-esteem and she had a hard time rallying. She went for job interviews but she couldn't hold it together to present herself as she must do, if she hoped to be hired. Her father suggested retraining, maybe enrolling in a program at the local college. She had tried cooking because her mother had said, "How hard can that be?"

It might not have been all that difficult if she had been able to get along with the male instructor. But she had made up her mind that most, if not all men were out to get her and she tended to see the instructor's behaviour in that light. She didn't make things easy for herself or anyone else. The program ended and she had no certification. Getting a job and being able to move out of her parent's house seemed like an impossible dream. She got depressed. She hated herself for what she was putting her family through. And she felt guilty that she wasn't there for Tabby because of the depth of her own self-pity.

Then one day her mom had come home with a plan. She worked for a lady whose sister knew of a place that wanted a cook. Brigit worried about facing another interview – about not being able to get it together and about disappointing her parents, yet again. In response to this fear, her mother had said that with any luck, there wouldn't even be an interview. However, she had explained, there was a catch. Brigit and Tabby would have to move to British Columbia. The job included accommodations and it paid well, but the Camp was located at the northern end of a place called Vancouver Island.

Brigit had broken down crying in her mother's arms. She didn't want to leave her parents or the neighbourhood or the city. Her mother had given her a shake and she had told her, "You need to take Tabby and get away from this place and all the bad memories that are dragging you down. Do you think I wanted to leave Haiti and come to this Godforsaken place where it's so cold half the time that I think I've landed on the moon? Well, I didn't and I cried in my own mother's arms the way you're doing now. She told me to think about the baby in my belly ... you ... and I knew I had to do it. You think about your child and you go and build yourself a new life in this British Columbia place."

True to her mother's word, there had been no interview – just a letter in the mail saying the job was hers and information on how to make the necessary travel arrangements. And now, she was Micah Camp's new cook – a woman who wasn't going to take a bit of crap from any man ever again, a cook who wasn't all that sure about how to cook, a mother who had the responsibility of making a decent life for her child. She definitely had her work cut out for her.

⛄⛄⛄⛄

After the kids were settled for the night, Izzy called Darlene at home. Without much preamble, she asked, "Why wasn't I told that Brigit Lafitte has an eight-year-old daughter that she planned to bring to Micah Camp?"

"A daughter? Hmmm ... I can't say that I knew about that either."

"Come on, Darlene. Stop playing games. How did the Board so quickly find us a cook willing to live at Micah Camp?"

A long, drawn-out silence on the other end of the line preceded Darlene's sigh. "Okay, okay, but what I'm going to tell you is confidential. This woman, Brigit, has no idea that any of us know anything about her private life. Her mother does housecleaning in Toronto for May Spencer's sister. You remember, May. She's one of the Vancouver Board members. The mother told May's sister Brigit's story. Later, when the sister phoned May, it just so happened that the news of the job was still sitting on May's desk. One thing led to another and the Board offered Brigit the position."

"That is the most ridiculously convoluted case of pulling strings that I've ever had the misfortune to hear. Is that how the Board generally goes about hiring people? Is Nick the son of a Board member's friend? Oh, never mind. Get on with the rest of it because I know there's more."

"I heard a bit about what happened to this Brigit woman and it really sucks. She used to be a cop in Toronto. She got pushed out of the job because she stood up to a few of the he-man types on the force. In the end, the lawyers wore her down until she took a crappy settlement."

Izzy's hand tightened around the phone. The last thing she wanted to hear was that a new staff member had a load of past emotional issues that she might be stuck dealing with. "At least tell me that she's had training as a cook."

"Oh yes, she did a community college course of some type. She also has a degree in criminology."

"If the steaks in the freezer go on a rampage and try to murder the pot roasts, I'll know who to call."

Darlene's deep laugh barrelled down the phone line. "Oh God, Izzy, you kill me with that wicked sense of humour. Look, I'm sorry about the fact that you didn't know she has a child. Is it really a big deal?"

"I'll handle it."

"Great. While I have you on the phone, three new residents will be arriving next week instead of the two we spoke of at our last meeting."

"How can you simply jam someone else onto the acceptance list like that? I haven't seen files or any documentation." Izzy realized she sounded as prissy and demanding of the necessary paperwork as Roland always had. Next thing she knew, she'd be walking around the Camp passing out thick binders of procedures.

"Don't shoot the messenger, Izzy. Oh ... there is something else. Dr. Rosemary spoke to town council last night about the need for an anger-management group for men but no one is qualified to facilitate the thing. The Board has been throwing around the idea that Micah Camp should be more of a presence in the local community. I thought that you could ask Nick to take this on. I do recall from his resume that he's had experience with that type of thing. The group would meet only one night a week and, of course, he would be compensated for the work."

Izzy sucked in her breath and practically sputtered, "You want me to ask Nick to start moonlighting?"

"I'll email you the details tomorrow. I've got to go. The Mayor has an episode of *Glee* all cued up on the TV for us to watch."

Liam paused on the top step from the back office and watched Izzy as she sat in the chair staring into space. He had been at his desk going over one of his wedding checklists while waiting for her to get off the phone. As his eyes lingered on her, he remembered how the idea of getting married had come about. It had been right after Christmas when they came home from attending Beulah and Bethany's wedding.

Izzy broached the topic by asking, "What are your thoughts on marriage, Liam?" When he didn't respond, more out of being stunned by her question than any thoughts he might have had about marriage, Izzy continued, "If you're not categorically opposed to the institution or anything like that, I'm thinking that you and I should get married. My reasons have to do with money."

Liam glanced up to the ceiling far above his head. "Now is the winter of my discontent made glorious summer by such an offer as this."

Izzy teased him back, saying, "I hope I'm not going to regret your Christmas gift." She had given him an iPod with hours of literary lectures uploaded onto the shiny silver and black object. Returning to the subject at hand, Izzy said, "I'm worried about what would happen if I died and you were left alone to look after Sophie, Robbie, this whole place and the sawmill. I want things to be secure into the future for you."

She kept talking as she curled up in one of the armchairs. "To be honest, it's about more than money. We're basically alone in the world. Well, you have your father. But we need to advocate for one another." To his bewildered stare, she elaborated, "Oh you know ... be there to pull the plug or not if that is what the other person wants. We're not getting any younger. So what do you say?"

Without hesitation, he answered, "No, I don't think so, Iz."

"You don't want to marry me?" She sat up in surprise.

He quickly reassured her, "I didn't say that, but I sure as hell won't marry you for the reasons you've given ...a few measly dollars and who gets to pull the plug.

Izzy laughed and said, "It's more than a few measly bucks and you know it. So, why would you marry me, then?

He drew her to her feet and kissed her. "I will marry you for the only reason that matters. You, Izzy Montgomery, are the love of my life. Nothing makes sense without you beside me." He let go of her to drop down onto one knee, grab her hand in his and ask, "Will you marry me?"

She pulled him up beside her. "Since it was my idea in the first place ... yes, I will. And just so you know, for future reference, I want you to pull the plug if I'm brain dead for more than thirty days."

Liam shook off the memories of their engagement day. He walked down the stairs and into the living room. "Penny for your thoughts," he said to Izzy.

She turned her gaze to his, "I'm not sure they're worth that much. This job is not what I thought it would be. I'm starting to understand why Roland acted the way he did. Working with the Board seems to be one headache after another."

Liam reached over to place the flat of his hand on Izzy's forehead, "Understand Roland? Who are you and what have you done with my soon-to-be wife?"

Izzy brushed his hand away and filled him in on the details of Brigit's arrival. "Though it was a shock – her showing up with a daughter like that – Tabby is so cute. She took to Robbie like they'd known each other forever."

"I wondered what Robbie was talking about at dinner. I assume she is the owner of the cat named Mr. Jangles?"

"Yes. I never saw the thing out of its cage but it sure made some screeching, angry noises. I've never cared for cats." With a thoughtful look on her face, Izzy asked, "Did Robbie have a cat before he came here?"

"No idea, you'd have to ask Dad but I doubt he has much of an idea what Robbie's life was like before he brought him to us." They both knew that Liam's dad, Alexander, had not seen Robbie since the boy was a baby. He had only landed back in his son's life when Robbie's mother had died suddenly.

Changing the subject, Izzy asked, "How would you feel about including Tabby in your home schooling program? It might be good for Robbie. Of course, it would depend on what Brigit thinks of the idea. I didn't make the best impression but I bet you'll charm her."

Liam brushed off the compliment, "While it is true that I can be charming, I don't see why I would want to charm my way into more work.

Home schooling means preparing lessons ... two kids equals twice the work."

"But you're a teacher and isn't your job a lot about adapting, taking advantage of teachable moments and going with what the child is ready to learn?"

Liam shook his head as he said, "Stop with the education babble. You are right about one thing, though; it could be good for Robbie."

They both looked up towards Robbie's loft. Izzy said, "He's slept through the night without any trouble for a few days now."

"Maybe it was a one-time thing," Liam added.

Izzy stretched in her chair and asked, "How is the wedding plan coming along?"

Liam grinned, "That is for me to know and you to find out. Will the dresses be ready on time?"

"Rest assured that the one thing that I am in charge of will be ready on time." Izzy shook her head as she remembered their earlier talk about wedding dresses. It had occurred a month or so after their decision to get married. Liam had caught Izzy by surprise when he asked, "What are you planning to wear for the wedding, Iz?"

She had looked up from digging one of Robbie's T-shirts out of the laundry basket, giving it a brisk snap, folding it and laying it on a pile of the boy's things. "Oh, I was thinking of not wearing anything at all. A naked wedding might be fun."

Liam pulled a magazine from a stack of things he'd brought home from the library that afternoon. He flipped it open to a page marked with a blue tab. "What do you think of a dress like this?"

Izzy took the magazine from his hands and sat down on the sofa beside him. She stared wide-eyed at the full-page photo of a young woman who stood facing the camera in an elaborate, formal garden. The model wore a traditional white gown; the low-cut bodice was scattered with pearls and the train swept across the lawn behind her. She held a massive bouquet of pink roses in front of her at waist level. The fabric behind the flowers took on a dreamy glow. Her eyes were downcast; thick lashes shadowed her glowing cheeks. Izzy swallowed in disbelief.

Liam pulled out another magazine, flipped to a similar blue tab and said, "Or maybe something like this?"

Izzy accepted the second magazine wordlessly. This time she saw a woman wearing a white, off-the-shoulder, peasant-type dress; her arms were filled with wild flowers and more of the same decorated her long hair. She was spinning around in a field. Izzy closed the magazine and placed both her hands flat on the top cover, trying to obscure the words, *Modern Bride*. She glanced at Liam for a moment to see if this was all part of some kind of elaborate joke. When it obviously wasn't, she said, "Have you lost your mind, Liam?"

"Don't think so. You did say I could plan the wedding." He pulled out another book and turned to a red tab. "Do you like the idea of fondant for the wedding cake? It looks pretty fancy." He flipped to another red tabbed page, "But this looks more like people could actually eat it. What do you think?"

Izzy reached past Liam to grab a notebook from the pile. She held it up and said, "What exactly do these colour-coded tabs stand for?"

Liam smiled as he began ticking off a list of things on his fingers, "Blue is for clothing, red for food and beverages, yellow for the service, green for music, purple for decorations and flowers, orange for the guest list and I think pink is for gifts and rings."

Izzy put the book down carefully. "No coloured tab for psychiatric institutions?" She threw the folded piles of laundry into the basket, got up and headed for their bedroom. As she yanked open Liam's dresser drawer to throw in his underwear, she heard him say, "I'm not sure you could pull off this sixties flower-child look anyway. The traditional gown has more class. What do you think?"

She balanced the laundry basked against her hip, walked out of their bedroom and passed him on the way down to Sophie's room. "I think you should make an appointment to see a doctor. You are way further gone that you realize, Liam."

The next day, try as she might, Izzy couldn't get the image of that traditional wedding dress out of her head. She waited until Liam had taken Robbie and Sophie to town. Then she rooted the magazine out of the pile on the desk in the library. She sat down, flipped to the photo and traced her fingers down the line of the bodice – a bit higher over the bust for sure and maybe the cap sleeves could drape a little. The top of her arms weren't as toned as they once had been. She looked critically at the long, sweeping panels of the skirt – she would like less fabric and no train. Still, the dress was gorgeous – especially the seed pearls that carried their way from the bodice down the front panel of the skirt. She flipped the page to see if she could find a back view. The dress laced down to a deep V. She would leave that. The pink roses were a bit much. Maybe white gardenias – they smelled so heavenly – mixed with some flower in a shade of deep purple. She'd have to think about that. She made note of the page numbers and the date of the magazine as she opened her laptop. She knew someone in Victoria who had an exclusive shop down on the waterfront. The woman designed a lot of the stuff she sold. She had created one or two dresses for Izzy over the years.

Later that night, she told Liam, "I'll take care of my own dress for the wedding."

"Something white, right?" Izzy murmured a yes. "And long, I'd really like it to be long." Then he asked, "What about the wedding party?"

"We're having a wedding party?"

Liam nodded and said, "I wanted to ask Dad and Cynthia to be our witnesses, if that's okay with you."

"Yes, I like that idea."

"We don't want to leave anyone out so I thought of Lisa and Bethany for bridesmaids, Beulah and Robbie for groomsmen and, of course, Sophie for the flower girl."

"She might not even be walking all on her own by the middle of July."

Liam shrugged, "Either way, she'll be cute."

"Okay, okay, I'll take care of all the dresses." Izzy thought of the email she would have to send the next morning. She would not only be looking for a designer wedding gown but also for dresses for a matron of honour, two bridesmaids and a flower girl. She fell asleep thinking of a knock-out dress in deep purple that could suit the ages and styles of Cynthia, Bethany and Lisa. Sophie would be so cute in flowing white satin with purple smocking, wearing tiny white shoes on her feet and a circlet of purple flowers on her baby curls.

❦❦❦❦

Robbie felt the impact as the cat pounced on the deer. The massive jaws closed around the deer's neck; the teeth ripped through the jugular vein while the claws raked up the animal's belly, travelling high enough to stab through the heart. A sharp, metallic smell filled the air and Robbie's stomach heaved as he tried to back away from the sounds of the animal feeding on the twitching body.

Later as the cat covered what was left of the carcass with branches, soil and leaves, Robbie revelled in the animal's satisfaction at finally feeling full, sated. He bowed down beside the cat's large head as the animal drank its fill from a stream that flowed down the mountain. From that vantage point, he could see a large, black pipe that lay alongside the stream. He stood on the mountain high above the sawmill where the micro-hydro pipeline that supplied all their power ran from an intake down to a turbine shed close to the cabin.

Robbie didn't wake up as Liam turned him away from the bolted door and walked him back to his bed.

NINE

Brigit sat cross-legged on the couch. She opened the book on her lap and started to make notes. She needed a plan. She wrote the word *Kitchen* across the top of a page and underlined it three times. She chewed the end of her pen while she puzzled over how to handle the day-to-day necessity of working with Dylan. He could definitely be a threat if he clued into her lack of experience. On the other hand, he could be useful if she played her cards right. She wrote rapidly for a few moments before flipping the page.

On the fresh sheet of paper, Brigit started a list of things she needed to do. *Stay in shape* – there had to be some sort of exercise room around this place, hopefully with weights. *Study* – she had all her textbooks and handouts from the cooking program and she knew she could get a ton of stuff off the internet. She also had several of her mother's recipes stuffed into a binder that she had tried to beg off bringing with her. What a fool she had been. Her mother often catered for large gatherings at the cultural centre. She had probably hand-picked certain recipes for Brigit – easy to prepare and bound to impress. At the bottom of the list, she wrote – *Be the best mom I can be.* Tabby mattered more than anything else in Brigit's life. Through all the dark days, her daughter had been the light that kept her going.

By the time Tabby walked out of the bedroom, rubbing sleep out of her eyes, Brigit was dressed and singing. She grabbed Tabby's hands and spun her around in a circle, "It's a new day, *Tifiyet* and Momma has a good feeling about this place. Let's go and get some breakfast. It will be the last meal we'll have that I won't be cooking."

Hand in hand with her mother, Tabby swung around the room. A big smile lit up her face. "Why do you and Grandma call me that ... *Tifiyet.*"

55

Brigit smiled down at her daughter. "It's an old Creole word that means little girl. Your grandma always used to call me that and I guess I thought I'd like to do the same with my *Tifiyet.*"

Later that morning, Brigit chopped vegetables at one of the kitchen's long counters. Dylan stood on the other side of the room preparing the chicken and spicy sausage for a jambalaya that would be dinner for the residents. Tabby was playing some sort of a game with her Barbie dolls, zipping them around the dining room and flying them to and from airports that were located at various tables. Brigit decided to let her play for a while before assigning her a couple of pages from one of the workbooks recommended by her teacher in Toronto.

Things were going well. Brigit had marched into the kitchen with the thick notebook under her arm, ramrod straight and ready to project an aura of complete self-confidence. Grabbing a clean apron off the hook, she deftly shook it out and folded it before tying it around her small waist and wrapping the ties snugly in front. She had learned to do that during her first week at cooking school. Then, adopting a no-nonsense tone – in imitation of a police academy instructor – she had said, "Okay, this is how we're going to do things. I'll be observing you for the next week. I want you to carry on as usual and think of me as your assistant. I'll be taking a lot of notes because that's how I remember things and I'll probably be asking a lot of questions." She had waited for him to nod his understanding before she said, "Let's get started."

Brigit learned fast; that ability had served her well over the years and she had picked up a lot more than she realized from her cook's training. She already had a few pages of notes on menu planning and grocery orders. She even had a sketchy idea of where most things were located in the kitchen.

For now, all she had to do was make it until two when Dylan would have everything organized enough to be off until five at which time he'd return to do the final dinner preparation. She hoped to explore the entire kitchen on her own while he was gone. She'd be in a far better position to act like she could run the show when she didn't constantly have to ask where things were.

She looked up from the pile of vegetables in front of her when Izzy came into the kitchen. She knew she needed to score some points with the boss so she smiled and called out, "Good morning." Brigit might have been tired when she arrived but she knew that her comment about preferring to work alone had not gone over well with Micah Camp's Director.

Izzy smiled back, "Morning. How is everything going?" Her voice reached out to include Dylan.

He turned from putting the large pan of meat in the fridge and said, "We are programmed and running full steam ahead." Brigit liked the sound of that.

Izzy looked back at her and said, "I have an invitation to deliver." Tabby came into the kitchen and leaned against her mom's leg. Izzy smiled down at the girl for a moment before saying, "Liam is taking the kids into Dearborn today to go on a tour of the museum. It has a lot of early logging and fishing stuff and I'm told they have a bunch of interactive activities for kids. He's leaving around two – when Sophie gets up from her nap – and he'll be back by five. Robbie wondered if Tabby could come along."

Brigit hesitated while Tabby's eyes begged her to say yes. Having her daughter occupied this afternoon would come in handy as Brigit tried to make the most of the time she would have alone in the kitchen. But she hadn't even met this Liam person.

As if reading the doubts flashing through Brigit's mind, Izzy said, "Why not meet Liam when he drops by later and decide?" She smiled and left the kitchen.

Dylan got the large commercial mixer out and told Brigit, "Chocolate chip cookie time."

Tabby's eyes sparkled as she jumped up and down, "Those are my favourites. Can I help?"

Dylan grabbed an apron from the hook on the wall and tied it around Tabby's waist. "Since your mom is my number one assistant, I'll have to make you my number two. How does that sound?" He looked over at Brigit and said, "Liam's a good guy. Izzy wouldn't be with anyone who wasn't."

Before Brigit knew it, Dylan and Tabby were busy with the cookie dough and she had been assigned the task of creating an uncomplicated bean salad to go with the hamburgers that were planned for lunch. She couldn't be sure, but she thought she had caught a knowing tone in Dylan's voice when he told Tabby that her mom was his assistant.

❧❧❧❧

Nick stood in front of his fancy coffee maker in the kitchen of his cabin. Months earlier, he had clutched the thing to his chest while his second Jennifer wife swooped around their Vancouver apartment laying claim to every object in sight. Hanging onto the appliance was all he'd managed when it came to sharing community property so the thing had taken on a special importance. As the whoosh of dark liquid filled the cup, a strange incident that had happened the previous afternoon during his first supervision time with Izzy tugged at his mind.

They had been watching one of his taped sessions when Izzy leaned forward to say something. At the same time, a bird flew against the window pane with a loud thump. Izzy had jumped up from her chair. Panic filled her eyes, the colour drained from her face and she threw her hand up to her chest as if to hold her heart in place. He had watched her struggle to get a deep breath.

Nick had stood up quickly and placed a steadying hand on Izzy's shoulder, "Hey, it's just a bird. Are you okay?" He watched her take a shaky breath and heard her brush the incident off, saying she had simply been startled. Nick knew startled; he also knew that what had happened to Izzy was more complicated than that. She had reacted like a shell-shocked person.

Nick grabbed the coffee and glanced at his watch. He had more than enough time to observe his new morning ritual. Soon he stood outside on the cabin's small deck watching the light tiptoe its way down the face of the mountain across the lake. His thoughts wandered as the trees opposite him turned from dark silhouettes to brilliantly lit spires of multi-hued green.

He had started booking appointments during the past week and he was definitely on a learning curve he hadn't fully anticipated. Working with younger clients was different, not the actual trauma issues – he was used to those. It was the emotional gut-punch of their presentations that was new to him. The way the kids approached their situations varied wildly from one circumstance to the next. Their attitudes about what they had been through were malleable and that was good; but these clients were also more upfront and graphic in their descriptions of their experiences than his older clients had ever been. They were volatile and vulnerable. He was glad to have Izzy's input because the margin for counsellor error with persons in this age group seemed slimmer than the leeway he was used to having.

✄✄✄✄

Bethany stopped in front of the door to her office. She knew it was her office because on the door, for anyone to see, a small black plaque with gold lettering read, *Researcher – Bethany Shannon.* Tears sprang into her eyes and she marvelled that Izzy could find the time to be this thoughtful when she had so many other things on her plate. Bethany opened the door, balancing a box on her hip. She saw a large bouquet of roses on the desk. They were a mix of red and pink and white, interspersed with wispy ferns and spikes of eucalyptus.

She walked over and plucked the small white envelope from among the stems. She pulled out the card and read – *To my beautiful and talented wife*

58

on her first day of work. (I saw Craig in town and he said to get flowers. The guy is a genius when it comes to women.) Love from Beulah.

The tears of emotion disappeared as she burst out laughing. Gordon walked by the door and he looked in on her. "Hi Beth, I heard you were starting today ... lovely flowers."

She turned to smile at him. There was something so comfortable and unthreatening about Gordon in his rumpled clothing and thick, black-rimmed glasses. She looked closely and wondered if she saw a mustard stain on his shirt. "Beulah sent them."

"Ah ... married life ... treating you well, then?"

"Oh yes –" Bethany noticed the sad look on Gordon's face and she quickly crossed the room to place a comforting hand on his shoulder. Gordon's wife had died of cancer a few years ago. It had been a long, drawn-out and painful death that no one would wish on a worst enemy let alone a partner of many years. Gordon had retired to care for his wife but once she died, the inactivity got to him and he had taken the job at Micah Camp. "How are you?" she asked.

"Staying busy. I'm looking forward to the book club in June; I'm the one who got to choose the book. Have you picked up your copy of *Paris 1919?*" Bethany smiled and avoided the question. She'd read over the back of the book's jacket and it didn't really seem like her cup of tea. Bogged down with research reading, she had a ready excuse for tossing the book aside. Gordon chatted on, "Have you met the new cook yet? She's a Canadian of Haitian descent." He smiled at Bethany and added, "I think that would be the politically correct way to say it. She's from Toronto and she has the most adorable daughter. Why don't you and I get Brigit to take a break with us later?"

※ ※ ※ ※

Liam found Izzy in her office sitting behind her desk. When she spotted him at the door she got up and said, "Is it that time already? Where are the kids?"

Liam walked over and tipped her face up gently so he could look into her eyes. "What's wrong?" he asked.

"How do you know anything is wrong?"

"Your lips are white around the edges."

Izzy sighed, "I am not having the best day. These expansion plans are sucking up all my time and I can't make head or tail of the budget stuff. I need someone to help me with these spreadsheets and I've already taken

Jeremy away from the computer lab more than I should. Promise me that you'll sit with me out on the cliff deck tonight and listen while I have a good rant about things."

He pulled her into a quick hug. "It's a date." As Izzy stepped back, he said, "I stopped in at the kitchen and met Brigit. We chatted. She's happy for Tabby to join us on the trip to the museum. The kids are in the kitchen eating cookies and Sophie is with Bethany in her new office. The sign on the door was a thoughtful touch."

A hint of a smile played around the corners of Izzy's mouth, "I thought she'd like it."

Liam leaned close to touch her lips lightly with his own. "I'd better get going."

"Tabby's adorable, isn't she?"

Liam nodded, "She is that and the way her face lit up when she saw Robbie was something."

"Well, there is a quality about you Collins men." Izzy's face now wore a relaxed smile. He held her gaze for a moment before she said, "You're right ... you should probably get going. I'll see you at dinner."

Later, with the kids chatting away in the back seat, Liam drove to Dearborn and considered Izzy's decision to take on the Director's position at Micah Camp. When she had first told him that Roland had suggested the idea he'd almost laughed out loud. He fully expected her to say that the very thought of such a thing was ludicrous. Izzy was a counsellor down to the marrow of her bones. She loathed anything to do with administration. But she had looked quite serious when she said she was considering the temporary assignment. She had spoken of career advancement, the natural progression of her work at Micah Camp and the degree of esteem that both Roland and the Board obviously had for her in offering her the position.

None of that reasoning had rung true to Liam. He believed a combination of factors had maneuvered Izzy into a spot where giving up trauma counselling seemed like a sound idea and he thought the list of those factors probably started with guilt and ended with fear. But Liam was wise enough to keep his mouth shut and wait things out.

✄✄✄✄

Dylan appeared back in the kitchen as promised, at five. He looked like he had come straight from a shower. His hair was slicked back behind his ears and a soap smell wafted around him. Right away, he began giving directions about the dinner. Brigit felt comfortable after her uninterrupted exploration of the kitchen and a lively afternoon coffee break with Gordon and Bethany.

As she dumped the pots of rice into the serving pans, she decided to initiate some casual conversation, something that would lighten the tone between the two of them. It was all fine and dandy to take control but she didn't want to alienate the guy. She would need him on her side for some time to come. "This place is sure a change from the precinct in Toronto."

Dylan continued to stir the pot of jambalaya. "The precinct? You used to cook in a cop shop?"

Brigit laughed. "No. I used to be a cop. It turned out not to be the life for a single mom with a dependent child. I decided to retrain for something else." Dylan gave her a look of combined surprise and admiration. She changed the subject. "Is there any place to work out around here? I'm used to hitting the gym a few times a week."

As he talked, Dylan did a quick check of all the food waiting to go out to the dining room, "There's a big exercise room downstairs with all kinds of equipment. Three evenings a week – Monday, Wednesday and Friday – it's girls only. The rest of the time is co-ed. I work out down there all the time and it's never crowded." He appeared to be running through a mental checklist. He smiled over at her, "We're almost ready." As he pulled the salads out of the fridge he told her, "I run every afternoon ... got up to six kilometers today without stopping."

"That's great. I used to run quite a bit."

After all the food had been delivered to the waiting residents, Brigit started on the clean-up while Dylan brought out tubs of vanilla ice cream and assembled a sundae making station complete with cookies, whipped cream, nuts, sliced bananas, candies, chocolate syrup and marshmallow cream.

"Tabby's going to go crazy when she sees all of that." Brigit surveyed the brightly-coloured array of sweets.

Dylan grinned, "The desserts are my speciality. This is nothing. Wait until you taste my triple-layer, chocolate-silk cake."

A tall man walked into the kitchen. He reached out a hand to Brigit, "We haven't been formally introduced. My name is Nick Anderson and I'm the Camp's trauma counsellor."

Brigit sized the man up. Her hand went instinctively to her waist where her gun used to nestle against her hip. She had always liked to drop her hand casually onto it when anyone tried to intimidate her. It was only a gesture, of course, and since she hadn't carried a gun for several years, a useless one at that. But Nick was a big guy. He could be the type who would give a woman a hard time. Well, she wasn't going to take any of that. She stared him in the eye as she gave his hand a brisk, no-nonsense shake. "Good to meet you, Nick." Then she turned to Dylan and said, "I'll start collecting the tubs of dirty dishes."

TEN

The smell of bacon wafted on the morning air as Alex opened the kitchen door. He let Cynthia scoot past him and enter the room first. She was loaded down with parcels which she deposited in the corner. Alex leaned close to Liam to touch his forehead to his son's then he pulled his granddaughter into his arms. The baby was having a great time pulling on Alex's long braid and knocking at the feather that hung down from the shorter hair at the side of his head.

Cynthia reached out to tickle Sophie and said, "Wow, this one has really grown and she's cuter than ever." She turned to Izzy and the two women hugged one another tightly.

Stepping back, Izzy asked, "Did you guys drive through the night?"

Cynthia shook her head, "We arrived late so we parked the camper at the top of the road and waited until this morning to drive down." She made a face, "God, I'm so sick of that camper. I'm looking forward to sleeping in the guest cabin tonight."

Alex reached out his arm to drag Cynthia closer, "I could have sworn you loved that camper. All those nights in that little bed –"

"That's enough from you," she pointed a stern finger at Alex.

"Coffee, Dad?" Liam held the pot in the air.

Alex nodded, "Where is Robbie?"

Adding more bacon to the frying pan, Izzy said, "He'll be back any minute. He went over to the Camp to see if our new cook's daughter could come for breakfast."

No sooner were the words out of Izzy's mouth than the two kids charged through the door. Alex got up to wrap his son in a tight hug. As Cynthia moved in for her turn, Alex hunched down beside the girl who had a large, gray cat draped over her arm, "Well, hello. What is your name and who might that be?" Alex pointed at the cat.

"My whole name is Tabitha Grace Lafitte but I like it when people call me, Tabby. And this is Mr. Jangles."

Alex shook Tabby's hand. He then reached out to give the cat's paw a shake and Tabby burst into a fit of giggles. He said, "I am Robbie's father and you can call me Alex."

Cynthia went over to the counter to help Izzy slice up some fruit for breakfast. "What a beautiful little girl. How old is she?"

"She just turned eight. She's taken to Robbie in a big way and he seems to like having another kid to hang around with." Izzy fanned out the melon slices on her side of the platter.

Cynthia added a section of sliced strawberries. "When does Lisa-Marie get here?"

"We're expecting her later this afternoon." Izzy glanced into the large open area of the kitchen to make sure Robbie was occupied. "Robbie did it again the other night. That's three times now." Izzy had shared her concerns about the boy's sleepwalking with Cynthia, via email hoping the woman's past experience as a nurse might put her in a position to offer some advice.

Cynthia frowned, "And he doesn't remember anything about it when he wakes up?"

"No ... nothing. I still want to wait it out a bit. If we take him to a doctor when he doesn't have any idea he's been doing it, the whole situation could end up being blown way out of proportion."

"I wish I knew more about this sort of thing. As long as you're sure he can't hurt himself."

"The lock on the back door is doing its job. The last two times we've gently turned him around and he has gone right back to bed."

Izzy carried the fruit to the table and glanced around the room from Alex, to Liam to Robbie. She was always struck by the likeness between the three of them. She put the tray down and said, "The rest of the food will be ready soon." She took Sophie from Liam and plunked the child into her high chair.

Robbie slipped over to his father to ask, "You said you were bringing me a drum, can I see it?"

Alex gestured for Cynthia to pass him the large bag she had set down in the corner. He opened it up and began to dig inside. He pulled out at a small cylindrical drum with a single eagle feather painted on the top. He passed it to Sophie who immediately began banging it against the tray of her high chair.

Next, Alex retrieved a much larger drum, flat and round with a painted scene of horses spread across the cowhide top. He handed that one to Liam.

Liam looked surprised, "I wasn't expecting this."

Alex laughed, "The best gift is an unexpected one. And drumming is good for the soul." Digging into the bag again, Alex brought out a drum a bit bigger than Sophie's that had a pattern of red thread woven up and down along the sides. He passed it to Tabby, "A gift for our guest." Tabby's eyes were huge as she took the instrument from Alex's hands and held it. He removed the final drum from the bag. It was slightly smaller than the one he had given to Liam and it had a painting of a mountain lion leaping from a rock ledge.

Robbie took the drum and stared at the picture for a moment. A strange expression crossed his face and he shook his head as if to ward off something. He smiled broadly at his father. Both Robbie and Tabby sat down and began to thump on their drums while Sophie continued to bang hers. Mayhem ensued and when Izzy gave Alex a sharp look, he smiled innocently.

Cynthia handed a long, slim box to Izzy. "Accept this as a peace offering for having brought such noisy gifts into your house. I saw it at a little shop in Taos."

Izzy sat down and opened the box. Inside she found a bracelet of pounded silver medallions that matched the necklace she wore so often. She picked the shiny object from the box and held it over her wrist, "Cynthia, thank you. It's beautiful. I wouldn't be surprised if it was made by the same artist who did my necklace."

With breakfast in full swing, Izzy pulled Alex aside and asked, "How did you happen to have a drum for Tabby?"

Alex smiled, "I couldn't decide on the right size for Robbie and the guy selling them out of the back of his truck said he'd give me a deal for the four of them. Seems like it was meant to be because having a gift for an honoured guest is not a tradition you want to mess around with."

Alex sat down, sipped his coffee and stretched out his long legs under the table. He looked over at Liam, "I've got news about your sister, Fiona."

Izzy had returned to her spot next to Sophie's high chair. As she tried to coax the baby to finish her breakfast, she considered the fact that it didn't seem to matter at all to Alex that Liam had never laid eyes on Fiona and that she was not his biological sister. Alex had met Fiona's mother when she was pregnant with the girl. He had hung around and been the only father Fiona had ever known. As Izzy looked at Liam's face she realized Fiona's absence from his life and her parentage made no difference to him either. If his father said Fiona was his sister then Fiona was his sister. She pondered anew how different her concept of family had been from Liam's only a year ago when Sophie and Robbie had come into their lives. She had to admit, she was finding her way closer and closer to Liam's worldview.

"She's been looking for a family practice internship," Alex leaned down to show Tabby how to hit the top of the drum with the flat of her hand. "I told her all about Dearborn and how you guys are getting married – now everything's arranged."

Liam gave his father's a quizzical look as he asked, "What's all arranged?"

"Fiona is coming to Dearborn for six months to intern in Rosemary's practice and I thought she could probably stay in the guest cabin. She'll be here in plenty of time for the wedding." Alex turned to Izzy, "That is, if you have no objections."

Izzy shrugged and glanced at Cynthia, "I guess your days out of that camper are numbered." Both the women laughed and Izzy said, "No objections at all, Alex. It's a great plan. I look forward to meeting Fiona. She won't find a better family doctor to learn from than Rosemary."

Alex slapped his hands down on his thighs, "Great. Well, that brings me to the second big piece of news." He smiled broadly, "Cynthia and I have decided to settle down together. We plan to build a place."

Cynthia added, "Not a mansion or anything but something definitely bigger than a camper or even the guest cabin. I need a room I can go into and shut the door." She gave Alex a pointed look.

Alex crossed his arms over his chest and looked up at the ceiling. "We have just one big problem at the moment. I'm not sure we can get our hands on the piece of property we have in mind."

Izzy wasn't surprised that Cynthia and Alex were taking such a serious step. She and Cynthia had become close since the author had rented the guest cabin over the past summer and had gotten involved with Liam's father. When Cynthia and Alex left for their five-month trip travelling around the American southwest, Cynthia and Izzy had kept in touch by email.

Izzy paused as she raised a spoonful of scrambled eggs to Sophie's mouth. She frowned down at Robbie and Tabby who were on the floor drumming, "Do you guys have to do that in here? I can't hear myself think." Glancing past the two kids, Izzy watched Tabby's cat delicately dig into a dish of dog food. "Should Mr. Jangles be eating dog food?"

Tabby shrugged and Liam got up to put the dog's dish out of reach. With all attention diverted from her, Sophie grabbed the spoon from Izzy's hand and sent the egg flying. Dante caught the food mid-air. He lingered always at attention near Sophie's chair, seemingly relaxed but ready for anything.

Izzy glanced at Liam, "Good God, this dog must have put on ten pounds since Sophie started eating solids. Why can't he take a page from Pearl's book and stop lurking around like he's starving?" Pearl raised her head at the sound of her name. Somehow her restraint served to emphasize Dante's greed.

Izzy smiled in Cynthia's direction, "So ... the wanderers are ready to settle down together. I suppose congratulations are in order. I hope this piece of property isn't too far away. We like having you guys around."

Alex gave Cynthia an I-told-you-so look.

Izzy leaned down to rob Dante of a piece of toast that Sophie had handed to him. "Dante, lie down, right now." She turned to Robbie and Tabby, "Stop laughing at Sophie when she does stuff like that. She'll never stop if you think she's funny." Robbie and Tabby grinned as they continued to drum.

Izzy glanced over at Alex, "Where is this property that you're so excited about?"

"Oh, just through the orchard there," he pointed out the large window, "about two minutes into the evergreens, right at that rise overlooking the lake before you start down the trail towards Beulah and Bethany's A-Frame."

Izzy's eyes widened as she looked from Liam to Cynthia and back to Alex. Finally, she asked, "You want to build here?" Only Cynthia smiled uncertainly.

Standing up, Alex walked over to Izzy and leaned down to take her hands and draw her up to her feet, "If you'll have us."

Izzy smiled, "The idea is more than okay with me." She looked over at Liam, "What do you think? Do you want your dad living right next door?"

Liam reached out to shake his dad's hand and turned to hug Cynthia. Sophie looked up at the activity all around her. She clapped her hands before grabbing her dish of scrambled eggs and winging it onto the floor right beside Dante's nose. The dog slurped up the largess while Robbie and Tabby burst out laughing. Sophie, looking extremely proud, patted her food-smeared hands in her hair.

Alex grinned broadly, "Well, I guess that's settled then. I'll go out to the truck and get the plans."

⚬⚬⚬⚬

Lisa-Marie hopped out of her cherry-red Jeep Wrangler at the bottom of Izzy and Liam's driveway. She pushed her sunglasses up onto her streaked hair. She had whipped it into a thick French braid that morning. A seven hour drive up the Island, most of the way under clear, blue skies with the jeep's top rolled back, meant the style was a bit windswept with wisps of brown and gold hair flying loosely around her heart-shaped face. She leaned into the vehicle to grab her bag. Her T-shirt rode up to reveal a butterfly tattoo in the middle of her lower back, right where her designer jeans sat low on her hips. An expensive bangle watch slid up and down on her bare forearm. Dropping her keys and iPhone into the bag, she hooked it over her shoulder and walked across the gravel driveway to meet her welcoming committee. She smiled broadly and her brown eyes shone with excitement.

Robbie held one of Sophie's small hands as the baby toddled along. When Lisa-Marie spotted her little girl, everything and everyone else faded into the background. She dropped her bag on the ground, scrunched down to Sophie's level and held her arms out. Robbie let go of Sophie's hand. Proudly propelling herself forward two steps, the baby landed safely in her mother's arms.

Lisa-Marie swung the child up close to her as she breathed in the powerful baby smell – new skin, clean clothes, everything sweet and soft. Staring into Sophie's eyes with tears shining in the corners of her own, she said, "Oh Sophie, Sophie ... you are so perfect." Dark eyes narrowed and the baby's lower lip began to tremble. She turned away to hold her arms out towards Liam.

A quick look of disappointment scampered across Lisa-Marie's face before she shrugged and forced a smile that didn't reach her eyes. "I know the drill, Little Miss. You need to get used to me all over again." She handed the baby to Liam, "I'm glad I've gone through this a couple of times now. It isn't so devastating."

Ignoring the look of sympathy in Liam's eyes, Lisa-Marie turned to Izzy who pulled her close then held her at arm's length to say, "Talk about looking perfect. Like mother, like daughter. You look gorgeous." Izzy pointed to the tote lying discarded on the ground, "Is that a Dolce and Gabbana bag?"

Lisa-Marie grinned as she shook her watch-bangled wrist and pointed to the sunglasses on her head. She turned to hug her Aunt Beth, getting a slap on the back from Beulah into the bargain. Then she stood in front of Justin and looked up into his eyes. The tears she had been holding back brimmed over. She moved closer and his arms came around her as he returned the intimacy of her greeting. She reached up to bring his face down close to hers. She let her lips brush his cheek, feeling the tickle of soft, blonde whiskers.

She backed up slightly with his arm still around her and said, "Oh my God, I've missed you." Keeping her body pressed close to his side, she reached behind her back to hold the hand that rested on the warm, bare skin of her waist. She blinked the tears from her eyes and turned to the rest of the group. She chatted happily with everyone as they moved toward the door of the cabin that she had come to think of as home.

⚜⚜⚜⚜

Sitting in the comfortable rocker down in the sun porch turned nursery, Lisa-Marie held her clean, pajama-clad daughter in her arms. She fed Sophie her bottle, cuddling the child close and singing *Puff the Magic Dragon*. Dark eyes stared at her face from under heavy lids as the baby slurped greedily and held onto Lisa-Marie's hand.

She continued to rock her long after she knew Sophie had fallen asleep. The weight of the baby against her was a comfort she had never expected to feel. Only a year ago she had given birth to this child with nothing on her mind but leaving her with Izzy and Liam so she could get on with her life. She'd had no intention of being a seventeen-year-old mom.

Lisa-Marie let her mind wander as she looked around the sun porch. This room had been something different each summer she had been here. The first year it was truly a sun porch. She remembered sitting here with her dish of food at one of Izzy's book-club, potluck gatherings. She had looked up from her meal and had felt her heart beat wildly when she saw Justin walking out to join her.

The next year the sun porch had become a work area for Izzy's father, Edward, as he raced to finish his book on photography before being overtaken by the cancer that had spread through his body. Lisa-Marie had spent many hours working with him. Up the three stairs, past the French doors, was where Edward had died making a heroic stance against Willow's insane boyfriend.

Lisa-Marie shivered with the memory. Izzy had said it would be fine to remember the good times she'd had with Edward and not dwell on that horrific afternoon. He had taught Lisa-Marie so much about the art of photography. And he believed in her talent. He had left her a substantial amount of money so she would be able to take advantage of any opportunities that came along. Edward had sent letters of introduction for her to a number of his contacts in the field of photography and journalism. During the past fall, she had been able to follow up on those leads while she travelled around Europe. It had been through one of Edward's contacts that she had gotten the information about an internship at Vogue's London office and had been given a stunning letter of reference.

This year the sun porch had transformed itself once again. Pushed up against the wall was a heavy, dark-wood crib with a quilt tossed over the side.

A matching change table, dresser and armoire completed the furnishings. Lamp, rug, and bedding all took up the theme of colourful owls in shades of brown and creamy yellow. On top of the dresser sat a framed photograph of Lisa-Marie and Sophie, along with owl bookends that flanked several children's books. One wall featured a framed poster of Monet's water lilies with the words, *The National Gallery*, on the bottom. The windows and their expansive views of Crater Lake were covered now by heavy, moss-green curtains. The combined shades of green, the dark wood and the owls made Sophie's nursery look like a clearing in the forest.

Holding the baby close, Lisa-Marie got up to walk across the room and place Sophie on her back in the crib. She tucked the baby's pink bunny under her arm and pulled the quilt over her. Staring down at her daughter, she felt a satisfying ache in her chest that she now knew to be love. When she was away from Sophie, she missed her night and day. Even so, she doubted Liam's insistence that one day her love for Sophie and her life circumstances would be such that she would want to care for her child full-time. She did love Sophie but there were so many things she wanted to do.

✄✄✄✄

"That was quite the greeting Lisa gave Justin, hey?" Izzy said as she slipped into the bed beside Liam.

"Maybe she doesn't know about the girlfriend."

"Well it certainly seemed as though his girlfriend was the furthest thing from his mind." Izzy adjusted her pillow with a sharp whack and settled down under the blankets. "I'm glad she's home. And did you see how fast Sophie came around this time? It was like Lisa had never left."

Liam pulled Izzy close and they settled into a comfortable silence, wrapped in their own thoughts. He stared up at the ceiling of their bedroom. The cabin and his life were full of people – Izzy in his arms, Lisa back in her upstairs loft, Robbie sleeping in the room next to her and Sophie snug in her crib. His dad and Cynthia were down the path in the guest cabin; Justin was not far beyond that; Beulah and Bethany were in their A-Frame. Soon his sister Fiona would arrive. A fierce love for and commitment to all these people had crept up on Liam and had loosened the tight rein he had kept on his emotions for years. He felt fully alive and he thanked the Creator every day for the chance to be part of something – a family – that, more than anything else in his life ever had, was stretching him to become the man he knew he could be.

ELEVEN

Izzy sat at her desk and scrolled through a long list of emails. Her mind wandered. Finally, she closed the lid to her laptop and stared out the window. A nagging question that begged for her attention hovered, as it often did, just below her busy thoughts. Why hadn't she known about Willow's violent and insanely possessive boyfriend? She'd missed a huge piece of the puzzle while working with the girl last year and because of that, she had put her entire family in the path of a gun-wielding madman. Her father had died and the fact that he would have succumbed soon enough to the cancer consuming him was little consolation.

She didn't want to think about her father's death or the guilt she felt about that afternoon, so her thoughts jumped to another gut-wrenching question. Why had she thought Maddy was ready to leave the Camp two years ago? And when she came back with her life in a mess, why hadn't Izzy seen the hopeless corner the girl had backed herself into? The memory of the night Maddy almost succeeded in killing herself haunted her.

As much as she griped about the responsibilities of Roland's job, a part of her had been relieved to wrap up her active counselling of clients, to move into the Director's role and pass all the residents' collective trauma onto Nick's wide shoulders. It meant she would not have to sit in the chair across from a client and second guess everything she said or did. Thankfully, her thoughts were interrupted by a knock at the door.

Lisa-Marie poked her head into the office and said, "That big desk suits you."

"Hmm ... I wonder about that." Izzy gestured for the Lisa to come in. "What's going on at home?"

71

"Sophie walked halfway across the living room all by herself. Liam wants to know if you're coming home for lunch. And he says to send Robbie and Tabby back after their math class. He and Auntie Beth are going to take them into Dearborn to go swimming this afternoon. The outdoor pool just opened and Liam thinks he can get both kids into lessons. I said I'd stay home with Sophie and wait for the guy who's coming from the internet place to look at the satellite dish."

"He'd better show up." Izzy made a face, "I'm sick of the bloody internet going out every second day."

"I hear you. It totally cramps my style. A text from Maddy got through last night saying she and Jesse will be here for the wedding. I'm so excited about seeing her again."

"I am too." Izzy smiled before a quick frown crossed her face, "Tell Liam I probably won't make it home for lunch."

Lisa-Marie held up a poster, "Is it okay if I put this on the bulletin board? I'm trying to get a few people to volunteer to sit for portraits so I can practice." To Izzy's nod, she added, "Josie called and asked me to stop by the paper and soap shop. If you see Robbie and Tabby, tell them to meet me there and I'll walk back with them."

The phone on Izzy's desk jangled to life. Lisa-Marie waved and headed for the door, calling out as she went, "Heavy is the head that wears the crown, hey?"

Izzy picked up the phone and had a brief but polite conversation with the person on the other end. She hung up and stared into space for a moment. This job was certainly proving to be one for which the ability to juggle should be number one on the list of qualifications.

She headed to the kitchen. Dylan stood by the stove and Brigit rolled out pie crust on the counter. She smiled over at Izzy, "Tabby loves that drum. She's been at it non-stop."

Izzy gave Brigit a quick look of compassion. "I'll understand if you don't want to thank us."

Brigit shook her head, "I'm glad to see Tabby excited about trying out new things. Robbie took her to your place earlier to study his frogs. He says Liam has assigned them a paper to write. When they left here, they were arguing about who would do the writing and who would do the drawings." Brigit locked eyes with Izzy, "I don't know how to thank Liam for including Tabby in all the great things he has Robbie doing." She looked around the kitchen, "I could have kept her busy while I worked, but Liam's style of active learning is so much better."

"This is as good for Robbie as it is for Tabby."

Brigit deftly pulled up the pie crust and fit it into a pan as she spoke, "I've had a couple of ideas of my own. There's no reason Robbie and Tabby can't have a cooking class with me here in the kitchen. I'll teach them how to make rice with red beans and fried plantains."

"Great idea." Izzy hesitated for a moment then walked over to Dylan. The Board had hired a new cook but for all appearances, Dylan still seemed to be running the kitchen. "I have a huge favour to ask." He glanced at her and continued to stir the thick meat sauce in the pot as he listened. "This is short notice but I need a special lunch served in the small dining room at around twelve-thirty."

Dylan frowned, "You won't want sloppy joes like everyone else. How many guests?"

. "Four."

He gestured back to Brigit where she worked at the counter and said, "I'll grab some of that pie crust, make a quiche and serve it with a Greek salad and fresh buns. How does that sound?" Izzy smiled as he added, "And for dessert, home-made raspberry sherbet with biscotti."

As she gave Dylan a grateful pat on the arm, Izzy looked up to see Alexander coming through the side door with Robbie and Tabby. He called out to her, "These kids are on their way to math. Hey, I heard through the rumour mill that Muriel Abbot is going to be here for lunch today. She's an old friend of mine."

Izzy smiled at Robbie and Tabby as they scooted past her. She grabbed Alex by the arm. She wouldn't even ask how on earth he got his information – smoke signals no doubt. "You know these people?" To his nonchalant nod, Izzy said, "Will you join us for lunch? And would you mind stopping by the bakery to let Arianna know they're coming to see her?"

Alex grinned, "I'll do you one better. I'll talk to Arianna now and when the guests arrive, I'll take them over to the bakery so they can meet Beulah. Then we'll all come back together."

"That's a great idea. Thank you so much." Izzy turned to Dylan, "Make enough food for five people, okay?"

❧❧❧❧

Lisa-Marie strolled down the breezeway that connected the main Camp building with the workshop and pushed open the door. A familiar scene of organized chaos met her eyes and she smiled. Josie hovered near the large vats at the back of the shop. Kids worked at the long tables packaging items for shipment and laying out herbs and flowers in the drying racks. A guy hauled in boxes of supplies through the service entrance. A clang echoed around the room as someone banged a couple of empty soap forms into the sink.

Entering the shop felt like another homecoming to Lisa-Marie. Two years ago, Josie had given her a job, accepting her at face value as Bethany's niece from Kingston visiting for the summer. Her tortured three years of high school had not followed her to Crater Lake. Here she was not treated like a social pariah; nor was she made to look like a slut. No one thought of her as an ugly, pathetic loser. She had been allowed a second chance.

Josie spotted her and waved as she threw off her black apron and gloves. She gave some quick instructions to the kid who stood by the vat, then walked across the workshop to open her arms for a hug. Stepping into the embrace, Lisa-Marie said, "You probably won't believe that I miss this place, but I do."

Josie gave her a wide smile, "That's good news. Come into my office. I have something I want to run by you."

The word office was a misnomer. The cubbyhole was big enough for a small table wedged into the corner, a chair and a file cabinet. Yellow sticky notes decorated every surface. Josie leaned against the file cabinet and motioned for Lisa-Marie to sit. She dug through a pile of things on the table. "How is Sophie?"

"Starting to walk and driving everyone crazy trying to keep up with her."

Josie passed Lisa a photo, "My grandson. He's three weeks old."

"Ahh ... he's so cute."

Josie grinned, "He sure is. Listen, I'm wondering if you'd be willing to supervise the shop a couple of days a week." Seeing Lisa-Marie's look of surprise followed by an expression of self-doubt, Josie added, "Come on. You've worked here for two summers. If you were to come in on Monday and Tuesday, I could spend those days with my grandson. I'd make sure that I ran the batches of soap and paper later in the week so you would mostly have the easy stuff to oversee." Josie's tone wheedled as she said, "Say you'll give it a go. Two days of full-time supervising will pay more than the part-time work you did last summer. I know the money you'd make isn't a fortune, but supervisory work experience looks good on a resume." Josie waved her arm to indicate the room they were in, "And you'd get to sit in this office."

Lisa-Marie burst out laughing. "Like sitting in this closet is any kind of an incentive. All the time I've worked with you, this is the first time I've ever seen you in this office." She looked out to the shop, "I'll give it a go but I'm not sure anyone is going to listen to me."

Josie grinned, "Oh, they'll listen or they'll be out on their ears. You channel me when you're in charge and you won't have a bit of trouble."

· · · · ·

Izzy found herself enjoying the impromptu lunch gathering. She would have preferred a bit more notice but it seemed to be going well. Alexander had brought the guests back from the bakery with Arianna in tow. A tour of the Camp facilities had followed with Arianna showing off her cabin. The lunch was perfect. Dylan served them like they were at an exclusive restaurant and, in the process, he managed to say a few things about his own experience at the Camp and his future plans. Muriel Abbot chatted back and forth with Alexander; they seemed to have friends and acquaintances in common all across the country. The quiet, older man beside her ate and smiled. Arianna was polite, speaking when she was spoken to. Muriel praised Izzy for having found such a great work-experience placement for Arianna.

As Dylan cleared away the sherbet bowls, the older man pushed back his chair and folded his hands over his belly. He looked at Izzy, "This is a good place. You have taught our girl many things. When will she be ready to come home?"

Izzy straightened in her chair, "Arianna has two more exams to write and she has agreed to work at the bakery full-time through the summer. After that her time here will be completed."

Arianna squirmed in her chair and flashed a quick look at Izzy before she glanced over at Muriel. "I'm not sure about going back to the reserve ... not right away. I know you have a job waiting for me but something else has come up." Her hair hung in a sheet around her face as she turned away from the woman's steady look and stared down at the floor.

Alexander addressed the elderly man, "We can leave you now if you would like to speak to Arianna in private."

The man shook his head. He looked out the window to the lake. He spoke slowly and the soft syllables of his words were like musical notes rising, falling and filling the room. "We do not want to lose our young people. Too many leave the reserve and don't come back. They are lured by many things and your world takes them away." His eyes found Izzy's for a moment. "All too often, they end up on the streets. Drugs and alcohol find them ... they become slaves to addiction. Our young men end up in jail and our young women are forced to sell themselves to survive. They are lost on all the highways of tears out there. This is a pain not easily spoken of." He sighed heavily as his hand waved in the direction of unknown and distant places. "All journeys have their risks. I don't pretend our world offers any guarantees of an easy or safe life. Sometimes we lose the young people who choose to stay home." He reached over to tip up Arianna's chin so their eyes met, "Why don't you want to come home?"

Arianna dug in the pocket of her jeans and pulled out a battered and folded envelope with the UBC logo in the corner. She drew an official paper from the inside and passed it across the table to Izzy. Pulling her glasses down out of her curls, Izzy quickly read the letter. As she did, her eyebrows lifted in surprise. She passed the piece of paper to Muriel Abbot and gave Arianna a quick smile.

Muriel in turn scanned the letter. Then she jumped off her chair to pull Arianna up and into a tight hug. "My God, girl, why didn't you say something?" She turned to the old man and a stream of their own language flowed from her. She used words punctuated with arm gestures in a conversation that ended when she threw her head back and laughed like she might burst.

A grin broke out on the man's face as he stood up, put his hands on Arianna's shoulders and turned her to face him. "Sometimes our young people go away and they rise high on the winds of hard work and good fortune. They remember where they came from and the people who helped them. They send good messages out into the world for all of us." Holding onto Arianna's gaze, he said, "We hope that someday you return to us. But we understand you must choose your own path. What is ahead is not yet known."

Tears glistened in Arianna's eyes as she looked from the man, to Muriel and finally to Izzy who felt her own eyes fill with tears. Muriel dropped an arm around Arianna's shoulder and stroked the girl's long hair, "Accepted with a full-scholarship to university ... your auntie will be so proud."

ᑭᑭᑭᑭ

Lisa-Marie gazed up at the good-looking guy who had finished readjusting the internet satellite. He was tall, well-built and had a sexy tool belt slung around his jean-clad hips. Wild, blonde curls framed a face that contained movie-star, blue eyes. She couldn't help but notice that those eyes were not even trying to hide the fact that they were impressed with what they saw.

He leaned against the door jam, "I've readjusted things and your signal reception is good. Now I need to come in to take a look at your modem." He grinned as his gaze swept over her. "My name is Zach Sampson, by the way."

76

As he walked through the door, she caught a whiff of some type of spicy, male cologne.

"Lisa-Marie Shannon," she told him. "Follow me." She led him upstairs to the hallway across from her bedroom door, which she closed quickly. She turned to point out the electronic equipment that sat on the shelf. The look on his face told her he had caught more than a passing glimpse of her clothes strewn around the room, including the lace bra draped over the back of a chair.

Zach grinned and turned to gaze beyond the railing that ran the length of the hall. He whistled, "Whew, quite the drop. This place is something. Are you related to Izzy?"

"No. My aunt Bethany lives next door. Sorry, but I have to get back downstairs. I'm right in the middle of baking some pies." She turned and walked away, resisting the urge to fan herself. Who knew the satellite repair guy would turn out to be so cute?

A few minutes later, Zach clumped down the stairs, "The modem is shot. I've got a new one in the truck." As Lisa-Marie rolled out a pie crust, he passed behind her and stopped to sniff appreciatively at the bowl of apples mixed with sugar and cinnamon. "A pretty girl who can bake a pie ... my, my."

Looking over her shoulder, she tried to frown but she ended up grinning at him. "Flattery won't even get you a piece of pie. Hadn't you better get back to work?"

Later, when the repairs were done, she walked Zach out to the kitchen deck, hoping that Sophie would stay asleep a few minutes more. He smiled down at her, "How about you and me hanging out together on Friday?"

"I don't even know you," she told him.

"I can fix that. My mom and dad are friends with your aunt and Beulah. My brother, Mike, works up at the sawmill. I worked up there summers, too, for a few years. Izzy and Liam know me." He hitched up his tool belt and added, "I'm a good guy. Ask anyone. Hand me your phone." He held out his hand and Lisa-Marie silently pulled her phone from her back pocket. He took it and whistled before he said, "Nothing but the best, hey?" He punched in a few numbers and handed the phone back. "Friday night ... come to my house for dinner. My mom will love you. Then we'll watch something. We've got the best movie room in town. Text me."

When Zach got to the driveway, he called back, "I'm betting this Jeep Maverick is yours?" Lisa-Marie laughed as she heard him call out, "Hot chicks always have hot wheels." He waved as he got into a company truck, started the engine and chugged out of sight up the driveway.

Sophie started to cry and Lisa-Marie checked the pies in the oven before hurrying down to the sun porch. She lifted the little girl out of the crib and hugged her close, "You have the best timing. Shall I tell you all about the good-looking guy who said your mom is hot?"

※ ※ ※ ※

Justin dug into his third slice of left-over, cold pizza chased down with warm Coke. A knock sounded and Lisa-Marie strolled in with a fresh-baked apple pie in her hand. He wasn't sure for a moment what was more enticing. He could actually smell the pie but Leez wore an attention-getting, tight shirt with the top and bottom buttons undone. Her belly button ring flashed against the smooth skin above her jeans and the lace edge of her bra was visible when she leaned over to put the pie on the table in front of him.

She grinned at him as she turned to grab a clean plate and fork from the kitchen. Of course, she knew her way around the place. She had shared the cabin with him the previous summer for a few weeks, as his roommate only.

Pulling up a chair, she sliced the pie, handed him a piece and said, "Why are you here all by your lonesome, eating cold pizza for supper? Why didn't you come over to Izzy and Liam's? We had barbecued steaks."

"I can't be scrounging off them every night." Justin dug into the pie. "This is good." He grinned suddenly, "I'm definitely not above having dessert delivered, though."

"You can take some for your lunch tomorrow, too." Lisa-Marie sat by and watched as he single-mindedly devoted himself to eating the pie. As he pushed away the plate, she said, "Hey, guess what happened today? Josie offered me a job supervising in the paper and soap shop two days a week."

"That's great but I don't suppose you really need the money."

"What do you mean?" A frown drew her eyebrows together.

"The car and the fancy new iPhone and your clothes. I'm just saying that it looks like Edward's money has moved you into a different economic bracket."

"I wasn't going to touch the money at all but Izzy said that would be stupid. She said I should have an allowance and buy the jeep."

"Some allowance." Justin stood up. "It's none of my business. It's your money." He headed over to the living room and sat down in the rocker.

Lisa-Marie followed him and curled up in the corner of the sofa. She looked a bit like a kitten getting ready to lick cream from her paw. She smiled over at him, "Maddy texted last night to say she and Jesse will be here for the wedding. It's going to be just like last summer ... the four of us together again."

She laid her head on the arm of the sofa, presenting a nice view down her shirt as she wiggled around to get comfortable. "Remember when we all went to the *Sea Shed* for my birthday and danced at the hotel afterwards." She laughed before adding, "Remind me never to drink beer straight from the pitcher again. God, I was so sick."

The desire to laugh with her and remember the good times they had spent together was tempting. Then he would want to go to the sofa and pull her into his arms. He put the brakes on that thought before it got going. "I have a girlfriend. Her name is Lauren." The words spilled out of his mouth like the confession of a sin.

He watched her turn away quickly to hide the stunned look on her face. She fiddled with the watch on her wrist. When the silence had gone on as long as he could stand, she sat up suddenly and hugged her arms around herself. "Does this mean we aren't friends anymore?" she asked him.

The distress in her tone made him feel off-balance and guilty – as if he had done something wrong. "Of course we're still friends. It's just that ...." He lost his train of thought and stared at the girl across from him for a moment. The memory of the things they had been through together, the secrets shared, hit him so hard he struggled to take a deep breath. "Things aren't the way they were last year. It won't be you and me and Maddy and Jesse hanging out. Lauren will be here for the wedding."

Getting off the sofa, Lisa-Marie crossed the room and leaned down to kiss him on the cheek. She straightened up and he thought he saw the sheen of tears as she said, "I'm glad nothing can come between us, Justin. You mean so much to me."

He lost himself in her eyes for a moment before answering, "You mean a lot to me, too, Leez."

"I've got to get back so I can bathe Sophie and put her to bed. See you tomorrow." She waved as she went out the door.

ᑫᐤᑫᐤᑫᐤᑫᐤ

Lisa-Marie came up from the sun porch and closed the doors behind her. Izzy watched the young girl walk across the living room texting on her phone as she went. She plopped down on the sofa, stretched out and stared at the device for a minute before dropping it face down on her stomach.

"Sophie sure goes down well for you." Izzy marked the page in the book she was reading as she spoke.

"*Puff the Magic Dragon* ... I'd be nothing without that song." Lisa-Marie stared up at the cedar ceiling far above her head, "I'm going to go out on Friday night if that's okay with you guys."

Izzy nodded silently. Liam, sitting in the chair next to her, looked over the top of his journal and asked, "Where?"

Ignoring his question, Lisa-Marie added, "And I've asked someone to be my date at the wedding."

Izzy marvelled at Liam's tenacity when she heard him ask, "Who?" She recalled that last summer he had been the one who had insisted that having Lisa stay with them meant they were responsible for her. But the girl was almost eighteen years old now. Izzy hoped that Liam realized Lisa would be well within her rights to tell him that who she saw or where she went was none of his business. She watched the subtle yet obvious dynamic that played out between the man in the chair and the girl lying on the sofa.

"The satellite repair guy." Lisa-Marie gave in and provided an answer, of sorts.

Liam bit the hook, "You asked the satellite repair guy to be your date for the wedding?"

"Ya ... his name's Zach Sampson. He said you guys know him."

Liam smiled and Izzy felt her eyebrow twitch up for a moment. She reined in the expression as Liam said, "Sure we know Zach. He's a great kid."

"I'm going to his house Friday for dinner and a movie." She pointed to the book in Izzy's hand, "Is that the novel for the next book-club night?"

"We won't be doing this one until into June but it's a bit of a different read so I started it early." She held the book out so Lisa could see the cover, "*Paris 1919 – Six Months that Changed the World* by Margaret MacMillan. It's nonfiction, all about the peace talks that followed the end of the First World War. It's a bit dry in spots and I doubt if anyone other than Gordon and I will actually have read it by the time we're supposed to discuss it."

Liam glanced at Izzy, "I'm going to read it. I like history."

"Well, that will make three of us. I'm almost finished if you want to start it next."

Lisa-Marie's phone chirped. Moments later she was lost in the world of texting. Liam went back to the pages of his journal and Izzy studied the girl on the sofa for a moment. She found herself wondering if she had ever been that young. She opened the book and tried to read but her thoughts were scattered. She suspected Lisa had found out about Lauren and that her discovery precipitated her desire to find a date for the wedding. She could be heading for a painful fall if her goal was to make Justin jealous.

Izzy couldn't count the number of times she had watched as clients walked willfully into painful situations. It was always a difficult thing to witness, though the client often learned valuable life lessons. As a counsellor, she'd had the sense to remain objective. But objectivity was not an option for her with Lisa-Marie. From the moment of Sophie's birth, the girl had become like a daughter to her. If Lisa got hurt, Izzy was going to hurt, too. The pain was no different than the tug she felt whenever Sophie cried or the constant heartache she suffered over Robbie's unexplained compulsion to sleepwalk.

⁂

Dear Emma:

Justin has a girlfriend. Her name is Lauren. When he told me I thought I would throw up but I managed to play it cool – like it didn't matter. Like all I cared about was if he and I were still friends.

Lisa-Marie stopped writing and stared at the words on the page. There is was – so stark and simple, really. Justin had a girlfriend. When would she outgrow her obsession with the guy? He had never once acted like he wanted to be more than friends with her. At the end of the previous summer, he had told her to get on with her life. He had asked her not to text or call and she hadn't. And she'd had a great year – travelling in Europe on a school exchange trip, dating more than a few good-looking guys; and with any luck, she'd soon be accepting a kick-ass, one-year internship with Vogue Magazine in London. The fact that Justin had a girlfriend shouldn't matter to her at all. But the way she'd felt when she actually saw him again changed everything.

She glanced out the window to the moonlit view of the pond overhung by dark evergreens. She had started keeping this particular journal almost two years ago, addressing all her entries to Emma, the character from Jane Austin's novel of the same name. She had hoped Emma's land-on-her-feet attitude would be inspiring. Instead, she seemed to be advising herself in Emma's know-it-all tone and she didn't like what she was hearing. She ripped into the page with her pen, anxious to set the record straight.

I never stopped thinking about Justin. I love him, I'll always love Justin. I thought he meant for me to get on with my life until we would be back together again for the summer. I never thought he would have a girlfriend. I can't stand the thought of him being with someone else.

I've asked this Zach guy to be my date at the wedding. I can't show up like a big fifth wheel to sit with Maddy and Jesse – couple number one – Justin and this Lauren chick – couple number two. I'd look like a pathetic loser.

She slammed the journal shut and tossed it on the floor. She flopped down onto the bed and buried her face in a pillow as tears leaked from her eyes. How could Justin have a girlfriend? How could he do this to her?

TWELVE

I zzy pulled out a chair and sat down in front of the three young people who had gathered in the skills lab. She crossed her legs and tapped the papers in her hand against her knee as she said, "Let's get to know each other before we go over the Residents' Contract. Introduce yourself and tell us one interesting thing that we might not know by looking at you. I'll start." She paused for a moment. "My name is Izzy Montgomery. When I was ten years old, I nearly drowned and I've been scared of the water ever since." A slight frown narrowed her eyes as she attempted a smile. "Sort of crazy since I live right beside a beautiful lake and everyone raves about the swimming."

The slim young man sitting in between the two girls jumped out of his chair and made a graceful, sweeping bow as he introduced himself. "Ethan Black." He put his hands over his head, pulled one foot up the inside of the opposite leg and spun around in a slow pirouette. When he was facing Izzy again, he said, "I've been out of the closet, loud and proud since eighth grade."

The girl to his left burst out laughing. "You were supposed to tell us something we might not know by looking at you." She stood up and added, "My name is Wynter Snow." With a rueful look, she shrugged, "Go ahead and laugh, everyone does. It is the most ridiculous name. I grew up in Ontario, in a place called the Peach Valley Commune. Until I was twelve years old, I never saw a piece of meat or even knew that cows and chickens could be food for humans."

Ethan shuddered and patted Wynter on the arm as she sat down, "I hear you, sister ... meat, totally gross. I'm a pesco-ova-vegetarian myself but sometimes I eat chicken."

Izzy looked at the girl to Ethan's right. She was thin and the T-shirt she wore hung off her shoulders like a shapeless sack. The sickly pale colour of her face did her no favours. She scratched nervously at a patch of angry red skin on the inside of her elbow. Her dull brown hair hung limply over part of her face and she squinted through a pair of thick eyeglasses that squeezed the sides of her head.

Izzy couldn't help but contrast the way Ethan and Wynter looked with the appearance of the third new resident. It was as if a different species of creature had slouched into the room to sit with two angels. Without a doubt, Ethan was the most beautiful young man Izzy had ever laid eyes on. He had ash blonde hair and midnight blue eyes shaped like almonds in a face almost elfin in the delicacy of its features. And Wynter would take anyone's breath away. Her eyes were such a deep shade of blue violet that Izzy assumed they must be enhanced by contacts. Thick, wheat coloured hair cascaded down Wynter's back and she moved like royalty. Sitting there, she was a picture of perfection.

Rachel continued to scratch at her skin as she twitched uncomfortably. Izzy was about to call the whole icebreaker activity off – it had been meant to help people relax, not make anyone break out in hives – when the girl spoke in a quiet voice, "My name is Rachel Franklin. There is nothing interesting about me at all."

Ethan stared up at the ceiling with a look on his face that suggested he might start humming the tune from *Twilight Zone*. Wynter carefully studied her manicured nails.

Izzy shuffled the papers in her hand and got up. "Okay then, let's get started on this paperwork."

Later, with the signed contracts in hand, Izzy pulled out the room assignment roster and glanced at Wynter and Rachel. "You two will be in the same cabin – number eight, right at the end of the row. You'll be rooming with a girl named Arianna." When she turned to address Ethan, a thought she couldn't quite catch danced around the edge of her awareness. "You're in cabin number one," she told him as she got up. "Take the rest of the morning to settle in and get unpacked. You'll find a ton of information to go over in the orientation package." She glanced at her watch, "Probably the most important thing you'll want to know is that lunch is in an hour."

Izzy left the skills lab and crossed the massive living room of the Camp's main building. She stopped for a moment to imagine how the space was going to look in a few short weeks when Liam had it decorated for the wedding reception. It wasn't until she got to her office and picked up the phone that she caught the thread of thought that had nagged at her the moment before she'd assigned Ethan his room. It was the name of the other resident who lived in cabin number one.

✄✄✄✄

Dylan stood by the counter covering a number of marinated steaks with plastic wrap and shifting the trays to the fridge. Brigit walked into the kitchen from the pantry. Her voice snapped out at Dylan like a wet rag, "Why didn't you wait until I got here to mix up the marinade."

Dylan shrugged as a look of impatience crossed his face. "It needed to be done. Where have you been for the last hour?" For at least a part of every day, working with this woman was driving him crazy.

Brigit stared back towards the pantry for a moment before she said, "I didn't know it was going to take so long to do the inventory before I could finish the shopping order, did I?" She smacked the clipboard she was holding against her leg.

"I need a break." Dylan tugged off his apron, threw it on the counter and headed out the door. In a few minutes he was next door at Beulah and Bethany's bakery. He leaned against the wall and watched Arianna stack freshly baked loaves on the cooling rack.

He shook his head, "I don't get what's up with her. One minute we're working like a team and I'm doing exactly what she has asked me to do – act like I'm in charge and she's my assistant until she gets the hang of things. The next minute she's taking my head off like she's got a broom shoved up her butt. If she wanted to be around when I mixed up the marinade, she should have realized it had to be done this morning and not wasted an hour banging around in the pantry."

Arianna looked over at him, "Do you think that could be it? I mean the broom-up-the-butt thing."

"Ha, ha ... I don't get why she acts like she's schizoid."

"Maybe that's it." Arianna grinned, "She could have multiple personalities like you see in freaky movies ... a Cook Jekyll and Cook Hyde sort of thing. Or maybe she has a twin no one knows about ... one minute you see the nice twin; the next minute you see the mean one."

Dylan laughed, "You're not helping. There is no way she has ever run a kitchen on her own before. She doesn't want me to know that but it's so frigging obvious. She has no idea of scheduling. She needs my help. I don't get why she doesn't come out and admit it so I can get on with training her. It's like she deliberately wants to make things difficult." Dylan shrugged and changed the subject, "If you're not busy later, come over and work out in the gym with me. I'm supposed to be getting a new roommate today but we can still go back to my cabin afterwards."

Arianna shoved the last loaf onto the rack. "I can't. I've got to study."

Dylan nudged her, "Okay, Miss Genius. If you change your mind and need a break, you know where to find me."

He got back to the Camp and looked at his watch. He'd been gone fifteen minutes. He thought he'd leave Brigit to sweat it out on her own in the kitchen for another fifteen minutes at least. Let her stew over the mess she'd be in if he chose not to come back at all. He headed for his cabin, thinking he might lie down for a power nap.

As he went through the door, he heard someone singing loudly in the bathroom. He passed the open doorway on the way to his room and stopped dead in his tracks. A guy stood beside the sink with one foot propped on the edge of the counter; the long leg attached to the foot was covered in shaving cream. Clad in nothing more than a pair of comic-covered boxer shorts, the guy held a razor in his hand.

"Hey, I'm Ethan Black, your new roommate," he smiled over at Dylan then turned to draw the razor in a straight line up the length of his leg, leaving a track that looked like a newly ploughed road in a snowstorm.

Dylan stared blankly into the bathroom for a moment before he said, "What the hell are you doing?"

Ethan threw his free arm up in the air in a dramatic pose, "Well, honest to God, boyfriend, what does it look like I'm doing?"

Dylan backed up a step and turned to head for the outside door. As he crossed the room he heard Ethan call out, "Body hair is so 1980's don't you think?"

⚜⚜⚜⚜

Izzy stared out the window of her office as she waited for Darlene to come to the phone.

"Hey, Izzy. What can I do for you on this fine morning?"

"I need Rachel Franklin's file. I have some concerns."

"Rachel will take some explaining." Izzy waited while the sounds of Darlene settling into a chair and gulping some beverage came down the phone line. "Remember how I told you the Board wants to change the narrow focus on talent as an entrance criterion?"

"Are you saying the girl has no talent?"

"Well, I wouldn't put it as bluntly as that." Darlene took a deep breath before she went on. "I pulled some strings to get Rachel into the program. She was the first foster kid I ever had and she has struggled the past few years because she's been bounced from one place to the next. I haven't laid eyes on her since she was much younger but I've tried to keep tabs on her. Micah Camp could give the kid a much needed boost. Since enrollment is going to increase, I didn't think including her would hurt anyone else's chances."

"Unbelievable. Why wouldn't you come and talk to me about this girl? Why dump her on us with no warning and no file?

"I didn't want to take the chance that you'd say no and I thought that once she was there, you wouldn't be able to turn her away. Okay, I'll understand if you want to hang up on me now."

"I'm not going to hang up on you but get me that file, Darlene. I mean it."

"I will. Even if I have to light a fire under every social worker up and down the Island. I better sign off. The town council meeting is starting in a few minutes and if I don't get in there early, there won't be a decent seat to be had. And don't even get me started on how fast those piranhas can make a platter of pastries disappear. Honest to God, you'd think the lot of them were fresh off a Lenten fast."

Dylan walked into Izzy's office as she hung up the phone. He gestured towards the door as he spoke, "How could you put that guy in my cabin? Are you trying to play matchmaker or something? Do you think a little fairy who shaves his legs is my type?"

Izzy pointed to a chair, "Calm down and think before you say another word."

Dylan huffed loudly and thumped his body down into the chair. He folded his arms tightly over his chest; his whole demeanour was thunderous.

Izzy closed her office door and sat down across from him. "Of course I'm not trying to play matchmaker. I asked Nick to figure out the room placements and honestly, I had completely forgotten that you're in cabin number one."

"Move him to another cabin."

Izzy sat silent for a moment before she said, "I can't do that, Dylan –" she held up her hand. "Let me explain. I would be breaking a rule that every resident knows about. We don't allow cabin reassignments. People are going to wonder why an exception would be made in this case. Do you think any of the other guys are going to want to room with him when they figure out you didn't have to? The whole situation could badly affect Ethan and I won't take that chance."

Dylan stared at the floor for a minute. He looked up at Izzy with an air of pissed-off resignation. "A little warning might have been nice."

Izzy nodded her agreement, "You're absolutely right and I'm sorry I didn't see this coming."

"It's not like I want to see the guy persecuted or anything. You know what this means, though; don't you?" Izzy shook her head. "Even if I wanted to come out while I'm here, I couldn't do it now. Everyone would think he and I were together and the thought of that makes me want to pound the shit out of something."

Dylan got up and paced the length of the room before he turned back to Izzy. "I've got to say this out loud. That guy is not my type. If he and I were the last two gay guys on this planet, he would not be my type."

※◇※◇※◇※◇

Lisa-Marie stared into the baby monitor before passing it to Izzy. "Am I seeing what I think I'm seeing?" She had just put Sophie down for her afternoon nap. Izzy was home early and they were about to look at photos of the wedding dresses on the laptop. An email from the designer was open and several of the attachments were waiting to be clicked.

Izzy glanced at the monitor and studied the grainy image. "I saw her trying to do this a few days ago." Spread-eagled on the thick corner post of her crib, Sophie was trying to squirm her way over the top. Izzy walked quickly down to the sun porch. Lisa-Marie continued to look at the small screen. Izzy moved Sophie off the post, deposited her back in her crib and handed her the soother. In a no-nonsense voice, she told her to go to sleep. Sophie gave an offended whimper before she grabbed her bunny and settled down.

Liam and Alex walked into the living room as Izzy closed the French doors to Sophie's room. Liam caught the pinched look on Izzy's face. He glanced over at the laptop. Lisa-Marie had a picture of her dress open on the screen. "Is something wrong with the dresses, Iz?"

"The dresses are fine. Good God, Liam – there are more important things happening in the world than our upcoming wedding. We just saw Sophie climbing up onto the corner post of her crib. A few more wriggles and she'd have fallen onto the floor."

Liam frowned, "That sounds dangerous. Maybe it's time to convert her crib to a toddler bed?" Both Izzy and Lisa-Marie stared at him with looks of horror on their faces.

Izzy shook her head, "No way. She'd be able to get out whenever she felt like it."

Lisa-Marie nodded her agreement, "It's bad enough with Robbie wandering around at night like the living dead; we don't need Sophie getting up and down whenever she pleases."

"We can still move the mattress down another notch. Hopefully that will deter her for a while," Izzy suggested.

Alex laughed, "You two sound like a couple of old hens. What's the big deal? Liam never had a crib at all; he slept in a basket on the floor and when he outgrew that ...." Alex paused to think. "I can't remember where he went then, but I know we didn't have a crib. Fiona slept in bed with me and Kate ... Robbie, too ... well, not with me and Kate. That would have been me and Marsha." He shrugged, "Sophie's been penned up long enough and that's why she's making a break for it. I think it shows she has fighting spirit."

Liam could almost feel the temperature in the room go up a few degrees. He thought it best to get his father out of sight before Alex discovered what the fighting spirit of two women who valued the break time provided by Sophie's nap would look like. Liam imagined a freight train blasting down the tracks full steam ahead. "Come on Dad, you said you wanted to talk to Reg about a lumber list for the new cabin. Let's go."

※※※※

When he got off work at two, Dylan had managed to avoid his new roommate. He'd spent some time in the weight room and run until he couldn't go any further. Then he'd killed another hour up at the sawmill, yakking with Mike and Justin. Now he was back at his cabin with just enough time to shower, change and get over to the kitchen. The bathroom door was shut and he could tell Ethan was in there, again. Dylan raised his fist and smashed on the door three times.

Ethan's voice drifted out, "Okay, okay. I hope you're pounding on the door like that to warn me the bloody place is on fire."

Dylan waited impatiently. As he was about to bang on the door again, it opened and Ethan emerged from the steamy room with a towel wrapped around his narrow hips. Dylan pushed by him, "Do you think you could speed up your fucking beauty queen routine? Some of us have to get to work."

Fifteen minutes later, Dylan came out of his room in a hurry to get back to the kitchen. He was concentrating on snapping his watch on his wrist. In a split second, Ethan, who had been sitting on the sofa flipping through a magazine, got up and aimed a well-placed kick to the back of Dylan's knees. His legs buckled under him and he fell flat on his face on the living room carpet. In no time, Ethan had an arm wrapped around Dylan's neck and a knee pushed into his back.

It took a few seconds for Dylan to get over the shock of the attack but when he did, he pushed back against Ethan's body, choking out the words, "Get off of me, you fucking maniac" Dylan's size and the thirty or so pounds he had on Ethan quickly won out.

Ethan broke the hold around Dylan's neck, did a quick sideways roll and stood up. Hardly short of breath, he said, "The next time you consider calling me a queen, think twice. Or better yet, take a look at yourself in the mirror."

Dylan straightened out his shirt. He had a scowl on his face as he muttered, "Mental case, I ought to smash you." Then Ethan's last few words registered. "Look at myself in the mirror? What the fuck is that supposed to mean?"

Ethan took his time answering, studying his fingernails with fascination. He finally glanced over to Dylan and said, "I know your big, dark secret."

Dylan stared at the guy. Mesmerized, he felt like the jungle boy, Mowgli, gazing into the snake's eyes, unable to look away. "How the hell would you know anything about me?"

Ethan shrugged, "The browser history on your laptop was a giveaway."

Shock replaced anger. "You touched my laptop?"

"Oh please, not even bothering to delete your browser history? It's like you wanted me to know." Ethan flicked his hair out of his face as he said, "I had my suspicions so why not find out for sure? Naturally, I recognized more than a few of *those* sites."

Dylan was so stunned by Ethan's nonchalant admission of sneaking around his bedroom and touching his laptop that he couldn't form a coherent thought. Finally, a few of Ethan's words registered. "Why would you have any suspicions about me?"

Ethan started to laugh, "I like guys, remember? I'm used to taking a close look and something about you made me look twice. That doesn't usually happen with a straight guy."

Dylan had moved from anger to stunned surprise to shock so quickly that all he wanted to do was get the hell away from Ethan as fast as he could. He turned and headed for the door.

Ethan called out, "Relax. It's not like I'll tell anyone. I don't out other guys. But why are you keeping it a secret? How do you ever expect to get laid?"

Dylan stopped with his hand on the doorknob. He turned back, "It's easy for you ...."

Ethan's chin came up, "Because I look like a pansy? Is that what you were going to say?" He moved across the room towards Dylan.

"Don't even think about it. You got lucky last time, sneaking up on me and hitting me from behind. If you try anything like that again, I'll thump you." Dylan glared at Ethan, "Keep your hands off my things." He walked out of the cabin and slammed the door.

♥♥♥♥

Ethan straddled a weight bench in Micah Camp's downstairs exercise room. He wiped the sweat from his forehead with a gym towel as he watched Wynter walk through the doors. He grinned, jumped up and walked over to an empty corner where a dance bar ran along a mirrored wall. He jammed his iPod into the dock that sat on the shelf and spun the dial as he turned towards Wynter, crooked his finger at her and said, "Girl, you are perfection in those yoga pants. Get your pretty self over here."

Wynter strolled over as music filled the room. Ethan reached out his hand, "Let's dance."

After an intense thirty minute workout, Wynter gasped, "Okay, enough. I'm not in as good shape as I thought. Whew ... you are one fine dancer, Ethan." She reached for her water bottle and towel and sat down on the floor to lean against the wall.

Ethan joined her. "Practice makes perfect." He glanced at Wynter and asked, "Where did you learn to tango like that?"

"My grandmother insisted I take all kinds of dance lessons."

Ethan gave the girl beside him an appraising look, "It shows." He changed the subject, "How do you like the place?"

"It's as good a place as any to kill some time. I'm here only because the lawyers in charge of my grandmother's money don't have a clue what to do with me until I turn nineteen. The cabins are nice. I'll get some work experience with the paper and soap business. The career counsellor says they'll find me a French tutor and I'm enrolled in two university transfer courses." She dabbed at her neck with her towel as she asked, "You're rooming with the guy who works in the kitchen, right?"

Ethan put his hand to his forehead and moaned, "Hands off, girl. I fell hopelessly in love the minute I laid eyes on him."

"He's gay?"

Ethan laughed, "What's that got to do with my grand passion?"

"You'd fall for a guy who isn't gay? Sounds like a stupid thing to do."

Ethan shrugged, "I like falling in love ... all the emotional drama. An unrequited, hopeless love is that much more of a kick." He gave Wynter a sideways glance before asking, "What's the story with that Rachel girl? She looks like something the cat dragged through a knothole backwards."

It was Wynter's turn to shrug, "No idea. After dinner she was in the bathroom of our cabin barfing her brains out."

Ethan whistled before he asked, "You think she's a stuff-and-chucker?"

"I asked her if she was okay and she said the dinner didn't agree with her stomach. I feel sorry for her. She's always twitching and scratching and peering out of those ugly glasses like she's half blind." Wynter got up and stretched, "I'm beat."

Ethan rose as well. "How about we do this again?"

"Sure, that was an awesome workout ... exactly what I needed. I'll hit the weights on the girls only nights and save my aerobic workout for the dance floor with you on the co-ed nights."

ᴎᴑᴎᴑᴎᴑᴎᴑ

Robbie gasped in admiration as he moved with the cougar through the broken terrain, up and down the steep slopes, easily maneuvering around, over or under fallen trees, rock outcroppings and thick brush. The cat had been created to traverse such a landscape as it sought a glimpse or sound of its prey.

Using agility, cover and darkness, the cougar had spotted a deer and they had been stalking it for some time. Now, crouched down low in the brush and hidden from view, the cat waited for the graceful animal to bend its neck to drink. Robbie knew an absolute stillness he had never felt before. Then the cat's muscles tensed; power surged and quivered through the animal. They were poised on the very precipice of the pounce that would end the deer's life. At that moment another animal leapt out of the brush from behind them. The tawny body of a full-grown, male cougar brought the deer down in an instant; gleaming teeth and sharp claws did the work they were created to do.

Standing over the kill, the larger male looked toward the place where Robbie and the intruder cat lay hidden. A low-throated growl conveyed a simple message – You do not belong here. A frustrated anguish gripped Robbie. The cougar had to eat or it would die. He moved off with the cat down the mountain toward the familiar smells of dogs and people.

Lisa-Marie was pushing up against the edge of sleep when she heard Robbie's door open and Dante's low whine. She quickly got out of bed and walked into the hall. The boy had passed her bedroom with the dog in close pursuit. Gently, she reached out a hand to take Robbie's arm. The vacant look on his face was spooky. As she tried to turn him back towards his own room, he shook all over and stared at her. She stepped back as a shiver of fear shot up her spine.

"It's coming closer, Leez."

"What's coming closer?"

Robbie eyelids fluttered up and down. He finally focused on Lisa-Marie. "I'm starving. Do you want to come downstairs with me to get something to eat?"

"It's late, Robbie. I've got a chocolate bar. I'll get it for you." She grabbed the KitKat from her desk then watched as Robbie stood in her doorway and wolfed it down. "Better?" she asked as he licked his fingers.

He smiled his regular Robbie smile at her, "Yup. That hit the spot. See you in the morning." He walked back to his room. Remembering how she'd compared Robbie's sleepwalking to the living dead, Lisa-Marie was tempted to close her door tight and jam a chair under the handle. She shook her head at the thought as she climbed into bed

THIRTEEN

"**E**xcuse me." The sound of a voice outside the open door of Josie's office distracted Lisa-Marie from the task of sorting a pile of order forms. The elegance of the girl standing in the doorway took her breath away. "Hey, I'm Wynter. I'm supposed to start working here today."

"Give me a minute to push my eyes back into their sockets. I suppose you hear this all the time, but you're beautiful." Riffling through one pile of forms, she said, "I'm Lisa-Marie. I'll be supervising the workshop a couple of days a week for Josie, so I guess I'm the person you need to see."

Wynter unfolded the piece of paper in her hand and held it out, "The same Lisa-Marie who is looking for people to pose for portraits?"

"Yup, that's me. Are you interested? It would be amazing if you were because I'm already itching to get my hands on a camera and take your picture."

Wynter paused for a moment before asking, "Are you any good?"

"I am good but I need to practice. I'm waiting to hear if I'll be accepted for an internship year at Vogue in London."

Wynter's eyebrows rose, "Impressive. Did you see the cover they did last year on Cate Blanchett?"

"Since I made the shortlist, every back issue of Vogue is like my bible."

"I was part of a photo shoot they did up at Whistler a couple of years ago. I didn't get featured or anything but I made it into a couple of shots." Wynter shrugged, "I'll be spending this year applying to various modelling agencies. I'd love to get my portfolio updated to give me a more mature look. The last time I had it done, I was sixteen. It really needs a few tasteful nudes. Maybe we can help each other. I wouldn't mind shots of me appearing in your portfolio for Vogue."

Lisa-Marie reached over to shake Wynter's hand. "The only volunteer I've had so far is my one-year-old daughter and that is hardly what I'm after." Grabbing the nearest pile of order forms, Lisa-Marie led the way out to the workshop, "Let's get you started on something a bit less glamorous than high fashion. We have a ton of stationery orders to package today."

⁂

Mike stopped by Justin's desk before heading out for his run. "Next time you'd better be coming with us. When I get back, why don't you come into town with me and have supper at my place? Then we'll hit the liquor store, stock up on snacks and head back out here for poker night."

Justin nodded, "As soon as I can get caught up on all this stuff Reg has me doing, I promise, I'll be running, too ... maybe just to get away from the boss." He looked up quickly to make sure Reg wasn't anywhere around. Mike slapped him on the back and headed out to the road where Dylan waited.

An hour later, Justin had finished the latest batch of paperwork and cleared off his desk. He grabbed his jacket and went outside where he spotted Mike and Dylan jogging back into the yard at a leisurely pace. At the same time, Ethan was walking away from a huge pile of neatly stacked lumber. He was singing a song and slapping his work gloves against his leg. The guy had such a lift in his step that he seemed to be dancing.

When Ethan had arrived that morning announcing that he was the latest Micah Camp resident to be assigned to the sawmill for work experience, Reg had stood in front of the young man with a dumbfounded look on his face. Justin had thought the wildly rotating toothpick in the man's mouth would fly right out. Setting his newest employee such a heavy task on his first afternoon had to be Reg's way of making the kid see he wasn't cut out for this type of work. By the looks of the piled lumber, the plan had backfired.

Ethan caught up with Justin and pointed over to the yard, "Think that will satisfy Reg?"

Eyeing the lumber piled neatly by size, Justin nodded and said, "Looks good."

The joggers slowed their pace to a walk as they drew near. Dylan glared at Ethan, "What the hell are you doing up here?"

Ethan put his hand on his hip and raised his voice to a high falsetto, "Why, little old me has done got himself a job at the sawmill, sugar."

Dylan shook his head in disbelief and turned to the others for confirmation. Justin nodded and said, "I'm assuming you two know each other?"

"Ya, meet my new roommate."

Justin chuckled and dropped the subject. "Mike and I are going into Dearborn for dinner and supplies. We'll see you down at my place at eight." He slapped Dylan on the arm and turned to walk towards Mike's truck.

Ethan put his fingers to his lips and gave a sharp whistle that sounded like an air-raid siren. "Time out, boys," he yelled while parodying a linesman's stance on a football field. When three sets of eyes turned to stare at him, he said, "A social gathering of co-workers has been arranged and the gay guy has been left out." Ethan crouched down, crossed his hands in front of his body several times and shouted, "Foul." He dropped his gloves on the ground as if they were a yellow flag and walked over to Justin. "Looks like homophobia, to me. You're outta the game, big feller."

Justin laughed; the guy was a regular riot. He slammed the wiry young man on the back, "My cabin, eight o'clock, poker night ... Dylan knows where it is." He started to walk away then suddenly turned back. "You're nineteen, right?" Ethan's head bobbed up and down. "Okay, good. I won't serve alcohol to anyone from the Camp who's underage. See you guys later."

Ethan called after him, "When you're grabbing those snacks, just so you know, I'm gluten intolerant. Read the labels." Justin waved his hand over his head as he got into Mike's truck.

Ethan smirked broadly at Dylan. "Want to walk home together, sweetcakes?"

Without saying a word, Dylan shook his head and walked away. He kept up a fast pace until the two of them were about to turn onto Micah Camp's paved driveway. He spun around, grabbed Ethan by the collar of his work shirt and stared into his face, "None of your bullshit jokes and asshole nicknames when we're at Justin's. Got it?" The last two words were accompanied by an extra shake before he let Ethan go.

Bouncing back on his toes, Ethan made a production of straightening his shirt collar. "I told you, I don't out other guys and I meant it."

Dylan was already walking away.

⚜ ⚜ ⚜ ⚜

Mike had driven a few minutes down the road before Justin noticed the pinched look on his face. "What's eating at you?" he asked.

Mike shifted gears and shrugged, "You and Dylan and me ... we know each other. We don't know this Ethan guy at all."

Justin laughed, "We're going to play cards with him. We'll get to know him." He changed the subject, "Is your mom going to be okay with me showing up for dinner unannounced?"

Mike grinned, "You don't know my mom. She's going to love you. She thinks anyone who is pursuing higher education has a halo glued over his head. Mark my words, sometime during supper my mom is going to say, *Well, let's hope your ambition for higher education rubs off on our Mike.* Then my dad is going to say, *Give it a rest, Helen. No offense Justin, but I've managed a building supply store for twenty years and I've done fine without a university education, thank you kindly.* The two of them are like broken records." Mike tipped his head to one side, "Do you hear that knocking sound in the engine?"

"I wouldn't know a bad engine sound from a good one."

"I leave most of that to my dad but you have to keep tuned into an old truck like this or you'll end up stranded somewhere." Mike downshifted, slowed for a tight corner and returned to the subject of his parents and higher education. "You should hear my mom go on about Zach and how he's going to BCIT. It's like he's the second coming or something. Believe me, ninety percent of the time that guy is as dumb as a post and no amount of higher education is going to change that."

Justin chuckled, "Sounds like you've got a good case of sibling rivalry going on."

Mike shook his head, "Seriously, the guy thinks with his dick twenty-four/seven. And for some reason, which is totally beyond me ... girls can't get enough of him."

Justin shifted the topic of conversation to what he hoped would be safer ground. "Did you talk to him about the ball team? I told Beulah both of you guys would be coming out."

"Oh ya, he's all for it. But, of course, he would be. He loves shit like team sports."

When they pulled into Mike's driveway, Justin looked at the comfortable two-story house with its landscaped yard and expansive deck that wrapped around to provide a view of the strait. A tree-covered island with rocky shores brushed by crisp, white waves dominated the horizon. At the back of a yard resplendent with flower beds, a vegetable garden and greenhouse, large cedars poked into the sky. Justin watched an eagle settle on the upper branches of one and preen feathers ruffled by the ocean breeze. "Nice place," he commented.

Mike led the way around the side of the house and up the back steps, "We've lived here since I was a kid." They walked into the kitchen and Mike went straight to the fridge, grabbed a beer for himself and tossed one to Justin. His mom turned to smile at both of them as she carved the ham. Mike pointed and said, "This is Justin, Mom. He's staying for dinner."

Helen Sampson gave Justin a big smile as she wiped her hands on her apron, put on a pair of oven mitts and transferred a pan of scalloped potatoes from the oven to the top of the stove. "It's nice to meet you, Justin. Any friend of Mike's is always welcome here for a meal."

Justin smiled back at Mike's mom. *Is this what's it like to have parents and a home?* He felt warm inside and uncomfortably empty all at the same time. He knew he didn't belong in this *Happy Days* scene where Mom makes dinner and friends are always welcome.

As Helen took a large salad from the fridge, she said, "We'll have a full table tonight. Zach has invited his new girl to join us."

Mike rolled his eyes, "What happened to Gigi or whatever her name is? That lasted all of two weeks, right?"

Helen gave her son a severe look, "Mind your manners, Mike."

Craig Sampson walked into the kitchen from the other side of the room and scooped a piece of ham from the platter into his mouth. His wife slapped at his hand, but he ignored her and pulled open the fridge to get a beer of his own. "Nice to see you, Justin."

Justin had met Craig a number of times up at the sawmill. He felt relaxed with Mike and his dad and the three of them gravitated to the dining room. They were shooting the breeze about cars when Zach came up the stairs laughing and holding the hand of the girl behind him.

Justin and Lisa-Marie stared at one another. "What are you doing here?" Their voices echoed in stereo across the room.

Zach laughed, "I guess you two know each other." Still holding tight to Lisa-Marie's hand, Zach headed into the kitchen, "Is supper ready? Can we do something to help? I'm starving."

Justin practically gawked at Lisa-Marie as she smiled over her shoulder at him. Soon she was chatting with Mike's mom and being given a pile of cutlery for the dinner table. The blonde guy who was slapping plates on the table was obviously Mike's brother, Zach. That piece of the puzzle made sense. But the part of the picture that explained how the hell Zach, the guy who thought with his dick twenty-four/seven, had ended up with Lisa-Marie by his side was clearly missing.

A few minutes later, with everyone seated at the large dining room table, Justin served himself from the dishes of food that were being passed around. He couldn't help watching Zach. The guy was a show-off, but not the kind who didn't have the smarts to back it up. Zach had confidence; he liked to laugh. Things came easily for him and he was riding the wave. He fit into this *Happy Days* family like it was tailor-made for him.

Craig interrupted Justin's thoughts by launching into a series of non-stop questions about the price per board foot of several types of lumber and whether or not Justin thought the cost would go up or down. When he took a breath for air, Helen jumped in with questions about Justin's university program. She ended by saying, "Well, I hope some of your educational ambition will rub off on our Mike."

Mike began to bob his head as he alerted Justin, "What did I tell you? Wait for it."

He pointed at his dad and, as if on cue, Craig said, "Now Helen, there you go again. No offense intended, Justin, but I've managed a building supply store for twenty years and made a good living without a university education."

Craig was interrupted by a young girl who breezed in and plunked herself down beside him. She had Zach's blonde hair in a curling mass down her back and a face that contained Mike's dark eyes. She dressed the way Justin had seen a thousand young girls dress – glitz and grunge fought for supremacy over fashion and girlish charm.

Helen gave her daughter a stern look, "Glad you could make an appearance, Hannah. We've only been having dinner in this house at six since you were born."

Hannah rolled her eyes and stared across the table at Lisa-Marie, "Are you Zach's new girlfriend? Is that a designer watch you're wearing?" She turned to her brother, "She's out of your league, Zachariah. Does she know you fart so loud at night it feels like the house is about to collapse?"

Pandemonium erupted around the table as Zach pointed at Hannah and said, "You're such a little b –"

Helen glared at Zach and said, "Don't you dare say that word at my dinner table."

Hannah smirked and Mike burst out laughing. Zach mouthed the word, *bitch* at Hannah before turning to his brother and grabbing him by the arm, "What's so funny, loser? When's the last time you invited a girl over? Oh, let me think ... never."

Craig held up his hand and said, "Enough, all three of you. What will our guests think?" He looked at Hannah, "Apologize to Zach and mind your manners. You don't talk like that at the table." He stared at Zach, "Let go of your brother, this minute."

Zach jerked Mike's arm before he let go of it. He shrugged and returned to eating a large slab of ham. Soon he joked with Hannah about someone they knew and the two of them were laughing like a pair of hyenas.

It wasn't until Helen served the dessert that Justin had a chance to say, "So, Zach, how did you and Lisa-Marie meet?"

Zach smiled at Justin as if they were best friends, "I was out at Izzy and Liam's the other day to fix their satellite dish. We met there." He draped an arm around Lisa-Marie, "She played a bit hard to get at first but, what can I say? I charmed her. Then she asked me to be her date for Izzy and Liam's wedding." He smiled his baby blues down on the girl beside him and said, "Right?"

Helen clapped her hands, "Oh, that's great. We'll be at the wedding, too. Wait until you see the cake I'm decorating according to Liam's very specific instructions."

Justin couldn't stop staring at the way Zach's arm draped over the back of Leez's chair. He almost missed what the guy said to him. "When is Beulah planning to start the ball practices? Slow pitch, mixed league ... it'll be a riot." He hugged Lisa-Marie closer, "You're going to play, right? The team is the Crater Lake Timber Wolves and you live right there. You have to be on the team."

Lisa-Marie looked at Justin and smiled before she turned to Zach and said, "Of course I'll be on the team. There is no way that Beulah would want a team without me. I really rock at slow pitch."

Justin felt something strange welling up in his gut that said get out of here right now. He caught Mike's eye and dipped his head towards the door.

Mike got up as Justin turned to Helen and said, "Thanks for a delicious dinner, Mrs. Sampson. I'm stuffed."

Mike hugged his mom where she still sat in her chair, "I'm staying at Justin's tonight so don't worry about me. I'll be home tomorrow morning."

Zach followed his brother and Justin into the kitchen. He pushed Mike in the arm and said, "Have fun playing poker with the guys. And while you're doing that, you can think of me cuddled up downstairs with the hottest girl around, watching some chick flick and I'll let you use your imagination for the rest. I know you're good at that." He laughed as he headed back to the dining room.

100

Lisa-Marie took the rinsed dishes from Mrs. Sampson's hand and loaded them into the dishwasher. Up until the awkward moment of seeing Justin in the dining room, she had been having a great time with Zach. He was cute and funny and he didn't talk about himself all the time like a lot of guys she'd met over the last year. He asked her questions about school and what her plans were for the future. He'd hardly batted an eye when she told him she had a year-old daughter that Izzy and Liam looked after while she was away at school.

He'd told her, "A couple of girls in my grade twelve class brought their babies to grad."

When she had driven up earlier, Zach's dad had insisted that she pull her jeep into his garage so he could put it up on the hoist and have a look. Zach said, "He does this sort of stuff. You'll have to humour him." The vehicle was still there. He'd said something about doing an oil change after dinner.

Zach had invited her inside the house and shown her around his home. She had been stunned at how perfect it all seemed. Not beautiful, fancy home perfect – it was more like the way she had always dreamed a real family home would be. The place smelled of food and fresh laundry. The rooms were comfortable and inviting. There were plants everywhere, pictures on the wall and photos of Mike and Zach and Hannah all over. It was the kind of house that said, come in, sit down, make yourself at home.

Coming back to the reality of the kitchen, Lisa-Marie heard Mrs. Sampson speaking to Hannah. "I know you girls voted for a beauty pageant, but the idea is all wrong for the theme of Dipsy-Doodle Days. No one on the committee will take it on and without an adult to organize things ... well, the event can't happen."

Hannah huffed and did a dramatic pout as she slammed the broom into the closet by the fridge. "This is bullshit. First you tell us to participate and vote for what we want to do then you say we can't have what we all agreed to. Talk about being phony. We voted for a beauty pageant and we should be able to have a frigging beauty pageant."

Mrs. Sampson raised her voice slightly. "Watch it, Missy. You're not too big to be sent to your room." She looked at Lisa-Marie and made a face, "She's right, though. We've made a real mess of things. The committee wanted to increase the participation of high school kids and getting their input seemed like a good idea at the time. Now we're caught looking like a bunch of turncoats."

Lisa-Marie closed the dishwasher and looked from Hannah to her mom. "I might have a solution. There's this new resident out at Micah Camp. Her name is Wynter and she's had modelling experience ... including a few professional shoots. If anyone could organize a beauty pageant it would be her. She's over-the-top gorgeous so she's got the beauty part down. How hard could the rest be?"

Mrs. Sampson smiled, "I'll call Darlene Evans and ask her about this girl. You say her name is Wynter? That's quite unique, isn't it?"

Lisa-Marie raised her hand in a high-five to Hannah as the girl walked out of the room. Zach came bounding up the back steps and into the kitchen. He threw his arm around Lisa-Marie. "We finished changing your oil and I backed your car out into the driveway. It's a sweet, sweet ride. Maybe you'll let me drive it someday?"

His grin was infectious and she found herself smiling back, "Maybe."

He grabbed her hand, "Come on. Let's go. You can pick any movie you want to see and I won't complain, promise."

⌁⌁⌁⌁

Justin had been hitting the vodka hard and he wasn't feeling any pain. He narrowed his eyes to focus on where he was dealing the cards. The cabin was dense with cigar smoke, the table littered with money. Drinks and half-eaten bowls of chips made it a challenge for Justin to send the cards flying over the surface of the table. He pushed aside a pile of beef jerky wrappers to drop a card in front of Dylan. He flipped a card up for himself and peered under the edge of the one that faced down in front of him. Keeping his face neutral, he glanced at Mike and waited while Mike pondered his card, opened his mouth, closed it and started the whole routine again. "Oh for Christ's sake, stop being such an old lady. Do you want a card or not?"

"Ya, ya ... okay." Glancing at the card dealt to him, Mike threw his hand on the table, "Busted again."

Justin looked across at Ethan who squinted at the card held close to his chest. He wore a Vegas style dealer's visor on his head and he had the sleeves of his white shirt rolled up to reveal wiry arms with sharply defined muscles.

Ethan wiggled his fingers, "Hit me."

As Justin slid the card over, he said, "Why don't you tell us something about yourself?"

"Is that some kind of distraction technique? Don't you already know all that a bunch of straight guys would want to know? I'm gay." Ethan held up his hand as Justin made to give him another card. "I'll be sitting pretty on these."

Dylan waved his hand over his cards to indicate he was good. Justin dealt himself another card face up. Everyone laid down his cards and Dylan laughed as he pulled the cash in the middle of the table towards him. Mike gathered the deck and started to shuffle.

Justin stretched. His chair teetered back on two legs as he stared at Ethan. "Did it ever occur to you that some of us Neanderthal straight guys might be interested in something other than your sexual orientation?"

Ethan grabbed a pepperoni wrapper and carefully read the label on the back. He threw it down on the table in disgust. "Gluten, it's everywhere." He looked at Justin, "Nope, can't say that thought ever did occur to me. What do you want to know?"

"How did you manage to stack all that lumber this afternoon? Reg was yanking your chain, trying to prove you weren't cut out for the job. I'm not sure I could have got through all of that in the time it took you."

Ethan grinned, "I did show Reg, didn't I?" He shrugged, "I've been dancing since I was four years old. I've done tap, ballet, jazz, modern ... you name it, I dance it. I work out every single day. Believe me, hefting a few of those delicate-looking, tutu-wearing ballerinas up over your head about a million times during rehearsals will make you think that stacking a bunch of lumber is a fucking picnic. They might look all feathery light but it's still bulling up a hundred or so pounds in the air."

"See, that wasn't so hard, was it? How did you end up at Micah Camp?"

Playing his way through another hand and dealing the next, Ethan talked, warming up to the topic as he went. "It's an ugly story of a custody battle taken to extremes that seriously defy common sense. When I was fourteen my parents decided to pull the plug on their marriage. They're both lawyers and a more pigheaded pair of people probably doesn't exist anywhere else on this fucking planet. I was like a UPS parcel going from house to house following one court order after another. Finally, a judge looked through my file and said, shit, neither of this guy's parents is fit to have a goldfish, let alone a kid. I had been staying with a friend from the dance studio and her dad talked to someone about getting me into this program at a place called Micah Camp. I had done shit in school for my whole grade twelve year and didn't have a hope in hell of graduating. At the interview, they told me I could do all my upgrading here, apply to dance schools and have a place to stay until I turned nineteen."

Justin reached across the table and grabbed the bottle of beer from in front of Ethan, "I thought you said you were nineteen."

Ethan shrugged and threw his cards down on the table to win the hand. "I lied." He raked in the cash.

A couple of hours later, Justin stood outside wishing to hell he was upstairs sleeping. In a somewhat drunken haze, he had seen Dylan and Ethan out the door and straightened up the cabin. Mike had flopped onto the sofa and was snoring within a matter of moments.

He thought about walking over closer to Izzy's house to see if he could pick up enough of an internet signal to text Lauren. He'd tried to get her a couple of times when he had been in town but she hadn't responded. He decided against the idea of going next door. It was a hell of a lot of effort in the dark. Plus he didn't want to get the dogs barking and end up being taken for some kind of prowler.

It came to him suddenly that he was lonely; well, to be more accurate, horny. It had seemed all well and good to maintain his self-imposed, monk-like existence, carefully sidestepping any girl who offered a no-strings-attached hook-up because he didn't want the complications of that oxymoron. But he had been having sex with Lauren for a couple of months before he left Vancouver. It was something a guy got used to and he was finding it harder to do without than he had imagined it would be.

His thoughts wandered to the way Leez had looked curled up on his sofa the other day. Shit, he was as pathetic as Zach had accused Mike of being, conjuring up the sight of smooth skin below a belly-button ring and imagining how warm that skin would feel as he slid his hand down the front of her faded jeans.

He leaned into the porch railing and listened to the night sounds – a rustling in a nearby bush, a flutter high above in one of the trees, the hoot of an owl in the distance, all against the steady backdrop of noise made by the waves lapping onto the rocks below.

He saw headlights flash through the thick trees up on the road. He watched as the light snaked in and out of view. He heard the engine go into low gear as the vehicle turned and began to ease down Izzy's steep driveway. He looked at his watch. Must have been a double feature or maybe Leez had been kept out late by what Zach had boastfully left for others to imagine. He took a deep breath. To his surprise, his body slowly unclenched. At least she was home. He relaxed and yawned as he turned to go back into the cabin.

FOURTEEN

Fiona grinned as she got out of the front seat of the Highlander and took in the view of Crater Lake beyond the expanse of the woodland garden. The sunshine scudded across the water in ripples atop the row after row of wavelets. She slowly turned in a full circle to see the clean lines of the large, cedar-shake cabin, the greenhouse and the trees that overhung the steep driveway and continued on up the mountainside. The grandeur of the place went beyond Liam's humble description, though he hadn't been able to contain his pride when he talked about the home he shared with the woman named Izzy.

Her heart had pounded with excitement when she'd crawled out of the plane at the Cedar Falls airport and strolled into the waiting area, glancing from side to side until she spotted Alexander, Liam and Robbie standing together. Alexander pointed to her and smiled. Her welcoming committee was a trio of guys whose appearance had seriously tempted her to throw aside all dignity and push past the slower passengers so she could break into a gallop and rush towards them.

But she had kept pace with the others. When she finally arrived in front of Alex, she waited silently for him to bow his forehead to touch hers. Placing his hands gently on her arms, he had drawn her close, into the circle of power that she had always felt around him. Alex was the only father she had ever known, the father who chose her to be his daughter. He alternately awed her and infuriated her even as she felt a love for him that was so fierce she couldn't really describe it.

She had turned from Alex to greet Liam, the brother she had tried so many times to imagine. When she was young, Alex had often spoken to her of Liam – of the boy Liam had been, of a father's pride in his eldest son's accomplishments, of the frustration and sorrow at not being able to find Liam for so many years. As a solitary child, Fiona had clung to the thought of this brother out in the world somewhere.

She supposed Liam bore a resemblance to the younger Alex she had grown up with, but as she got older Fiona realized that Alex's aura had always made it hard for her to see him as he really was. Liam was different. Where Alex was a fortress of strength, there were no walls guarding Liam. His face, his demeanour, the way he held himself – everything was an invitation for her to come closer. He had opened his arms to her in greeting and when she rested her face against his shoulder, the soft material of his jean jacket caressed her. She felt the wet prick of tears in her eyes and she had to swallow hard.

Covering her emotions, she had stepped away and squatted down to grab Robbie and tug him close. A year ago, when Robbie and Alex had shown up at the door of her small apartment in Montreal, she had fallen head over heels for the kid. He would be the brother she could know and care for as he grew up. She promised herself that she and Alex would never lose Robbie the way Alex had carelessly lost Liam for so many years.

They had left the small airport and piled into the SUV for the drive back. Alex, Robbie and Liam competed with one another in their efforts to point things out to her and tell her as much as they could about northern Vancouver Island, Cedar Falls, Dearborn and Crater Lake. She let it all wash over her with no need to understand or question. Not yet. The sound of their collective voices was enough. She laughed out loud a number of times as she stretched back to touch Alex or Robbie, or reached across to lay her hand on Liam's arm as he drove. These men were her people and she couldn't take the smile off her face as she thought of the coming months. She was away from school at last; she was finally on her way to becoming a real doctor in a real community. She'd have time to spend with Liam and Robbie. She'd settle herself under Alex's sway, as she always did. And from what she could pick up from the conversation, there were women and children for her to meet – Izzy, Cynthia, Lisa-Marie, Robbie's friend Tabby and a special little girl named Sophie. Wedding bells were in the offing. She could hardly wait.

❦❦❦❦

Izzy crossed the driveway to meet the group of people piling out of the Highlander. Sophie was in her arms and Cynthia was right behind her. She watched Fiona spin around trying to see everything at once. The young woman was striking – a dark flow of shiny hair draped over her shoulder in a thick braid and beaded hoop earrings flashed against her skin. As Fiona turned, Izzy saw her wide, clear forehead, her prominent nose above a generous mouth and her easy smile which revealed the sparkling white of her teeth. She noticed the young woman's eyes. They drew her forward into pools of darkness under strong brows. Izzy caught herself thinking, Frida Kahlo after a good eye-brow waxing. All of a sudden, the sun of Fiona's features went behind a cloud brought on by a slight pursing of her lips and a mere narrowing of her eyes. The shadow lifted as quickly as it had appeared but it was obvious that something about Izzy didn't meet with Fiona's approval.

Liam stood beside Izzy, pulling her close as he said, "Fiona, this is my bride-to-be, Izzy Montgomery." The moment of chill passed as the younger woman shook Izzy's hand. Fiona's arms reached out instinctively for Sophie and Izzy passed the baby over. When Fiona met Cynthia the clouded look was once again evident. Soon enough they were all chatting and moving into the garden and over to the cliff deck to admire the view of the lake. Quite content to be pulling on Fiona's thick braid, Sophie smiled and chattered away.

❧❧❧❧

After a day's work at Micah Camp's paper and soap shop, supervising supplies coming in and orders going out, Lisa-Marie strolled along the path that wound through the trees on her way back to Izzy and Liam's. When she got to the curve that allowed a clear view of her aunt and Beulah's A-Frame, she spotted Arianna sitting on the back steps of the bakery building. Lisa-Marie waved and called out hello. She left the path to cut across the driveway and walk past the outdoor oven. She climbed up the stairs and sat down beside Arianna. "I was hoping to see you. I've got a favour to ask. But first, how are you doing?"

Arianna grinned and shrugged, "I'm studying for my math and English finals until my head is about to split."

Lisa-Marie nudged the other girl with her shoulder, "Auntie Beth said you got accepted to UBC. That's amazing. Who knew you were such a smarty pants?"

Arianna loosened the ponytail that danced high on her head and ran her hands through the length of her hair as she grinned, "Took me by surprise, too. So, what's the favour?"

"I've met this guy named Zach."

"Is he cute?"

Lisa-Marie fanned herself as she said, "Oh ya, he's super cute. He's going to be on Beulah's new ball team and I sort of ended up bragging about how I'd be on the team, too."

"Is he any good at ball?" Arianna's sudden excitement at the prospect of recruiting a talented player for the team was replaced quickly by a frown as she asked, "Beulah said you could be on the team?"

Lisa-Marie laughed. "Her exact words were – *when hell freezes over I'll consider it.* That's why I'm here. I was hoping you could help me convince her."

Arianna thought it over for a minute and Lisa-Marie could tell that friendship had won out over good judgement when her answer came. "Sure. I'll tell her I won't be on the team if you're not."

Lisa-Marie grinned, "That was sort of what I had in mind."

A few minutes later Lisa-Marie was back on the path. When she came through the orchard, she could see people sitting in the chairs on the kitchen deck of Izzy and Liam's cabin. Sophie was clutching at the edge of her playpen and throwing toys out of the enclosed space as fast as the adults surrounding her could throw them back. Lisa-Marie's heart thumped as Sophie spotted her, lifted her arms and smiled brightly. She walked over, raised her child from the playpen and held her close. Tickling the baby's tummy, she asked, "How is my little girl this sunny afternoon?" She hoisted Sophie onto her hip and turned to meet Fiona.

Liam had already stood up to make the introductions. "Fiona, this is Lisa-Marie, Sophie's mother. Her Aunt Beth lives next door."

Lisa-Marie smiled at Fiona as she bumped Sophie up and down and twisted the fingers of her free hand through the baby's dark curls. She was not surprised by the startled look on Fiona's face during Liam's introduction. Izzy and Liam often left people to think what they wanted about Sophie.

"Hey," Lisa-Marie said as she reached for a slice of fruit from the nearby tray, "I've never met anyone who was going to be a doctor. Do people start telling you what's wrong with them all the time? You don't look very old. I thought you had to go to school forever to be a doctor."

Fiona tossed her braid over her shoulder as she smiled, "I'm twenty-eight and that means I've done nothing but school for the past twenty-three years. Being a doctor is what I've always wanted and most times I don't even care if people tell me what's wrong with them."

Alexander got up from where he was lounging on a bench beside Cynthia. "I'll walk you over to the guest cabin now, if you like, Fi. You'll have some time to get unpacked and settled in before dinner."

After a quick stroll through the garden and down the path, Fiona barely glanced around the cabin that would be her home for the next six months. Instead, she rounded on Alex and pointed a finger at him, "What the hell is going on here? My brother appears to be playing houseboy to a colonial, white woman who owns all the property around here for as far as the eye can see. And why, by the way, are you building a house on her land? What's Robbie to her? How come she and my brother are acting like that young girl's baby belongs to them?" Alex dropped Fiona's bag on the floor with a clunk. She didn't give him a chance to respond to any of her questions. "And you're shacked up with another white woman who is old enough to be my grandmother. Are there no Indian women in BC?"

Alex leveled a stern look her way, "Mind what that sharp tongue of yours deals out when it comes to Cynthia. And that goes for what you say about your brother and Izzy, too; your mom didn't raise you to be so damn disrespectful. Izzy's been like a mother to Robbie this past year and she is exactly what that kid needed. As for Sophie, if you want to know any more about that, you'll have to ask one of the parties involved." Alex crossed his arms over his chest and said, "Behave yourself." Then he grinned, "And for your information, I'm old enough to be your grandfather. It never seemed to bother you or your mother, for that matter."

Fiona took a deep breath, shrugged and managed a half smile of her own. The normality of being put in her place by Alex was comforting in an odd way. She turned her attention to the guest cabin. It was more than nice. They had walked across a large cedar deck to a sliding glass door that opened to a comfy living room and small dining area. Both commanded wonderful views of the lake. A winder staircase led up to a loft bedroom. She wandered through the small but efficient-looking galley kitchen and took note of the bathroom and storage area nestled behind the living room. It would be perfect for her and she did feel grateful that Liam and this Izzy woman would offer to let her stay here.

When she returned to the living room she found Alex standing in the same spot watching her. She smiled a mischievous grin at him. "You behave yourself, too or I'll let your girlfriend know that in my medical opinion, a man of your advanced age should certainly see a doctor for a prostrate exam."

With a look of horror on his face, Alex said, "You wouldn't dare."

"Oh, don't be too sure about that and you know how persuasive I can be." She walked over to the sliding glass door with him pretending all the while that she was snapping on latex gloves and wiggling her middle finger at him.

❧❧❧❧

Cynthia settled herself on the camper's tiny sofa. She was none too happy about giving up the guest cabin to Fiona and landing back here in this cramped camper but she took it with good grace. It would be some time before the new cabin she and Alex envisioned would be finished, but at least there was light on the horizon. She looked over at Alex and asked, "What's up with Fiona. She definitely gave me and Izzy the cold shoulder. I thought I had imagined it but Izzy noticed, too."

Alex shrugged, "Fiona's a bit militant ... a chip off the old block and all of that."

Cynthia's eyes widened, "Coming from you, the term *a bit militant* is just plain scary."

Alex smiled as he sat down beside her. "Fi can take some time to warm up to people."

"She seemed perfectly warm and friendly to everyone else and I'd suggest that having to take time to warm up to people will make for a poor bedside manner." Suddenly, she turned to push Alex's arm, "She said something about me, didn't she? What is it?" An expression of distress crossed Cynthia's face, "Oh my God ... she's read one of my books and she thinks I'm a sex maniac –" Cynthia's shoulders drooped. "Or she thinks I'm a hack."

Alex laughed as he pulled Cynthia close. "I doubt Fiona's had the time to read anything but medical textbooks for the last five years. The problem is much more basic. You are too white for Fiona's taste. I had hoped she would have gotten over some of her more non-compromising attitudes."

"She has something against white people?"

"Not in general. It's a more specific issue. She's opposed to mixed-race relationships."

Cynthia actually sputtered as she tried to get her words out, "But that's ... that's ... reverse discrimination."

She watched as Alex burst out laughing. He actually doubled over and had a hard time getting his breath. Finally he got control of himself and said, "Oh, that's rich. Promise me you'll be patient with Fi, and please, please ... never say those words again. I'm too old to be cracked up by a white woman of position and influence screaming discrimination."

Cynthia shrugged, "Oh, whatever ... Izzy's going to love this when I tell her."

"Don't you two be ganging up on wee Fi. She's not as tough as she thinks she is."

Cynthia held out her arm, "I'm surprised she was on to me so fast."
Cynthia held out her arm. "People are always saying I have such a great tan."

※※※※

Marking the page in his book, Liam closed it and turned to Izzy in the bed beside him. "I think we should ask Fiona to be part of the wedding party. Can you get her a matching dress?"

Izzy shrugged and closed her own book. "For the right price, anything can be had. But maybe she won't appreciate being asked at the last minute."

Liam considered that for a moment. "I think she'd want to be included."

Based on the cool way Fiona had behaved towards her on and off for most of the evening, Izzy wasn't as convinced but she wouldn't argue the point. "I'm sure the designer can make another dress in time. Fiona would suit the same style as Lisa. It might not be ready for when we go down to Victoria for the final fittings but I'm sure Bethany could take care of any last minute alterations."

With a broad smile on his face, Liam said, "That's great because I wondered if Tabby could be a flower girl. She asked the other day whether she could do anything for the wedding and I didn't know how to say no. Wouldn't she look adorable in a dress like Sophie's?"

"The more the merrier, I suppose, but we're getting a bit unbalanced on the men's side."

"I'm working on that. I asked Justin to be one of the groomsmen. Are you okay with that?"

Izzy set her book on the night table and reached to turn off her lamp. She settled down in the bed as Liam did the same. He put his arms around her and she breathed in the scent of him as she nestled closer. "Why not ... I'm sure Lisa will be tickled pink."

FIFTEEN

Izzy was on her way to work when she spotted Alex out on the site that he and Cynthia had chosen for their new cabin. The land had already been cleared and stacks of building materials were peeking out from under tarps. Alex was sitting in a lawn chair, enjoying the view. An old thermos sat on the ground by his chair and thick curls of steam drifted up from the cup in his hand. Alex waved as Izzy picked her way carefully across the cleared space. Through the trees, she noticed the beginning of what would become a driveway cutting across from the curve at the bottom of her and Liam's road.

Alex got out of the chair and grabbed a nearby round of firewood for himself to sit on. He held up the thermos, "Want some. I've got another cup around here somewhere." Izzy nodded, sat down in the chair and watched Alex unfasten an old tin cup from the side of his nearby pack. He wiped it out with the end of his shirt and poured her a coffee. "Right where you're sitting, that will be the view from the main windows of the place."

Izzy took a drink of the surprisingly delicious brew and enjoyed the view. Every spot around Crater Lake provided a unique vista and Alex had chosen well. From this perspective, nothing could be seen except the curve of the shore past Micah Camp as it wound in and out of numerous coves. In spots, the trees marched right down to the water's edge in impenetrable ranks of multi-hued green. In other places the waves lapped up against shores littered with logs bleached gold by the sun. The silence in the clearing was broken by the loud squawking of ravens circling above and lighting in the trees.

Izzy lowered the cup and said, "Fiona isn't too keen on me."

"Did Cynthia send you to talk to me?" Izzy nodded. Alex was silent for a moment, as if he weighed up a series of pros and cons in his head. Finally, he said, "Let me tell you a story."

Encouraged by Izzy's nod, Alex leaned back and stretched out his legs. As he spoke, he narrowed his eyes to cut the glare of the morning sun slanting off the water. "Fi had this friend back on the reserve, her name was Poppy. They grew up together ... chummed around since toddler days. The first summer Fi came home from university, she reconnected with Poppy. Kate phoned me a couple of times to say that Fi was acting strangely – anxious all the time, going into town every weekend. That wasn't like Fi at all and her mom was worried. It turned out Fi was trying to protect Poppy but it wasn't long until she figured out the job was too much for her and she got scared. She told her mom everything.

Poppy had been drinking, doing drugs and running with a bunch of town boys. There wasn't a hell of a lot Kate could do. Poppy was nineteen and her own parents didn't give a rat's ass what she was up to. Fi went back to school and that fall Kate got a call to identify a body that had been found in a ditch out on the edge of the reserve. It was Poppy. She'd been raped, beaten up bad and left to die like a dog in that ditch. The police got the boys who did it. They went to jail and I'm talking about them doing serious time, but that wasn't enough for Fi. I don't think she's ever gotten over what happened to Poppy."

Alex sat forward, "She blamed her mom for a long time. She said that it wasn't any use being a reserve cop if her mom couldn't do something to protect one young girl." Staring over at Izzy, he went on, "I'll be honest with you. Fi's always been the unforgiving type. The time she spent with me when she was young opened her mind to a lot of stuff and I'm not sure, in retrospect, that it did her any good. What happened to Poppy dug a deep pit of anger in her." Alex shrugged, "Anyway, to wrap up a long story, Fi's developed a strong bias against mixed-race relationships when it comes to native men and women."

Izzy finished her coffee and handed the cup back to Alex. "Thanks for telling me. It's always good to know that things aren't personal. I can understand how Fiona feels. Anger is a stage."

She watched as a range of emotions darted across Alex's face. He obviously cared deeply for Fiona. Finally, he shrugged and said, "Then she's been stuck in that stage for a hell of a long time."

"She'll come out of it when she's ready." Izzy looked curiously at Alex, "Weren't you ever angry?"

The man's face went still. "Sure, but prison cured me of wasting my time being angry." He shook his head as he continued, "It wasn't an easy lesson. At first, I didn't know what to do with the feelings I had about rotting away in Springfield for a crime I didn't commit. Before that, all my righteous anger had been about the big causes but I have to say, I never really felt the injustice personally. Things changed when it was my life leaking down the drain year by year. I found out quickly that anger wouldn't get me through that experience and letting go of it made me a hell of a lot better at what I've done ever since."

⁂

Bethany checked the small digital recorder for the third time. The batteries were fine, the machine was working. She realigned the supplies on the table. Everything was in order. She felt nervous. She'd watched Jillian conduct research interviews many times but she'd never done one on her own. It felt like a huge responsibility. She grabbed her research journal and wrote the date and time at the top of a page. Under that she wrote: *Rachel Franklin - First Interview*. A knock on the door had her wiping her suddenly damp palms on her pants. She closed her notebook and got up to usher Rachel into the room.

Thirty minutes later, Bethany watched as Rachel finished up the main task of the interview – a large map covered with post-it notes that detailed her hopes and fears about her time at Micah Camp. She had observed the girl's painstaking struggle as she wrote on each note, squinted at the papers in front of her and rearranged them in various categories. And through it all, Rachel's constant scratching at the dry, red patches on the inside of her arms made Bethany cringe.

When Rachel sat back, finally satisfied with her work, Bethany invited her to talk about the map, beginning anywhere she liked. Realizing that the young woman had deliberately skipped over a couple of the notes, Bethany pointed to the fears category and asked, "Can you tell me about this one – *never be able to eat right again?*"

Rachel squirmed in her chair and scratched a bit more before she shrugged her thin shoulders. "I used to be fat. Then I lost weight and now I can't seem to eat right anymore. Lots of foods make me feel sick to my stomach."

"Can you tell me a bit about what it was like ... losing weight?" Jillian had always made this part of the interview look easy as she drew the kids out to talk about specifics. Now Bethany was discovering for herself the challenge of coming up with the right question and asking it in the right way.

Rachel shrugged again. "There isn't very much to tell. I was in a foster home for about two years and the woman there never cooked. We were always snacking on chips and pop and cookies and she got us fast food take-out meals all the time. I really packed on the weight when I lived there. Then I went to a group home where the rules were super strict about food. The fridge had a lock on it and some of the cupboards did, too. Anyway, I lost a bunch of weight there ... I think about sixty pounds. It wasn't hard. All we got to eat was exactly what was put on our plate at each meal and we weren't allowed snacks at all."

Rachel had gotten more and more uncomfortable as she talked. She fidgeted and scratched and made the behaviour all the more obvious by trying to hide the fact that she was doing it. Bethany recalled that Jillian often said – *the interview is meant to explore what the kids want to share; it is not meant to satisfy our curiosity.* The last thing Bethany wanted to do was make Rachel even more uncomfortable.

Shifting the focus, she pointed to the hopes category – a note that contained a picture of a pair of running shoes. "What can you tell me about this drawing?"

A tentative smile brightened Rachel's face. "I'll be working with Penny for twenty hours a week. When I get my first pay cheque, I'm going to buy a new pair of running shoes." She held one foot up in the air. "At the group home they gave me these. Another girl left them behind. They're too tight for me."

As Bethany turned the digital recorder off to signal the end of the interview, she made a quick decision. She pointed at Rachel's arms and said, "Scratching at a rash like that isn't good. You could get an infection. Do you have any ointment you're supposed to put on it?"

Rachel's face turned beet red and she hung her head. Her limp hair fell over her face as she mumbled, "Sorry. Everyone says the scratching is bad but my arms are so itchy all the time."

Bethany's heart went out to the girl. "Don't apologize. I had eczema for years and it was awful. You really need to see a doctor and find out what is causing the problem." She picked up an envelope from the table and passed it to Rachel. "This is a twenty dollar gift certificate for the local drugstore. It's our way of saying thank you for giving up your time to do this interview."

Rachel hesitated then reached out to take the envelope, "Gee, thanks. I wasn't expecting anything like this."

After her first research participant had left the office, Bethany carefully filed away the girl's map, downloaded the recorded interview onto her laptop and backed it up on the external hard drive. She sat down to complete her post-interview notes. When she finished up, she went over what she had written. She rubbed at her forehead as she reviewed her role in the interview process. *Why did I ask Rachel to talk about losing weight instead of about eating as one of her current fears? Did I follow the wrong thread? Should I have been more proactive about her rash? Where is the line between being a research interviewer and a concerned adult? And if there is a line, should there be one?* She wished Jillian were easier to get a hold of. She would have liked to discuss these questions.

Bethany closed her journal, stretched and decided a short break was in order. She made her way to the kitchen, poured a cup of coffee and glanced over at Brigit. "Am I on the right schedule for your break?"

Brigit finished swiping out the sink and tossed the cloth in the laundry hamper in the corner. "You bet. I'll meet you out in the dining room and I'll bring along a plate of scones."

Settled at the end of a table that nestled close to one of the large windows, Brigit sipped her coffee and nodded her head towards the wide sweeping lawn. Nick was cutting across the grounds with a golf bag over his shoulder. "Does he think he's at a country club or something?"

Bethany watched Nick disappear around the corner. "I suppose he takes his breaks around his client schedule. He and Jim have built themselves a crude sort of driving range out past the greenhouses." She smiled at the idea.

The look on Brigit's face made it obvious that she didn't find anything humorous about Nick. "He acts friendly enough but I've met men like him before." A knowing look came into Brigit's eyes, "You never know when that type will turn on you."

Bethany spread a small corner of her scone with butter. She'd struggled for years to get over her fear of men but that didn't mean she had an axe to grind about men in general. "I don't know Nick well but he seems nice and Izzy thinks highly of him."

"Oh ya ... they all seem nice." Brigit pushed her coffee cup away and folded her arms across her chest. She pointed back to the kitchen, "Dylan seems nice, too. But I'm not banking on his staying that way."

"Are you not getting on well with Dylan? I've known him since he arrived here and I've always found him to be a very respectful young man." Bethany chewed on her lower lip for a moment as she tried to read the look on Brigit's face. "Is something wrong? I don't want to push in, so please tell me to mind my own business if you want me to stop."

Brigit fiddled with a spoon lying on the table. "No, that's okay. I brought it up." She shrugged, "I'm having a few issues getting up to speed on the job. It's nothing I can't handle but Dylan is the take-over type and that's making it hard for me. If I'm not where I should be at exactly the right moment, he's gone and done something without me."

"Could you talk to him about that?"

"Not without looking like I don't have a clue about what I'm doing." Brigit looked miserable as she gazed out to the lake. "I need to make a go of it here." She shook her head and her eyes glistened suddenly with tears. "For Tabby's sake. She's settling in so well and I don't know what would happen if I uprooted her again."

Bethany reached across the table and squeezed Brigit's hand. "Talk to Izzy. I know she's the director and that can seem intimidating, but Izzy isn't that kind of a boss."

"No." Brigit sat up straight in her chair. "It may come to that but I want to keep trying on my own for now." She glanced back at Bethany, "Sorry if I seem abrupt. I like being able to stand up on my own and I'm usually the one helping others. I'm not so used to accepting help."

Bethany nodded her understanding. She was well acquainted with take-charge women. "Why don't you and Tabby come for dinner some night? You can meet Beulah and if baking bread is something you need some tips on, we can certainly help you there." Bethany smiled, "And I promise, the help will be painless."

⚜⚜⚜⚜

From the doorway of the shop, Fiona spotted Liam where he was leaning against the workbench. He shook his head and smiled at something he was reading. She cleared her throat and called out, "Mind if I come in?"

He closed the red exercise book in front of him, pointed to a nearby stool and gestured for her to sit down. "How did you sleep?"

Fiona stretched her arms over her head, "Like a baby. The guest cabin is a slice of heaven. Thanks so much for letting me stay there."

"It's our pleasure." Liam sat down. "I hoped I would get a chance to talk to you before you headed into Dearborn. I wanted to ask you something." He smiled, "Would you be a member of the wedding party?"

Fiona felt her mouth drop open for a second. She snapped it closed and said, "Yes, of course. Thank you. I'd love to."

"Good. Let Izzy know your size. She's taking care of all the dresses." Liam reached for a set of keys from a hook on the wall and held them out to her. "You're starting tomorrow at the clinic, right? Here are the keys to that new truck out in the driveway."

117

Fiona shook her head, "I can't take your new truck, Liam. I'd be fine driving that old beater out there ... if it still runs, that is."

Liam grinned, "Absolutely not. You have no idea how much I have wanted an excuse to get back into that old beater, as you call it. And I guarantee you, it still runs fine."

Fiona took the keys. "Okay then, the Sierra it is but only because you insist." She smiled at him and asked, "What were you reading when I came in?" She gestured to the array of exercise books on the work bench.

"Bits and pieces from some journals written by the man who built this whole place ... his name was Caleb and he was married to Izzy. We were all friends forever. That old Dodge was his truck. He died in a logging accident almost four years ago. I found his journals a while back. I take a look through them every now and then."

Catching some emotion she couldn't quite name in his tone, Fiona asked, "This man named Caleb ... he was more than a friend, wasn't he?"

"Have you ever studied Shakespeare, Fi?"

Fiona shook her head, warmed by the way Liam had so easily taken up Alex's shortened way of addressing her. "I'm more of a sciences girl."

"Good thing for a doctor, I suppose." Liam packed the journals away into the lower drawer of the desk. "When you read Shakespeare's tragedies you discover that any character left standing at the end of the play has been irrelevant in the grand scheme of things. That's how my life was before I met Caleb – a Shakespearean tragedy with me, despite my best efforts to fall, left standing through it all. Caleb pulled me out of my irrelevancy. He saved my life." Liam's gaze went past Fiona to something she couldn't see. He shook his head and smiled at her, "It's that simple and that complicated, I suppose."

Fiona reached over to put a hand on Liam's arm, "And now you're going to marry his wife?"

He nodded, "Funny how life works out, isn't it?"

She stared at this man she had always thought of as her brother. She suddenly realized how much she needed him to acknowledge their connection. Though she had lived with the thought of him her whole life, he had not heard of her until recently. Would he accept her as his sister? She took a deep breath and said, "I have a question and if you don't want to answer, I will understand." Liam simply leveled his dark eyes at her and waited. She swallowed hard and went on. "Will you tell me about Sophie? I asked Alex but he says it isn't his story to tell."

Liam looked down at his hands. His voice was slow and measured. "It's only partially my story but I'll trust you with it because you're family." Her breath caught sharply at the word, family. She had to lean forward to hear his next words. "Sophie is my daughter." Liam raised his eyes to Fiona's, "Outside of our family we don't talk about who Sophie's dad is. Everyone knows Lisa is her mom and everyone knows Izzy and I are helping out by looking after Sophie while Lisa goes to school. We leave it at that."

Fiona sat back on the stool and swung her dark hair out of her eyes. One long feathered earring danced across her cheek. "Eventually you'll have to say something. As Sophie gets older, people will be able to tell she's your daughter."

Liam shrugged, "We'll cross that bridge when we come to it and the decisions about what to say and when to say it are up to Lisa."

As she tried to process the details of what Liam had told her, a part of the story didn't fit. "And Izzy accepts Sophie as your daughter?"

"In the beginning, she hoped that we would adopt Sophie and raise her as our own. I didn't agree. I couldn't do anything to take Lisa's child from her. I made the decision that we would look after Sophie until Lisa is ready to be a full-time mom. Izzy accepted that."

Fiona couldn't stop the frown that drew her sweeping brows together as she realized that she agreed with Izzy's take on things and not Liam's. She blurted out, "Then one day you'll let Lisa walk away with your child?"

"This is Lisa's home now. I don't believe she'd ever take Sophie away. Not completely. But yes, if that's what she wants. She is Sophie's mother."

Fiona shook her head, "I'll respect your privacy but I don't think you're doing the right thing. What Izzy wanted would have been a better choice. Sophie is your child. It isn't right for you to hand her over to white people. If you had adopted her, she would always know who her father is and that she is First Nations."

Liam took his time forming his next words. Fiona knew when he began to speak, from the tone of his voice and the expression on his face that, while Alex would have told her exactly how to think, Liam sought only to instruct. "My mother left my father to return to a reserve in Northern Manitoba that had no running water or sewer because she believed it was right to raise me there among her people. It meant that growing up, I barely knew my father. Later, I was sent south for school because my mother thought that was the right thing for me to do. Even later, on her death bed, she urged me to come home. Your mother granted Alex the privilege of being your father, over many other choices she could have made. She let him raise you as his own because she thought it was the right thing for you. Robbie's mother sent Alex

119

away when Robbie was only a baby because she felt that, for her son, an absent father would better than a part-time one."

Liam spread his hands, "All our mothers made the best choices they could and somehow those choices brought us together today as a family. Would you change any of that?" Fiona shook her head, slowly. "It's no different for Lisa. It will be the same for you when you're a mother. You'll make the best choices you can." Liam spoke with a conviction that commanded Fiona's full attention, "And no matter where Sophie goes or who she's with, nothing can change who she is."

※ ※ ※ ※

Brigit tucked Tabby into bed and told her, "Don't you worry about Mr. Jangles. He's a smart cat. He knows who feeds him every day. You wait and see. He'll be back here bright and early meowing by the door for his breakfast."

Walking out to the living room, she cursed the bloody cat for dashing out the door earlier in the evening. He'd done disappearing acts like this several times at her parent's house and he always found his way home. She supposed he'd do the same here. But Tabby worried. She loved Mr. Jangles to the point that Brigit had been persuaded to let her bring him along to their new home, even though travelling halfway across the country with a cat was a major pain in the butt.

She turned on her laptop and settled down on the sofa. She'd found a ton of cooking resources online – articles, recipes and YouTube videos that showed step-by-step instructions on how to do any number of cooking related things. She spent a couple of hours every night studying. But no matter how hard she tried to expand her skill set, she was not yet at the point where she could comfortably run the kitchen on her own. She knew she was missing the complete picture of what it meant to be a cook. When she was a cop she'd always been able to think three or four steps ahead and yet stay in the moment, ready to adjust to any situation. Every now and then she got a tantalizing glimpse of the underlying flow that made the kitchen function efficiently; but when she tried to grasp that flow and list it down on paper in easy to remember steps, it slipped away like the tattered edges of a dream.

As much as she put on a show of knowing what she was doing, she wasn't ready to allow Dylan to go back to the assistant role in the kitchen. Her ruse of having him stay in charge while she got the hang of things had stretched out now for way too long to be believable. What was she going to do if Dylan called her bluff?

Brigit wasn't totally sure why she'd confided in Bethany, except that the other woman's warmth and quiet demeanour seemed to draw the words out of her. And she was smarting from having come close to disaster with the breakfast that morning. Dylan had no sooner rescued a huge pot of oatmeal from the stove when he had to clear the kitchen of smoke rising from bacon that was blistering on the grill. By flicking the exhaust fan up to high speed, he had kept the smoke alarms from blasting but he couldn't stop his eyes from rolling back in disbelief.

Brigit considered Bethany's advice. Should she speak to Izzy? If she decided to go that route, there was no going back. It would involve explaining how she had exaggerated her qualifications and that would lead to disclosing what had happened to her in Toronto. After those revelations, Izzy would never look at her the same way again. It could work out but then again, it was a risk. Talking to Izzy and coming clean had to be a last case scenario. She would definitely follow up on Bethany's dinner invitation and if she could learn anything valuable about cooking in the process, all the better.

Hours later she got up from the sofa and stretched. It was time to call it a day. With the instructions running through her head on how to make a hollandaise sauce, she walked across the living room to open the window. Hopefully that pain-in-the-ass cat would make its way back before Tabby woke up.

ᔕᕋᔕᕋᔕᕋᔕᕋ

Robbie's bed had become, in his dream, the thick bushes that lined the slope up from the sawmill. He was close to the large cat; he could feel the curiosity that came over the animal as together they watched the dogs in the sawmill yard running back and forth, barking loudly and occasionally making wild leaps, as if they would scale the fence. The dogs definitely knew they were out there.

Robbie whispered, "They can't get out. Look ... they're behind a fence." The large cat rose slowly, driven forward by hunger. The past two weeks had been lean ones with no more to show for nights of hunting than a marten, a grouse and the rotting carcass of a deer – road kill spotted in a ditch near the gravel turn-off to Dearborn. The cougar silently padded out into the open and walked a wide circle around the sawmill yard, keeping near the trees and the parking area. The dogs went mad as they raced around the inside of the fence. Rain had fallen earlier and the cougar's large paws left a clear trail.

A flash of movement and a tinkling sound caught the cougar's attention. Now they were moving through the thick brush towards Micah Camp as if the

121

dark, rugged maze of uneven ground and massive stumps were as wide and easy to transverse as the logging road they had left behind. Coming into the open, they circled the main building and Robbie followed across the back lawn that skirted the lake and along one of the paths. He recognized Tabby's cabin as the cougar went into a low crouch prepared to pounce.

Mr. Jangles darted across the gravel path heading for the cabin porch, the bell around his neck jingled as he moved. The cougar sprang forward. Robbie screamed, the animal hesitated and Mr. Jangles cleared the porch steps in a single bound. His next jump took him through the partially-open, living room window and into the cabin's safety. The cougar stared at Robbie with confusion in its eyes.

Robbie woke up with tears pouring down his face as he wrenched on the cabin door and looked wildly around the entry way. He let go of the door and tried to figure out what was going on.

Izzy came out of the bedroom. She put an arm around Robbie and pulled him close, "What's wrong? Did you hurt yourself?"

He shook his head and stared at her. "Why am I down here? What's going on?"

Izzy led him out to the darkened living room where she guided him to the sofa. "You've been sleepwalking. Were you having a bad dream? I heard you scream out and you've been crying."

"I don't remember." He swiped at the tears on his face and shook his head. "I was sleepwalking? That's weird. Why would I do something like that?"

Izzy shrugged, "I'm not sure. You've done it a few times in the last little while."

"No way ... why don't I remember?" Robbie shook his head in disbelief then he realized he was starving. "I'm hungry. Can I have something to eat?"

"Come out to the kitchen and I'll make you a sandwich and a glass of milk."

SIXTEEN

R eg stood by his truck jiggling his keys. He saw fresh cougar prints
tracking across the muddy, open space beyond the fenced yard. The
ruts the dogs had made by running back and forth around the inside of the
fence were obvious. He stooped down and sized up the paw prints.

As Liam and Justin walked across the logging road to join him, Reg stood
up and pointed down at his feet, "Cougar tracks." He gestured to the mess
around the inside of the fence. "There's no goddamned way a cougar should
get this close. I know my dogs. You can tell by those ruts that they were
carrying on like their balls were in a crusher." He turned to spit a stream on
the dirt behind him. "You run into a cougar that ain't afraid of a dog and you
got a shit storm of trouble coming at you. A cougar like that would be one
spherical bastard." Seeing the confused looks on Liam and Justin's face, Reg
laughed. "A bastard from any angle."

Liam smiled at Reg's turn of phrase before voicing his concern, "It'll be
after the chickens. I'm surprised they've made it this long since Pearl isn't
wandering around my old place anymore."

Justin stared over his shoulder nervously when Reg said, "We'll leave one
of my dogs down there for a few nights. But you listen up good," he pointed a
finger at Justin, "if that dog starts barking, you let him out and you stay put in
the cabin." As Justin's frown deepened, Reg reached out and slapped him on
the back, "Hey, it's nothing to get your shorts in a twist about. The dog will
tree the cougar somewhere and wait it out until I come along in the morning."
Reg parodied taking aim with an imaginary rifle and pulling the trigger.

Justin stared from Reg to Liam and back to Reg. "You're allowed to shoot
a cougar?"

123

Reg jammed his ball cap up and down on his head. "I used to go out cougar hunting a fair bit. Not so much anymore. Times are changing and Josie doesn't like the idea of it. Whenever a conservation officer isn't in the area, I get called by the locals if there's a sighting near a school or if a cougar's treed in a back yard." Reg shrugged, "As far as I'm concerned, the only good cougar is a dead one. And you can quote me on that."

"But you said this cougar isn't afraid of dogs."

Reg unlocked the gate and swung it open. He whistled loudly. "Well, I did say that, you got me on that one but my dogs are special. These two," he reached out to grab the collars of the dogs that had come at a run to his call, "they're my last two cougar hounds and they know their stuff." He headed back out to his truck with the dogs behind him. "See you guys later. I'm going to try to pick up the trail."

Fifteen minutes later, Reg knelt in the soft ground outside of Brigit and Tabby's cabin and studied the perfect print mark sunk into the dirt. The dogs sat at attention nearby. The cabin door opened and Brigit and Tabby came out onto the porch. The woman stopped and stared at Reg as he rose from his crouch. The cat draped over Tabby's arm meowed loudly and the dogs whined. Reg gave his animals a stern command, "Stay."

He walked up the porch steps and stuck out his hand, "Reg Compton, Ma'am. You must be Brigit. You might have heard my better half, Josie, mention my name." He smiled broadly as Brigit reached out and shook his hand.

"Oh, yes. Josie did mention you ... more than once." Brigit smiled back, "It's nice to meet you, Reg. This is my daughter, Tabby. What can we do for you?"

Reg looked at Tabby. "Where were you thinking of going with that cat, little lady?"

Tabby clutched onto Mr. Jangles, "He likes to go with me to the dining room for breakfast."

Reg looked over at the living room window half open to the breeze with the screen lying against the side of the cabin. He addressed his next words to Brigit. "I'm going to ask you to put the cat inside and close the window so he can't get out. After you do that, I'd like to show you something."

Brigit's lips pursed together but she turned to do what Reg had asked. Tabby opened her mouth to object but shut it quickly when she saw the look on her mother's face. They went back inside the cabin and while Tabby held Mr. Jangles, Brigit closed the window. Tabby put the cat down. On their way back outside, Brigit shooed the animal with her foot so she could shut the door behind them. She turned to Reg, "Okay. What do you want to show us?"

He walked down the porch steps and crouched again beside the print. As Brigit and Tabby leaned over, he said, "This is a cougar print ... a young male, probably about a hundred and fifty pounds." Looking at Tabby, Reg said, "My guess is he was after your cat for his supper."

Tabby's face fell and her mouth opened in what would have become a howl if Brigit hadn't pulled her close and given her another look. Turning back to Reg, she said, "No one told us there was any problem with Mr. Jangles leaving the cabin."

"I don't suppose you know much about cougars or living in the wild for that matter, Ma'am. Josie says you come from Toronto." Reg smiled as he added, "Love those Leafs though they sure don't do a hell of a lot to deserve it." He shrugged and went on, "I'm not saying it's a common thing to see a cougar. Most folks around here are never even going to catch a glimpse. And I'm not saying you've got to look over your shoulder all the time. But I don't like the thought of a cougar so close to where people live."

Brigit lowered her voice, "Tabby loves that cat. Tell us what to do to keep him safe."

Reg pulled a toothpick out of the pocket of his shirt and began chewing it, swinging it around in his mouth in an action that fascinated Tabby. "Get the screens back on the windows and make sure they're secure. That cat does not leave your cabin. He's the bolting type. I saw that when the little bugger tried to get past you now. You put him in a bedroom or the bathroom before you open the doors." Reg looked stern as he said, "And you never allow that child to walk around outside holding that cat. The only thing a cougar likes better than a cat is a kid. Got it?"

Brigit pulled Tabby even closer. "Yes. Alright, we'll do that. Thank you."

By the time Reg had stopped to have a visit with Josie and made his way to Izzy's office, the Camp was abuzz with the rumour that a cougar was stalking the trails. Izzy had no idea how news spread around the place the way it did but she sure as hell wished it didn't.

Ushering Reg in, she pointed to a chair, "You could have come and talked to me first before getting Brigit all worked up."

Reg fiddled with his hat and bounced his knee a few times before answering. "Caleb always said it was pointless trying to get you to take cougars seriously but there's no goddamned way - excuse the French - that you should be letting that little girl walk around here carrying a cat. She might as well be in a lion's cage with a raw steak plastered to her butt like a bull's-eye." Reg shook his head, "You know better."

Izzy sighed as she sat down. "Spare me the colourful analogies, okay. I've lived here for over nineteen years and you know how many cougars I've seen? The answer is zero. It's hard to take that kind of threat seriously."

"It ain't the cougar you *see* that's the problem. They're elusive animals." Reg shrugged, "A cougar was up at the sawmill driving the dogs into a fit last night and I tracked it down to Brigit's cabin. She admitted the kid's cat was out. The cougar stalked it back to her door. I'm betting Mr. Jangles used up one of his nine lives last night."

A look of concern wrinkled Izzy's forehead as the importance of Reg's words sank in. "Okay ... okay. I'm responsible for the safety of the people here at the Camp. I know that. I'll gather everyone in the dining room if you want to stay and give the cougar safety talk. But do me a favour, Reg ... lay off the *only good cougar is a dead cougar* line. A lot of the residents are sensitive to issues around the killing of wildlife." Izzy shivered and hugged her arms around herself for a moment. "I never thought about Tabby carrying the cat around. I get your point. There is no need to take unnecessary risks."

Reg looked thoughtful. "Having kids here is new. First there's Robbie wandering back and forth, now this Tabby girl and her cat. And you've got Sophie to think about. It won't be long before she's out and about. Small pets and kids can cause problems when it comes to cougars."

Izzy's shoulders slumped. "You're right. Looks like I have to write a new protocol. What about our dogs? Is it safe for Robbie and Tabby to be out walking the trails between the cabin and the Camp if they have one of the dogs with them?"

"Better if they're always with an adult. But the dogs are good. Even for yourself. Don't walk around without another adult or a dog. I know it's useless to suggest that you might consider carrying a knife. But make sure you wear a whistle, take the walkie-talkie and carry a walking stick with you. An air horn is great. Then there's bear spray."

Izzy made a face as she left her office to gather everyone in the dining room. She had never felt the need to walk around armed and she wasn't about to start now.

⚔⚔⚔⚔

"Dr. Wells, welcome aboard." Fiona turned from studying the poster on the office wall. In the picture, Dr. Rosemary Maxwell was surrounded by a bunch of black kids outside a village medical clinic. She was kicking a soccer ball.

The Doctors Without Borders logo graced the lower right-hand corner of the poster. Fiona reached for the woman's outstretched hand. The doctor smiled, gave her hand a quick shake then moved to the desk to grab a thick file. "I believe in jumping in with both feet." She passed Fiona the file. "Give this a look-see and meet me in examining room three."

Hours later, the two doctors sat across from one another at a desk littered with patient files. They were eating sandwiches as they reviewed the day's events. Fiona had sat in on several appointments during which Rosemary examined patients with complaints ranging from a minor sore throat to sudden chest pains. They had immediately ordered an ambulance to take the latter patient, a middle-aged man, to the hospital in Cedar Falls.

Fiona's attention shifted back and forth from her sandwich to the piece of paper in her hand to Rosemary. The older doctor continued to eat as she spoke. "We could spend time chitchatting and getting to know each other and I could ask you what you expect of your internship," she waved her hand to dismiss the idea. "Waste of time. We are going to get to know each other, probably more than we want to. I've been at this for some time and I'm in a better position to tell you what to expect than you are to tell me what you want." Rosemary pushed her plate aside, "Complete immersion in what a rural, family practice involves ... that's what is in store for you. You'll see patients with me and later, on your own, but a well-rounded family practice is much more than that. I want you helping at the addiction center at least two mornings a week and manning the high school's drop-in clinic one afternoon a week." She paused a moment before adding, "The fact that you are First Nations is a bonus for me but it's going to add to your workload. It actually bumped your application to the top of my list."

Fiona nodded silently. She didn't waste her time feeling badly because her gender or status gave her an advantage. The pendulum had to swing and if it shifted in her favour then that was justice, plain and simple.

"I'll have you in Cedar Falls one day a week doing home visits at the reserve and facilitating a young mom's support group. And when I say young, I mean fifteen and sixteen-year olds. Once a week, you'll do a twenty-four hour stint on call at the hospital in Cedar Falls – don't worry – there's lots of room to stay there. I'm booked, day after tomorrow, to do my annual *Sexual Health in Your Twenties* talk at Micah Camp. Since you're staying out that way, I'll dump that on you. There's also a men's anger-management group starting up here in Dearborn. I want you to sit in on at least one of those sessions to get a feel for the scale of a problem like that in a rural community, though you'll see evidence of it soon enough in the clinic and the hospital."

Rosemary paused to gulp down her cold tea. "Then, of course, you'll have your own reading and researching to do. That will be based on the cases we're seeing. There's more, but I don't want to have you on your knees gibbering for mercy." She smiled over at Fiona, "At least not on the first day."

Fiona's mind raced. Were there enough hours in a week to support the schedule Rosemary had just outlined? She'd have to do the math. She'd make it work by pulling as many overnighters as she had to. Being introduced to patients as Dr. Wells was the most exhilarating thing that had ever happened to her and she didn't think the thrill would ever wear off.

Rosemary got up and glanced out the office window to the back parking lot where Fiona had parked Liam's truck. "Glad to see you're driving a reliable vehicle." She laughed, "And, I'm not surprised Liam found an excuse to get back into Caleb's old Dodge." She headed for the door, talking as she went, "You're lucky to have landed in Izzy Montgomery's circle. We go way back. If you have any emotional issues at all, don't hesitate to talk to her. The woman's a brilliant counsellor. Don't be afraid to find what you need by digging around in the office files or asking the girls at reception. If you get Myrna one of those fancy coffees every now and then, she'll do anything for you."

A cell phone chirped. Rosemary pulled the device out of her pocket and spoke briefly to the person on the other end. She reached over her desk to grab her car keys, "Come on, Dr. Wells. You can follow me up to Cedar Falls. We've got a baby who's decided to make an appearance this afternoon."

❧❧❧❧

Izzy grabbed her latte from the counter of Dearborn's new and trendy coffee shop located near the boardwalk that stretched out along the waterfront. She walked over to a table where Beulah sat reading the local paper. Izzy had her own copy tucked under her arm. She put down her latte, pulled out the paper and pointed it at Beulah, "Why didn't you ask me about this memorial ball tournament idea before you went ahead with it?"

She had thumbed through the paper while waiting in the grocery store checkout line and had been stunned to see the large half-page ad with Caleb's name in bold letters running across the top of it. Her heart had thumped in an odd way when she saw the picture of him under the caption advertising the ball tournament. He was crouched behind home plate. His catcher's mask was thrown back and his gloved hand was up in the air. Obviously, the catch was good and Caleb looked happy.

Beulah stared at the folded newspaper Izzy was waving in her face. "You saw the ad? It's great, isn't it?" She shrugged in the face of Izzy's silent stare. "I thought you would love the idea."

"Well, I don't," Izzy voice shook and she took a deep breath as she sat down.

Beulah seemed truly surprised as she asked, "Why not?"

Izzy forced herself to remain calm as she gathered her thoughts. There was no point going off the deep end with Beulah. Doing that would only make the woman more determined. "It's ghoulish. It's too soon. People don't get memorialized until they've been dead for years and years."

"Caleb's been dead for almost four years. No one thinks it's too soon to remember him in a way that would have meant a lot to him."

Against her best resolve, Izzy dug her heels in. "I don't like the idea. You should have asked me first."

Beulah shrugged, "Well, it's too late to do anything about that now. All the advertising is out and I've already started signing up teams."

Izzy stared out the window at the harbour. Sunshine danced above the surface of the choppy water and glinted off the metal of the boats jostling against the dock. The white bodies and yellow beaks of seagulls stood out against the clear blue sky as they swooped and set up a raucous cacophony of sound. Beyond the tightly packed pleasure boats, the fishing fleet was coming in. Grey, hulking seiners lumbered past the breakwater towards the commercial wharf. Hemmed in by massive creosoted pilings, the wide structure dwarfed the vehicles and people that moved about on it like so many colourful playthings being pushed around on a toy room floor. The already noisy harbour was suddenly dominated by the roar of a seaplane. Wide pontoons skimmed the waves before the plane lifted into the air on wings buffeted to and fro by the wind.

Izzy knew it would take her days to get over the shock of seeing that picture of Caleb in the paper the way she had. The ground had dropped right out from under her feet. She was angry at being put in such a position; but directing that anger at Beulah would do no good. Though Izzy believed she was justified in being upset about not being informed, she also knew she didn't own exclusive rights to Caleb's memory.

Sipping her latte, Izzy said, "Don't even ask me to bankroll all the trophies because the answer is no." She took childish comfort in the comical giveaway look on Beulah's face – she had obviously been planning to stick Izzy with the bill for the trophies.

❦❦❦❦

Justin knocked on the door of the tiny office to get Lisa-Marie's attention. She had herself crammed up against the wall, trying to file invoices. "Looks like a great place to work, Leez." He smiled as he leaned against the door jamb, "Do you want to come over tonight to watch a movie? I borrowed a few DVDs from Mike and we can make ourselves some microwave popcorn."

Lisa-Marie closed the file cabinet. "Geez, Josie really has no idea how to file. What a nightmare." She walked over to the door and glanced out to the paper and soap shop to survey the activity as she spoke, "Can't ... sorry. I've got a date with Zach tonight."

Justin's eyes narrowed and his smile disappeared, "Ya, sure ... maybe another time." He pushed away from the door, "I better go. I told Lauren I'd call her after work and I promised Liam I'd help him get the dock into the water and anchored. We're going to freeze our butts off doing that job." He waved and strolled out of the shop, taking a moment to smile and say hi to Wynter who was sorting dried flowers into a tray at one of the butcher block tables.

As soon as the workshop door closed, Wynter leapt from her stool and practically ran across the room to confront Lisa-Marie. "Who was that guy? Is he yours? Quick, tell me everything. I almost fainted when he said hello to me."

Lisa-Marie stared at Wynter. "You almost fainted when he said hello to you? Oh my God ... guys must fall over themselves to say hello to you all the frigging time."

Wynter sighed, "Not as often as you'd think. Anyway, who is he?"

"His name is Justin and no, he doesn't belong to me. He has a girlfriend named Lauren and he's gone in search of a cell phone signal so he can call her."

Wynter's eyebrows rose as she made a scratching gesture in the air, "Hello Kitty. I love your claws."

"I have a date tonight with Zach, remember? Justin and I are just friends."

"Oh well, he does get the heart fluttering ... that scruffy beard look is so hot. You'll be picking me up at six-thirty, right?"

"Yup. I don't envy you ... upstairs in a committee meeting with Zach's mom while I'm downstairs having fun."

Wynter's eyes lit up. "Promise you'll tell me everything when we drive home. Have you and Zach kissed yet?" She held her hand up suddenly,

"Don't say anything until later. I can't handle all the excitement when I'm supposed to be working."

❧❧❧❧

Mike came in from an after dinner run at the track. He strolled through the dining room on his way to the kitchen where a cold bottle of Gatorade awaited him. He waved casually at the gathering of women at the large table – just another one of his mom's meetings.

He was almost out of the room when he spotted a young woman sitting at the far side of the table. He stopped and stared as she met his gaze by slowly raising the most stunning pair of violet eyes surrounded by thick, dark lashes. He felt himself flush a deep shade of red. He stumbled a bit as he moved quickly into the kitchen. His mother followed right behind him. She shuffled through a pile of papers by the phone. Mike edged around the room, trying to keep out of sight. He nudged his mom with his elbow and whispered, "Who's the girl?"

Helen pulled a list out of the pile. "Here it is. Thank God." She looked up at Mike, "What did you say, dear?"

Mike pointed towards the dining room, "The girl out there ... who is she?"

"Do you mean Wynter? She's from Micah Camp. She's the young lady Lisa-Marie said might help with organizing the beauty pageant and she's going to be perfect. I couldn't be happier. Do you want to meet her? Come out and I'll introduce you."

Mike shook his head wildly. "Are you nuts? Look at me, I've just run ten K. I'm sweating like a pig and probably smell like one, too."

Helen laughed, "You always look perfect to me." She turned and headed back to her meeting.

Mike made a dash for the hallway and on to the bathroom. He hurried through a shower. In his bedroom, he tugged on a clean pair of jeans and in an agony of indecision, discarded one shirt after the other. By the time he got back to the dining room, it was empty. He could hear voices at the bottom of the stairs near the landing. As he rounded the corner, he saw his mom close the front door.

"Where is everyone?" he asked.

"Oh, the meeting is over, dear. Zach and Lisa-Marie took Wynter down to the waterfront with them. You could probably catch them if you hurried."

Mike shook his head – as if he would risk meeting Wynter with that asshole Zach around. The guy was sure to make some kind of butthead comment and ruin everything.

SEVENTEEN

D ylan caught up with Arianna as she left the exercise room. "Can you come for a walk?"

The ground outside was wet from an earlier rain, though the sky was now clear as they strolled down the darkened path towards a picnic table out on the grass. Stars winked out between sweeping clouds and the rhythm of waves brushing softly over the rocks on the nearby beach kept time with the creaking and swaying of the tree branches overhead.

The table was soaked and Dylan said, "Let's go down to the boathouse."

Arianna's heart thudded painfully. The only time she had ever been at the boathouse was with Dylan. The memory of that one night almost a year ago still made her feel cold with sadness and regret for how things had worked out. She followed him silently. Once inside the cozy space, he sat down on the wooden bench against the wall and she joined him.

Dylan looked at the floor as he spoke, "Have you met the new guy ... Ethan?"

Arianna laughed, "Sure I've met him. He's really out there, hey?"

"I might kill him and ask you to help me cover it up. I want to be a chef, not end up in prison."

Arianna giggled then narrowed her eyes, "You're not serious, are you?"

Dylan glanced over at her, "He knows I'm gay."

"Did you tell him?"

"No, I did not tell him and I'm not going to tell you how he found out because it's embarrassing."

Arianna stifled her curiosity and asked, "Are you worried he'll tell everyone?"

"He says he won't and he hasn't so far. It isn't that ... the guy bugs the absolute crap out of me. Every time I see him I want to thump him."

"Cause he's gay in a different way than you are?"

"Well, when you say it like that, it sounds stupid." Dylan was quiet for a minute. "I keep thinking that if people know I'm gay and rooming with him, they'll all think – two gay guys together in the same cabin, they must be at it every chance they get – and that makes me want to kill Ethan."

"Stop saying that, Dylan. You wouldn't kill anyone. People aren't as stupid as you think. I've met lots of guys here who are straight and I sure wouldn't want to have sex with every one of them." She pushed away the thought of wanting to be intimate only with the guy who sat beside her. "I certainly wouldn't be thinking about going to bed with a straight guy simply because we were in the same cabin. You have to be attracted to the person you're having sex with. People know that. I don't see why being gay should change any of that."

He smiled over at her, "That was quite the speech." He dropped an arm around her and pulled her close, "Thanks. You always make me feel better. I don't know how I'm going to keep my head on straight when I'm in Montreal and you're in Vancouver."

She sighed and said, "Texting."

❧❧❧❧

"Zach has a brother, right?" Wynter sat on the passenger side of the jeep as Lisa-Marie manoeuvered her vehicle around the sharp curve that led from the paved highway out of Dearborn and onto the gravel road to Crater Lake.

"Ya, his name's Mike. The two of them don't look like brothers at all, though."

"He walked through the dining room while we were having the meeting. He looked like he might be about to faint or something. Does he run?"

"He probably got a glimpse of you among his mom's cronies." Lisa-Marie glanced sideways at Wynter, "You really don't get the way you turn guys into puddles of desire, do you? And yes, he does run ... all the time, apparently. He's entered in some marathon race in August. He's got Dylan and Justin running with him."

"You're wrong about the effect I have on guys. I'll tell you something if you promise not to laugh at me?

"Of course I won't laugh at you. We aren't in high school."

"I've never been on a single date. No guy has ever asked me out. I didn't even go to prom because no one asked me. I've never had a first kiss. I might as well look like one of Cinderella's ugly stepsisters for all the attention my so-called gorgeousness gets me."

Lisa-Marie kept her hands tight on the steering wheel; driving on the gravel was tricky, especially going around the corners. She glanced quickly over at Wynter, "You can't be serious."

"I am." Wynter reached up her hand to cross her heart.

Pondering Wynter's words, Lisa-Marie hit her open palm on the steering wheel. "Maybe you're too beautiful. You might be intimidating the guys ... like they think they could never ask you out because you'd say no, on account of the fact that you're so freaking gorgeous."

"Stop calling me gorgeous and tell me everything you know about Mike."

"Okay, but it isn't much. He's really quiet. I've stayed for dinner more than once. They have these great sit-down meals ... with the whole family around the table, talking and stuff. Just like a sitcom on TV. Mike's never said one word directly to me. I think he's pretty shy around girls. Zach says Mike was super skinny in high school and he used to have bad skin."

"You'd never know any of that now, would you?"

"You like him?"

"I don't even know him and judging from the way he bolted out of the room after taking one look at me, I doubt I ever will. Anyway, I should have more important things on my mind right now than a guy. Thanks to you, I am stuck with eight, wannabe beauty queens to organize and a committee who insists that I cannot have the contestants do one thing that could be construed as demeaning to the ideals of feminism."

Coming into a tight corner, Lisa-Marie slowed down as she said, "Feminism ... that was big in the sixties, right?"

Wynter opened her window to let the fresh breeze off the lake fill the vehicle. "I could end up stepping into some kind of frigging minefield with this project. Let me tell you ... these women were really riled up when they talked about feminism. And get this ... it can't be called a beauty pageant, though everyone knows that's exactly what it is. It will be billed as *The Young Women Shine Cooperative Competition.*"

"How can you compete and cooperate at the same time?"

With her face partway out the window like a dog sniffing at the breeze, Wynter held her thick hair away from her face. After a moment, she ducked her head back into the jeep and said, "I love the way things smell around here. Good question. Their vision is that the girls are to be showcased as the professionals of tomorrow. You won't believe the stuff they suggested. The girls could job shadow the doctor, stage a mock town council meeting with one of them acting as Mayor, compete in the loggers' sports competition, catch a bloody fish. I'm telling you, Leez, these women gave me a spooky feeling. It was like they all might as well have come from the Peach Valley Commune. I bet every one of them needs a good leg waxing."

Lisa-Marie burst out laughing. "Stop, already ... I'll drive off the road. You're obsessed with people's body hair."

Wynter dug in her purse and pulled out a fancy tube of lip gloss. She applied it to her lips and pursed them together. Throwing the gloss back into her bag, she said, "You don't know what kind of culture shock I felt when I came out of the commune to live with my grandmother."

Lisa-Marie glanced quickly at the girl beside her and asked, "What was the commune like?"

"It wasn't anything dark and terrible, if that's what you think. No guru guy abused kids while he went around acting like God. A bunch of throwback hippies just decided they wanted to build solar-powered houses, grow their own food, be vegetarian and raise all their kids together. They bought a chunk of land that had been part of a huge peach orchard in the Niagara area and they did their own thing. It was a great place to grow up. As far as I know, they were all good people."

"How did you end up leaving?"

Wynter sat up straight and folded her arms around her body. "My mom was older when she had me ... like forty. I was her last chance baby. I don't have a clue who my dad is. He must have been one of the men in the commune because my mom never left the place. No one ever told me his name and it didn't seem like a big deal. There were more than enough parents to go around. Mom had a lot of health issues ... even before I was born. My grandmother always begged her to leave the commune and come back to Vancouver but she was stubborn. I guess she thought all the organic food and healthy living would cure her. In the end, it turned out she had this rare type of cancer in her blood. We both came back to my grandmother's after Mom was diagnosed but she died within the year. So ... that left me with my grandmother."

"Gee, that's sad. Sometimes I get down because I didn't know my mom but you lost a mother who loved you and you'd had her in your life for years. I start to think maybe it was better never to have known my mom at all.

Wynter shook her head, "No, don't say that, Leez. I'm glad I knew my mom and I'm glad she chose to bring me up where she did. It was sure a shocker, though, when I landed in the real world."

Lisa-Marie grinned. "Because of all the body hair issues?"

Wynter grinned back. "That and a whole bunch of stuff ... like TV and cell phones and eating meat and school and how mean the other kids were and living in a big city in a mansion – my grandmother has scads of money."

"Lucky you. My grandmother raised me and she didn't have much of anything. Remind me to tell you what I know about mean kids someday. My first three years of high school were not a lot of fun." They rounded a corner and the view of Crater Lake opened up past a steep cliff. Lisa-Marie pointed to her right, out the passenger-side window. "Look at that moon over the water, hey?" Returning her eyes to the gravel, she pumped the brakes quickly as the headlights caught the movement of an animal loping across the road. Slowing the jeep, Lisa-Marie gasped, "Did you see that? What was it? It wasn't a deer or a dog."

Wynter shook her head, "I didn't see anything. I was looking at the moon."

"Maybe it was that cougar everyone at the Camp is talking about. I only got a glimpse of it. Whew ... freaky." Lisa-Marie resumed her speed and asked, "Where is your grandma now?"

"A couple of years ago she was diagnosed with Alzheimer's. It wasn't all that obvious at first but she could tell she was going down fast. She settled all her affairs and then checked herself into a high-end, care facility somewhere in Europe. She told me not to expect to see her again."

"That sounds kind of cold."

"Not for her. It's the type of woman she is. Even when I first met her, she was almost seventy but she looked like a movie star to me in her sparkling jewelry, fine clothes and soft furs. Her hair was always perfectly styled and she stood so tall and straight. She had been a model for years." Wynter laughed suddenly. "I remember the first time she saw me. I'd never had my hair cut and it was all tangled and down past my butt. I had these bushy eyebrows like Hermione Granger in the *Harry Potter* movies. I was tall for my age and I slouched a lot. I wore oddball, round John Lennon glasses and my teeth were crooked. I think the only thing I had going for me was that I had clear skin. Grandma stared at me like I was an alien. Then she turned me around slowly, tipped my head up and looked at me from different angles. Finally she said – *I think I see some potential here. I'll clean you up and see what I can do with you.*"

Lisa-Marie stared at Wynter for a second before she returned her eyes to the road to turn into Micah Camp's driveway. She swung the jeep to a stop by the path that led down to Wynter's cabin. Smiling at the girl beside her, she said, "Well, whatever she did ... it sure worked."

"I suppose it did." Wynter stepped out of the vehicle. "If you ever get a chance, will you introduce me to Mike?"

Nodding, Lisa-Marie said, "Sure."

"See you tomorrow, Leez. Thanks for the ride."

✿✿✿✿

Beulah dropped her robe over the chair in the corner and got into bed. Bethany was flipping through photocopied pages of small print that made Beulah's eyes water. "What are you reading?" she asked as she adjusted the blankets and reached for the book on her night table. She had to admit that there was no way she would make it through *Paris 1919.* The bloody book was better than a shot of whiskey for putting her to sleep.

"It's an article I downloaded from a journal on how kids in care sometimes fall through the cracks of the medical system."

Beulah tried to stop her eyes from rolling. "Hmm ... interesting."

Bethany underlined a section of print with her highlighter and dropped the pages onto the bed. "It is interesting." She glanced over at Beulah, "Listen ... I want to run something by you. There's this girl I interviewed the other day. She's thin as a rail and she says all kinds of foods make her sick. She squints and acts like she can't see; she was scratching at a rash on her arm so much through the whole interview, I thought I might scream." Bethany frowned, "How can I put this? Everyone sees her but it seems like no one notices that something isn't right. Anyway, she had an appointment this morning with the career counsellor who comes to the Camp once a month. I'm allowed to read the girl's regular Micah Camp file. It contains everything except Nick's notes. The career counsellor suggests a bunch of tests I've never heard of. Her report reads like she's already made up her mind that the girl is mentally challenged. The only work assignment she recommends is with the cleaning lady."

"I gather you don't share her opinion?"

Bethany shook her head and her frown deepened. "No, I don't. There wasn't much in the file from the teachers. To be honest, all the time I was working with Jillian and looking at files, I never saw anything written by Jeremy. Gordon wrote that he had no idea where to begin with math upgrading and Maryanne put down something rude about not even scheduling time with this girl until she has access to her past school records." Bethany ran her hand through her hair as she continued, "Maybe the girl's glasses aren't right. That could explain why she has so much trouble reading. What about the eating issue and her rash? Why hasn't she seen a doctor? And now that she's at the Camp, who keeps an eye on her health issues? This article says kids who've been in the system may not have had proper medical care because they're always being bounced around from place to place."

"So, what are you going to do?"

Bethany stumbled over her words, "I don't know. I could be out in left field. I've got one year of university ... what do I know?"

Beulah grabbed the article from the bed and shook it in Bethany's face. "You know a hell of a lot. You worked with these kids all last year with Jillian and from what you're saying, it seems you are the only one who is really seeing this kid."

Bethany grabbed the article from Beulah's hand, "Be careful, you'll knock the paperclip off. Geez, I didn't know you could get so hyped up about what I know."

Beulah reached out to tip up Bethany's chin and turn her face towards her, "You care about those kids and you have good instincts. Go and talk to Izzy. You owe it to this girl you interviewed."

"Okay, okay." Bethany smiled and cuddled close to Beulah. She spoke against the warmth of Beulah's neck, "I'll try to talk to Izzy when we're down in Victoria for Lisa's grad this weekend."

"I hope she'll be in a better mood than she was today. She bit my head off at the coffee shop this afternoon. It turns out she doesn't love the idea of *The First Annual Caleb Jenkins Memorial Ball Tournament* and she isn't going to pay for the trophies." Beulah stretched and groaned as Bethany's lips began a slow trek.

Bethany shook her head as she tugged her top off. "I knew she wouldn't," she whispered as she stretched out on the bed and let Beulah pull her close.

EIGHTEEN

Nick pressed a button on the remote control to pause the videotape, "Right there ... did you hear the question I asked her? That's not me. And my tone ... shit ... I can hardly believe it." He tapped the controller against his leg and frowned. "I'm not one to hang much on Freudian jargon but I do think he was onto something with the concepts of transference and counter-transference." He watched Izzy's eyebrows go up as she listened to him. Nick ignored her look and plunged on, "Rachel has me pegged as someone who will pick on her and I'm living right down to her expectations."

He got up and paced his office, stopping to look out the window at the crisp whitecaps that danced along the surface of the water. "I've tried to get in touch with what I was feeling when I asked her that question." He turned to face Izzy who sat composed and quiet in her chair. "And I hate to admit it but I was thinking that I really didn't like her. The way she fidgets around all the time gets on my nerves." He sat back down and pressed play. He pointed the remote at the computer screen on his desk, "See the look on her face. She totally expected me to talk to her like that." Nick clicked stop and reached over to close the lid on his laptop. "I've got to follow my gut on this one. I don't want to work with her."

Izzy crossed one of her slim legs over the other; her foot, in a designer pump, moved up and down. "That's a rather quick decision, Nick. You've only had two sessions with her. There's no rule that says we have to like all our clients."

"Well, you have to admit, it does help."

Izzy shrugged. "I'm wondering why your first reaction is to get out of

139

working with Rachel. From my perspective, this seems like an excellent opportunity for you to explore some of your own reactions."

Nick hadn't anticipated being challenged on his request to pass Rachel off on Izzy. He had a very full client load and it seemed logical to him that Izzy could take some of the pressure off. He forced his voice to remain calm. "I don't have a good feeling about working with this girl. I'm thinking about what's best for her."

Izzy straightened in her chair, a hint of something crept into her voice that Nick had not heard before. "You are in no position as Micah Camp's only trauma counsellor to refuse to treat a specific client."

Nick stared at her, "Are you seriously suggesting I continue to counsel a person with whom I am uncomfortable? Why can't you take her on? You have more experience than I have with young adults. What gives? Roland saw clients and did the director's job. I've read his case notes."

Izzy stood up. "The fact that you lack experience with a client like Rachel is reason enough for you to continue. Believe me, she is not unique and, as you say, I do have more experience, so you can trust me on that. Meeting with a supervisor gives you the chance to work out what to do next, not dump your responsibility." Izzy's voice had a steely quality that stunned Nick. If he weren't getting pissed off by her attitude, he'd have admired her control. "If you don't want to do your job then write up your resignation and I'll take it to the Board." She turned and left his office, closing the door firmly behind her.

❦❦❦❦

Fiona stepped into one of Micah Camp's classrooms, stripped off her sweater and placed her bags and papers on the desk at the front of the room. She looked around for a piece of chalk and scrawled on the board – *Sexual Health in Your Twenties*. Under that she wrote – *What is still your best friend?* She underlined her question several times before she turned to face the assembled residents. Pushing her long braid back over her shoulder, she leaned against the edge of the desk and introduced herself. "Hi, I'm Dr. Fiona Wells." She pointed over her shoulder to the question on the board, "Hands up ... tell me what you think."

One guy at the back laughed loudly and called out, "A virgin?"

"The question is *what*, not *who*. Anyone else?"

A girl in the front row said, "Stick with girls." To the giggled whispers around her, she answered, "If it works for you ... you won't get pregnant."

Fiona raised an eyebrow, "The if-it-works-for-you is a limiting factor and again, *what*, not *who*."

Another girl raised her hand to say, "Abstinence?"

Fiona spoke above the moans and groans, "A possibility but probably less doable in your twenties." She got up and pulled a basket from her bag. She put it on the desk, grabbed another bag and tipped out the contents. Small, brightly coloured foil packages showered and shimmered into the basket until it overflowed. She grabbed a handful, letting them cascade back into the basket and onto the desk in a sparkly waterfall. "Condoms. These simple devices can be your best friend throughout your twenties. I expect this basket to be empty by the time I leave this room."

To the hoots and hollers that followed her comment, Fiona motioned for silence and said, "I need a male volunteer ... upfront right now." Ethan was the first to bounce out of his chair and dance his way to the front. Fiona gestured to the basket, "Take your pick and show us how it's done." She reached into her bag to pull out a banana. While her back was turned, the room erupted into laugher. She looked over to see Ethan pretending to do a striptease. He was rotating his hips and he already had his hand on the zipper of his jeans. She burst out laughing and passed him the banana. "Let's keep this G-rated please."

❧❧❧❧

Nick had stewed for a while over Izzy's refusal to take Rachel off his hands. He didn't spend any time worrying about the way she had tossed out the suggestion that he could leave if he didn't like his job. She was obviously not serious. People say things they don't mean when they're challenged. But why she'd gotten so worked up over the mere suggestion that she take on a trauma client was beyond him.

He checked his day planner and realized he had the rest of the morning free because all the residents were attending the local doctor's sex talk. That certainly seemed more interesting than his paperwork. It occurred to him that he might help out with crowd control and the idea put a smile on his face.

Nick slipped into the classroom and stood by the back wall. For some reason, he had expected the doctor to be male and old. The attractive young woman at the front of the classroom did not need help engaging the residents in a conversation on sexual matters. He watched her field a comment with a challenge of her own, "Okay, let's talk about the whole idea of friends with benefits. Who is being a friend and who is getting the benefits?"

He leaned against the wall, folded his arms over his chest and enjoyed the show. His mind wandered. He wouldn't mind playing doctor with her; she had something that put her beyond being simply attractive. The air around

141

her sparked with energy. The way she tossed her thick braid of hair over her shoulder made loose strands dance around her face. Her crisp, white shirt accentuated the brown of her skin. Her black jeans were tight in all the right spots and the spiky heels on her classy, leather boots clicked over the hardwood floor as she moved about the front of the classroom.

Lost in his evaluation and not yet at the point of reminding himself to avoid getting involved with another woman, Nick snapped back to reality. The doctor's voice was directed his way.

"You there ... against the back wall. Who are you? Are you part of this workshop?"

Nick laughed, "It's been awhile since I needed to think about sexual health in my twenties." A few of the residents laughed with him and he could see the doctor's eyes smoulder as she glared at him. He straightened up. "My name is Nick Anderson and I'm a counsellor here. I thought I'd drop by to make sure this crowd was behaving for you." He smiled across the room at her.

She did not return his smile. "Yes, I see now that you are well beyond belonging to this age group. Please don't feel obliged to stay ... unless, of course, you think you could use the review."

Taking with good grace the tittering laughter that sped around the room, Nick said, "I think I'll pass. I will leave the residents in your capable hands, Doctor." He nodded his head at her and left the room thinking that he'd be her friend with benefits any day of the week.

⁕⁘⁕⁘⁕

Fiona waited in the food line-up, feeling her stomach rumble and savouring the delicious smells wafting her way. She glanced over and saw one of the young women from the workshop walking towards her. The girl thrust her hand out and said, "I'm Arianna. May I sit with you at lunch?"

Fiona smiled, "Hey, Arianna. Where are you from?"

"The Osoyoos Band."

"I've seen your chief on television. He's sure got things right with regard to economic development. Did you want to talk about a health issue? If so, you should come to the clinic."

It was her turn at the food and Fiona didn't waste any time in filling her plate. She couldn't remember the last time she'd eaten a hot meal. Grabbing sandwiches and washing them down with cold tea had been a recurring theme since she had started her internship. Looking over her shoulder, she continued her conversation with the girl behind her, "The food looks great. Do you guys always eat so well?"

Arianna smiled, "My friend Dylan does most of the cooking and he's awesome. What I want to talk about isn't a health issue."

Izzy stepped into the food line between Arianna and Fiona. "Excuse me, Arianna. Please feel free to sit at the staff table, Fiona. I'm sure everyone there would like to meet you." She pointed to a table in the corner by the window.

Fiona's eyes were on the penne with alfredo sauce and Caesar salad already on her plate. She felt like drooling. As she reached over to grab a chunk of garlic bread, she saw, beyond Izzy's shoulder, the way Arianna's face fell. It looked like the girl might burst out crying. Fiona glanced at the staff table – that Nick guy sat there large as life. "I'll stop by and introduce myself but I already promised Arianna I would sit with her. She'd like to talk to me about something."

Izzy nodded and said, "Come by my office before you leave. I have a small thank you gift for you." She turned and left the dining room, obviously not intending to stop long enough to enjoy lunch with the others.

Seated at a table with Arianna, Fiona dug into her lunch. The girl's words rushed out, "I want to be a doctor. I want to be like you. Oh my God ... I want it so much. I've never said those words out loud to anyone but when I saw you today, it was like, wow, wow ... I have to talk to her. Maybe it's not impossible. I looked at you and I felt like my dream smacked me right up the side of the head and started shouting, go for it, go for it."

Fiona grinned and continued to eat. "Don't mind me, stuffing myself while you talk. If you ever make it to medical school or internship," the doctor stopped to point the fork at her, "and that is entirely possible, you'll find that when a good meal comes along you don't let much get in the way of your enjoyment." She waved the fork around, "Talk, tell me everything about your dream."

"When I was a little girl, I always used to say I'd be a doctor when I grew up. Then I sort of forgot until I came here and I really got to think about the rest of my life and what I could be. I found out I've been accepted to UBC on a full scholarship. I've always wanted to help people. For a while, I wasn't on the right track; counselling made me see that. I was too much into helping people so they would like me. I don't do that anymore. Instead of trying to please everyone else, I want to do something that matters to me. I told myself that if I actually got accepted to UBC, that would be the first step. Now I have to think of the next step and the next. What courses should I take? What happens after I get an undergrad degree? When should I be thinking of applying to medical schools? How long will it all take?" Arianna put her hand to her chest, "My heart is thumping; talking to you about my future is so exciting. Am I crazy? Do you think I could really do it?"

Fiona burst out laughing. "Well, I don't know if you could really do it but I'll tell you how it can be done." She gulped her tea and continued, "I went right from high school to an undergrad degree at the University of Toronto, studying sciences all the way. I wanted to apply to medical schools right after I graduated but I got some good advice about that. I was pretty young – only twenty-one. I did a Master's Degree in Pharmacology and tuned up my applications. For my thesis, I interviewed a bunch of Elders from my Band on how traditional medicine compares to pharmacological approaches. The master's took me two years and I felt old and seasoned at twenty-three. I was chomping at the bit to send off those applications I'd been working so hard on. My mentor asked me to wait one more year. I had an opportunity to go up north as a member of a research team studying the high rate of diabetes in native communities. During that year, I finally got to mail out all those applications and I ended up snagging a spot at McGill. Then came four of the most gruelling years of my life ... no one can describe to you what that's like. You just have to get through it. I applied to the Family Residency Program and I'm now in my internship year. I'll spend six months here learning everything I can about a rural, family practice then I'll do six months at a street clinic on the Downtown Eastside of Vancouver. After that, one year of residency and I'll be able to apply for my license to practice medicine in Canada." Fiona stared at the girl across from her. "If that rundown doesn't scare the shit out of you, it should. But if you've got the fire in you to see it through, then I'm here to tell you it can be done."

Fiona watched as wide-eyed looks of fear and wonder chased across the girl's face. She knew exactly how Arianna felt. She had been fortunate to take her early dreams of becoming a doctor to someone who honoured and nurtured them. Now she was happy to pass that experience along. "They'll be tough years but if you want it badly enough, you'll get there. I promise you. And the fact that you are a First Nations woman is in your favour. Our communities are screaming for doctors. If you want to help, you'll find a well that isn't going to run dry for a good number of years. There's no limit to the number of places you can go and things you might do to help our people. I'll be happy to talk more to you about all of this. I know it's a lot to take in. I'm over at the guest cabin past Izzy and Liam's. I don't have a ton of time but if you're serious, I'll make time for you. There are all kinds of things you can be doing every step of the way to strengthen your medical school applications when the time comes for you to submit them. In the meantime, you need good mentoring and contacts to make those things happen."

Tears shone in Arianna's eyes as she stared at Fiona. "Thank you. Thank you so much."

Fiona reached over and covered the girl's hands with her own. "We pay it forward. If this road is for you, someday you'll be doing the same for someone else."

After a brief round of introductions at the staff table, Fiona excused herself and headed down the hall to the washroom. The door had hardly closed behind her when she heard the sound of someone being violently sick in one of the stalls. She rapped on the door and called out, "Are you, okay? Do you need help?"

The toilet flushed and a thin girl came out holding her hair away from her face. She shook her head as she walked over to the sink to splash cold water on her face. After gulping a bit from her cupped hands and rinsing her mouth, she turned and said, "I'm fine, thanks. Something I ate made me sick to my stomach."

Fiona's eyes narrowed as she stared at the girl's pale, sweaty skin. "Something made you sick or you made yourself sick?"

The girl blushed, shook her head and stammered out a reply without meeting Fiona's gaze. "No, it isn't like that. It was something I ate."

"If you're sick you should see a doctor. What's your name?"

The girl stared at the ground as she said, "Rachel Franklin."

"Okay, Rachel. I hope you're being honest when you say you are not making yourself throw up because that type of behaviour is very serious. If you continue to feel ill, you need to come to the clinic in town so we can find out what's wrong with you. Your colour is not good and you look too thin to me."

Rachel continued to stare at the ground. Fiona frowned as the girl left the washroom.

❧❧❧❧

Bethany did a double take when she looked up from her transcribing to see Rachel standing in the doorway to her office. She pulled off her earphones and said, "Come in Rachel. Gee, your hair looks nice. Did you get it done?"

A half-hearted attempt at a smile flitted over Rachel's face as she said, "No, I bought some hair products at the drugstore with my gift card and Wynter showed me how to scrunch dry this style so all the curl would come out."

"What can I do for you?" Bethany pushed back from the desk and pointed to a chair. Rachel sat down, removed her glasses and rubbed the pressure grooves left by them. Bethany frowned and asked, "When was the last time you had a new pair of glasses?"

Rachel looked confused, "What do you mean?"

"A new pair of glasses ... those seem small for you."

"I got these when I was in grade five. But I'm not sure they work very well anymore because they seem to give me a headache and I can't see out of them very well."

Bethany's mind reeled at that statement. Before she had a chance to follow it up, she noticed tears in Rachel's eyes. She got up and moved across the room to shut the door; then she pulled a chair up beside the girl. "Hey ... what's up?"

"I'm sorry for crying. Right after lunch, I ran to the bathroom to throw up ... I told you the other day that so many things make me feel sick to my stomach. The doctor who did the workshop this morning was in the bathroom. She asked me if I was making myself sick – like making myself throw up." The tears were coming faster now and Rachel's voice choked up as she said, "I would never do something like that. I'm not lying, Ms. Shannon. Throwing up is horrible. Dr. Wells looked at me like she didn't believe me."

Bethany decided the time had come for her to act. "Rachel, I need to talk with Izzy about this, right now. Maybe it would be best for you to go to your cabin and lie down. I promise that I'll come and see you as soon as I can."

Rachel shook her head, "I don't want to cause any trouble. I like it here. I don't want to get sent away." She got up and backed towards the door.

Bethany walked over and put her hands on the girl's arms. "You are not causing trouble. I believe that you're not making yourself throw up. I'm more and more convinced that you have a health issue that needs to be taken care of. We are here to help you, Rachel. Please believe me on that. No one is sending you away. Okay?"

Rachel didn't look convinced but she agreed to wait in her cabin. Bethany gathered up her notes and headed for Izzy's office.

⚶⚶⚶⚶

Izzy cleared the top of her desk and spread out the large, site plan drawing that the architect had dropped off that morning. She leaned over it, imaging how the placement of the new cabins would change the overall look of the grounds. A sharp rap on the door had her raising her eyes as Fiona strode into the office. Izzy could see a cloud of trouble in the woman's sweeping

146

brows and snapping eyes. Being around Fiona was like standing under high voltage wires – she buzzed.

Izzy pushed the plans aside and reached for the gift bag on a nearby shelf. Hopefully the gift would cut the current. "Fiona, please accept this small token on behalf of Micah Camp. We really appreciate the time you took to come out and talk to the residents. From the comments I heard when I walked through the dining room, I'm convinced you were a hit."

The expression on Fiona's face revealed her impatience but she politely took the bag, pushed aside the tissue paper and pulled out a black mug. The words Micah Camp were written under an artist's rendition of a stylized owl in a deep shade of red that carried over to the interior of the mug. "Thank you. This is beautiful."

"Isn't it? A local artist does the design."

Fiona stuffed the mug back into the bag. "Just now, one of the residents, Rachel Franklin, was throwing up her lunch in a washroom stall. Does the girl have an eating disorder? She denied it. Said she had an upset stomach from lunch but she doesn't look well to me. If she's ill, why hasn't she been to the clinic to see a doctor? Who keeps track of the health of these kids when they're here?"

Izzy took in the information and felt yet another red flag go up. She tapped her fingers on the desk for a moment. "Thanks for coming to me with this, Fiona. I've been hearing a few things about Rachel over the past couple of days. She was already first on my agenda for next week but I think I'll have to review her case this afternoon."

A quiet knock on the door sounded and Bethany walked into the office. "I'm sorry to disturb you Izzy, but I've got a serious issue concerning Rachel Franklin that I need to discuss with you."

Izzy held up her hand and said, "Hold that thought for about two minutes, Beth." She reached for the phone on her desk and quickly punched in a number. "Darlene ... I need you at the Camp right away. I'm about to call an emergency meeting to discuss Rachel Franklin and I think you'll want to attend. When was the last time you saw her? Okay ... well, I think it would be a good idea for you to touch base with her before the meeting." Izzy looked down at her watch, "It's one o'clock now. We'll meet at two-thirty. That will give you time to get here and see Rachel."

She hung up the phone and turned to Fiona. "What's your schedule like this afternoon? I'd appreciate it if you could stay for the meeting."

"I was going home to do some research then get a couple of hours of sleep. I'm on call tonight at the hospital but I don't have to leave until six. If you can set me up with a computer somewhere, I'll stay here and work until the meeting."

Izzy turned to Bethany. "Can what you want to tell me wait until the meeting? It will be better if we can air our individual concerns when we're all together."

Bethany nodded. "Yes, that will work. Rachel's a bit upset so maybe I'll go back to her cabin and keep her company until Darlene shows up."

"Sounds good. Come on Fiona, there's an office next door that you can use."

❦❦❦❦

Darlene burst into the meeting room. A large woman who had no trouble making her presence felt at the best of times, she was now flushed and upset. Her eyes searched out Izzy at the head of the table and her voice boomed, "Why didn't you call me to see Rachel before this? The kid's as thin as a rake and as pale as a ghost. What the hell is going on?"

Izzy pointed to an empty seat, "Sit down, Darlene. That is what we are here to find out." She glanced around the table. Bethany sat beside Fiona. Darlene took the empty chair next to Nick. Izzy looked over at Bethany and asked, "If you wouldn't mind, Beth, could you start things off?"

Bethany glanced at her notes. She looked around the table of professionals and willed herself to calm down and tell them what she knew, clearly, unemotionally and as concisely as she could manage. "In my first research interview with Rachel, I asked her about a rash she had. She had not been to a doctor and she had no medication for it. During the interview, she indicated that one of her concerns was that she couldn't eat properly – that many foods made her feel sick to her stomach. I didn't follow that up at the time and I regret that."

Bethany pulled out the article that she had downloaded and passed it around the table as she talked about what she had learned. "After I read this article, I began to question what kind of medical care Rachel has been receiving. I also wondered about her glasses – whether they're the proper prescription." Bethany took a deep breath and tried not to think about how everyone's attention was fixed on her. "I asked her today when she'd last had her eyes checked or been prescribed new glasses. She has never been back to an optometrist and she is wearing glasses she got when she was ten." She looked quickly around the table, "Rachel came to see me after lunch. She had vomited in the ladies washroom and Dr. Wells asked her if she had made herself throw up. She was very upset and denied that she would ever do something like that. I believe her. I don't think she has an eating disorder. I think she's ill."

Fiona leaned forward with a frown on her face. "Did she tell you anything more about this stomach problem?"

Bethany checked her notes quickly. "She said she had gained a lot of weight in one home then she had been sent to another home where she lost a lot of weight ... about sixty pounds. Since then, there are all kinds of foods that make her feel sick."

Fiona smacked her hand on the table, "The kid could have a gallbladder problem. It isn't common in someone this young but it can happen when a person has gained weight then dropped it quickly. The sooner we get Rachel to the hospital in Cedar Falls for a blood work-up and ultrasound, the better."

Darlene shook her head, "I should have come to see her right away. I don't know what she's been through over the last few years but it seems clear that she has been neglected big time. I'll get to the bottom of this." She looked at Izzy, "I know I bear the responsibility for not rounding up her file and forwarding it to you sooner." She pulled a green folder from her brief case, "I've got it now for all the good it does. But maybe there's something in here that will help." She passed the folder across the table to Izzy.

Izzy glanced around, "Does anyone else have anything to add?"

Nick reached for the file. "I'd like to be the first to go through this, if you don't mind, Izzy. I didn't make the best counselling start with Rachel. Maybe this will give me some insight."

Izzy spoke to Fiona, "Shall we wait to get an appointment at the clinic tomorrow or take her up to the hospital this afternoon?"

"I don't think we should wait."

Darlene straightened in her chair, "I'll drive her and make myself available for whatever else she needs. I can't tell you how bad I feel about all of this."

Izzy met Darlene's eyes and nodded. "I think we all have a lot to learn from what has happened here." Her glance took in the group around the table. "The public health nurse comes in every few months to talk with the residents but I think we'll have to recommend a scheduled appointment with her for each new resident. A thorough health screening is supposed to be done before a resident gets here but Rachel's case tells me that we can't just assume that this criterion has been met." Izzy shrugged with frustration. She looked over at Bethany and said, "For now, I want to thank you, Beth. We are all grateful for the relationship of trust you established with Rachel. You followed up on your instincts and you reported what you discovered in a professional manner."

Bethany blushed as everyone around the table nodded.

⚬⚬⚬⚬

As Fiona pushed opened Micah Camp's heavy doors she felt someone leaning close from behind, taking their weight from her. She stepped outside and turned to see Nick standing there.

"I wanted to apologize for interrupting your workshop earlier," he said.

"Why did you?"

"I was curious and it sure beat doing paperwork. I'm sorry if we got off to a bad start. Let's begin again." He stuck his hand out, "Hi, my name is Nick Anderson."

Fiona ignored the outstretched hand. "Apology accepted but there's no need for us to get off to any kind of start. I don't date white guys."

Nick backed up a step. He looked at her with surprise and puzzlement. "I'm not looking for a date."

Shaking her head, Fiona said, "Holding the door for me, offering an apology where none is expected, suggesting we should start again ... I could be wrong but you seem interested in me and I don't want to mislead you. Goodbye."

As she walked away, she heard him calling out. "Your bedside manner could use some work, Dr. Wells."

⚬⚬⚬⚬

Izzy picked up the phone on her desk and called Liam to tell him she was going to be late. She felt shitty about doing it because it meant sticking him with a bunch of extra work packing for the trip down Island in the morning, but he was good about it. She closed the blinds on her office door and pulled out her bin of collage materials from a drawer. Spreading on the table an assortment of pictures cut from old magazines, she let her mind wander as she kept or rejected one image after another. When she was satisfied with her small pile of choices, she began to arrange the images on a piece of paper. She shuffled them around, grabbed some scissors to trim one and cut out a few words from another. Finally she glued everything down and sat back to take in the finished product.

A number of impressions danced their way through the opening steps of awareness and she found herself in the arms of ghosts she didn't want to face. She shivered as she ran her fingers over the picture of a woman with terrified

150

eyes and screaming mouth. The woman's image dominated the others – the smiling family around a table, a plush armchair, wedding bells, the thick forest, a coffin and a heavy gate.

She slid the collage into an envelope and put it in her drawer. The building was quiet; supper and the subsequent clean-up were long over. She left her office and walked out of the side entrance to stroll down the tree-lined path to Nick's cabin. She knocked on the door and when he answered, she noted the surprised look on his face as he invited her in.

"I came over to apologize. I had no right to end our supervision session with such a heavy-handed ultimatum." Izzy crossed the room and sat down in one of the living room chairs as she spoke.

Nick raised his hands palms up, "I have a lot to learn. I shouldn't have been in such a rush to get out of working with Rachel. I've gone back over the tape a few times and there's more there to pay attention to than what I interpreted as transference/counter-transference issues."

"In our next supervision session, I'd like to work with you on what you've discovered. Right now, I need to tell you something, Nick." She raised her large, dark eyes to his. "For a number of reasons that I'm not ready to discuss, I don't feel competent to see clients at the moment." She folded her arms around herself as her eyes filled with tears.

Nick leaned forward, "Is there anything I can do?"

She shook her head, "No, I need some time to figure out how I'll deal with this." She got up and walked to the door. "But thanks for the offer."

NINETEEN

L iam turned from watching the patterns made by the street lights shining through the thick foliage of the Gary Oak trees that overhung the house like a dark, rustling roof. He glanced at Izzy. They were enjoying the night's warmth on the balcony off their bedroom on the third floor of Tim and Marlene's home in Victoria. "When are you going to tell me what's bothering you?"

"Hmmm ...." Izzy murmured as she sipped her wine.

Liam changed his strategy. He got up and moved behind her chair to place his hands on her shoulders. Izzy lifted her hair and he began to work gently at the muscles of her neck. When he felt her relax, he asked, "Are you enjoying the weekend?"

"Last night, I worried that Robbie might wander but Lisa-Marie says she checked on him a few times and he was sleeping like a log. It's nice to get away, isn't it? Maybe we should do this more often."

On the drive to Victoria, in a caravan of vehicles, Liam had wondered how Tim and Marlene could possibly accommodate their group of nine. The place was perfect. The house itself had three floors with empty bedrooms on the upper two. Several of the windows offered views of the ocean through the trees and the yard was beautifully landscaped. No wonder Lisa had enjoyed boarding here. He and Izzy had the top floor to themselves with a spacious bedroom and private bathroom. Lisa-Marie slept down one floor, sharing her old room with Sophie. Robbie bunked in the room next to her and the baby. Beulah and Bethany were across the hall. Another bedroom on the main floor had been set aside for Alex and Cynthia but they had chosen to stay with friends across town.

Izzy reached up and stroked Liam's hand, "How was your afternoon?"

"Great. I confirmed the delivery date for all the suits and I managed to find everything on my decorating list. Dad introduced us to some interesting people at the university. Then we all went down to the waterfront and hung out. There was an Elder there selling cedar baskets. She fell in love with Sophie. She dressed her up in a little button blanket and a cedar hat. Sophie strutted around in front of the booth and had the tourists going wild." Liam worked the massage deeper as he said, "Robbie spent a bunch of time with the Elder. He helped her make about a hundred cigarettes with one of those rolling machines." Liam laughed.

Turning her head slightly towards him, Izzy said, "Rolling cigarettes isn't exactly the best thing for Robbie to be learning how to do."

"He was chatting a mile a minute the whole time. When I asked him later what they talked about, all he said was - spirit guides." Liam slowed down the motion of his hands as he asked, "How did the dress fitting go?"

"Good." Izzy stretched in the chair. "Bethany got all kinds of tips on last minute alterations. Fiona and Tabby's dresses will be couriered up next week. I had lots of time this afternoon to shop. I wanted to pick out gifts for everyone myself."

"Speaking of gifts," Liam squeezed Izzy's hand and held it as he moved back to his chair and sat down, "the pearls *we* gave Lisa for her graduation are lovely."

Izzy smiled, "They are aren't they? The grad ceremony dragged on but I'm glad we were all there for her. And wasn't Sophie priceless?" When Lisa crossed the stage to get her diploma, Alex had hoisted the child up onto his shoulders. Sophie got so excited at the sight of her mother that she belted out a string of baby talk that had the people sitting around them in stitches.

"Sure was a great dinner afterwards," Liam said.

"I hope it wasn't too over the top."

He found himself laughing, "I don't know if the meal was over the top but I do know that we all felt on top of the world." Izzy had rented a private balcony at a small restaurant that jutted out over the cliffs near the summit of the Malahat Drive. Tim and Marlene had joined them along with two of Lisa-Marie's school friends and their parents. The food was first class and the setting was stunning. All the guests had spent the evening circulating between the small tables - visiting, eating and watching the sun set across the water.

Izzy shrugged, "Graduation is special. I wanted Lisa always to remember with pleasure the celebration at the end of her high school years."

The gentle sound of the waves on the beach carried across the quiet street to their balcony. The sweet smell of the honeysuckle bush that draped over the front entrance filled the air. Izzy sighed and closed her eyes. She spoke softly, "I snapped at Nick the other day when he tried to foist one of his clients onto me. I was seriously out of line. That's why I stayed late that night. I had to figure out what the hell was going on with me and," she looked over at Liam, "I didn't like what I discovered."

Meeting her gaze, he said, "Whatever you need ... I'm here, Iz."

"I know you are."

❧❧❧❧

Nick clicked the remote and the golf DVD stopped. He chugged down the remains of his beer as he glanced at his watch. Ten-thirty on a Saturday night and the best thing he could think of doing was hitting the sack. It was true that he didn't want any emotional entanglements, but he hadn't bargained on entering a social no man's land. He thought about his earlier stroll across the Camp with Brigit. He could believe the rumour that she had been a cop; she certainly carried herself that way. As they walked, she was constantly scanning the area like she was about to carry out single-handedly a major drug bust. She was slim and compact but it wouldn't have surprised him to discover that she had the strength to slam him up against the nearest wall and cuff him. The thought of that made him laugh right out loud.

He stretched and considered what the good Dr. Wells might be up to on this fine Saturday night. She wasn't wearing any rings – so she was likely single. Izzy had explained that Fiona had only recently arrived to stay in their guest cabin while she did her internship in Dearborn. She'd probably had no time yet to meet anyone. It was a shame she didn't date white guys. Their proximity out here in the middle of nowhere might have been handy. He pictured the way her hips had swayed in her tight, black jeans as she walked away from him. He screeched the brakes on that thought.

She had him pegged to the wall and squirming when she had recognized his smooth introduction for what it was – an attempt to get to know her better on the chance that he could ask her out. Now he considered himself lucky to be white and off her social calendar. It seemed to him that the number of relationships he had jumped into without testing the waters had not taught him a damn thing.

❧❧❧❧

Fiona sat in her snug living room and stroked her bare foot over Dante's silky fur, digging her toes in to rub behind the dog's ear. Pearl lay close by, snoring peacefully. Looking after the dogs wasn't a bad job at all. She was glad to have their company and relieved that Justin was right next door. If she had been the only one out here in the wilderness on this piece of property, she'd have been uneasy. She had run into Justin on his way home from working at the sawmill. A large dog trotted beside him and they had joked about the benefits of dog-sitting.

She wondered if everyone was enjoying the weekend down in Victoria. She was still trying to process Liam's admission about Sophie. What she had trouble grasping was how Izzy had so completely accepted Lisa-Marie and Sophie into her family and how she was moving forward as the happy bride-to-be as if nothing out of the ordinary had happened in her life. A few discreet inquiries and a quick bit of math made it clear that Sophie had been conceived before Liam moved in with Izzy ... but still, Liam seemed to have landed himself one very forgiving woman.

She dropped the book onto her lap and closed her eyes. *Paris 1919* had not grabbed her attention. She was beyond tired but her mind wouldn't turn off. She went from thinking about Izzy to recalling the awkward moment that Rosemary had said Rachel was being sent down Island for surgery because blood work and an ultrasound had indicated an inflamed gallbladder. The older doctor had congratulated Fiona on a good call. She'd had to admit she immediately suspected an eating disorder and that she'd actually accused the girl of making herself sick. Rosemary had shrugged and said, "Examine the physical possibilities before you consider the psychological ones."

Challenging was a word that didn't even begin to describe Fiona's internship. Her time at the addiction center had been an eye-opener. A few years before, because of a sizeable alcohol and drug problem, the decision had been made to turn Dearborn's small hospital into an addiction center that could meet the needs of the whole area. The flip side of that decision was to make the hospital in Cedar Falls serve both communities. The model seemed to be working. All dollars allocated to the region for healthcare went directly to the hospital in Cedar Falls and the region tapped into other sources of funding for the addiction center in Dearborn. A wide array of workshops and day programs went on at the center and the people in the area had access to several de-tox beds. But the waiting list for those beds was as long as her arm.

Friday night and into the late hours of Saturday, Fiona had been on call at the Cedar Hills Hospital and the calls were fairly steady. She had seen three drunks – one a young man who had to have his stomach pumped. A woman had stumbled into the emergency on her partner's arm; her nose was bleeding and she had a cut over her eye that required stitches. She insisted she had fallen down the stairs. The male nurse rolled his eyes as if he didn't believe her. Fiona didn't think the injuries were caused by a fall either, but the woman resisted any attempts the doctor made to get a different story. A young mom arrived with a crying infant, flushed with fever. A car accident had forced Fiona to call an air ambulance for the driver who had a serious compound fracture.

Her favourite patient of the night showed up with a puncture wound that had barely missed an artery and had gone almost deep enough to graze a nerve. She stitched him up and asked him how the injury had happened. He had accidently driven a pair of garden shears into his wrist while doing some clipping. When she asked him why he had been clipping at night, she had expected him to hem and haw and maybe own up to having a basement grow-op or something. He had looked at her steadily and said, "I won't lie to you Doc ... with the job, the kids and the wife to deal with, the only time I have to clip the hedge is after midnight."

Fiona had finally made her way to the small cot in a back room of the hospital. She had fallen exhausted into a fitful sleep when a bang on the door woke her up and sent her back to the emergency room. There, she met a police officer who informed her that a boat had sunk; two fishermen who seemed to be suffering from hypothermia were on their way. She had no sooner sorted that out than she got a call saying that an air ambulance was on its way from one of the coastal villages with a woman in early-stage labour. It turned out she was far beyond early labour and a healthy baby boy was born about five minutes after the woman was transferred to the emergency room bed. Never a dull moment, it seemed.

Fiona's mind returned to the present moment and the comfort of her own living room. She wondered what Nick Anderson did to keep himself occupied every night over at Micah Camp. He was older than she was, obviously, but not that old. Was there a social life to be had out here in the woods? Did he go to Dearborn ... and do what? He didn't seem the type to spend an evening drinking in the Dearborn Hotel. She opened her eyes and sat up in the chair. The guy knew how to dress; he had a body that he kept in shape and a smile that could make a girl's heart hammer unexpectedly. It sucked that he was white because otherwise she might have shown him that her bedside manner didn't need any work at all.

Fiona got up and checked the lock on the sliding glass door. She turned off the lights and made her way up the steps to the loft bed with Dante trotting right behind her. She fell asleep and dreamed about Poppy. They were together down by the river, digging their toes into the wet mud on the bank and laughing at the squishy, slapping sounds their feet were making. A fish jumped in the slow-moving water and Fiona watched in fascination as concentric circles fanned out across the dappled green and brown surface. She wanted to tell Poppy that they should bring their fishing rods the next time; then she remembered they hadn't been down to the river to fish since they were kids. The sky darkened and huge rain drops began to splatter over the surface of the water. She turned to grab Poppy and make a run for home but her friend was gone. The prints of her feet in the soft mud quickly filled with rain.

Fiona woke up to the sound of an animal howling somewhere in the distance. Her face was wet with tears. Dante stood by the bed and nuzzled her shoulder. She sat up; her heart beat loudly as she strained to hear anything else. After a few moments of silence, she patted the bed beside her and said, "Come on up, boy." In a moment the dog was curled beside her. The animal's warmth combined with the sound of the rain on the cabin roof, lulled her back to sleep.

✻ ✻ ✻ ✻

Justin woke to the absence of sound. He reached for his watch on the ledge above the bed and cursed when he saw it was already seven-thirty in the morning. He was halfway out of bed before he remembered it was Sunday. He lay back down and thought about Liam's rooster. Every morning that rooster screamed out its presence at six a.m. The thing was better than an alarm clock.

Justin considered pulling the blankets over his head and going back to sleep but after the events of the early morning hours, he knew he had to get up. The frantic barking of Reg's dog had wakened him at around four. He had stumbled downstairs where the dog was making a terrible racket throwing its body against the door and clawing at the wood. He'd let the animal out and stood on the small deck to watch as the dog made a dash up the hill toward the chicken coop. The wild sound of frenzied barking went on for quite a few minutes and just as Justin turned to go back inside, he heard a high-pitched, hair-raising howl. As the eerie sound faded and the whole area slipped back into silence, he stood on the porch and tried to decide what to do. Reg had said to stay put and he thought that was probably sound advice. First light would be soon enough to investigate.

He got up and yanked on a pair of jeans and a T-shirt. Grabbing the large stick from near the back door, he headed up the hill to the chicken coop. What he saw looked like the contents of a few feather pillows, doused with a bucket of blood and stomped all over with mud. He counted at least seven chicken carcasses scattered over the yard. Though he didn't hold out much hope for the two dozen chickens that occupied the inside of the small building, Justin unfastened the gate to walk across the space and take a look inside. It was only when he got closer that he saw Reg's dog lying on the far side of the yard against the fence.

He knelt down in the earth wet with a combination of the rain and the blood that had run freely from the slash marks along the side of the animal's head and front quarter. The dog's eyes slowly opened and it let out a low-pitched whine. "Hang on boy; I'll be back as soon as I can."

He sprinted down the path and headed for Liam and Izzy's. Once there, he got Reg on the phone. He told him what had happened then made his way back to wait with the injured dog. Reg must have pushed the boundaries of safety in getting from Dearborn to Crater Lake. It wasn't long before Justin saw him making his way up the hill from Liam's cabin to the chicken coop. He was carrying a rifle.

Moving aside, Justin watched Reg kneel by the fence. He gently stroked the dog's fur and assessed the extent of the animal's injuries. He stood up and said, "You might not want to see what comes next. Give me about ten minutes. I'll help you clean up this chicken massacre after that."

Justin turned around to head back to the cabin. Halfway there he heard a rifle shot echo through the bush. He gave Reg fifteen minutes for good measure and by the time he got back up to the coop, the dog's body was wrapped in a couple of old, chicken feed bags and loaded into a nearby wheelbarrow. His boss had a rake in his hand and had started to scrape up the mess in the yard. He pointed to a shovel, "Grab that and toss some dirt over here."

Justin did as he was told. "Are we going to bury what's left of the chickens?"

Reg shook his head, "No. We'll bag them up and burn the whole goddamned mess in the barrel out back of the sawmill."

Later, Reg poked at the flames that were licking around the jumbled carcasses in the burn barrel. "No fuckin' way a cougar should attack a dog like that. That dog weighed over a hundred pounds. Damn near the same size as that cat. A dog that size chases after a healthy cougar and that cougar goes up a tree. It doesn't run and it doesn't attack. That ain't natural behaviour. This cat is acting desperate and that makes it one dangerous son-of-a-bitch."

Justin waited until after dinner to give Liam and Izzy a chance to get settled in before he dropped by to let them know about the chickens. There were a few suitcases stacked in the entrance when he went into the cabin but he found Izzy and Liam relaxing in the living room. Lisa-Marie sat on the floor playing with Sophie.

He got right to the point. "You were right about a cougar going after the chickens, Liam. Around four this morning, I had to let Reg's dog out and when I went to check things at seven ... well, the chickens are all dead and Reg had to put his dog down. The cougar had clawed him up badly."

"All the chickens are dead?" Robbie had walked into the room while Justin was speaking.

Lisa-Marie stared, looking every bit as shocked as Robbie. She glanced over at Liam, "All this talk about cougars is serious, then?"

Izzy waved for Robbie to come over and sit beside her in the big armchair as Liam replied, "Very serious. Robbie and Tabby aren't to be walking back and forth between the Camp on their own." He spoke directly to Robbie, "If you and Tabby are outside, around here, you must have both dogs with you and stay back from the trees ... stay in the open." Robbie nodded and Liam continued, "Dawn and dusk are the times for all of us to be cautious. I don't want Sophie outside unless there are at least two adults to keep an eye on her. Lisa, and you too, Izzy ... if either of you has to walk over to the Camp, make sure someone is with you." He gave Izzy a quick stare, "I know you won't even consider this, but Lisa," he turned to the young woman, "why don't you drive back and forth for now?" Liam took a deep breath, "I won't replace the chickens until this whole thing is resolved. We don't need anything luring the animal closer."

Izzy stroked the hair back from Robbie's face and frowned, "You feel clammy. Are you okay, Robbie?"

Robbie shook his head, bolted up and ran for the bathroom. Izzy followed him and waited while he was sick over the toilet. She wet a cloth and passed it to him and poured him a glass of water. "Sip it slowly. Maybe you better go and lie down for a bit."

When she left the bathroom, Izzy made a face at Liam and said, "I hope he didn't pick up some kind of bug that we're all going to get."

Liam shrugged and lifted Sophie up from the floor, "Time for your bath."

Lisa-Marie said, "I'll do it."

"No, you stay and talk with Justin. I never get a turn at bath duty anymore."

Justin sat down and asked, "How was graduation?"

"Great. I wish you could have been there for the dinner. Izzy rented out this fancy, private patio with the best view over the ocean." She smiled and relaxed on the sofa. "Sounds like you had a horrible weekend. That must have been awful ... finding all the dead chickens and Reg's dog." She rubbed her hands up and down her arms and shivered.

"Ya, it was gruesome. Don't take any chances, Leez. Reg thinks this cougar is a real problem."

"I don't know why Izzy's so stubborn. I'll drive around to the Camp until we get the all-clear." She pushed her hair back from her face, "How will that happen? Will someone come and shoot the cougar with a tranquilizer gun and take it somewhere else?"

Justin shook his head, "I don't think so. Reg looked like he'd hunt the thing down and kill it."

"Wow ... that sounds harsh. Maybe we shouldn't be living out here in the middle of cougar land and tempting wild animals with things like chickens."

"I guess you should have told that to Caleb." He glanced at her and smiled, "I seem to recall that you and I have a date set up for next week ... Wednesday, right?"

Lisa-Marie stared at him, "You remembered."

"Of course I remember ... your eighteenth birthday, you and me at *The Sea Shed* for dinner, but no drinking beer straight from the jug at the Hotel afterwards for you." He got up, "I better get going. I'll pick you up next Wednesday at six-thirty."

"We can take my jeep."

"No ... I'll borrow Izzy's Highlander. See you then."

※。※。※。※

Robbie tossed back and forth in his bed, caught deep in his dream. He stood outside the chicken coop watching as the cougar ripped aside the fence and scrambled inside the yard. The wire snapped back into place behind the animal. The rooster squawked and the chickens clucked as the cat burst into the coop building. A snowfall of feathers whipped around in the wind as the birds spilled out into the yard. Robbie wanted the frenzied killing to stop but he understood the cat's need to eat. Quelling the hunger was everything to them now. The barking of a dog got the cat's attention. It came out of the building and spun around seeking a way out of the yard.

Robbie recognized Reg's dog from the sawmill. He tried to call to it – to distract it – but the animal was focused on one thing only. The scent of the cougar brought the dog right to the rip in the fence. It burst through and made straight for the cat. Trapped and with no room to make the leap to the top of the chicken coop, the cougar retreated into the confines of the narrow, dark building in the middle of the yard.

Drool whipped back from the attacking dog's mouth. Snarling and barking, it pushed its head and front paws into the coop until it was almost nose to nose with the cat. The cougar did the only thing it could do, what instinct demands of all cornered animals – it fought back. The cat raked out a huge paw, clawing at the dog with desperate strength and laying open a series of jagged wounds along the side of the animal's head and front leg. Robbie heard the dog howl an unearthly yelp of pain as it skittered backwards. Fear and pain propelled it into a wild spin that took it out the door of the coop and halfway across the yard.

The cougar moved cautiously out of the building, keeping its eyes on the dog that lay against the fence whimpering a low and continual litany of pain. An easy jump took the cat to the roof of the coop and one more leap landed it safely on the other side of the fence. Leaving the carnage of the chicken yard behind, Robbie loped easily alongside the cat as they moved into the bush where hunger would once again become a constant companion.

As Robbie tried to open the door to get out of his bedroom, the trap he had set for himself sent a large book tumbling off the door's upper ledge and crashing down on his head. It bounced off his head, smacked his nose and fell to the floor with a thud. He came awake to the sound of Dante whining beside him. His eyes smarted with quick tears as he touched his nose. His mouth dropped open in disbelief as he backed up and sat down on the bed. It was true then. He really had been sleepwalking. It wasn't that he thought Izzy had been lying to him; it was just hard for him to believe he could be doing such a thing without knowing at the time or remembering afterwards.

He rubbed at his sleep-crusted eyes and felt hot tears stream down his face. Why couldn't he remember?

The thudding sound that came from Robbie's room made the pen in Lisa-Marie's hand skid across her journal page. She jumped off her bed and ran out to the hallway. His door was closed. She walked over to stand close and listen. She heard a quiet sniffing sound. She opened the door and in the moonlight streaming in through the skylight she saw Robbie sitting on the bed, crying. She sat down beside him. "What's wrong? Do you feel sick again?"

Robbie turned his dark eyes to her, "I don't know. I've been sleepwalking."

Lisa-Marie stared from Robbie to the book on the floor. "Was that the noise I heard?"

"I made a trap to wake me up if I tried to get out of the room. I didn't really believe I was sleepwalking but I guess it's true."

"Ya, it is true. I've turned you around and sent you back to your bedroom a few times." Lisa-Marie drew back the quilt and said, "Come on. I'll tuck you in."

As she turned to go, Robbie said, "Leez, can you stay here until I fall asleep?" She nodded and Robbie moved over so she could stretch out on the bed beside him. When Dante jumped up and squirmed between them, she ran her hand along the dog's fur. Lisa-Marie waited patiently for the boy to fall asleep.

TWENTY

Justin sat in the living room of Izzy and Liam's cabin and waited for Lisa to make an appearance. The kitchen and the deck outside the cabin were crowded with people gathered for the book-club potluck. Robbie strolled into the room and flopped into one of the armchairs. He stared at Justin, "How come you're all dressed up?"

"Leez and I are going to *The Sea Shed* for dinner ... for her birthday." A burst of laughter came from the kitchen and Justin asked, "What about you? Are you stuck here for the book club?"

Robbie shook his head, "Liam's walking me over to the Camp to have dinner and I'm staying overnight at Tabby's. Dylan's doing make-your-own sundaes for dessert and Jeremy says he'll set up the big screen for us to watch the new *X-Men* movie."

"Sounds like fun."

Robbie picked at the threads around a rip in the knee of his jeans. "Did you see all the chickens when they were dead?"

Justin shook his head at the memory, "Ya, what was left of them. It's not something I want to remember."

"I guess not." He went silent for a moment and when he spoke again his voice was low, "The way they were all spread out in the rain and the mud, with blood and feathers everywhere. And Reg's dog all cut up."

"How did you know that?"

"I must have heard you telling Leez."

"I never told her how gruesome it was. God, that's the last thing you'd tell a girl."

Robbie stared at the ground as he said, "I never liked Reg's dogs and I don't care that one of them is dead."

"Hey, that's not fair. The dog did what Reg trained it to do. It wasn't the dog's fault."

Robbie was on the verge of tears. "Then it's Reg's own fault that his stupid dog is dead." He got up and walked away.

❦❦❦❦

Izzy moved Sophie's hand away from pulling at the neck of her dress. She tugged the silky fabric back up over the top edge of her bra as she carried the child across the deck to welcome Gordon and Nick. She smiled at Gordon and gestured towards the kitchen, "You can take the food inside. Liam's in there. He'll tell you where to put it." She looked over at Nick and asked, "Would you like a drink?"

"A beer would go down well." Nick followed her to the drinks table. He took the ice cold bottle from Izzy's hand and twisted off the cap. As he looked around the spacious cedar deck his eyes were drawn to the lake shimmering in the late afternoon sun. He admired the sleek, majestic lines of the cabin and the soft colours of the flowers that dotted the planters and pots. "Your place is really something." He reached over to touch Sophie's dark curls, "And this little one ... what might her name be?"

Sophie took one look at Nick then hid her face against Izzy's neck. "This is Sophie." At the sound of her name, Sophie snuck a quick peek at the man beside her. "You'll have to excuse me, Nick. I need to check on some things in the kitchen." She turned to wave Bethany over, "Beth, can you make sure Nick is introduced to everyone?"

Bethany took Nick on a circuit of the deck, introducing him first to Liam who had just come out of the cabin. He now held the baby whose dark head was close to his own. Nick was immediately impressed by the man's quiet voice and the air of stillness that surrounded him. He seemed like a guy who could absorb the vibes of power that emanated from Izzy, a guy who wouldn't have any ego issues in being married to such a woman.

Bethany next introduced Nick to Liam's father, Alexander, and his partner, a wonderfully vibrant woman named Cynthia whose silver hair perfectly complemented her brown eyes. As Alexander moved off, Nick chatted with Cynthia. He was fascinated to learn that she was a writer of medical mysteries and a published author. Still, his mind wandered from their conversation. He couldn't take his eyes off the beautiful Dr. Wells. She stood close to Liam and reached out to take the baby from him. She rubbed noses

164

with Sophie and laughed as the baby played with her thick braid of hair.

Robbie came out onto the deck and walked over to Alexander who pulled the boy close and leaned down to ask him something. Now Nick stared at the group of them – at their strong faces and wide smiles, and their dark, glossy hair shining like the pelts of midnight black cats basking in the sun.

Cynthia followed his gaze and excused his distraction. "They are an impressive bunch, aren't they?" All Nick could do was nod.

Bethany returned hand-in-hand with a tall, thin woman. "Nick, I would like you to meet my wife, Beulah."

Beulah reached out to give his hand a firm shake. He was still in conversation with Beulah about the bakery when Gordon joined them. "Isn't this a delightful place, Nick? I love these gatherings. I've only been coming for the last few months. For personal reasons, I didn't feel up to it, even though I had an open invitation from Izzy. Mind you, I've never read the assigned book before tonight. The others choose novels. Not my thing. I'm a military history buff. My name got drawn to choose this month's selection and I'm quite excited to hear what people think of *Paris 1919.*"

Nick kept quiet about not being able to finish the book. When he caught Beulah's eye he knew she was thinking the same thing. Gordon went on chatting, "Izzy and I have an odd sort of bond. My wife died the very same week that Izzy lost her husband, Caleb. In that first year, one of us always seemed to sense how the other was feeling. Everyone who knows her is thrilled about how she has moved on in her life with Liam and a big family." Gordon's hand gesture took in all the people on the deck, "What a bonus." He caught sight of Izzy and Bethany carrying out two large trays of hors d'oeuvres. "I better nip over and sample the snacks."

❧❧❧❧

Arianna breezed into the kitchen as Dylan and Brigit were cleaning up after dinner. She had only a couple of minutes to spare because she had promised Robbie she'd watch the movie with him and Tabby. She waved at Brigit then scooted up to sit on the counter close to Dylan who was busy scrubbing pots. He smiled over at her and said, "What's up, Ari? Every time I see you lately you've got a big smile on your face."

"Did you see me having lunch with Dr. Wells the other day?"

He nodded, "I thought you might know her from home or something."

"Ya, right. As if all of us Indians know one another. Geez, Dylan, she's from a reserve outside of Toronto." She reached over and playfully punched his arm. Then she flashed him a huge smile and lowered her voice so only he could hear her, "I am always smiling and it's because Dr. Wells is going to help me with my plans to be a doctor."

Dylan dropped the scouring pad and turned to stare at her. Matching her low tone, he said, "Since when have you wanted to be a doctor?"

"Since I was a kid but I couldn't think about it until I got accepted to UBC. It seemed so crazy that I couldn't say it out loud ... not even to you. I asked Dr. Wells to tell me if it's possible and she really encouraged me. Not like pie in the sky stuff either ... she actually scared the shit out of me when she talked about everything I'll have to do. Even knowing all that, I still want it ... more than anything. She's says if I can stick it out, she'll help me."

Dylan wiped his hands on his apron and threw his arms around Arianna, lifting her off the counter to spin her around. She clung to him and laughed as she buried her face in his neck and took a deep breath. Pathetic ... but she'd take what she could get. Lowering her down to the floor, he said, "I'm really happy for you."

Ethan had walked into the kitchen as Dylan was spinning Arianna around in his arms. When she landed on her feet, Ethan pulled her into a quick dance step across the room. "By the way, what are we celebrating ... a possible ménage a trois?" He batted his eyelashes in Dylan's direction.

Arianna broke away and gave Ethan a stern look, "Never mind. Behave yourself. Are you coming to watch the X-Men?"

Ethan fanned himself, "Does the Pope wear a funny hat? I wouldn't miss Hugh Jackman without his shirt on." Arianna flounced out of the kitchen with a big grin on her face.

Ethan slid up onto the spot Arianna had vacated on the counter and whispered, "What gives, boyfriend? That was quite the hug ... are you swinging both ways these days?"

Back at work on the pots, Dylan didn't even bother to look at Ethan, "Get your butt off that counter. We prepare food in here, you know."

Brigit had finished unloading the dishwasher. She grabbed a towel and started to dry the pots that were draining in the sink. She smiled and told Dylan, "Put that poor girl out of her misery. Anyone with eyes can tell she's crazy about you. Why don't you ask her out?"

Ethan smirked as he hopped off the counter and started to walk away, "Ya, Dylan. Why don't you ask pretty little Arianna out on a date? She's so hot."

Dylan turned and heaved the scouring pad at Ethan's head. It sprayed water across the room. "Get the hell out of this kitchen before I thump you."

Ethan jumped out of the way of the wet projectile. He stuck his lip out in an elaborate pout and hung his head as he left the room.

Brigit stared from Ethan's retreating figure to Dylan. She dropped her towel and folded her arms across her chest. "That was completely uncalled for. Don't ever talk to anyone in my kitchen like that again."

Dylan backed up from the sink. "Your kitchen? I'll tell you what, Brigit ... when I get through catering Izzy and Liam's wedding reception this weekend, I'm done. I don't need this shit anymore. I'll get a job up at the sawmill until I leave here. The kitchen will be all yours, and it's about time." He walked out and didn't look back.

❧❧❧❧

When Fiona saw Nick with two beers in hand making his way across the deck towards her, she looked around quickly. If she tried to slip away before he got to her, she'd look stupid. And why should she avoid him? She smiled and took the beer he offered.

He smiled back and said, "I come in peace and I assure you, I am not looking for a date."

"Well, I hope it isn't medical advice you want. I'm off duty." She glanced over at Alex who sat relaxed in a deck chair holding Sophie in his arms. He waved, pointed to her and Nick and gave her a thumbs up. She raised her hand close by her side and gave him the finger. She turned away and leaned against the deck railing as the sound of Alex's deep laughter carried across the space between them.

Nick leaned beside her. "Let's be friends."

"I'm not trying to be difficult." Fiona gulped at the cold beer in her hand. "I really have no time for friends. I'm coming off ten straight days of work and I'll be back at it day after tomorrow. I'm pulling eighty-hour weeks."

He met her gaze, "Everyone needs friends."

"A friend is a luxury item and right now I can barely manage the essentials like eating and sleeping."

"Since you're fresh out of medical school, I imagine you're used to long hours. What's the biggest challenge so far?"

The curiosity and interest in his voice snagged Fiona's attention and she found herself considering the question. "My first reaction is to say that the work is so disjointed ... chock-a-block, non-stop, one different thing after the other. I can be checking a sore throat one minute, stitching a cut the next, then trying to decide between heartburn or a possible heart attack right after that. I literally scramble around in my head like I'm thumbing through a whole reference library, skidding from shelf to shelf to dig out what's stored in the grey matter." She tapped her head and smiled. "Besides the long hours,

167

I'm used to a fast pace and a wide range of medical issues being thrown at me. Probably the hardest part is handling the sense of being an imposter." Nick nodded and sipped his beer as Fiona continued. "For hours, I won't think of the importance of the job I'm doing then out of the blue someone will say Dr. Wells or ask me to clarify what I'm saying and imposter syndrome will slam me like a tidal wave." She shrugged, surprised at the honest response his question had garnered.

"I had a similar experience when I started counselling clients on my own." He paused and shook his head slightly as he added, "I'm not trying to imply that saying the wrong thing to a trauma client is like failing to properly diagnose heart failure – though there are times when it might be as fatal. I'm more getting at that sense of having pulled the wool over everyone's eyes and the fear of being found lacking."

Fiona nodded, "Yes, that's it exactly." She sighed, "Then there's that startled reaction when a patient sees me walk into the room and realizes that the doctor about to conduct the examination is a First Nations woman."

Nick frowned, "Rural communities aren't known for their liberal ideas and open-minded acceptance."

"It isn't always sexism or racism. Sometimes it's just a case of never having been exposed to a possibility."

※※※※

Beulah ticked off names on her fingers, "Dylan will be pitching, Justin in the catcher's box ... Fiona, can I count on you for third base?"

Fiona pushed her plate away, totally stuffed. The food had been delicious and, thank God, it had consisted of more thoughtful contributions than the bag of tortilla chips she'd grabbed off the grocery store shelf. "I'll be there unless I get called for some type of emergency."

Beulah laughed, "I guess I'll have to accept that condition if I'm going to get a girl who was good enough to play ball at university. And having a doctor on the team has got to count for something." She returned to her list, "Where was I? Right ... Arianna on second. Josie and Reg say they'll come out for the team. That will work out well. We need a few older players who still remember how to do the Timber Wolf howl. Josie will be at shortstop and Reg in center field." She raised her eyes to the ceiling in a gesture of forbearance, "I'm less than thrilled to announce that, thanks to Arianna's blackmail, Lisa-Marie will also be on the team. I'll bury her way out in the field and hope Reg can cover her area as well as his own. I'll round out the fielders with Mike Sampson and put his brother Zach on first. But that leaves me with no one to spare. If one person doesn't show up, we'll be screwed."

Nick came over to the table from where he had been sitting in the living room chatting with Cynthia and Alex. He grabbed another piece of chicken and asked, "What's all this baseball talk?"

Beulah looked him up and down before she said, "I'm putting together a team – mixed slow-pitch. Have you ever played?"

Nick smiled, "Not for a few years but I grew up playing ball. Where do I sign on?"

Izzy listened from the kitchen as Beulah continued to hold court around the dining room table, talking non-stop about *The First Annual Caleb Jenkins Memorial Ball Tournament*. Her irritation grew in direct proportion to the number of times Caleb's name came up and the night was still young. Beulah's multiple strolls down memory lane were more than enough to get on Izzy's nerves without Liam's leaps into every lull in the conversation with a quote from Caleb's journals.

Right before she left the room she'd heard him saying, "You wouldn't believe the way Caleb kept track of baseball stats. He had lists and lists of them in his journals ... year after year."

These mystery journals were bothering her more than she thought they would. She realized that she had far too quickly brushed off the whole issue of Liam's discovery of Caleb's journals. A week ago, she had walked into the workshop and found Liam thumbing through one of them. A whole stack of the things sat near his arm. All of a sudden, it struck her that it might not be right for Liam to read any of the personal things that Caleb had written about her. On the other hand, what if Caleb hadn't mentioned her at all? She had a hard time deciding what might be worse.

That day in the workshop, Liam had stared at her with a look of naked loss on his face. "Listen to what Caleb wrote after I moved here, Iz. *My handyman is none too handy but I will have him as my friend. I'll take that as a fair return on my investment.*"

Unable to think of a single thing to say, she had walked out of the workshop to wander around the garden. Caleb was dead. They had all lost him and it had taken a lot of effort over the past four years for her to bring her life back into balance. Why couldn't Liam leave the past in the past? Life was moving on the way it was supposed to. The more she thought about it, the more morbid the whole idea of the journals became. And seriously, all this talk about Caleb was getting totally out of hand. She was marrying Liam in a few short days and the conversation over dinner had revolved completely around Caleb. It made her shiver at the way the man could make his presence felt from beyond the grave. Was he going to show up like some spectre on her wedding night? Her worst fear was that Liam would be more overjoyed to see Caleb than he would be saddened by the loss of intimacy with her on that special night in their lives.

She snapped out of her thoughts when Fiona passed her a plate. Izzy put the dish in the dishwasher as she said, "Darlene called today to say Rachel's surgery is booked for tomorrow. She's also taking her to an optometrist, a dentist and a skin specialist while they're down Island. Rachel will be staying in town with Darlene and her husband for a couple of weeks after that. I'm not sure what the actual recovery period is for the surgery but I think Darlene wants to pamper her a bit."

"Barring any complications, she'll be having a laparoscopic surgery so it shouldn't be too bad but she'll still have to take it easy for a while."

"Can we talk outside on the deck for a minute?"

Fiona nodded and followed Izzy outside. The stars glittered above their heads against a sky so black it seemed to press right down to the deck. Izzy leaned against the railing and said, "I know Robbie's over at the Camp spending the night at Tabby's but I didn't want anyone else to overhear. Liam and I are worried about him and I wondered if you might be able to give us some advice."

"What's wrong with Robbie?"

"He's been having episodes of sleepwalking for weeks now. At first he didn't remember anything about it – except that he keeps talking about being thirsty and hungry. During the most recent episode, he woke up and he was really upset. He can't recall any specific dreams. He isn't himself lately and he threw up the other day for no reason. I thought maybe he was coming down with something but the next day he was fine."

Fiona's weighed the various options. It wasn't that long ago that Robbie had lost his mother and only last summer, he'd lived through a traumatic shooting. Alex had filled her in on all the details of that. Then Rosemary's words came back to her. Rule out the physical possibilities before getting into the emotional ones. "Have you taken him to see Rosemary?"

"Maybe I should have before now. But when he didn't remember anything about the sleepwalking, I didn't want to upset him. Liam and I both hoped the problem would go away but that's not happening. Now he knows and he's setting up traps in his room so he won't get out. I think he's embarrassed and scared."

Fiona shook her head, "Poor kid. Look, I don't know much of anything about sleepwalking. He's a growing boy so it makes sense that he's hungry all the time. Kids throw up for all sorts of reasons. None of his symptoms have to point to anything serious but I certainly think you should get him in for a checkup and see what Rosemary thinks. Robbie's how old now?"

"Nine and a half."

"Old enough for hormones to be circulating. Lots of things can go haywire at puberty."

Izzy looked quickly at Fiona, "He's just a boy."

Fiona shrugged, "Kids grow up fast these days."

"I'll make him an appointment at the clinic. Thanks, Fiona. I appreciate your take on this."

"You should have told me right away. Robbie is my brother."

Izzy let Fiona's accusative tone slide. She placed a hand on her arm, "You're right. I'm sorry." Izzy smiled, "Quick change of subject. Your dress arrived today. The dark purple is going to look lovely on you. I'm glad you're going to be part of the wedding."

Izzy watched as emotions raced across Fiona's face and she wondered if she'd be successful in her efforts to charm Liam's sister. Finally, Fiona looked away and said, "I want to be part of this family." Her voice shook and Izzy thought about reaching out and embracing the young woman. But her instincts told her – not yet, it's too soon. Instead, she said, "Come on, let's go back inside."

❧❧❧❧

Justin sat across from Lisa-Marie at a small table in *The Sea Shed* restaurant thoroughly enjoying himself. He was making good on his promise to take her out for her birthday. He had been at Crater Lake for almost two months and this was the first time he'd been out on the town ... even a small town like Dearborn counted. The beer on tap was excellent and he'd been served a mouth-watering steak, smothered in fresh shrimp and scallops. The girl across the table smiled at him like no one else existed in the world. Candlelight softened the features of her heart-shaped face. She wore a tight, black dress and her hair hung loose around her shoulders. A choker of pearls lay in the hollows near her throat and glowed against her tanned skin.

Guilt slammed him like a punch in the gut. He shouldn't be looking at her that way and he shouldn't be enjoying himself quite this much. He said the first thing that came into his head. "Lauren has a pearl necklace just like that one."

Lisa-Marie's hand came up to touch the necklace. She coloured slightly as she carefully put her wine glass down and dabbed at her mouth with a napkin.

171

"Zach loves this necklace. He says it makes me look sophisticated and sexy. He wants me to wear it all the time."

Justin pushed his plate away and upped the ante by launching into the story of how he had met Lauren. He described her apartment in Vancouver, talked about her desire to become an architect and bragged about her mother's architectural firm in Ottawa.

The waitress arrived at the table asking if they wanted her to bring over the dessert trolley. They both shook their heads and Justin asked for the bill. As the waitress walked away, Lisa-Marie raised the stakes herself by saying, "It can't be easy ... being with a girl like that, right?"

Justin's eyes narrowed, "What do you mean?"

"Being with someone who's so different ... imagine the look on her face if you told her about your mom?"

He felt the colour drain from his face. Then he got angry because she had named his own fears out loud. He struck back without thinking. "That's rich coming from you. What about imagining Zach's face if you told him about your life in Kingston?"

The minute the words were out of his mouth, he knew he'd gone too far. Tears shimmered in Lisa-Marie's eyes. She got up and walked out of the restaurant. He grabbed the bill from the waitress' hand as her eyes shifted from him to Lisa-Marie's departing figure. He dropped a few bills on the table and headed for the door.

Lisa-Marie sat in the passenger side of Izzy's Highlander and stared out the window as Justin got in. Without a word, he started the vehicle. She sat equally silent as he drove along the waterfront to the deserted turnaround at the end of the road. She knew where they were headed. She'd been here a couple of times with Zach. He cut the engine. He reached out to touch her arm, "Leez, look at me. I'm sorry. I should never have thrown Kingston in your face."

She turned and slid across the seat towards him. He put his arms around her and stroked her hair. Her hand crept up along his arm as she nestled against him. He tipped her face towards him and kissed her. Her heart thumped and she returned the kiss, overwhelmed by how she was feeling. Being kissed by Justin made what she had been doing with Zach seem like child's play.

A vehicle raced down the street toward them. Bright headlights raked through the inside of the Highlander as the car turned at the end of the road. The driver honked and sped away. Justin pulled back and slammed his fist against the steering wheel. "Can you just forget this happened? Please."

Lisa-Marie stared at him for a moment. She smiled as she moved to her side of the car and adjusted her dress. "No worries ... it was just a kiss. I know you have a girlfriend." As he started the car, she reached over to fiddle with the radio. Music flooded the space between them as Justin drove back to Crater Lake.

⚜⚜⚜⚜

Nick called out across the room, "I'll walk you over to the guest cabin, Fiona." He watched her shrug and head for the door, so he rounded up a flashlight and followed her.

As they walked along the darkened trail, she said, "You must be really short on friends to be this persistent."

"Well, I am new here and Micah Camp is an isolated spot compared to Vancouver."

"Did you get on the ball team because of me?"

Nick burst out laughing. "Full of yourself, or what? I like baseball and I thought it might be a good way to meet people." He was silent for a minute as they maneuvered a dark corner in the trail. "I seriously just want to be friends."

"Hmmm ... I've heard that one before. But you've been warned, right? I can't do any more than that."

When they reached the stairs to the deck of her cabin, he leaned against the railing and asked, "Why won't you date a white guy? I'm curious."

She looked him in the eye for a moment. "Okay ... it's like this. Say you and I date for a while and we like each other. Maybe it goes a bit further and we get serious, get married and have a child. I'm a full-blood Anishinaabe, a status Indian according to Indian and Northern Affairs and that means the government of Canada is obliged to honour my treaty rights. My child with you is only half Anishinaabe because one day, way back when, I decided I would go on a date with a white guy. But my child is still a status Indian. Now because this child is half white, it's raised in two worlds. That means there's a pretty good chance my son or daughter ends up saying yes to a date with a white guy or gal. And the cycle of friendship, marriage and parenthood happens all over again. But now my grandchild is no longer a status Indian." Fiona paused to stare at Nick, "That's this country's cleaned-up version of assimilation ... No residential schools to beat the Indian out of the child, take kids away from their parents and their traditions, rob them of their heritage, their language and their dignity ... No child raids to put Indian children in white foster homes ... Just a slow and steady, generation to generation, loss of status and rights." She shrugged, "And all because I decided to date a white guy."

Nick felt stunned by her long-winded explanation. "I'm glad I only want to be friends because I just saw my whole life race past me." He reached out a hand to touch her arm, "I'm not trying to make a joke out of what you're saying. I understand you're describing a serious issue."

Fiona shrugged, "We could be friends but like I said, I don't have much free time." She stared at him for a moment, "What's your story? Why are you up here in the middle of nowhere all by your lonesome?"

"Thirty-six, divorced twice and financially strapped. I think that about covers it."

Fiona laughed, "I'm glad you're white because you don't sound like much of a catch." She stepped closer to him and he felt hard hit by the way she stared at him. Her lips were parted slightly and her eyes were large pools of liquid blackness, darker than the night that surrounded them. She put her hands on his chest and kissed him. The surge of his own passion crashed headlong into the reckless emotion that stirred in her. As quickly as she had moved towards him, she retreated.

Off balance, he asked, "Do you always kiss your friends like that?"

She shook her head, "Nope. Only the white ones I'm sure I won't ever date." She walked up the stairs and called over her shoulder, "Good night, Nick."

※ ※ ※ ※

Dear Emma:

For two whole summers I've been agonizing over what Justin felt for me. I wanted him to want me so much, but I could never figure out if he did. Well, he wants me now and I know it. If that car hadn't driven down the road when it did – he wouldn't have stopped. He wanted me that much. That kiss was like something from a movie.

Lisa-Marie stopped writing and tapped her pen back and forth between her fingers. He did stop, though didn't he? Was it because of Lauren?

He loves me. I know he does. He doesn't love Lauren. How could he love her and kiss me like that?

She read over her last words. The big problem was that Justin didn't know that what he felt for her was far stronger than anything he felt for Lauren. She wasn't entirely sure how she knew that but she did know it.

I'll keep the pressure up and eventually he won't be able to hide from the truth of things.

She slammed the journal shut at the same time as she pushed aside the thought that her plans could backfire. Not this year. This year things were going to work out.

TWENTY-ONE

Izzy called out, "Are you guys ready? I've got to get to work."

Liam came up the stairs to the kitchen, carrying Sophie and wearing the baby carrier on his back. He passed the child to Izzy, "Put her in for me, okay?" Liam raised his voice to shout up the stairs, "Come on, Robbie. Izzy's got to get going."

Robbie clattered down the stairs. "After we get Tabby, can we play for a while before we do reading?"

Liam rolled his shoulders to adjust the baby carrier on his back and glanced around the kitchen. "You'll have to. I need to clean this place up before we get started." The canister of bear spray on his belt banged against his leg. On the way out the door he grabbed a large walking stick.

As they strolled through the orchard toward the path that darkened with the overhang of evergreens, Izzy glanced at the grey sky. "The forecast calls for rain over the next few days." Liam turned briefly from his position in the front of the group to look over Robbie's head and smile at her. She raised her voice, "That doesn't concern you at all? I thought you were planning the wedding ceremony for the garden?"

"The bride shouldn't worry. All will be well."

Izzy decided that all she could do was accept the inevitable. "Okay, okay but I'm telling you right now, a yellow raincoat will not go well with my dress."

After Liam, Sophie and Robbie had walked Izzy to her office door, they stopped at the kitchen to collect Tabby. As they went out of the Camp's main building, Tabby asked, "Liam, can I get Mr. Jangles and bring him to your place? I'll keep him in the carrier all the way there."

"No ... don't bring Mr. Jangles." Robbie's voice was sharp.

Tabby's bottom lip came out, "I thought you liked him."

The boy shrugged, "I don't want him at my house."

Liam watched the play of emotion on his brother's face – an odd mixture of stubbornness and something else ... fear, maybe. He patted Tabby on the arm, "Probably not a good idea, even with the carrier."

They headed along the trail from the Camp and Liam heard Tabby tell Robbie, "Mr. Jangles probably wouldn't want to come to your house anyway. He thinks Dante and Pearl smell."

Robbie's mood seemed to have improved because he laughed, "Maybe they do ... to a cat. It will be better without Mr. Jangles, though. We won't have to worry about him getting out, right? Do you want to build with Lego when we get to my place?"

Liam finished emptying the dishwasher. He put a load of laundry in the dryer and started the spaghetti sauce for later. Robbie and Tabby were building a space station on the kitchen table and Sophie stood in her playpen, none too happy about the confinement. Liam didn't want her playing underfoot or crawling around the room where she could pick up one of the small building blocks and choke on it. Robbie and Tabby were doing a good job of distracting the child.

As he chopped vegetables, Liam tuned his wandering thoughts to the children's voices. He heard Robbie say, "Okay, Sophie, we'll tell you a story. Once upon a time there was a baby named Sophie who hated to be in her playpen."

Tabby started to laugh, "And that baby decided to turn herself into a big, old, black raven and fly right out of that playpen."

Robbie flew his spaceship toward Sophie. "But something went wrong with her spell and instead of turning into a raven she accidently turned herself into a very teeny-tiny frog that went ribbit, ribbit." He leaned over her playpen to make the noises.

Liam shook his head as the story carried on to more and more ridiculous heights and Sophie's gaze went back and forth between the two older children as if they were relating information vital to her future. He was browning the hamburger when a thought came to him that was so inspired he dropped the flipper and hooted out loud.

Robbie, Tabby and Sophie all looked over at him. Liam smiled at them, "I just had a good idea for the wedding." Robbie reacted like nothing could be more boring and the kids went back to playing with Lego and entertaining Sophie. Tabby wove into their story a theme that included a cat wearing a flower girl dress.

Liam had been struggling for weeks to come up with vows for the wedding ceremony. He wanted to write something that would ring true for each of them – something that would honour their past and express what it meant for them to be together. He had made several attempts and had scrapped all of them. Everything he wrote sounded maudlin, superficial or way too personal. But if he were to write an allegory – a once upon a time fairy tale – he might be able to speak the deeper realities. After all, a story is a powerful thing. He could see that now. Though Sophie couldn't understand much of what Tabby and Robbie were saying, she was entertained by her storytellers and wanted more.

❧❧❧❧

Dylan skewered cubes of frozen cake, swirled them in a bowl of icing and gently set them on a drying rack. He was into his fourth shade and the racks of petit fours decorated the kitchen counter like brightly painted children's blocks. Concentrating on the job at hand, Dylan ignored Ethan who had slipped into the kitchen and slid up onto the counter nearby. He had more important things on his mind than Ethan's bullshit antics.

He and Brigit had been walking wide circles around each other all day. She was leaving the wedding arrangements to him and he was supposed to be leaving the preparation of the Camp's meals to her. He seriously regretted his words about quitting his job in the kitchen but had no idea how to admit that to Brigit without suggesting that she wasn't ready to run the kitchen on her own. He knew she was going to town in the afternoon. He worried that she would leave without doing a dry run on the béarnaise sauce. That wasn't a good idea since she'd obviously never done one before. A sauce like that could be tricky but he hadn't been able to think of a way to tell her that.

Dylan watched as Brigit stood on her tiptoes and stretched for the corn starch high on the shelf next to him. He stepped over, reached behind her and grabbed the canister. When he turned to hand it to her, she backed away and snapped at him, "Did I ask for your help?" She pulled her apron off, threw it on the counter and headed out of the kitchen.

Dylan turned suddenly on Ethan. "What are you doing in here, anyway?"

"I like the view." Ethan batted his eyes and smiled.

"Knock it off and get your butt off that counter. I've told you before –"

"You prepare food in here. I've got that figured out ... this is a kitchen." Jumping down from the counter, Ethan said, "Someone's in a pissy mood. What's the problem? Is your nonexistent love life getting you down?" Ethan skirted around the back of Dylan and tried to dip his finger in the bowl of

178

icing. Seeing the look on Dylan's face, he said, "I know, I know ... back off or you'll thump me." He leaned against the counter and asked, "Seriously, though ... what's up with you and Brigit? A guy could gag on the bad energy between the two of you."

Dylan pointed in the direction Brigit had gone, "She pissed me off so much the other day that I told her I'm going to quit and get a job up at the sawmill for the rest of the summer."

"Say it isn't so. I don't think I can handle that kind of excitement." Ethan fanned himself dramatically.

"Only thing is, if I do that, she's going to lose her job. Why doesn't she let me help her?"

"You really don't know what's up with her?"

"Why do you say it like that? How would I know? I'm not a fucking mind reader."

Ethan shook his head as he raised his eyes to the ceiling, "You intimidate her. You're too good at what you do in here. She's a woman who likes to be on top and I'm not talking about in the sack ... though that could be true, too." Ethan's face wore a thoughtful expression before he went on, "She isn't the type who likes to admit she needs help."

"I don't know why I tell you anything." Dylan shook his head in disgust, "You're an idiot. If anyone is intimidating it's Brigit. She used to be a cop. It's worth her while to let me help her because I know what I'm doing in the kitchen and she can learn from me."

Ethan shrugged, "Well, I don't care if she can arrest a whole biker gang and whip their collective asses. She's intimidated ... and being a cop is not exactly a qualification for cooking." Ethan pushed away from the counter, "Tell her which way you lean and see how fast she gets on side with you. She's a person who loves to be on the side of the underdog. Look how she stuck up for me." With complete confidence in his take on things, Ethan strolled out of the kitchen.

Dylan finished the icing and left the racks of delicate, coloured cake cubes to set. He was looking forward to the decorating. He considered getting out the ingredients to begin the first sheet of cheese cake squares - he'd start with the strawberry swirl. Then he decided he had time to make the béarnaise sauce himself and stave off any problems Brigit might have later.

As Dylan moved the sauce to a back burner for cooling, Robbie and Tabby came into the kitchen with a huge pad of paper and a bucket of felt pens. They eyed the petit fours like they had walked into heaven. "Don't even think about it," Dylan warned.

179

Robbie gave Tabby a nudge. She stepped forward to smile at Dylan as she said, "Just one each, please."

He frowned then gave into her smiling, pleading face. "Okay, one ... but only touch the one you want."

"Can we work in here on the big table? We're drawing the solar system." Robbie was already setting up on the table.

When Brigit made an appearance back in the kitchen, she took one look at the pot on the stove and said, "I better not look in that pot and see the béarnaise sauce."

Dylan narrowed his eyes, "Well, I guess you shouldn't look, then."

She glared at him, "We had an agreement about how to handle the cooking today."

"I'm trying to help out here ... okay? You don't need to snap my head off."

Brigit turned to Tabby, "Come on, it's time to get ready to go to town. Jim said he would drive us and we don't want to keep him waiting." Her tone got sharp, "And I have to get back before someone steals my whole dinner right out from under me."

Tabby raised her head from colouring dark yellow rings around a planet, "I don't want to go. Can't I stay here with Robbie?"

"We already talked about this. How am I supposed to get you runners and a bathing suit if you aren't there?"

"But Mom –"

Brigit gave her daughter a stern look, "Now."

Robbie nudged Tabby in the arm, "The other day when Izzy was shopping at Fields, she got Sophie a pink Minnie Mouse bathing suit with ruffles on the bum. Don't get one like that."

Tabby made a face by sticking her tongue out, "Of course not. That's for babies." She turned to her mom, "Can I get Spiderman runners like Robbie's?"

"You can get whatever fits you." Brigit looked over at Dylan, "I will be back in less than two hours. Do not do anything else for the dinner preparation."

After Tabby and Brigit had left the kitchen, Robbie kept working on the solar system poster. He glanced at Dylan a few times. Finally he said, "Don't be mad. She's scared of you."

Dylan dropped the whisk in his hand. It skittered off the counter and splattered cheese cake on the floor. He was shocked to have Ethan's pronouncement echoed in Robbie's words so he checked to make sure he'd heard right, "Tabby's mom?" Robbie nodded.

Dylan picked up the whisk and rinsed it off. He walked over to the table, pulled up a chair and sat down. "Why do you think that Tabby's mom is scared of me?"

"Her light, it's all spiky and shaky." Robbie kept colouring, "I see light around people. It tells me things."

Dylan tried to decide if the boy in front of him was a snoop who had overheard his conversation with Ethan, a kid with an over-active imagination or someone with serious problems. Robbie looked at him and said, "You used to be scared of me. Every time I came into the kitchen, I saw that light. You were mean to me, just like Tabby's mom is mean to you sometimes." Robbie tipped his head to the side and studied Dylan, "Why did you stop?"

Dylan sat back in his chair feeling more than a bit stunned. "Did Izzy tell you I was scared of you?"

Robbie returned to his colouring, "Nope. Izzy never talks about kids at the Camp. Once I asked her about Willow because looking at that girl made my stomach hurt but she said she couldn't talk about any of you guys. It was the light, like I told you."

He believed what Robbie said about Izzy; he knew he could trust her. He shivered at the thought of Robbie knowing there was something off about Willow. And the kid certainly had him pegged. His question deserved an answer. "I stopped because Izzy helped me see that it wasn't you I was scared of ... I was scared of myself and she showed me I didn't need to be. I'm sorry I was mean to you because of that."

Robbie shrugged off the apology. "Maybe Izzy could help Tabby's mom. Do you think I should ask her?"

Dylan shook his head, "Better not. Sometimes it's not a good idea to poke your nose into other people's business. Let me see if I can do something to work out the kitchen problems before we bring in the big boss."

❧❧❧❧

Wynter sat on a chair on the stage of the Dearborn Community Hall surrounded by eight girls whose voices echoed around the empty building. They all had strong opinions on what they didn't want the beauty pageant to be. Most of their thoughts had to do with not allowing their show to be run by a bunch of old women who didn't have a clue.

Wynter got up and clapped her hands. When everyone stared at her, she said, "Okay, I get that you don't want to do anything that would make your moms happy. Fine. What you need to tell me is what you'd like to do instead."

Fifteen more minutes were wasted as the girls chatted, laughed and bickered back and forth. Wynter grabbed a notebook out of her bag. She pulled out eight blank pages and passed them around. "Rip that page into four pieces and write one idea on each piece." She looked sternly at the girls, "Move apart ... there's lots of room. And no talking until everyone is finished." The stage grew quiet as the girls hunched over the papers, some thinking, others scribbling rapidly.

Wynter wandered over to an old desk at the back of the stage. She opened the top drawer and found a package of stick pins. Perfect. She pulled the thick and dusty purple curtain across part of the stage and told the girls to pin their ideas up on the curtain. When all the slips of paper were in view, she set them the task of eliminating any duplications and grouping similar ideas together. By the time they finished, they had four categories with about five slips per category. They then voted on the best idea from each category. All the other slips were set aside and the four chosen ideas were now displayed.

The girls were hopping off their seats with excitement. Shouts of *yes, right on, exactly,* rang out. Hannah got up, grabbed a chunk of paper and hastily wrote out some words that she pinned at the top – a title and a pledge. The girls all started high-fiving each other and dancing around the stage. Hannah ran over to Wynter and hugged her. "It's perfect ... exactly what we want. Thanks for helping us figure it out."

Wynter smiled at the girls' enthusiasm despite her worries about the ideas displayed on the curtain. The girl's grabbed their bags and began heading out. Wynter was halfway across the hall, chatting to Hannah, when she saw Mike push open the main entrance door and walk into the hall. Her heart thumped and she felt suddenly overwarm. She resisted the urge to fan herself.

Hannah spotted Mike and called out, "Right on time, big brother," as she walked towards him. Wynter followed a few steps behind, feeling as though she were being pulled forward by a force outside herself. She tried not to stare but she got various impressions as she approached him. Taller than her, he was slim but not skinny and he had dark hair that brushed against his collar. His shoulders looked broad under the shirt that was rolled up at the sleeves and tucked into a pair of dark jeans.

Hannah shoved her brother in the arm, "What are you all dressed up for? Are you going somewhere?"

Wynter looked away. He probably had a date. He would drop off his little sister then go out on a date ... with someone else.

Mike cleared his throat and looked like he wanted to say something. Then he seemed to change his mind because his mouth closed firmly. He cleared his throat and tried the whole routine again with much the same result. Hannah frowned, "What the hell's wrong with you? Let's go." When Mike didn't move, Hannah stared from him to Wynter. She stepped back and grinned suddenly. "Do you have a ride back out to the Camp, Wynter? Mike could take you if you don't." Twin waves of colour banked up both Wynter and Mike's faces.

At that moment, Lisa-Marie came up the stairs of the community hall. If Wynter could have twitched her nose and made the other girl vanish into thin air, she would have. But Lisa-Marie was already calling out, "Ready to go, Wynter?"

Mike turned and walked away, saying over his shoulder, "Come on, Hannah. I don't have all night."

Lisa-Marie passed Mike and Hannah at the top of the stairs. She gave Hannah a push with her hip and the girl laughed. Walking into the hall, she said, "How did it go?"

"Great ... until you showed up." Wynter's lip stuck out in a childish pout.

Lisa-Marie slipped her watch around her wrist and glanced at it, "You asked me to pick you up at eight."

"Hannah said Mike could drive me back to Crater Lake; then you walked in and now I'll never know if he would have said yes or no." She stared wistfully down the now empty stairs. "He looked really cute, didn't he?" To Lisa-Marie's shrug, Wynter said, "He probably had a date. He was probably going to say no."

"I bet you ten bucks he doesn't have a date and another ten that he got himself all spiffed up because he knew he was going to see you. Let's wait about fifteen minutes then we'll drive up to his place and say we dropped by to say hi. We can hang out with Zach and Mike will wander in and ... voila."

Wynter shook her head, "No, no, no. I can't do that."

"Chicken."

Wynter walked back up to the stage and Lisa-Marie followed her. They both stared at the slips of paper on the curtain. Lisa-Marie mouthed the word – *WOW.*

"I know. This is sure to give Mrs. Sampson and the other women on the planning committee heart failure. What guy would ever ask out a girl who was the cause of his mother's heart stopping?"

The title proclaimed, *Show them the meaning of GIRL POWER.* Wynter unpinned each slip and stared at the words before tucking them in her notebook. *Lots of dancing – preferably hip-hop numbers. Costumes – they have to be sexy. Turn their ideas upside down. No winners and no losers.*

❧❧❧❧

Robbie tossed restlessly in his bed. In his dream, he followed the cat. They ranged along a path near a jutting overhang that led down to a stretch of beach not far below. It had been a long night of hunting with nothing to show for the effort.

Dawn's light greyed the sky and the rain fell in a steady sheet. Robbie wiped the drops from his face. The cougar's head came up suddenly. A scraping, scrambling sound carried clearly on the morning air. The cat moved with stealth as it picked its way down the slope. A few silent steps took the animal into the shadow of a large, beached log. There they crouched on the rocks of the beach, virtually invisible, downwind from a mother bear and two cubs. The mother wandered ahead, reaching up the overgrown cliff side to gorge on the ripe salmonberries that grew amidst the salal. One of the cubs lagged back, rolling on the beach to overturn a small log and dig through the debris beneath.

Focussed only on the cub, the cougar stayed hidden and edged slowly and silently along the length of log. When the cat was close enough to pounce, Robbie whispered – *now* – his voice rang loud in his own ears. At that exact moment, the mother bear dropped down on all fours and spun around. The cougar sprang, sinking its teeth deeply into the cub's neck. The mother bear moved faster than Robbie had ever imagined an animal of that size could move. A frantic moment of indecision motivated by hunger kept the cougar crouched over the dead cub for too long. Realizing its own danger, the cat dropped the cub and spun around, making a leap for the brush-covered slope.

The snarling mother bear closed in and swiped at the cougar, slashing into its moving haunch. The blow caught the cat in mid-leap, heading for the cliff. The swiping force spun the cougar around in a complete circle so that it landed on the beach meters away and stumbled over the rocks. Back on its feet, without thought for the wound it had received, the cat leapt for the trunk of a tree growing at an angle out of the slope.

The mother bear skidded to a halt as the cougar gained the safety of the tree. She turned back to the small heap of fur abandoned on the beach. She prodded her cub, sniffing and licking at the body. Her deep-set eyes returned constantly to the tree where the cougar clung onto a branch that hung over the beach. The bear pawed at the rocks, rolled her large head dripping with rain and growled. She snarled as she started toward the tree only to turn back to check on her last remaining offspring and re-examine the dead cub. Her other cub stood like a statue on the beach, staring as if mesmerized by the sight of a once lively sibling so quiet and still.

Finally, the mother bear gave the dead cub one last shove with her large snout and ambled quickly down the beach keeping what she had left of her family close to her side.

Robbie had teetered alongside the cougar out on the branch as the rain fell steadily down on them. Together they watched and waited. When the mother bear finally disappeared around a rock outcropping, Robbie felt the ripping pain of the cougar's wound as the cat crept down out of the tree and slunk low along the beach to retrieve its kill.

Robbie woke up suddenly. He was in bed. The early morning light leaked through the skylight over his head and the sound of the rain beat steadily on the roof. He looked over quickly to check for the book on the ledge above the door. It was in place. He hadn't been sleepwalking. He curled into a ball and tried to remember what he had been dreaming about. Threads swirled back and forth but he couldn't catch one of them. His feelings were all mixed up – he was sad and scared.

He could hear movement down in the kitchen. He got out of bed and staggered with a sudden, burning pain in his hip. He rubbed it and stumbled around his room trying to walk off what he imagined must be a cramp. He frowned. It was Friday and tomorrow was Izzy and Liam's wedding. He would have to get all dressed up in that stupid suit. He headed for the door. At least his suit wasn't as bad as the lacy dress Tabby had to wear and he'd already made up his mind that no one was coming near his hair.

TWENTY-TWO

I zzy sat in the glider rocker in the corner of the large kitchen and listened to the sound of the rain beating down on the roof above. Rain this time in July wasn't all that unusual, but still ... what was she to think when the sky darkened to multiple shades of grey on the eve of her wedding? It was a good thing she wasn't the superstitious type.

Liam came into the kitchen with his wedding planner notebook in hand. The coloured tabs were looking the worse for wear and the cover was ripped but the book seemed to have held him in good stead. He sat down in the matching rocker across from her. "It's time to let you in on a few scheduling details, Iz."

She smiled, "You were certainly burning the midnight oil last night. Last minute planning?" To Liam's grin she said, "I suppose it's now or never."

"The inclement weather situation has altered the garden ceremony plan. Both the ceremony and the reception will now take place at the Camp." Liam looked across at her with a shrug. He passed her a piece of paper. "Here's what I've put together as an itinerary for today and tomorrow." Studying his own copy, he said, "Rehearsal tonight at the Camp, seven o'clock, with snacks and a gathering afterward at our place. Dylan will deliver the food while the rehearsal is going on."

"Who's invited to this gathering?"

Liam flipped to a section of his notebook. "Only the wedding party but I told Justin he could bring Lauren." Izzy cringed at the thought of how that would sit with Lisa. Maybe she should suggest Lisa invite Zach. No – it was probably better not to get involved. She tuned back into Liam's voice. "I'll be staying over at the A-Frame tonight with Robbie. You'll have Bethany here. I

186

thought you might like to have some time with the women after we guys leave. I put some extra bottles of your favourite wine in the fridge." She smiled over at him. Liam was always considerate of other people's drinking habits even though he never touched a drop of alcohol himself.

All business now, he continued, "So ... onto the big day. The guys will be getting ready at the A-Frame – the girls, here. Dylan will bring lunch over at around twelve-thirty. Oh, he'll be walking Tabby over, too. Beulah is picking up the flowers in town then she'll drop them off here. The couple taking our wedding photos will arrive after lunch. The woman will be here with you and her husband will come over to the A-Frame. I've washed the vehicles. Dad will drive you, Sophie, Cynthia and Bethany in the Highlander. Lisa, Fiona and Tabby can go in her jeep." Liam looked up from the notebook in his hand. "That's all I've got. Am I missing anything?"

"Rings and vows?"

He grinned, "Surprises ... I'll give you a copy of the vows after the rehearsal and you'll see the rings tomorrow."

It was Izzy's turn to grin, "And how about our wedding night? Will we be spending it here with a cabin full of kids?"

Liam shook his head, "All taken care of. We'll be at the guest cabin. Dad and Cynthia are going to stay here to hold down the fort and Fiona can bunk in Robbie's room. He'll be staying over at Tabby's." Liam stared across at her for a moment before he sighed deeply and said, "I don't know how I can wait until tomorrow to see you in your wedding dress."

Izzy sat up straight and caught her breath, "Stop that. I have to go to work." She got up and gazed at Liam as he looked at her with a type of concentration that never failed to enchant her. She leaned over and stroked his face before she kissed him lightly on the lips. He got up quickly to grab her, bend her over his arm and deepen the kiss dramatically. She came up for air as he raised her back to a standing position. Hitching her breath, she said, "You are ...."

"The man you are about to marry." He chuckled and said, "You better get off to work now, the clock is ticking."

⚜⚜⚜⚜

Izzy moved across her office to embrace the tall, young woman whose spiky hair showed bright pink streaks against inky black. She stepped back and smiled warmly. "It's so good to see you, Maddy. Are you and Jesse all settled into the guest suite upstairs?"

Maddy rolled her eyes, "We sure are. Jesse couldn't believe you'd give us the best room in the place." She looked around the large, director's office, "Congratulations on moving into Roland's job. I bet the kids miss you as their counsellor, though."

Izzy shrugged and gestured to the two comfortable chairs by the window, "Some days I find myself sounding a bit like Roland and it worries me." She grinned at the young woman across from her, "Can you imagine his face if he knew Jesse was staying in the guest suite?"

Maddy grinned back, "Thanks so much for inviting us to the wedding."

"I hoped you'd be out in time to come. I wanted to see you again and Lisa is really excited you're here."

"All the letters you sent to me while I was in treatment meant a lot." Maddy made a sweeping movement of her artist's hands and the scars on her wrists were a visible, silvery white in the afternoon light. "Other people got letters from home and I knew there would be nothing like that for me but whenever they handed me something from you, I knew someone out in the world cared about me. Hearing everyday things like what you made for dinner or the new sweater you were thinking of getting or what Sophie and Robbie were up to - made me feel part of something that was normal and cozy."

"I enjoyed writing to you and I'm glad the letters helped."

A quick drop of moisture glistened at the corner of Maddy's eyes. "I've said this before in my letters but I wanted to say it again, in person." The girl took a deep breath before going on. "Please, don't blame yourself for what happened. I ran back here last year begging you to help me but I wasn't up front with you when you tried. I deliberately misled you. What I did - trying to take my own life - I did that to myself. No one else is to blame ... certainly not you."

Izzy stared at Maddy, "I regret not understanding sooner that you needed more help than I could give you. I'm sorry for that."

"If you had referred me out right away maybe I wouldn't have gotten into the great program that I did"

"I suppose you could be right about that. We never know how things will unfold, do we?"

"Over and over in my therapy we went back to the skills I'd learned when I worked with you. I wouldn't have made the kind of progress that I did if it weren't for my counselling time here."

Izzy reached over and touched Maddy's hand, "I'm glad that you were able to draw on the progress you had already made." Changing the subject, she said, "So, catch me up on everything you've been doing since you got out."

Twenty minutes flew by and Izzy suddenly looked up when Dylan knocked on her office door. He leaned in and said, "Everything's ready for the staff meeting."

Maddy got up, "I'll get out of your hair. I'm heading over to your place to hang out with Leez and Sophie for the day. Leez is going to do some portrait shots of me."

Izzy laughed, "I'm sure she's glad to have a new victim. If you want my advice, refuse to do anything that involves being draped over the top of the piano. It's way more uncomfortable than you might think." Maddy was on her way to the door when Izzy said, "We have the rehearsal tonight and a gathering at the cabin afterwards. Why don't you and Jesse come?"

"Sure, that would be fun. See you later."

Izzy grabbed her notebook and a sheaf of papers from her desk and headed to the dining room for the staff meeting. She passed Dylan in the kitchen. "I want to thank you for all the work you're doing for the wedding. I had no idea you would also be preparing food for tonight's gathering and lunch for tomorrow."

"I'm enjoying it and what you guys are paying me makes working the extra hours well worth the effort." A buzzer sounded and Dylan turned away quickly to grab a pair of oven mitts.

The staff meeting was, as always, the regular blend of shared information, new red flags, large and small complaints and increased work assignments. All of that was mixed with the irritation, distraction, tedium and humour that Izzy had come to expect during any gathering of the entire staff. At least sitting in Roland's chair gave her the advantage of being able to move things along.

She had called for the adjournment of the meeting when Gordon stood up and asked for a moment of her time. He walked around the corner of the dining room into the kitchen and came back pulling a flat dolly with a large, oddly-shaped parcel on top. He parked it near Izzy and passed her a card. "On behalf of the staff," he smiled at her, "a small, but awfully heavy token of our appreciation on the eve of your nuptials." He leaned forward to kiss her on the cheek. Izzy looked into Gordon's eyes and an unspoken message passed between them – his pleasure at seeing how she had moved on and his own conviction that, for him, a day like this would never come.

Izzy took in the smiling faces that ringed the large dining room table. "If this is how you guys get around the *absolutely no gifts* request, I need to work on how I deliver my directives." She walked over and bent down to pull off the wrappings. A large, concrete, smiling Buddha emerged. Clapping her hands in delight, she turned to everyone, "Thank you. I know just the spot in the garden for this."

Gordon folded his hands in front of his paunch and rocked back on his heels as he said, "Many people say the only Buddha statue one should ever choose is the smiling one for of what use is it, if it doesn't make a person feel happy?"

⁓⁓⁓⁓⁓

Lisa-Marie sighed with relief as the rehearsal gathering at the cabin wound down. After doing a quick look around to make sure Justin and Lauren were elsewhere, she joined Jesse and Maddy in the living room. She had managed to make herself invisible for most of the evening – dealing with Sophie, helping Izzy and Liam serve people, hiding in the bathroom. As she sat down, she kicked herself for the thousandth time for not inviting Zach. That would have at least been a distraction from having to watch Justin fawn over Lauren.

Liam was busy ushering out everyone who was heading over to the A-Frame. Jesse called to Justin, "Come over for a few drinks with the guys. Lauren wouldn't mind staying with the girls, right?" He flashed a persuasive smile in Lauren's direction.

Lisa-Marie watched as Justin started to nod. He looked quickly down at Lauren who shook her head ever so slightly and let her lips form a sexy pout. Justin told Jesse, "I'll pass. Thanks anyway." Winding his arm tightly around Lauren's waist, he moved around the room, saying good night to everyone.

Jesse leaned close to Maddy's ear and said, loud enough for Lisa-Marie to hear, "Pussy whipped."

Maddy elbowed him, "Come on ... be fair. She's only here for two nights. Do you think she wants him to spend one of those nights drinking with the guys?" She looked quickly at Lisa-Marie, "I'm sorry, Leez, but both of you ... give Justin a break."

Jesse shrugged and grinned at Lisa-Marie, "A chick like that is not my type, for sure."

Maddy made a face at him, "Why don't you sleep in that big guest room by yourself tonight and I'll stay here with Leez. I think she could use the company."

"Ya, right. There's no way that's happening. We've got the best accommodations at the Camp and we're going to make the most of them. You saw that bathtub with the jets, right?"

Lisa-Marie nudged Maddy, "I'll be fine." She looked over at Jesse, "Come back at around midnight to get her." Lisa-Marie got up and gathered a stack of dishes to take to the kitchen as Jesse and Maddy cuddled together and kissed goodbye.

❦ ❦ ❦ ❦

Izzy grabbed her bag from where she had tossed it on the floor by the piano. She pulled out the envelope that Liam had given her at the end of the rehearsal. Things had gone off without a hitch as they walked through the wedding ceremony. Liam seemed to have things completely in hand. The gathering at the cabin afterwards had been fun, though she definitely picked up on Lisa's avoidance tactics throughout the evening and she felt for her. As much as Izzy had tried, she found herself not liking Lauren. The slightest air of snobbery surrounded Justin's girlfriend.

Izzy chased thoughts of Lauren out of her head. She was biased, plain and simple, and she was reading too much into a very short acquaintance. The all-girl party had certainly been fun. Lisa may have drunk a bit too much but she was among friends.

Leaning against the piano, Izzy tore open the envelope and drew out the two sheets of paper on which the vows were written. She started to read.

When Bethany walked past her a few minutes later, she put one hand on Izzy's arm as she asked, "Are you crying or laughing? I can't tell."

Izzy shook her head, "I'm not sure myself." She folded the papers in her hand and looked around at the group of women. "Who's staying here tonight? I've got vows to practice and a speech yet to finish. I think the party is over."

"I'm in Robbie's room," Bethany said as she headed up to the kitchen.

Fiona got up and stretched, "Alex's coming at midnight to walk me back to the guest cabin." She looked at her watch, "I should say, any minute."

Cynthia frowned, "And to drag me back to the camper."

"You can stay here and bunk with me if you like," Izzy told her.

Cynthia nudged her arm, "We can lie awake and compare father and son stories."

"No thanks." Izzy pushed back with her own arm. "I wouldn't want to read about my love life in your next book."

"Oh, by the way, speaking of your love life ...." Cynthia grinned as she said, "We girls have arranged a bit of a surprise for you. You'll find it tomorrow night over at the guest cabin." Everyone started to giggle as Alex's voice boomed from the entry way, "Whoever wants a walk home, let's get going. A man my age needs his beauty sleep."

Jesse called out, "Come on, Maddy. The guest suite awaits us."

191

TWENTY-THREE

Izzy fastened the necklace clasp and Lisa-Marie spun around wide-eyed as she touched the delicate rose coloured, gold chain dotted with glittering Swarovski crystal. Her hair was done up on her head and thick, shiny tresses cascaded down, framing her face. The photographer crouched nearby and captured a few shots of the moment then jumped up to move to another spot in the room; the camera shutter snapped over and over.

"Oh my God, Izzy ... this is so beautiful. Thank you."

Lisa-Marie turned away as Fiona held a pair of shoes up high and called out, "Leez, are these yours or mine?"

Izzy occupied the middle of the living room feeling as though she stood in the eye of a tornado. Sophie clung to the edge of her playpen looking like a dark haired angel in her frilly white dress with its delicate smocking and the wide purple sash. But Izzy had to admit that the child's angry face and her hollering voice worked against the angelic image. In a matching dress and with nothing on her feet, Tabby sat on the floor, colouring. Her hair spun around her face in a halo of loose curls. A smaller version of the necklace worn by all the other women glittered at her neck.

Bethany struggled with the zipper on Cynthia's dress. Sipping champagne, Cynthia looked over her shoulder and said, "Just yank it; I'm sure it will come up."

Bethany frowned. "Suck in your breath. I told you I should have let this dress out a smidge." The zipper flew up and both women burst out laughing.

Having sorted out their shoes, Lisa-Marie deftly wound purple ribbon through Fiona's thick, black braid while Fiona adjusted the skirt of her dress down over her hips. Lisa-Marie stood back and scrutinized the woman in front of her. "I hope I look as hot in my dress as you do in yours. Wow."

Fiona smiled, "If I'm hot, you're sizzling."

Her bridal attendants whirled around her as Izzy patiently waited for Cynthia to pin the veil in her hair. The incapacitation of wearing a wedding gown was surprisingly nice. All she could do was stand and wait. Her silver medallion necklace and matching bracelet flashed with reflected light. She glanced out to the entryway table and saw the bouquets of flowers all lined up and ready to go. Sophie's bag sat near the door, stuffed with a variety of necessary baby paraphernalia. The living room was a mess of discarded clothes, make-up bags, bottles of hair products, blow dryers, curling irons and straighteners scattered all over. She felt fortunate to be walking out of the place and not coming back to face the clean-up.

Izzy glanced at the clock. They were going to be a bit late but that would be fine. What bride worth marrying would show up on time? All she had to do was slip on her shoes and she'd be ready.

Alexander and Justin walked through the door. They both stopped when they saw Izzy. She stared at them, equally transfixed. They were extraordinarily handsome dressed in matching black tuxedos with purple vests and ties.

Alexander shook his head slowly and smiled. "I've seen some sights in my life Izzy, but in that dress, you take my breath away."

Justin glanced around the chaotic room looking for Lisa-Marie. She was leaning against the piano, knee bent, one foot behind her, slipping on her shoe when she saw him in the doorway. The naked, longing look that passed between them made Izzy swallow hard. It was going to be a long night for them.

Justin picked his way across the room to Lisa and kissed her on the cheek as he said, "You look beautiful. Liam said I should drive the jeep ... so you don't wrinkle your dress."

Alexander reached into the playpen and lifted Sophie into his arms. At the same time, Cynthia rushed over with a cool cloth to wipe the child's face. Sophie batted away Cynthia's hand and pulled Alex's tie askew.

Tabby got up and took the hand Alex held out to her. He laughed as he said, "Now that I have commandeered the two prettiest girls in the room, shall we go?" He glanced down at Tabby's bare feet and asked the women gathered around him, "Is this one supposed to go barefoot?"

❦❦❦❦

Liam stood in front of Micah Camp's massive fireplace. The centerpiece of the large room was flanked by floor to ceiling windows that drew into the high-ceilinged space the view of Crater Lake and the tree-clad slopes that lay beyond. His father stood beside him and next to Alexander, the groomsmen ranged down in a line, each one standing tall and straight.

Liam had an unimpeded view through the building to the large, wooden entry doors. He savoured the quiet moments of waiting and enjoyed the results of the busy morning setup. His plan had been to bring the garden atmosphere inside. The wedding aisle was marked by pot after pot of miniature evergreens festooned with purple and white ribbons. Squat glass vases spilled flowers over the tops of pedestals between the trees. More flowers decorated the wide mantle behind him. Miniature white lights draped down the walls and glittered in the corners. Between the flowers on the mantle stood thick, white candles casting their warm glow over the hearth.

The woman who sat at a piano to Liam's left cleared her throat and shuffled the sheets of music in front of her. A younger woman stood beside her, flute in hand. She bent to consult the pianist in a low whisper then turned to her music stand to make a quick notation.

On either side of the aisle, rows of chairs were filled with guests, gathered and waiting. A low hum of conversation and the occasional ripple of laughter filled the room. The Marriage Commissioner busied himself setting out the marriage certificate alongside a fancy plumed pen he must have brought himself for the occasion.

Liam caught sight of Maddy cutting through the dining room from the kitchen. She whispered to the Marriage Commissioner who then smiled and signalled to the pianist. Within moments the first notes of music caught everyone's attention. Whispers ceased, chairs scuffled to quiet and all eyes turned to the aisle. Liam felt his throat go dry as he swallowed. He glanced quickly at his father who reached over to squeeze his shoulder.

A collective sigh accompanied the music as the doors swung open and Sophie toddled through the entryway and down the aisle, clutching a tiny bouquet of white flowers with trailing purple ribbons. The small, patent leather shoes on her feet made a smacking noise that she obviously enjoyed causing as she walked along. In her matching dress, Tabby appeared behind Sophie, strewing flower petals from the basket in her hand. The sighs were now joined by oohs and aahs. Brigit wiped a tear from her eye as Tabby passed her, walking with more dignity than most eight-year-olds could manage. Liam glanced down the row of groomsmen and saw Robbie grinning at his friend.

When Sophie finally made her way to the front amid the snapping of photos, she did a complete turn to look back at everyone who was staring at her. Her bottom lip came out and she spun around to look down the row of men lined up in front of the fireplace. Her face broke out in a large smile. She walked over to Justin and raised her arms, making her demand obvious for all to see. He grinned and swung her up beside him, whispering to the child as she tried to get his boutonniere out of his buttonhole.

There was a subtle shift in the music and Lisa-Marie appeared, framed by the doors. As she started to move, Justin pointed and Sophie turned to watch her mother come down the aisle. When Lisa-Marie neared the front, Sophie began to squirm for Justin to put her down. She toddled over to her mother and together they took their places. After Fiona, Bethany, and Cynthia had made their way up the aisle, the music faded and a solemn, expectant quiet filled the room.

Liam's heart started to pound as the first notes of the *Wedding March* sounded. Then he saw her. Izzy stood still at the end of the aisle; the long white dress fell in rich folds of satin, lace and luminescent pearls. Her head was bent, as if her attention were caught by the huge bouquet of flowers she held at waist level. Dark hair curled around her bare shoulders. She raised her eyes and looked at Liam and he felt as though his heart would explode with love. He drank in the sight of her as each step brought her closer. She passed people and acknowledged them with a smile that could light up a room. Her eyes searched the crowd, catching a look here and a nod there.

Finally, she stood in front of Liam. He took her arm and they turned to face one another. He reached out to brush the veil aside so he could touch her face and she leaned forward and whispered, "I will get even with you someday, Liam, for these vows."

The Marriage Commissioner made his preliminary remarks, speaking about the sanctity of marriage, the necessity of commitment in a world that at times seems bent on running out of control. Liam knew the man wanted to say much more but they had been over the ceremony several times and Liam had insisted that he keep his remarks brief.

Liam nodded to Robbie and the boy stepped forward holding his hand out for Tabby to join him. The two children stood in front of Izzy and Liam, facing the guests. Robbie spoke, his young voice clear and strong, "We will now have the story of, *The Beautiful Queen and the Wise Prince.*" In unison Robbie and Tabby bowed and turned to face Izzy and Liam.

Whispers and shushing sounds fluttered through the group of guests. Expectancy hung in the air and people moved to the edge of their seats. Liam smiled at Izzy as he began.

"Once upon a time there was a beautiful Queen who ruled over a kingdom that lay along the shores of a crystal lake. The people of the kingdom were a fierce, independent group who worked hard. They were loyal to the Queen and they loved the land near the lake and the mountains. The Queen served her people well though she was not always as happy as a queen should be. She was under a spell that made many of the things she had once loved seem grey and dreary to her. She still smiled and she even laughed but sometimes her days dragged and her nights were lonely. The seasons came and went and all the people enjoyed the flowers of spring and the sunny skies of summer but the Queen found her thoughts straying more often to the dull days than to the sunny ones." As if to emphasize the atmosphere of the fairy tale, the rain dripped continually outside the large windows and the sound filled the room.

The guests glanced from one to another, some smiling, others with bemused looks on their faces. Izzy turned her gaze from Liam to the room full of people and took up the tale. "There was a man who came to live beside the crystal clear lake. He was a prince with great wisdom but he had forgotten his true nature. For many years before coming to the kingdom, he had been lost in a dark land, wandering and trying to find his way out. One day he discovered the path that led out to the light. The huge, black dragon who ruled the dark land was angry that the man had found a way to escape. As the man slipped down that path towards the light, the dragon reached out a slender, magic claw and stabbed the man's heart. This was a subtle wound and the man was not even aware he now carried this trace of dragon poison in his heart. Every day he worked hard and he grew close to the people of the kingdom. He grew to love the land and the lake."

Liam bowed his head slightly as he spoke and his voice tremored with emotion, "Time went by and the man tried to be as happy as all the other people in the kingdom but it was as if there was a wall around him that kept him from finding true happiness." He raised his glance to Izzy, "One day he woke up and realized that he had fallen in love with the Queen. He didn't know what to do because he felt sure a queen could never love an ordinary man like him." He shook his head sadly.

Izzy moved a step closer, "The Queen had a powerful gift of healing. One day she looked inside the man's heart and she saw the wound the dragon had inflicted. The Queen desired that all her people would be whole and happy.

She reached out and took the man's hands in her own." Izzy stretched out her hands and clasped Liam's.

His voice took over, "And in the moment that the Queen held the man's hands and looked into his eyes, the dragon wound was healed and the Prince knew of his wisdom and his strength." He stood taller and smiled.

Izzy's eyes looked into his as she said, "And in the moment that the Queen held the Prince's hands the spell on her own heart was broken and the sun shone through the clouds and she knew that she could love this man."

All the guests seemed to hold their breath as Liam stared into Izzy's eyes. Then Tabby and Robbie turned and proclaimed in unison, "And so the Beautiful Queen and the Wise Prince got married and they lived happily ever after, all of the days of their life." Robbie took Tabby's hand and together they did a sweeping bow. The guests broke out in loud applause.

The Marriage Commissioner took his place in front of Izzy and Liam and asked that the rings be brought forward. Alexander dug in his pocket and passed a ring to Liam while Izzy turned to give her bouquet to Cynthia. Liam reached for Izzy's hand and, as he slid the ring on her finger he said, "With this ring, I thee wed, Isabella. And may I always see you with the eyes of love I see you with today."

Izzy gazed at the exquisitely carved silver ring on her finger; the delicately etched lines of the killer whale design danced around the circle. Alexander passed her a matching ring and she slid it onto Liam's finger as she said, "With this ring, I thee wed, Liam. And may I always appreciate your wisdom and your strength."

"By the powers invested in me by the Province of British Columbia, I now pronounce you husband and wife." The Marriage Commissioner smiled and said, "You may kiss the bride."

Liam leaned forward and kissed Izzy's lips. Amid the laughing, clapping sounds of joy in the room he knew the utter truth of their vows. When he gained the love of this woman he had finally broken free of every bond that had held him down.

TWENTY-FOUR

L isa-Marie deposited Sophie in her highchair at the table where Robbie and Tabby were sitting with Brigit, Beulah and Bethany. Her aunt circled Lisa's waist with her arm, "Away you go and enjoy the evening."

Lisa-Marie headed for the space at the table where Zach sat flanked by Justin and Lauren on one side and Maddy and Jesse on the other. Zach jumped up and pulled the chair out for her. He leaned in close to kiss her cheek, "You look totally gorgeous."

She sat down and tried to avoid looking at Lauren, though it was difficult. Her rival wore a tight, low-cut, sapphire-coloured dress. A diamond pendant dipped deep into her cleavage; matching stud earrings flashed whenever she turned her head. Her thick blonde hair was drawn up the back of her neck and she looked stylish and elegant. Both Jesse and Zach were being careful to make only the politest eye contact with Lauren. Their self-imposed restraint revealed more about where they would have preferred to be looking than it did about their manners.

Trying to focus her attention on Zach who looked quite handsome in his dark suit jacket and tie, Lisa-Marie couldn't help but hear Lauren whisper to Justin, "Thank God they didn't stick you up at a head table for the whole evening." Raising her voice, Lauren looked across at Lisa-Marie, "Your daughter is a beautiful little girl." She turned back to Justin, "And she seemed smitten by you."

Justin looked uncomfortable at the unspoken question in Lauren's tone. He shrugged, "Sophie and I go way back." Lisa-Marie tried to catch his eye but he refused to look at her.

A few minutes later when Justin had headed to the bar to get a round of drinks and Lauren went in search of the washroom, Jesse leaned close to Lisa-Marie and said, "If you could have seen that chick's face when Sophie walked up to Justin and held her arms out to be picked up ... she looked like she'd sucked an entire lemon." He laughed as he sat back in his chair. Maddy frowned at him and he held his hands up in mock innocence, "I was just telling Lisa how nice she looks."

"Everyone behave and get along, okay?" Maddy's eyes went from Lisa to Jesse.

At a table near the front, Izzy was thoroughly enjoying the meal, laughing and chatting with Liam, Fiona, Alex and Cynthia. Their conversations were interrupted by many episodes of clinking spoons on glassware that prompted the bride and groom to stand up and kiss. Izzy didn't mind at all since the wine flowed freely and the people surrounding her were having a good time.

She was amazed at how fast the Camp's living room had been transformed from the wedding ceremony site to the reception venue. During the hour that she, Liam and the others had spent posing for photos, Reg had taken charge of preparing for the reception. In his able but less than subtle manner, he had directed the dismantling of the wedding aisle and the setting up of tables complete with purple cloths, white runners, floral arrangements and candles. He and his enlisted helpers had also tastefully rearranged the tree tubs and flower pedestals.

As the dinner wound down, Alexander stood up and pulled the microphone from its stand. He walked to the front and tapped on the gadget to make sure it was working. When the sensitive mike popped and crackled, Jeremy cringed in the corner where he had set up his DJ equipment. Alex said, "Time for a few speeches." He cleared his throat and waited while people turned their chairs to face him. "Weddings are special public commitments that matter in this world. Words and gestures bind us together in social contracts that create communities of strength. We're born into a family and while we honour and always respect that, we move into the world and, if we're lucky, we create new families and new connections that bring life to ourselves and others."

He smiled over at Liam, "Shakespeare wrote, in *Twelfth Night,* that, *journeys end in lovers meetings, every wise man's son doth know.* I have the great pleasure of being blessed with a wise son, indeed."

Amid the clapping and cheering, father and son maintained eye contact for a long moment before Alexander went on, "We're here to honour and celebrate the marriage of Izzy and Liam and it's my great pleasure to be standing here before you to pay tribute to the bride." He bowed to Izzy and she smiled over at him. "We all know she's beautiful," Alex paused for the applause and whistles that erupted around the room, "but I'm guessing that not everyone knows she can swear like a trooper when it suits her." Several people who had clearly witnessed this trait of Izzy's, burst out laughing. "She's a professional woman but that doesn't stop her from exchanging her designer clothes for worn coveralls and going out to dig in the garden. She can rock a baby to sleep or read a child's story with such emotion you want to be that child sitting beside her." Izzy shook her head slightly and looked down at the table as she grabbed a napkin to dab delicately at the tears in her eyes. "There is something very special about this woman Liam has fallen in love with." Alex paused to let the silence in the room build to a high level of expectation.

He walked the few steps to Izzy's chair and reached for her hand. She stood up beside him. He looked into her eyes and spoke quietly into the microphone, "Izzy has a core of strength that runs straight through her, deep down into the earth that nourishes us all. The winds of life can come and shake her but she will stand firm. She's all a man could ask for in a wife - she holds strong to her beliefs; she plants and sows; she loves children. She suffers the slings and arrows that come her way without any compulsion to pass on the pain. She offers the solace of her own tears to those around her and, somehow," Alex shook his head in wonder, "through all of that, she manages to bear with us men." He leaned forward and gently pulled Izzy toward him so their foreheads touched. After a quiet moment of communion, he whispered, "Welcome."

Izzy kissed Alex on the cheek as she said, "Thank you." Before she could sit down another chorus of glass clinking rang throughout the room. Liam stood up and drew her close, wiping at the tear that lay on her cheek and kissing her yet again.

Beulah got up from her table and made her way to the front, straightening her shoulders and doing up the button of her jacket. She took the microphone. "While Alexander is a hard act to follow in the speech department, I'm going to give it my best shot."

Laugher greeted her opening words and Reg called out, "Give 'em hell, Beulah." The laugher increased as Josie smacked Reg and told him to watch his language.

"My job on this happy occasion is to pay tribute to the groom." Beulah nodded at Liam who had turned his chair so he could face her. "A few of us here got together many years ago for another wedding. Liam stood up for the groom that day. The groom said he chose Liam as his best man because Liam was the best man he had come upon in a long time." The sudden hush in the room caught Beulah by surprise. She drew herself up straight and said, "Liam is still the best man we've come upon." A burst of applause interrupted her. "Now he takes his place beside Izzy as her husband."

Beulah paused to steady her voice. "Alexander rightly said that Izzy is strong but even the strongest woman needs someone to lean on." She looked over at Bethany and smiled before going on. "There is something about Liam that invites those around him to lean on him, confide in him and trust him. He's the rare kind of man who sits quietly and listens. Liam isn't the type of guy to tell you what you should or shouldn't be doing. He helps those around him find their own truth." She shook her head, "Believe me, you can mess up big time when you're Liam's friend and he won't walk away from you. And you won't find a better guy to have close by in an emergency." She leaned forward to take a glass from the tray that Arianna had come forward with. "Raise a glass with me ... to my friend, Liam." Everyone joined in the toast as Beulah walked over to Liam who stood up and put out his hand to shake hers. She pulled him into a hug then she leaned over to kiss Izzy on the cheek.

When Beulah had made her way back to her seat, Liam stood and reached for Izzy's hand. Silence fell over the crowd as he looked at her and said, "Please, everyone, stand with me as I present a toast to my lovely bride." He raised his glass and glanced at his father, "Not to be outdone by my dad," he turned his eyes back to Izzy, "*I love you with so much of my heart that none is left to protest.*" Izzy bit her bottom lip to hold back more tears as she raised her glass to touch Liam's.

Alexander called out, "*Much Ado about Nothing*, right?" Liam smiled while the inevitable tinkling sound of spoons tapping on glasses surrounded them. He took Izzy into his arms and kissed her while another round of claps, whistles and hoots filled the room.

Not bothering to sit down, Izzy took a sip of her wine and reached for the microphone. She looked around the room and smiled, "I admit to being a bit overwhelmed by the task of saying thank you to so many of you. And since I don't have a Shakespearean quote on the tip of my tongue," she glanced down at Liam and over to Alexander, "I'll have to rely on my own devices." She called out, "Arianna ... keep circulating that wine. I have a number of toasts to make."

She raised her glass, "First ...to our wedding party" She waited until all of them were on their feet. "So many thanks to each one of you for standing beside Liam and me and making this day so special for us." Izzy looked to the guests, "And I have to say, I don't think any couple could have asked for a better looking group. A bride can't be full of herself with beautiful women like these standing beside her." She had to pause because further words were drowned out by the sounds of clapping and whistling. When the noise died down, she said, "And you guys ... they say the suit makes the man and maybe there's something to that. All I can say is ... wow." The women outdid the guys at cheering. Izzy raised her glass, "To our wedding party."

Moving gracefully away from her table, she asked, "Robbie, Tabby and Sophie, can you stand up?" Bethany lifted Sophie from her chair. Robbie and Tabby came forward holding Sophie's hands. Izzy scrunched down to eye level with the kids, "Thank you so much for being part of our wedding." She hugged the two older children and swung Sophie up beside her. Carrying the child and walking towards the middle of the room, Izzy pointed out the musicians and raised her glass in thanks. She turned to gesture toward the kitchen, "Our wonderful chef ... Dylan Sullivan, could you come out and take a bow?" Dylan appeared, wiping his hands on his white apron. He bowed and took a glass of wine from Arianna. Izzy walked over and clinked glasses with him and everyone clapped.

Depositing Sophie with Fiona, Izzy glanced around the room, a look of wonder on her face. "Thank you to everyone at the Camp who helped with the decorating. It's really so beautiful and perfect." She pointed to the wedding cake that graced a table near the front. "Our cake decorator ... Helen Sampson." The woman rose quickly and bobbed her head before sitting back down to the murmur of voices complimenting her on the elaborate cake with its layers iced in shimmery white and decorated with trailing flowers.

Izzy pointed to the sound system in the corner, "Our DJ for the evening, Jeremy Lewis." Suddenly Izzy laughed. She looked back in triumph at Liam and Alex, "I've got one." Waving her hand at Jeremy, she said, "*If music be the food of gods, play on.*"

Jeremy did an elaborate bow and Alexander called out, "*Twelfth Night ...* it doesn't count if you steal from the same play I used."

Izzy made a face at him as she walked over to stand beside Liam. "That leaves you." She reached for his hand and he stood up beside her. "To my husband, a wise Prince beyond measure." Her eyes sparkled and a smile played around her lips. She moved closer, "Thank you for standing here beside me today; thank you for knowing when to speak and when to remain silent; thank you for sharing this journey with me. I love you, Liam." She was in his arms and they were kissing, again.

Jeremy took the mike and announced, "The wedding party will now join the bride and groom on the dance floor."

Justin felt his body stiffen as Lisa-Marie got up and held her hand out to him. He'd have had to be stone-blind to have missed the pout on Lauren's face. He got up, took Lisa's hand and walked out to the dance floor as his gut churned with frustration. The weekend had slid down the crapper at a speed he hadn't anticipated. Lauren had been fairly steady in her complaints. It was a long drive all the way from Vancouver to this place in the middle of nowhere, she had told him. And what had she said about his cabin? It was a bit rustic for her taste and the bed wasn't really all that comfortable either. She hadn't thought they would spend all of Friday night with his friends and she did not appreciate the number of times he had stranded her today because he had things to do as a member of the wedding party. If she'd known he was going to be a groomsman, she probably wouldn't have come to visit at all.

With his girlfriend's eyes drilling a hole in his back, he resisted Lisa's attempts to melt into his arms. He held her stiffly and snapped at her, "Do you have to be such a bitch to Lauren? She doesn't know anyone and you're treating her like she's invisible."

He steered her around the dance floor, oblivious to everything but his mounting anger. Though he hadn't invited Lauren here solely to get laid, she had been too tired last night and would probably be too pissed off tonight to turn his fantasies into a shared reality. He suddenly realized that Leez was trembling. He heard her sniffle quickly a couple of times and felt a hitch in her breathing. She was crying and trying not to cry and she wasn't making a good job of it.

He looked down at her in shock and with more than a bit of panic, "Hey, don't cry. Shit, don't cry." He maneuvered her to the far side of the dance floor, keeping his back to the table where Lauren sat. He tightened his arms around Leez and stroked her back gently as he bent his head to whisper in her ear, "I'm sorry, I shouldn't have said that. It's not you. Please, don't cry."

She raised her tear-filled eyes to his. He could see Izzy staring at them over Liam's shoulder. The last thing he needed now was a scene like this. Thankfully the music ended and Lisa appeared to have pulled herself together. One minute she stood in his arms, the next she was being pulled away by Zach as the crash of music signalled the next dance.

Nick had smiled when Izzy leaned over and quickly whispered an apology for not telling him sooner that he was supposed to be Fiona's partner for the wedding waltz. He had enjoyed the dance immensely. Fiona danced the way she did everything – with an intense energy that lay just below the surface, smouldering. He had walked her back to her table and pulled up a nearby chair, "You don't mind if I join you?"

Alex slapped him on the back, "Great. I'm heading to the bar. Can I get you something?"

Nick smiled and ignored the frown that Fiona directed at Alex. "A beer, thanks."

When Alex was out of earshot, Fiona looked at Nick, "So, my friend, how are things?"

Nick sat back and folded his arms over his chest. He smiled at the woman next to him, "As your friend, I must tell you, I've thought more than a few times about the kiss you gave me the other night."

Fiona shook her head and the glittering chain around her neck caught the light. "That was probably an error of judgement on my part. You shouldn't read too much into it."

Nick couldn't help but admire the way the purple dress clung to Fiona in all the right places. "Error in judgement, hey? Or perhaps a deeply subconscious desire that rose to the surface of your awareness and I was right there, ready and willing and not a bad looking guy even if I do say so myself."

"Who is full of himself now?" Fiona drained her drink and got up. She held out her hand, "We may as well dance."

Once she knew Sophie had fallen asleep in her playpen in a darkened corner of the still busy kitchen, Lisa-Marie allowed Zach to get her a drink. The way Justin had ruined the wedding waltz and the sight of him and Lauren together were all proving too much for her to bear. She returned to the table with Zach after a particularly fast dance and let him kiss her right in front of Justin.

He grabbed Lauren's hand and said, "Let's get some air."

It felt good to make him pay for hurting her by calling her names and acting as if Lauren's bitchy behaviour was her doing. But she couldn't quiet her inner voice which actually sounded a lot like Emma telling her that by acting like this, she could get hurt way more than Justin ever would.

After Justin and Lauren had left the table, Maddy leaned close, "That was a bit obvious, don't you think? I know what you're doing and it's a not very nice."

Lisa-Marie shrugged and leaned back against Zach as she drained her drink. "Nice girls finish last, Maddy."

Maddy grabbed her arm, "Come with me to the ladies room." When they stood in front of the mirrors, Maddy fluffed her hair and locked eyes with Lisa-Marie's reflection, "I was serious out there."

Lisa-Marie looked back steadily, "So was I."

Knowing when to back off, Maddy leaned against the counter and said, "Do you like my hair like this? I think the pink really works."

As they returned to the table, the lyrics of The Police song, *Every Step You Take*, enveloped them. Maddy shimmied onto Jesse's lap and her short dress rode up her thighs. She wrapped her arms around his neck and laughed as she looked over at the others. "This is our song ... right, Jesse?" She put both her hands on his face to pull him close as she looked into his eyes and sang, "*Every step you take, every move you make, I'll be watching you.*"

Jesse held her gaze and sang along, "*Can't you see ... you belong to me.*" He kissed the girl in his arms and said, "Go right ahead and watch, Maddy. There isn't anyone else in the room for me when I know that I have you." The song ended and he scooted out from under her. "I don't know about you guys but I can't stomach any more hits from the eighties. I'm sure Jeremy must have something else up his sleeve."

Liam was passing the table just as Jesse made his comment about the choice of music and he stopped to tell them, "I researched this stuff. Seriously, these songs are the top one hundred of the most popular songs to be played at a wedding reception."

Jesse hooted with laughter as he slapped Liam on the back, "Voted for by people in their fifties, I'm betting."

Towards the end of the evening, Ethan snuck along the edge of the dark room, holding Wynter's hand. He tapped Arianna on the shoulder. She was leaning against the wall with a drink tray in her hand. She jumped and said, "What are you guys doing here?"

Ethan smiled as he grabbed a glass of wine and downed it, "Party crashers ... we've got some dance plans."

Arianna slapped his hand away as he tried to grab another glass, "You'll get in big trouble if anyone sees you here."

"Ya, right," Ethan pointed out to the partying crowd, "What's Izzy going to do? Drag me back to my cabin while she's all decked out in a wedding dress?"

"Well, maybe she won't do anything, but if Nick sees you drinking you'll be in big trouble. He can be pretty tough."

"Looks like he's got his hands full with the stunning Dr. Wells." Ethan scanned the room. He nudged Arianna with his elbow, "Who's that guy with the girl who's got those fabulous pink streaks in her hair?"

"That's Jesse. He was a resident here last year. He and Dylan roomed together."

Ethan was onto her tone in a flash. He got right up to her face and stared at her with eyes as large as saucers. She pushed him away, "Stop staring at me like that. Leave it alone and behave yourself. You're such a troublemaker."

Ethan grinned, grabbed the last glass of wine from the tray and hugged the wall heading towards the kitchen. Wynter stared out at the dance floor where Zach held Lisa-Marie in his arms. She sighed. Arianna looked at her and said, "What's your problem?"

"I wish I had a boyfriend."

Arianna shrugged and looked back towards the kitchen. "Ya, double that here."

Dylan had been going non-stop for hours. He'd finished setting out a long table of food for a midnight snack when Ethan waltzed in and leaned against the counter nearby. "I just saw Jesse." He drew the name out. "No wonder you're so cold to me. Who knew you were waiting in the closet for a man's man like him to show up?" He got closer and whispered, "Did the two of you have a thing going?"

Dylan shook his head and continued with his clean-up. "Get out of this kitchen right now, Ethan or I swear to God, I'll hit you so hard you'll be sitting on your ass up at the sawmill."

Ethan backed up with his hands in the air, "Oh man, you know that kind of rough talk gets me so hot and bothered. I have to dance."

He minced out of the kitchen and grabbed Wynter. "Come on, girl. Let's show these country bumpkins how it's done." Ethan gave Jeremy a signal as they moved past the DJ table. He then directed Wynter to the middle of the dance floor, proclaiming as he went, "Clear the floor, folks."

The opening notes of a sultry tango filled the air and people got to their feet, circling the dance floor to watch. Wynter was beautiful and sexy as she effortlessly performed the intricate steps but Ethan's passion turned all eyes towards him. He moved like a snake coiled to strike, draping Wynter over his arm and leaning close as if he would devour her. The next moment he snapped her away at arm's length as the tension built with the tempo of the music.

Arianna ran into the kitchen and grabbed Dylan's arm. "Come on, you have to see this." She pulled him to the doorway and pointed at Ethan, "I know you can't stand the guy, but oh my God, look at him dance."

Mike had arrived to pick up his parents. He walked over to the bar and asked for a Coke. He leaned back and looked out past the crowd of people standing around the dance floor. When he saw Wynter, he stared at her like he had been hypnotized. He watched her every move without even realizing he was holding his breath.

❧❧❧❧

Izzy lay across Liam's lap in the armchair of the guest cottage. She still wore her wedding gown and it billowed around her as she popped a chocolate-covered strawberry into her mouth. The newlyweds were wonderfully and completely alone, interrupted only by the sound of the rain pouring down outside. A black negligee was draped over a nearby chair. The bowl of decadent fruit, the garment and a container of speciality coffee beans for the morning were compliments of her wedding attendants.

Liam smiled down at her and asked, "What did you think of the wedding vows – would you have chosen anything like that?"

"Oh my God, no, never." Izzy licked chocolate from her fingers.

"What about the wedding waltz?"

Izzy rolled her eyes, "So sappy. Not in a million years."

Liam grinned, "What about my toast to the bride?"

"Quoting Shakespeare ... so very pretentious of you, wasn't it?"

"So you didn't like any of it?" Liam raised an eyebrow as he stared at the woman lying in his lap.

Izzy popped another strawberry into her mouth and savoured it for a moment. "I didn't say that. I wouldn't have chosen those things but they were absolutely perfect."

"That's a bit of an oxymoron." Liam pulled her closer.

"Not at all. I don't plan social events for a reason. I obviously have no idea what I would enjoy."

Liam leaned over to kiss her. He slowly pulled the sleeve of her dress down her shoulder. She stared up at him as he said, "I'll say this for you, Iz ... you may not know what you want out of a social event but you sure know how to pick a wedding dress."

TWENTY-FIVE

Brigit unlocked the side door of Micah Camp's main building and headed for the kitchen. She'd spent the night tossing and turning as she tried to figure out if she felt relief or anxiety about being left to run the kitchen on her own. She was glad she wouldn't have to hide her ineptitude from Dylan's prying eyes anymore but at the same time, she knew she wasn't ready. She had already asked herself what was the worst that could happen. First she had a vision of two dozen residents banging their trays on the tables demanding to be fed. Following on the heels of that, she imagined a worse scenario in which the same two dozen young people were screaming that the food sucked.

She rounded the corner to see the lights on in the kitchen and Dylan sitting at the table. He looked up when she came into the room and said, "I'd like to talk."

She nodded and walked over to the counter to pour a cup of coffee. It was strong, the way Dylan knew she liked it. She sat down at the table, sipped the dark brew and waited.

"I don't want to stop working in the kitchen and I'm sorry I got so rattled that I told you I'd had enough." Dylan stared into the creamy liquid in his own cup as he spoke.

Brigit felt off balance. A sudden realization hit her square between the eyes like a two-by-four getting the attention of a stubborn mule. He was a young guy with more than a trace of vulnerability in his voice. Dylan went on, "I'm going to tell you something about me that hardly anyone else knows." He looked up and before she could even think about stopping him, he said, "I'm gay."

That was about the last thing Brigit expected to hear and she sat back in her chair with a look of surprise on her face. Dylan shrugged, "I'm not ready to come out in a more public way. Besides Izzy, you're the first person I've told. Arianna knows because she really liked me and when I didn't come through for her, she guessed why. And that jackass Ethan knows because he's an irritating busybody."

Brigit scrambled to fit Dylan's confession – an admission that obviously put her in a position of power over him – into her paradigm of all men being out to get her but she couldn't find a way to make it fit. She felt like the robot on that old sci-fi show who kept saying – *that does not compute, that does not compute* – right before its circuits blew. She played for time, "Why tell me your secret?"

"Ethan thinks that if I confide in you, then maybe you'll trust me. And I need you to trust me. He says you like to be on the side of the underdog." Dylan shook his head, "Maybe the fact that I'm taking his advice will help you to understand how desperate I'm feeling right now."

Brigit's eyebrows rose high on her wide brow; then she shrugged and a slight smile tugged at the corners of her mouth. "He could be onto something about me."

Dylan eyed her steadily, "How much cooking experience do you actually have?"

"Besides what I've done here?" She made a face. "Honestly ... not much. I learned a few things growing up with my mother. She can whip up dinner for fifty without even breaking a sweat. I did part of a community college cooking course but I didn't finish. I've never had a job as a cook and I've certainly never managed three meals a day for thirty people."

"Do you want this job?"

Brigit's voice snapped with a tone more desperate that she wanted to admit, "I need this job."

"Then let me help you." Dylan put his hands flat on the table in front of him. "I can't show you stuff when you're always acting like you already know everything. Sometimes I can't even get you to see that there's a hell of a lot more going on than you realize. You just won't let me give you the benefit of my experience."

Brigit's sweeping, dark brows drew together, "Okay, but why would you want to help me when I've made your time in the kitchen difficult? Why not go and tell Izzy I've been misleading everyone."

"You're good for this place. The residents like you. You have a kid depending on you. I believe in the old saying, what comes around, goes around." He smiled at her, "Take your pick, but the answer is all of the above."

Brigit sat quietly digesting Dylan's words. Then she smacked her hands down on the table and said, "Okay, let's get to it, boss."

Dylan smiled and got up. He walked over to the fridge and said, "How about we give these guys a treat this morning and make eggs Benedict? You're on the hollandaise sauce." He pulled eggs out of the fridge and added, "For the record, there's nothing going on between me and Ethan."

Brigit grabbed a heavy saucepan from the rack, "I know that. He isn't your type. Ethan is going to reach the top with his dancing and he'll need to find a guy who can play second fiddle. I don't see you being that type of guy. You're going to need the whole spotlight for yourself, Dylan, my man."

❧❧❧❧

Mike leaned against the wall of the sawmill office and grinned at Justin, "How was the big weekend?"

Looking up from a pile of paperwork, Justin frowned, "The less said the better."

Mike raised an eyebrow. "I looked for you at the wedding when I came to pick my parents up, but I didn't see you anywhere."

"We left early." Well into the wee hours of Sunday morning, Justin had endured an endless stream of questions about his relationship with Lisa-Marie and though Lauren eventually initiated sex, he hadn't been the most engaging partner. The intensity with which she had grilled him had been less than a turn on.

"We practically had to drag that idiot brother of mine out of there. My dad threatened to make him walk home if he didn't get moving. He reamed him out all the way to Dearborn for getting Lisa drinks from the bar." Mike laughed, "It was great."

Reg walked in and pointed at Mike, "That saw's not going to be cutting those goddamned logs on its own. I better have the fuckin' wood for that special order so I can get it to the finishing guys before noon."

Mike pushed himself away from the wall, "I'm on it, relax. The stats on guys your age having a stroke when they get too worked up are sky high ... I'm just saying."

Reg let out a string of curses that had Mike doubled over with laughter as he headed out to the saw.

Ethan knocked then strolled into Wynter and Rachel's cabin. Wynter called out hello but didn't get up. She sat on the sofa staring at a YouTube video on her laptop. Rachel was curled up in a chair nearby, reading a book. She rose and headed for the small fridge in the corner, asking as she went, "Do you guys want a Coke or something?"

Ethan made his eyes huge and round as he stared at Rachel. He took a step back and slapped his hand over his mouth. He tiptoed over to her and reached out a hand to fluff his fingers through her shoulder length hair. He lifted his other hand from his mouth to whisper, "Nice style and I adore the streaks." He stepped closer, "Your makeup is perfect, that light touch on the mascara and the subtle eyeliner ... gorgeous." He ran a finger over her eyebrow, "I love the wax job, well done. Who knew your brows had such perfect shape?" He stared into her eyes and asked, "Are you wearing contacts?" As she nodded he grabbed her hand and spun her around, "Oh girlfriend ... that shirt and those shorts ... they really fit. You look smoking."

Rachel ran a hand down the checked, cotton shirt to smooth it over her black shorts. She grinned, "Oh Ethan, you're a scream. What guy talks about eyebrow waxing?"

"A gay guy, sweet pea." He flopped down on the sofa beside Wynter and glanced at the screen. "What's up? I didn't know you were a hip-hop fan. Who listens to Dr. Dre anymore?"

Wynter frowned and closed the lid of her laptop. "It's this beauty pageant thing. The girls want to do three dance numbers and a grand finale and I'm not sure about the music." Wynter stretched and shook her head in frustration, "They've got these wild ideas for costumes and the messages they're trying to get across but I don't have a freaking clue how to go from their ideas to dance steps."

Ethan took the Coke Rachel passed him, "I'll help. I've choreographed a bunch of dance numbers."

Wynter's eyes went wide, "You'd do that for me?" She reached over and hugged Ethan, "Thank you." She pulled out a page of notes from a binder. "This is what they came up with at our last meeting."

Ethan scanned the page and hooted with laughter. "Ooh la la ... this is going to be so much fun. I should be thanking you."

Maddy relaxed on the swing chair out on the cliff deck, held up her empty wine glass and waited for it to be filled. She watched as Lisa-Marie glanced over her shoulder quickly before pouring the wine. "Why do you keep looking at the cabin like you stole that bottle?"

Lisa-Marie laughed, "Izzy wouldn't mind but Liam can be touchy when it comes to alcohol."

"Shouldn't they be off on a honeymoon somewhere?"

"They spent their wedding night over at the guest cabin. I guess they don't see the need for anything more." Lisa-Marie filled her own glass and sat down on the chair across from her friend. "It's not like they're our age." She sipped the wine and asked, "You guys are going back tomorrow, right?"

Maddy nodded, "We'd have gone today but Jeremy asked Jesse to help him with a few things for the Camp website." She glanced out to the lake and asked, "Has Lauren gone?"

"She left Sunday afternoon." Lisa-Marie couldn't bring herself to discuss Justin's girlfriend at any length and she hoped she would not have to answer any more questions.

As if on cue, Maddy changed the subject. "I have an idea I want to run by you. I'm guessing that you have a ton of digital photographs."

"You can say that again. I had to get an external hard drive to hold them all because my laptop was too full. Well, I also archive all the camera cards to keep the originals but ya ... I have a lot of photos."

"I wondered if you would consider partnering up with me for an idea I have. A friend of Jesse's wrote this book he wanted to publish and he asked me if I could do the art for the cover. He had a photo he'd bought for fifty bucks from someone ... to get the rights. I did some interesting computer work with that photo by combining it with some of my graphic designs. Anyway, the guy was impressed and when he asked me how much I wanted for it, I had no idea what to say. Jesse popped up with five hundred and the guy paid that amount like it was nothing. He says all kinds of people are self-publishing books. They want professional covers and they'll pay big bucks for something original." Maddy raked her free hand through her spiky hair, "I thought I might set up a small business doing book covers and whatever else comes along. If I have access to your photo archives we could split the profits. What do you think?"

Lisa-Marie smiled, "Sure, why not? The photos aren't doing me any good sitting on a hard drive." She raised her glass, "Let's drink to a successful union of my photographic skill and your artistic eye."

Maddy leaned forward to clink her glass with Lisa-Marie's, "Salut."

Justin and Jesse came along the path toward the cliff deck from the direction of Justin's cabin. They each had a beer in hand. Justin was also carrying his guitar and the rest of a six-pack of beer bounced against Jesse's leg.

Jesse sat down beside Maddy on the swing chair and casually dropped an arm around her. She cuddled up to him while Justin made himself comfortable in the chair across from Lisa-Marie. As the four of them laughed and chatted, Lisa-Marie could almost make herself believe that none of the tension of the weekend – Justin's nasty words, her tears, Lauren and Zach – existed at all. It was her and Justin, Maddy and Jesse – two couples enjoying a visit together.

Maddy grabbed the bottle to pour herself some more wine, "Play us a tune, Justin."

He picked up the guitar and soon music drifted out over the water. Lisa-Marie had a hard time not staring at him. He seemed relaxed as he strummed the guitar and sang one song after the other. When he started in on Neil Young, Lisa-Marie leaned forward with a frown on her face and said, "You don't do *Cinnamon Girl* do you?"

Justin shook his head, "I never liked that song."

He ended an eclectic medley of tunes with, *Four Strong Winds* and Maddy leaned forward to sing with him. As the last notes faded away, Lisa-Marie had trouble keeping the tears from her eyes.

Maddy spoke softly, "Who would have thought we'd be here like this, together, after all the crap that happened last year?"

Jesse raised his beer, "Let's drink to us ... the survivors." They all raised their drinks and the clinking sound of glasses against cans joined the quiet hooting of an owl in a distant tree. The moon slid gracefully across the water as the sky darkened.

Justin looked steadily at Maddy and asked, "How are you doing?" His voice was filled with care. The question was one Lisa-Marie had struggled to find the words to ask all weekend. She had finally given up.

Maddy took her time answering. Her eyes strayed out to the wavering path the moon cut across the rippled water. The only sound was the creak of the chair she shared with Jesse, as it swung gently back and forth. Finally, she glanced at Justin and said, "I never thanked you for what you did that night. I know if it hadn't have been for you, I wouldn't be here."

Justin reached over and touched her hand as he shrugged off her thanks. Maddy smiled, "I'm much better. The treatment program was more intense than Micah Camp but it was what I needed. I'm on some anti-anxiety meds. It took me a while to get the dosage right, but they've really helped me. I'm picking up the pieces of my life. I've got a place in Vancouver and I'm back at school. I'm drawing again. I see a really great counsellor a few times a week. I've still got a long way to go but I feel like I'm on the right path."

Lisa-Marie cleared her throat as she saw how Jesse had his arm protectively around Maddy's shoulders. "Are you guys a couple now?"

Maddy burst out laughing. "Oh God, Leez, how many times did you ask me that last summer? You're hilarious." She shook her head, "I've only been out of treatment for a month. I'm not ready to be in a relationship." She paused before she said, "But me and Jess –" her words ran out as she reached up to stroke his face.

Jesse leaned over and kissed Maddy softly on the lips. He looked from Lisa to Justin, "I can't get this girl out of my head. What can I say?"

He then launched into a monologue description of how successful he had been over the last year, how he travelled back and forth between San Francisco and Vancouver, how fancy his car was and how expensive his suits. Lisa-Marie caught Justin staring at her and felt her heart thump. He smiled and she knew they were both thinking the same thing. Jesse was as full of himself as ever. Some things never change.

※◦※◦※◦※

Robbie was frantic in his dream as he ran through the bush. The cougar was calling to him. He needed to find the animal. Branches scratched at his face; he tripped and fell. He struggled to push his way through the thick underbrush. He crawled around a fallen log to the hollowed-out backside. Deep in the space he sensed the cat. He slithered on his stomach to get closer. The cat turned its eyes to his. He felt the pain that coursed through the animal's body and overrode the steady drum of hunger.

Robbie reached out and rubbed behind the cougar's ear. The animal relaxed for a moment as contentment replaced pain. Reaching his thoughts along the length of the cat's body, Robbie felt the jagged wound on the animal's haunch. He could see the dark track of the infection that moved relentlessly through the cat's body. He whimpered with the pain. He lay with the cougar for hours trying to convince the animal that it had to get up and hunt. When the cat finally rose to its feet, the pain that shot through its hind quarters let Robbie understand fully why the animal had resisted.

The cougar's slow and crippled efforts yielded a number of voles caught scurrying out in the moonlight and a small, dead fawn that had got its leg caught within a tangle of tree roots near the stream. It wasn't much but it was what could be had with a minimal amount of movement.

214

Robbie woke up when his hand touched his door knob. It was as if his body remembered the smack on the nose from the book above his head and refused to risk another encounter. Confused, he stood by the door and rubbed at the pain in his hip until the sight of his bed lured him back under the warm covers.

TWENTY-SIX

L iam glanced over to the playpen that sat in the corner of the workshop. Sophie was fast asleep. He had no idea what he and Izzy would do when Sophie outgrew all the playpens they had collected. The devices sure made life easier. If he brought Sophie out here before her nap time, plopped her into the playpen with her bunny, gave her a bottle and put on some background music, she was sure to be asleep in no time.

He turned back to the work bench and flipped the pages of the journal in front of him. He had already worked his way through the pile of exercise books at his elbow. In them, he'd found tips on growing tomatoes in the Pacific Northwest, an interesting article on pruning apple trees, an address for a place that did soil sample tests, and even some instructions on how to roast a whole pig on a spit. Scattered throughout the pages were bits of information including World Series statistics, baseball line-ups, gift ideas for various people, and random names and phone numbers. Caleb had also jotted down meaningful quotes from various sources, snatches of musical lyrics, several personal reminders to write to his mother, and a list of songs he thought he might be able to convince Izzy to sing on Karaoke Night at the Legion.

One of Caleb's journals contained a remarkably accurate sketch of how the main cabin and gardens would turn out. In others there were ads for saws, a Vancouver architect's name and phone number, a drawing of a stellar jay and a picture of a surfboard snipped from a magazine and stapled to a page. Liam's eyes had widened in surprise when, at the top of a page, he'd come to a notation of his own birthday underlined a couple of times.

He read detailed accounts of cougar sightings that continued for the first ten or so years Caleb had been on the property. As the place became more

216

developed, the number of sightings decreased. The year Izzy came to live with Caleb he wrote – *not one cougar sighting anywhere close to the cabin this entire year.*

Liam waded through pages of elaborate drawings of the micro-hydro system and examined to-do lists of ongoing projects. Hidden amongst all of the mundane things of everyday life, he discovered snippets of personal writing.

A few days after meeting Beulah, Caleb had written – *this woman, Beulah, she wants to buy that rundown A-Frame next door that I got from Weedy Wendell and turn it into an organic bakery. Of all the crazy ideas! But honest to God, she makes me laugh. What's in her that wants a fight so bad?*

When Izzy moved into the main cabin – *I am to be reduced to a man forced to take sanctuary in the workshop. She lays claim to everything she sees and challenges me to object. But it's a small price to pay to have her beside me – worth everything I've built here. Go ahead, take it all woman – none of it matters. Only smile and look at me the way you do.*

There were notes that made Liam feel like he'd peered straight into the heart of the man who had meant so much to him.

America – love it or leave it. What if you left it but you still love it? This should be home now after all this time, but California is truly the Garden of Eden and I'll never get over missing it.

On another page, Caleb had written, *I asked Izzy if she could help Bethany. If I cared to pray, I would ask the good Lord to find a way to make things right for that beautiful, broken woman. But since I'm a gambling man and not a praying one, I'll put my money on Izzy. If anyone can help Bethany, she can. And if you're listening Lord, listen good – don't ever let me cross paths with the man who hurt Beth so bad because if I do, I swear I'll kill him with my bare hands.*

Deep within the pages of one of the newer books, Liam found the following words. *It's pretty certain now, after all this time, that Izzy and I won't be having a family. She says it doesn't matter and I see in her eyes that she means that. Life goes on – you play the hand you've been dealt. But in these ragged pages I will say, it does matter. I wanted to be a father.* The last words made him ponder deeply the ways fatherhood had changed him and all that Caleb had missed.

Today, his eyes lit on a passage that brought a lump to his throat. He was near the end of the last journal and he glanced at the date. Caleb had written this only a few days before he died. *I've been sitting here thinking that my life has been one of exceedingly good fortune. I have this place, friends to share it with and a woman by my side who is more than my match. She still turns my head and makes my heart thud. I couldn't ask for more. Come home soon, Izzy. I miss you more than I can say. Oh, and I have baseball – can't leave that out.*

Liam closed the journal and slipped it onto the pile with the others. He opened the desk and dropped the whole stack into the bottom drawer. He wished he could share some of Caleb's thoughts with Izzy but she'd made it clear she wasn't comfortable with the journals. He didn't blame her. Reading them had been an emotional roller coaster.

He looked out the window of the workshop and saw Robbie standing in the driveway staring off into the brush that lined the road. He got up and went to the door, "Hey, Robbie. What's up?" The boy turned slowly and wiped his hands hastily on his pants. He had a strange look on his face that made Liam take a step forward, "Are you okay?"

Robbie's expression cleared and he smiled, "Ya, sure. When Sophie wakes up can we get Tabby and go swimming?"

Liam nodded. He had an uneasy feeling about Robbie's behavior but then he heard Sophie stirring and he turned to walk back into the workshop.

❧❧❧❧

Wynter stood by a large Spruce tree out on the gravel that led to the water. One hand rested on the trunk in front of her as she flipped her long hair over her naked shoulder and stared back at Lisa-Marie. "I'm not a complainer, Leez, but this tree bark is scratching me in places I don't want to mention and I think something just slithered over my foot."

Ethan laughed as he darted forward to pull a piece of hair away from her mouth, "Hang in there, Princess."

Lisa-Marie moved back a few steps and called out, "Okay ... no smiles this time. I want something more serious. Shift a bit to the left so I get only the curve of your breast."

Wynter did as she was told but she flinched as the bark dug into her skin. After a couple of moments, her attention was caught by a sound coming from the trees that banked up the hill away from the beach. She glanced away from the camera, in the direction of the noise. Her eyes widened as three guys burst through the tree cover and jogged into the open area near the water.

"That's perfect, keep looking that way." So intent on getting the right shot, Lisa-Marie didn't notice anything until Wynter's naked body skittered around to the far side of the tree. Then she caught sight of Ethan pointing at something behind her. She turned and saw Justin gasping for breath with

Dylan and Mike close behind him. "What the hell are you doing down here?" she demanded. "This lake is ten kilometers long. You'd think we could find a deserted piece of beach."

Justin stared as Ethan grabbed a robe from a low-hanging branch, moved over to the lone tree near the water's edge and passed the garment to the girl who was huddling behind the tree. He recognized her long, wheat coloured hair as belonging to the knock-out who worked in the paper and soap shop. He saw an arm shrug into the garment but she stayed behind the large trunk. They'd obviously seen all of her they were going to. He watched Lisa-Marie as she adjusted her camera. "I think a better question is what are you guys doing here?" he asked.

"I'm working on my portrait portfolio and Wynter is getting some tasteful nudes for hers." To Justin's blank stare, Lisa-Marie huffed and said, "She's applying to all kinds of modeling agencies. No surprise, right? Look, I'm going to lose this great shadow effect around the tree if I don't hurry. Take your little troop of running boys and get out of here."

Justin grinned at her irritation and waved the other guys back up the trail. As they jogged away, she turned back to the work at hand. "Come on, Wynter. Come out from behind there and get that robe off. Ethan, pull out that rose coloured scarf and let's have that trailing over her shoulder for the next few shots ... and get me the parasol. We might be able to get some interesting shadows with that."

Ethan gave her a quick salute, "On it, boss lady. You're going to owe me a whole portfolio of dance shots by the time we're done here." He began digging through the large duffle bag that lay near a log.

Back up on the logging road, the guys jogged on for another ten minutes before Justin gasped out, "I've got to take a breather."

Slowing to a walk beside Dylan, Mike asked, "Did we see what I think we saw down on the beach?"

Justin elbowed him, "Bet you wish you'd been out front." He chuckled as Mike's face reddened from more than physical exertion. He was well aware of Mike's obsession with the subject of Lisa-Marie's photo shoot.

Dylan thumped Mike on the back, "I was right behind him," he pointed at Justin, "And I didn't see anything much more than a blur of hair when Wynter ducked behind the tree."

They walked along in silence for a few moments then Mike asked, "What the hell was Ethan doing down there? Are you guys okay, hanging out with him, I mean ...."

Justin rubbed at a stitch in his side, "Because he's gay?"

219

"Ya, I suppose that's what I mean." Mike looked uncomfortable.

"Haven't you ever hung around with anyone who's gay?"

"I grew up in Dearborn. Are you serious? There aren't any gay guys in Dearborn."

Justin barked out a sharp laugh, "I doubt that. There are gay guys everywhere, Mike. Come on ... you sound like some sort of redneck."

Mike looked miserable as he glanced from Dylan back to Justin. "I know I do. Why do you think I'm practically whispering even though there's no one out here but us?"

Dylan pulled out his water bottle and took a drink. "At least that's what we thought ten minutes ago when we explored that deserted path."

Mike did a three-sixty just to be sure and turned back to Justin. "If my mom or dad heard me asking you a question like that they'd smack me. Last year I asked my dad if he thought it was strange hanging around with Beulah. He swore at me ... he actually used the f-word ... called me a fucking moron to ask a question like that. But shit, two girls together is sort of hot. Two guys ... that picture makes me want to puke."

Still short of breath, Justin stopped and leaned forward to rest his hands on his knees. He looked up at Mike, "You are further gone than I thought if you have to fantasize about Beulah and Bethany."

Dylan let out a loud hoot of laugher as Mike turned even redder and started to sputter, "You know I didn't mean them."

Justin gave him a serious look, "Ya ... I guess you meant the kind of crap you can see on the internet. Relax, man. I've hung out with a lot of gay guys – guys you'd never know were gay and guys like Ethan who like to play it up. Think of Ethan as a person you work with – period. What he does in his private life is no one else's business. And for frig sakes, don't get all uptight around him. One day you'll have to work close to him ... maybe on a saw, or on a piece of equipment or out in the bush. You don't want to give a guy like Ethan the idea he makes you nervous. He'll torture you. There are safety issues to consider. That's my management spiel." As Mike continued to look doubtful, Justin added, "Look ... even assuming Ethan was hot for you – and I seriously doubt he is – he's not going to try and grope you in a tight spot any more than you would push yourself on a girl who wasn't interested in you. Your straightness is safe."

Mike shrugged in embarrassment, "Okay, okay ... when you say it like that I get how stupid I sound. But I'll tell you one thing. Given the chance, I might trade in being straight if I could get as close to Wynter as Ethan did for that Tango number they did at Izzy and Liam's wedding. It looked like he was making out with her right on the dance floor. Man, oh man, what a waste. And now he's down there with her and she's got her clothes off."

Justin started to jog again and called back to Mike, "By the way, that part about what we do in private being no one else's business doesn't count if you ever have a date with Wynter. You're going to have to spill the beans on that one, man."

Mike shook his head, "Never going to happen, not in this life, so I'm safe to make that promise." They all started running again.

Dylan jogged along beside Justin while Mike took point. His stomach churned. Justin and Mike were good guys and he didn't hold anything against Mike for feeling uncomfortable around Ethan. At least the guy was honest and upfront about it, and that went a long way. Dylan realized that there was a chance he could be friends with both these guys even after he left Micah Camp and he felt like shit for misleading them. If they discovered that he was gay, they wouldn't appreciate the way he had lurked in on their conversation. And who could blame them? As he picked up his pace for Justin's sake, he wondered why life had to be so fucking complicated.

✻✻✻✻

Izzy came into the cabin sniffing appreciatively. "Wow, something smells good." She tossed her briefcase onto the chair in the corner and shrugged out of her sweater. She walked into the galley kitchen and peeked over Liam's shoulder as she slipped her arms around his waist. "Is that chicken?" she asked as she stared into the casserole dish. "I thought I took a roast out of the freezer last night."

Liam shoved his hands into a pair of oven mitts and grabbed the hot dish, "That's what you said but I couldn't find any roast." He gave her a stern look that was somewhat mollified by the red poppy apron he wore and the thick, insulated gloves on his hands. "You said you would make sure someone walked back with you. I didn't see you coming down the path with anyone." He moved past her to take the pan to the table.

Izzy opened the cupboard and grabbed a stack of plates, "I didn't even remember I'd said that until I was almost halfway home." She set the plates on the table as he passed her with a bowl of salad.

"You aren't taking this whole cougar thing seriously. I hope you don't live to regret that." He walked over to the stairs and called, "Dinner's ready, Robbie."

Izzy made a face, "Don't you mean you hope I do live?"

Robbie came into the room carrying Sophie. He sat the baby in her high

221

chair, looked at the table and from there over to Izzy, "You said we were having a roast. I wanted mashed potatoes and gravy."

Izzy adjusted the high chair strap around Sophie's squirming body as she said, "I'm pretty sure I took a roast out."

Liam sat down. "I didn't see any roast anywhere. What's wrong with chicken?"

Izzy walked over to the fridge, opened it and peered inside. She shut the door and moved back to the table. "I must be working too hard. I could swear I put a roast on a plate right on the second shelf of the fridge."

Liam waved a chicken leg in the air to cool it before he set it on Sophie's tray. "The plate was in the fridge but there was no roast on it. Your memory isn't what it should be, is it?" He gave her a stern look.

Robbie slammed a helping of the casserole onto his plate, "Are you trying to say I took it?"

Izzy's eyebrows went up in surprise as she laughed, "Good grief, why on earth would you take a raw roast?"

Robbie grabbed a bun, "It was probably Leez. She's always sneaking food for Justin."

"It was probably me thinking about it and not doing it. Where is Lisa, by the way?" Izzy asked as she dished out the salad. "I love this red lettuce. We should plant some more of it."

"She said she was going to be doing a photo shoot over at the Camp." Liam passed Sophie her sippy cup of milk and warned the child, "I've got my eye on you. Do not throw this cup." Izzy dug into the chicken casserole and laughed at the defiant Lisa-like look on the baby's face.

⚜ ⚜ ⚜ ⚜

Robbie got up and scrunched his feet into his old runners. He wasn't awake and he wasn't dreaming. He was simply moving. He reached up to remove the teetering book from its place above the door; he walked out of his room, down the stairs from his loft and through the darkened cabin. When he came to the kitchen door, he reached up and slid the bolt open. He was out in the pre-dawn light and running toward the driveway. Near the workshop, he stopped to grab a covered bucket out from where it was hidden in the brush. He ripped off the lid and pulled the piece of meat from inside. He walked over to the tap that was mounted against the workshop wall. His face was slack and his eyes unfocused as he filled the bucket with water.

He walked up the driveway that led to his father and Cynthia's building site. He held the raw roast in his hands; blood dripped down his forearm while the bucket sloshed water on his leg. He moved off the path and made his way over the uneven ground, pushing aside scratchy salmonberry branches and stepping through wet patches of fern. He came to the hollowed out log and knelt down in the dirt to lay the piece of meat at the opening.

He waited as a shadow moved in the darkness. The cat crawled out into the dim light and ravaged the offering. Gleaming teeth tore and gouged at the meat that was gone in moments. Eyes glittered as the cougar raised its gaze in an obvious plea for more. Robbie moved the bucket forward and tipped it so the cat could lap at the life-giving water. He dropped down by the animal's side and put his arms around its tawny neck, rubbing the spot behind its ear and whispering, "You have to get up and hunt." The animal moaned low in its throat. Robbie felt a sickness beyond hunger growing in the cat's body. It was a burning, pounding heat that reached deep fingers of hot pain through the animal's haunch. Tears fell unchecked down the boy's face. He burrowed closer to the animal, "Don't die ... please don't die."

Hours later and back in his bed, Robbie woke up and squirmed for a moment on the damp sheet before jumping up. He stared at his hands. They were covered in something dry and dark mixed with dirt that went deep into the creases of his skin. He wrinkled his nose at the strange smell in the room. It seemed to be coming from him. His pajama pants were damp and the knees were covered in dirt. He looked back at the bed. The sheets were a mess of dark streaks. Leaning over to pick up what looked like a squished salmonberry, his heart pounded and his mind went blank. He quickly pulled off his pajamas and put on some clothes. He stripped the sheets from the bed, wrapped his pajamas inside the ball of soiled fabric and headed straight for the laundry hamper and the shower.

TWENTY-SEVEN

Ethan cut the sound on the music. When he had the attention of all eight girls on the stage of the Community Hall, he struck a pose with his hands on his hips. "I don't know where you ladies learned to dance but we really have our work cut out for us." He looked at his watch, "Take five and when you come back I'll show you what I have in mind for the finale."

Chatter and laughter filled the stage as the girls rushed for water bottles and collapsed against the wall. Hannah mopped her face and grinned at Wynter, "We love Ethan. He's the best."

Wynter smiled and walked over to where Ethan fiddled with his laptop. "Geez, you really know how to get them to work. I thought they might mutiny but the more you insult them the better they like you."

Ethan grinned at her. "It's all in the tone." He pointed to his laptop and clicked play on a YouTube music video from the eighties. "What do you think about this number for the finale? I'll want you to come in as well as all of the girls."

Wynter's eyes widened as Boy George's face filled the screen. "I know this song. You want to dance to this in front of the whole town?"

"Why not? It's an anthem of sorts and I think it turns things upside down the way the girls want. They're going to love it; can you picture the costumes?"

His grin was infectious and Wynter caught herself smiling back. "How do you see all of us fitting in?"

"The girls will definitely be in the red can-can dresses and you'll be cross-dressing, wearing a fancy suit and stealing the girl's jewellery. It's going to be a total riot. You'll be my dancing partner – my lover onstage." He winked at her.

Wynter shook her head, "I think that's turning things way too upside down."

Ethan pouted, "You're being a prude. Let's see what the girls think."

The girls loved the idea and Wynter found herself, once again, caught up in the whirl of their planning. The whole beauty pageant had turned into a runaway train since Ethan came on the scene and there wasn't a thing she could do to slow it down. He had somehow managed to talk Maryanne, the English teacher at the Camp, into helping with the costumes and sets and, unfortunately, she was as wildly theatrical as Ethan. At their meeting that afternoon, when Wynter saw some examples of what the two of them had come up with, she was speechless. Ethan had also roped Jeremy into the planning and he had all kinds of ideas for a flashy light show and special effects. She had no idea if all the parties involved could pull everything together and she was in an agony of worry over the dress rehearsal. The girls were thrilled with all of Ethan's suggestions. Wynter could only hope Mike's mother would share those sentiments or, barring that, at least not want to murder her on the spot.

Mike continued to pick Hannah up after each practice and since he and Ethan knew each other from the sawmill, it was easy for Wynter to convince Ethan to ask Mike to give them a ride back to Micah Camp. Easy – yes – but not without the inevitable questions. Having to tell Ethan she had a crush on Mike hadn't been pleasant.

He had stared at her like she had sprouted a pair of horns, "Lord on high dressed in a G-string and heels ... are you nuts? He's B-team and that's being generous. Why are you even considering slumming with a guy like that? Don't you have a mirror, girl?"

Wynter had blushed, which made Ethan double over laughing. She told him to shut up. "I think he's cute. Come on. He's got nice eyes and I love the way his hair curls up at his collar. That's sweet, right?"

"Sweet is for puppy dogs, not guys. But if you want to waste your time on him, I'll do what I can."

While the rides out to Micah Camp appeared to be a regular riot for Hannah and Ethan, Wynter never got a moment alone with Mike. The others always encouraged her to climb into the truck first and though she was squished right up against Mike's arm, Wynter was so nervous she couldn't say a word. Mike didn't say anything to her either.

❧❧❧❧

Fiona pushed back from the small table in the corner of the Sea Shed restaurant and grinned sheepishly at the man across from her. "I should have warned you that I'm not the best company at meals." Her side of the table was littered with the remains of a late supper – a deep soup bowl that had contained clam chowder, a board covered with bread crumbs and an empty dessert plate that had earlier held a generous slice of coconut cream pie.

Nick smiled over at her from his relatively tidy side of the table and sipped a cup of tea. She had met him earlier in front of the Community College. He'd been taken aback to see her there, so she'd explained, "Rosemary asked me to sit in on one of your group sessions and here I am," she had told him.

She'd watched as Nick frowned, "This is our fourth session. The group is closed to any newcomers and the guys are starting to open up with one another. I wouldn't want anything to get in the way of that dynamic."

"What if you let me introduce myself and explain why I'm here? Then they can decide. If they have any objections, I'll leave right away." Nick had agreed. In the meeting room, she had told the guys sitting in a circle that it was important for her to face all the realities of a rural medical practice. She described the connection between men who lack anger-management skills and victims of violence who end up in emergency or in Rosemary's office. She stressed her need to understand the dynamic from their perspective and to become better informed as to what could be done to effect real change. The guys had all agreed to have her stay and she had blended into the woodwork and simply listened.

As the waitress cleared the table, Fiona sipped from a cup of steaming, black coffee and said, "Thanks for letting the guys decide if I could stay. The session was an eye-opener."

"I'm glad it was a useful experience. It's a difficult type of group to facilitate. Three of the guys are there on court order." As Fiona's eyebrows rose in curiosity, he held up his hand, "I won't say which ones but I think you'd be surprised. The group is also recommended for guys coming out of addiction treatment and a couple of them have been that route. A few saw the notice in the local paper and showed up ... so there are lots of mixed agendas and motivations for attendance. That's always a challenge. And it's a touchy thing to hold the group in balance – to leave things open enough so the guys can share but keep a tight rein on the ones who'll talk all the time and drag the discussion off topic."

"Ya, I could see the potential for problems a couple of times but you handled things well."

"It's not my first time out of the chute. I wouldn't have wanted you to sit in on the first group I worked with. I've done this several times in various settings ... prison, a military base, university, a big city. This is my first time in a small town, though."

She glanced down at her hands, wrapped around her cup, "The stats you mentioned took me by surprise. I had no idea that domestic violence could be so prevalent in what looks like an ordinary, rural community." She shrugged as she looked up at him, "I grew up on a reserve near Orillia. I witnessed enough violence there, for sure. My mom is a tribal cop, so the stories were always around. I was prepared for what I saw on the reserve out at Cedar Falls. I've lived in cities and seen lots of violence there, too. I suppose I had a warped idea about what rural life would be like in a picturesque, seaside town like Dearborn."

Nick pushed his empty tea cup aside. "I hate the term, domestic violence. When the guys can handle a bit more reality, I'm going to set them straight. Those words hide the perpetrator. We need to name things as they are ... male violence against women and children ... period. That's what we're talking about. But the whole thing is a process and you don't get the best results by moving too far, too fast."

Fiona looked out the window to the dark outline of the breakwater in the distance. "I shouldn't have been surprised about the violence. I've seen the waiting lists at the addiction center and the two seem to go hand in hand."

Nick nodded, "A lot of people would be surprised to know how much alcohol and drugs are consumed in a rural, resource-based community. Guys work hard and they party hard, too. There's stress related to the boom and bust cycles that seem to go with forestry, fishing, and mining. Lots of people aren't from around here so extended family networks are thin. That creates isolation. When people look around for a sympathetic shoulder to cry on they might not find anyone there. Then there's the ready access to firearms in rural areas. Stress, isolation, addiction and violence – none of those things mesh together well."

The waitress returned with the bill and Fiona insisted on giving the woman her credit card. "You hardly ate anything. This impromptu dinner is my treat." She glanced at Nick and asked, "Where did you grow up?"

"A cattle ranch in Alberta. I had a standard upbringing for that area ... lots of horse riding and 4-H club." He hesitated and his voice softened, "But I remember the time one of the ranchers stalked his wife all the way to BC after she left him. When he found her, he killed her and her sister for good measure."

Out in the parking lot near Liam's brand new truck, Fiona glanced at her watch, "I better get moving. I have to be on call at the hospital in Cedar Falls at midnight." Nick reached out and put his hand on her arm, a simple gesture. It could have meant one of many things. She hesitated as she looked up at him. The moment stretched out and the spark of attraction between them made her pulse quicken. She stepped away and reached for the door handle of the truck. "Thanks again for letting me sit in on the group."

He smiled, "No problem. Thanks for coming out with me afterwards. It was a nice change for me to sit down to a meal for two instead of having to eat dinner with two dozen young people. Drive safely." He waved and headed for his own car.

As she drove the dark and curving road from Dearborn to Cedar Falls, Fiona struggled with more than a few things. She'd already seen women and kids, in Rosemary's office and at the emergency room in Cedar Falls, who had fallen victim to male anger and she hadn't been particularly interested in the feelings of the men dishing out the blows. In her mind, they were guilty as charged. But nothing in life is so straightforward and she had picked up, even from the little she had heard tonight, that the guys were also victims – of their own pasts, of societal expectations and of a host of other things. Fiona already knew that violent behaviors have deep roots and the reasons behind them are complicated. Now she realized that these men would be her patients, too. She needed to open her mind to hear their stories.

Her thoughts turned to Nick as she flipped her lights to low beam and cruised by another vehicle. She could picture him growing up on a ranch and riding a horse. In the back-and-forth chit chat at the restaurant he had talked about his passion for golf and had kept her smiling with more than a few funny stories about living on-site at Micah Camp. He was easy to talk to and part of that ease came from their shared professional bond – they were both committed to helping people. She also liked that he wasn't a fellow doctor. Hanging out with too many doctors made her feel crazy. She never felt like she could get away from work.

She wished Nick were shorter, maybe balding, with a big gut and a beard. But he was actually quite attractive and she would have to keep a firm hold on her hormones or she'd end up where her mind told her she didn't want to be – naked in a bed with him beside her.

TWENTY-EIGHT

The red light on the video camera flashed and the machine whirred away in the corner on its tripod. Nick sat in his chair with his arms folded and an eyebrow raised as Ethan paced back and forth, always in line with the camera, throwing his arms out in dramatic gestures and striking elaborate poses. His voice rose as he pulled at his hair and declared, "I'm dying here, Nick, dying with heart-wrenching pain and lust for that guy and he hates me ... do you hear what I'm saying? He can't stand the sight of me." With that last line, Ethan clutched at his chest and fell back into his chair.

Nick walked to the corner of the room and shut off the camera. Ethan frowned and sat up straight, "Hey, what did you do that for? I've got lots more to say."

"Ya, I'm sure you do but I'm sick of the drama, Ethan. Today's Oscar performance is over."

"Is that any way to talk to a vulnerable, gay guy on the verge of absolute heartbreak?" Ethan's voice trembled with dramatic outrage.

"You won't get anywhere playing that card with me. When it comes to Dylan ... you're about as vulnerable as an alley cat." Nick sat down, "Come on. Get real. I'm thinking this grand passion you keep talking about goes about this deep." He held his thumb and forefinger a fraction apart.

Ethan sat back in his chair, folded his arms over his chest and smirked. "Okay, smart man ... if my issues don't stem from unrequited love ... what is my problem? That's your job isn't it? To tell me what's wrong with me."

"No way." Nick shook his head. "That's your job."

"There's nothing wrong with wanting to be in love."

"There's a lot wrong with making the object of your fake passions

229

uncomfortable and working yourself up over something you know isn't real."

Ethan rose and paced around the office, touching objects, singing snatches of songs under his breath and doing dance steps as he went. He stopped at the window and stared out at the lake. "Dylan's not really my type." He turned back to stare at Nick, "I'm not saying I wouldn't be all over him if he gave me even a hint he was interested. I suppose that's the alley cat in me. But you're right. I'm not in love with him."

"Why the game playing then?"

Ethan shrugged and walked back to his chair. He flopped down and stared at the ceiling. "Habit, I suppose. Love, passion ... it makes me feel alive. Artistic types need something to kickstart the creative juices." He glanced at Nick with an angelic smile on his face, "What if I said you were my type, Nick." He purred out the man's name.

Nick snorted with laughter, "I'd say bullshit."

Ethan looked surprised for a second then he burst out laughing, too. "You'd be right. Jock types who like golf are definitely not my thing. And you're taking the whole work casual look a bit too far. Seriously, how many different combos of golf shirts and Dockers pants do you own, anyway? Couldn't you shake it up now and then? I'm assuming you have a decent suit. And, please," Ethan drew the word out. "Don't get me started on that clean-shaven look. If I didn't know better, I'd take you for an off-duty cop."

Nick frowned down at his carefully chosen ensemble and ran a hand over his clean-shaven jaw, "Thanks for the tip, but we aren't here to discuss my wardrobe choices or facial hair." He glanced at the clock. "We've got plenty of time left in this session, let's not waste it. I want you to tell me something important about yourself that's real."

Ethan crossed his long legs and his foot tapped out some tune only he was aware of. Silence settled over the room. When the young man finally looked up, his eyes glittered but his voice was steady, "My first love was a disaster ... my dance instructor. I was fifteen and he was forty. It was a truly grand passion that twisted me around like a pretzel." He looked over at Nick and waved a hand, "It didn't turn into what you're thinking so forget about calling the cops. He tried to let me down easy with all this bullshit about our age difference and how he couldn't possibly get involved with a student. He told me to see a counsellor because he thought I might have a daddy complex."

"Did you? See a counsellor, I mean."

Ethan shook his head, "Why would I? I can't stand my father. I really don't see myself trying to replace the guy." He got up to pace again, shooting his words at Nick, "I suppose you're going to say that because of that stupid, immature crush, I'm afraid to fall for anyone – that I play games to protect myself."

"No I'm not. But I will remind you that you said you were in love ... not in the grip of a stupid, immature crush."

"Okay, okay ... it hurt, a lot and I don't want to get hurt like that again. I don't know if I could really like Dylan or not ... I don't want to get close enough to him or anyone else to find out." He sat back down, "And he's definitely not interested in me."

"Could you guys be friends?" The natural curiosity that made Nick a good listener and a good counsellor was obvious in his words.

Ethan made a face. "I've no idea but I'll tell you this, the guy could sure use a gay friend. He's scared shitless of who he is. It seems like it might take a backhoe to get him out of his closet." Nick raised an eyebrow and Ethan threw his hands up in the air, "I told him I wouldn't out him and I won't. Telling you doesn't count, right? Confidentiality and all of that." Ethan slumped in his chair and said, "I suppose you want me to drop all my bullshit and be the guy's friend?"

"That's up to you." Nick leaned forward, "You're a strong person, Ethan. You like to challenge the stereotypes by working up at the sawmill and getting in peoples' faces if you think they're discriminating against you in anyway. That kind of stuff matters. Every time you take a stand like that, you make it easier for other guys coming along behind you. Don't waste your time on games."

Ethan glanced at the clock, "Isn't it time for your end-of session spiel?"

Nick laughed, "No need. You seem determined to do all my work for me today."

Ethan stretched and pointed at the video camera in the corner, "Do you think I could see some of my footage?"

Nick waved his hand towards the door, "Get out of here. I'll see you next week and remember ... this office is now a no bullshit zone and I'm going to be holding you to that."

Ethan rolled his eyes, "Ya, ya, ya ... tell me about it," he said as he strolled out of the room.

❧❧❧❧

"I'd like to update everyone on Rachel Franklin's health situation." Izzy looked down at her agenda for the Direct Client Meeting. She ticked off an item and grabbed a piece of paper from a file. She pulled her glasses out of her hair and put them on to refer to the sheet. "According to Dr. Wells,

Rachel has made a complete recovery from her gallbladder surgery. She is no longer having any issues around eating and is headed for a normal weight. The rash that had caused her so many problems is being treated." She smiled as she looked around the table, "Darlene took her to the dentist and Rachel is booked for some long overdue dental work. She's also been to the optometrist and has a new pair of glasses and contacts as well."

Maryanne shuffled through a pile of papers in front of her and dramatically pulled one out to wave it back and forth. "Instead of waiting for the results of her recent educational testing," she shook her head, "you know those things take forever ... I did an assessment myself and the results are certainly at odds with her low school grades. I've got her working on two Grade Twelve English upgrading courses and she's more than capable of handling the assignments."

Gordon looked up from the folded newspaper in his lap and nodded his agreement, "She's meeting most of the requirements for upper-level math as well. There are gaps but we'll address them in one-on-one tutoring."

Izzy's eyes skipped over Jeremy who was slouching at the end of the table, typing rapidly on his laptop. She looked at Nick and asked, "Is there anything you'd like to add?"

"She and I are making progress on a number of fronts. I was wondering if we could get her a work experience placement that is in line with her emerging abilities. I think she can do something more formative than working with the cleaning woman."

"Perhaps something in the library would suit her." Maryanne glanced down at a paper in her hand. "The girl can write and she has a keen mind. I've given her a B+ on her analysis of Ian McEwan's novel, *Atonement*."

Izzy addressed herself to the end of the table, "Jeremy, what are Rachel Franklin's computer skills like?"

Jeremy looked up from his laptop. His glasses slid down his nose and he peered out, over the black rims. "Who?" As Izzy repeated the name, he returned his eyes to the screen and his fingers flew over the keyboard. "Basic. She can type at a pretty good clip, though." He looked up to glance around the table. "She's the girl who used to squint and twitch all the time, right? She told me that she was good on the keyboard because even with her old glasses, she could see the keys." He looked back down and shook his head, "I've pulled up the work assignment roster. The library position is filled for the next few months."

Bethany put her hand up to get Izzy's attention. "I've got an idea. I know she couldn't work with me on Jillian's research as it involves the other residents and the interviews are confidential but Nick has asked me to do some work for him," she smiled at the man across from her. "I'm hoping to get an extra course credit for organizing and analyzing some of his research data, searching for recent articles and doing other related tasks. Could Rachel help me with that work?"

Izzy tapped her pen on the table and considered the idea. "It's bound to expand her horizons more than scrubbing out toilets will do. Why don't you have her ease into it, Beth? She could start with you for five hours a week and continue with Penny for the rest. By the time the library job opens up you could have her for ten and she could work in the library for the other ten." Izzy stopped to sip her coffee and added, "Beth, I've looked over the entire folder of articles you've found on kids in care slipping through cracks in the healthcare system. Maybe you and I could work on a case study article for a peer-reviewed journal. Co-authoring would be a great experience for you." Izzy glanced at Nick and shrugged, "And your recent list of publications makes me realize that I would benefit from the inclusion of something recent on my CV."

❧❧❧❧

Mike spent the whole time at the Legion trying not to stare down the length of the table to where Wynter sat close to Lisa-Marie and Zach. She'd shown up earlier to watch the ball game and he'd made a fool of himself out on the field more than once because he couldn't stop looking up to the bleachers where she sat. Beulah had actually shouted at him to get his head out of the clouds. He only hoped her booming voice hadn't reached Wynter's ears but that was probably too much to expect.

He looked across the table at Dylan who sat comfortable and relaxed with his arm flung casually over Arianna's shoulder. Dylan's easy pose reminded Mike of a line from a Rod Stewart song – *Some guys have all the luck.* Arianna was a knockout as well as a kick-ass ball player and it was obvious she thought the sun rose and set on Dylan. Mike glanced down the table to Zach who was holding Lisa-Marie on his lap, tickling her, guzzling a beer and telling some joke. His brother made him want to puke. He had a good mind to tell their father that Zach was buying drinks for Lisa again.

Mike couldn't help but notice that most people were sitting in pairs. The doctor and the counsellor guy from Micah Camp looked cozy together. Reg sat down the table with his arm around Josie. Playing on a team with Reg had certainly provided comic relief. Though as demanding on the ball field as he was at the sawmill, Reg seemed downright human in his comical efforts to get

Josie's attention every chance he got. Mike looked around the crowded Legion and it seemed to him that he and Justin were the only guys in the place flying solo. Even Justin had his city girlfriend to dream about. Mike sighed heavily, finished his beer and thought about ordering a burger.

He watched as Justin made his way over to Zach and tapped Lisa-Marie on the shoulder. She smiled up at him and disentangled herself from Zach's lap. She and Justin walked away together. Lisa-Marie's empty chair yawned beside Wynter. Mike tried to picture himself casually strolling over and sitting down beside her. The fantasy ground to a crashing halt as Zach moved into the seat next to Wynter and started yapping to her.

Mike seemed doomed to be a lonely guy working at a sawmill for the rest of his life. Since he was already half out of his chair, he headed for the small, kitchen window at the back of the Legion to order that burger.

Justin led Lisa-Marie to a quiet spot in the hall near the cloakroom. The whole ball team had gathered around one table and the noise they were making filled the room. Justin watched from a distance as Beulah got up and raised her hands in the air for yet another Timber Wolf howl.

Lisa-Marie laughed as she followed his gaze, "Can you imagine what she'll be like when we get into one of the real tournament games? Anyway, what's up? What did you want to talk to me about?"

He leaned against the wall and paused for a moment. "I know it's none of my business but you and Zach ... things seem to be moving along pretty quickly between the two of you. Maybe you should slow down."

Lisa-Marie's eyes narrowed, "You're right, it is none of your business. I don't suppose you were thinking about slowing down when you had Lauren at your cabin for the weekend."

Justin grabbed her arm as she started to walk away, "That's different. Lauren and I are in a committed relationship. I think we both know what Zach's after." He watched emotions race across her face as she got ready to fire back a sharp reply. He let go of her arm and held up his hands, "Don't get mad. I don't want to fight. We're friends, right? Friends watch out for each other. I'm worried about you." He opened his arms and said, "Come here."

She hesitated for a moment then snuggled close to him and spoke against his chest, "You don't need to worry about me. Zach's a nice guy."

He leaned his face against the top of her hair, "I'm sorry I'm making such a mess of everything."

She backed away and looked up at him, "Hey, what's wrong?"

"Nothing. I thought we'd see each other more often. I miss you. We haven't been down to the lake swimming together even once." He grinned suddenly, "I wonder if I can still beat you out to the raft."

"I've been down at the beach with Sophie and Robbie tons of times. Come down any afternoon."

He dropped his arm around her as they moved back towards the table, "I will, I promise."

As the team gathering broke up, Nick followed Fiona out to the parking lot and leaned against the side of her truck, blocking the driver's door. She raised an eyebrow as he said, "Look ... I've always thought the honest approach is best. I'm attracted to you and I want to get to know you better."

"By getting to know me better I assume you mean sleeping with me." She gave him a long, appraising look.

Nick made a face, "Well, you've got me there. It has been on my mind to start at an advanced stage of the getting acquainted process and work backwards, but only if you're on the same page."

"None of what I said when we first met has changed."

"Let's not gaze into that crystal ball of yours that has our whole lives zipping by. Maybe we could focus on the present ... Dearborn, summer 2010."

He pulled her close and kissed her. "Let me come back to your place tonight," he breathed against her neck.

She pulled away. "I'm sorry, Nick. I really am. This is bad timing. I have to be up at the hospital in Cedar Falls tonight."

"Okay, but at least tell me you'll give me a rain check. A guy needs hope."

She laughed, "All I can say is that I'm tempted. Will that do?"

TWENTY-NINE

Reg walked into the sawmill lunch room and spotted Ethan, earbuds in place and iPod in hand, dancing across the floor. The young man's body was fluid and graceful as he spun away. Reg caught a snatch of lyrics. "*I'm a man without convictions; I'm a man who doesn't know ....*"

He glanced at the table where Mike and Justin were eating their lunch, either oblivious to the show or doing their damnedest to ignore it. He headed towards the coffee machine, grabbed his mug and muttered as he poured, "He can say that again. Jesus jumped up Christ in a handcart, if ever I saw a man without convictions, it's that one."

"What did you say?" Ethan pulled the earbuds from his head and spun around to face Reg.

Mike stuffed the last of his sandwich into his mouth and grabbed his lunch bag as Justin got up so fast his chair almost tipped over. They both vacated the room in record time. Reg took a gulp of his coffee and stared at Ethan who vibrated with anger.

"Where the hell do you get off making a butt-wad comment like that?" Ethan pointed his finger at Reg, "Get this straight. I'm as much of a man as you are. I piss standing up like you do. I've got a dick, like I imagine you do. Where I choose to put mine is none of your fucking business."

Reg held up his hand, "Okay, settle down there, Ethan." He was on the verge of saying – *don't have a hissy fit for shit's shake.* Instead he bit back the words and took a deep breath. "You're right to call me on that remark." He shrugged, "I razz all the guys about one thing or another and it's hard to resist when someone gives me the best opening possible. But I stepped over the line. I admit it and I'm sorry." Reg paused before adding, "Oh, and just so you know ... I have zero interest in where you put your dick."

Ethan sat down on the sofa and slowly wound up the cord of his earbuds. He folded his arms over his chest and stared at Reg, "I know exactly what you really wanted to say. *Don't have a hissy fit, Ethan.* Right?"

"I didn't say it, did I? That's what matters. A man's entitled to the freedom of his own thoughts. And I'm damn sure you were thinking that even if I have a dick I'm probably too old to get it up." Ethan choked on a laugh that indicated that was exactly what he had been thinking. "So let's agree to keep our thoughts to ourselves, how about that? Now get back to work before I fire your sorry ass."

Ethan danced out of the lunchroom as Reg hollered after him, "And you'd be wrong thinking something like that about me." He chuckled to himself as he recalled the other night and how much Josie appreciated what he could do with what he had.

෩෩෩෩

"You have to help me, Leez." Wynter flipped over onto her stomach on the raft that floated out in front of Izzy and Liam's place. She adjusted the waistband of her black and white polka-dot bikini bottom. "Mike has driven us back from rehearsals three times now and he hasn't said a word to me. I'm begging you ... please."

Lisa-Marie laughed at Wynter's wheedling tone and tried to stifle her jealousy as she looked down at her own body clad in a flashy tankini that was okay but not in the same league as Wynter's suit. Her stretch marks from being pregnant with Sophie were mere silver streaks now but she didn't feel comfortable enough to appear on the beach showing the amount of skin Wynter had on display. "I'll ask Zach when I see him tonight about setting up a double date with his brother and one of my friends but why can't I say you'd be Mike's date? I'm sure that would clinch the deal."

Wynter shook her head and the clip that held her hair at the back of her neck released strands of hair that danced around her face. "I couldn't stand it if Mike knew it was me and said no. I can't take that kind of rejection."

Robbie's voice carried from the top of the stairs, "We're coming down, Leez." Tabby walked beside him and Liam came behind holding Sophie.

Liam called out to the raft, "Are you guys okay with being down there with all three of them. I have to start dinner."

Lisa-Marie got up from the raft, "Ya, sure." She dove in and swam for shore. Wynter eased herself into the water and dog paddled behind her.

After playing around with Sophie in the shallows for a bit, Lisa-Marie filled a small, inflatable pool with water from the lake. She sat Sophie in it with a bunch of brightly-coloured buckets and rings. Wynter lounged in a beach chair working on her tan while Robbie and Tabby dove off the raft. Tabby tugged at her life jacket, "Lisa, can I take off this dumb thing?"

Lisa-Marie shook her head, "Nope. Your mom's orders, sorry." She looked up at the sound of a loud hoot from the top of the stairs on the far side of the beach and saw Justin making his way down as he shouted out, "I'll beat you to the raft, Leez."

Lisa-Marie jumped up and looked over her shoulder at Wynter, "Watch Sophie, okay?" Then she ran full speed for the water, dove in and started to swim for the raft.

Wynter removed her large sunglasses and got up from the lounger to walk over and sit cross-legged beside the kiddie pool. She glanced down the beach and gasped. Mike stood on the shore staring at her. Justin had already climbed up onto the raft. He reached out to help Lisa-Marie up as he called out, "Come on in, Mike. The water's great."

Mike hesitated, taking one more glance at Wynter before wading out into the water. He dove in and she watched the flash of his muscled arms as they carved through the waves. The sight of him without his shirt on had done something odd to her breath. It hitched strangely and Sophie stared at her from curious, dark eyes.

Wynter splashed the little girl, "Well, I can't help it. He's so cute." Sophie laughed and dumped a bucket of water over her own head.

After about ten minutes of crazed antics on the raft, Lisa-Marie took pity on Wynter and swam to the shore. She plopped down beside Sophie and said, "Go ahead, get out there."

Wynter shook her head, "I can't. I can hardly swim let alone dive. He'll think I'm an idiot." She had watched in fascination as Mike performed one perfect dive after another.

Tabby's voice called out from the raft, "Please Lisa. Let me take this off." She tugged at the life jacket like it might be throttling her.

"Mike was a life guard, Leez. I'm sure it's okay. We'll keep an eye on her. She can't even dive with that thing on." Justin pointed at the bulky life jacket.

"Oh, okay."

Wynter continued to watch Mike as she asked, "Is Justin really only a friend?"

Lisa-Marie was helping Sophie stack up the buckets and she looked up in surprise, "Why do you ask? I told you he has a girlfriend."

"There's something about the way you guys look at each other. Sometimes it seems like sparks are flying between you. And that hug he gave you down near the cloakroom at the Legion the other night made me think he must be more than a friend."

The buckets tumbled over and Sophie clapped. Lisa-Marie started to build the tower again, "We're just friends." Soon enough, Sophie started to fuss and Lisa-Marie picked up her daughter and called out to the raft, "I've got to take Sophie up to the cabin. Make sure Robbie and Tabby come in when you do, okay, Justin? And keep a close eye on Tabby. Her mom will skin me alive if anything happens to her because we let her take off that life jacket."

Justin waved his assent and Wynter tagged along after Lisa-Marie and Sophie. All the way up the stairs, she took longing glances out to the raft where Mike stood, shirtless and dripping with water. At the top of the stairs she said, "You won't forget to ask Zach tonight about the double date, right?"

Lisa-Marie hefted Sophie up on her hip and said, "Cross my heart, I'll ask. See you later."

⋇⋇⋇⋇

Dylan pulled a layer cake from the fridge in the kitchen of the A-frame and brought it to the table. Covered with buttercream flowers, the cake trailed streamers of icing down its sides. Across the top were the words – *Best Wishes Arianna*. Beulah and Bethany clapped and Arianna held her hands up to her cheeks. Her eyes were bright with tears.

She had been surprised when Dylan knocked on her cabin door right before supper and said she should come with him over to Beulah and Bethany's. "Why aren't you in the kitchen?" she'd asked.

He had grinned and said, "I've got the night off and you need to come with me."

When they got to the A-Frame, Dylan served all of Arianna's favourites for dinner – spicy, butter chicken and Caesar salad with Dylan's special dressing. He'd smiled and said, "You didn't think I would let you head out of here without a proper send-off."

Arianna had asked Beulah to let her quit the bakery job a couple of weeks early so she could spend some time at home with her aunt and her younger brother and sister before she headed to UBC. She planned to leave as soon as the ball tournament was over.

She smiled at Dylan through her tears and admired the cake. Beulah got up to get the dessert plates and when she returned she laid a small, gift-wrapped box in front of Arianna. She grinned, "Go ahead ... open it. We all chipped in for it."

Arianna took the small parcel and turned it over and over in her hand. Slowly, she tore off the paper. She opened the padded box and drew out a filigree chain and a tiny pendant. A gold stethoscope caught the light and glittered. "Oh, you guys. I love it."

Dylan nodded solemnly, "It's so you'll know we're always rooting for you."

Bethany reached over to pat Arianna's hand. "We'll have a hard time ever finding anyone else who is as reliable and responsible as you've been working in the bakery. I have no doubt you can do anything you set your mind to."

Beulah sniffed loudly and said, "Cut that cake, Dylan." She put her hand on Arianna's shoulder, "I might be looking for a good doctor in a few years. I'm not getting any younger. Don't let me down, kid."

Dylan held Arianna's hand as they walked back to the Camp on the dark trail. She leaned into him and said, "Thanks again for the dinner and the cake."

"I wanted you to know how much you matter to me. I wish now I'd applied to a culinary school in Vancouver. We could have roomed together."

Arianna moved away slightly and stared down at the wavering pattern Dylan's flashlight made on the trail as they walked along. "That wouldn't work. I couldn't live in a place as your roommate. You're my best friend and I love you, but I wouldn't be able to stop myself from wanting more. I still think about you ... that way. I can't help it." She shook her head and wiped away tears that had come out of nowhere. "It's better that there be some distance between us for a while." She pushed him in the arm, "Don't feel sorry for me and don't stop being my friend."

He pulled her close, "Never, I promise."

Later, in his own cabin, Dylan flopped on the sofa and watched Ethan block out dance steps across the living room floor. He was clutching his iPod and the earbuds were firmly in place; his eyes were intent on his feet. The guy was totally unaware that Dylan had even come into the room. When Ethan whirled around and saw him, Dylan shook his head and raised his voice to shout, "I could have been an axe murderer."

Ethan pulled out his earbuds and shrugged, "At least you'd be a good looking one." He collapsed into a chair and asked, "Where were you at dinner?"

"Doing a going away thing for Arianna next door. Was everything alright here?"

"If you mean the food, sure. I suppose the dessert didn't have your special touch but Brigit did fine." Ethan stared at Dylan for a minute, "What's up? You look like your dog died or something."

"I'll miss Arianna when we go our separate ways. She's the first friend I made here."

Ethan nodded knowingly, "But she's always wanted more than to be your friend, right? That's what's really got you so bummed out."

"If I wanted to talk to a counsellor. I'd go see Izzy. Mind your own business."

Ethan put up a hand to stop Dylan who was about to get off the couch and leave the room, "Wait ... I'm sorry. I'm not trying to bug you." All curiosity, he asked, "Did Izzy actually tell you what's wrong with you? I wish I was seeing her. Nick makes me figure out everything for myself. I am right about Arianna, aren't I?"

Dylan sat back and stared at Ethan for a moment. "It twists something up in me to know our friendship hurts her."

"Did you two ever have sex?'

"A fumbling attempt that wasn't anything like what she deserved. I was trying to figure stuff out." Dylan shrugged, "I don't know why I'm telling you any of this."

"Maybe it's because you need to be friends with a gay guy." Ethan got up and started to untangle his earbuds, "Getting my advice on clothing should be incentive enough but I understand other things, too."

❦❦❦❦

Lisa-Marie pushed Zach away and rolled off his bed to sit on the side with her back to him. "I'm not ready for this. I'm sorry." She pushed her long hair out of her face and straightened her top. She'd been letting things with Zach get out of hand. When they came out of the TV room in the basement and into an empty house, she should have said no to the invitation to see his room. He had every right to be angry with her.

She looked back over her shoulder and saw him grinning. He shrugged as he said, "Can't blame a guy for trying. It's cool, you don't have to apologize. Don't get me wrong, I'm crushed with disappointment, but it's cool." He slid over to sit beside her.

She frowned, "I thought you might be angry. I didn't mean to lead you on."

"You're not leading me on. You let me know loud and clear when you wanted to stop."

"You're a nice guy, Zach."

He shrugged, "Nice because I get the fact that no means no? I'm not sure what other kind of guys you've dated, but my parents taught me to respect girls." He got up and held out his hand, "Come on, let's go for a ride in your fancy jeep. If you let me drive, I'll take you on a tour of Dearborn and tell you some urban legends." He laughed, "Well rural legends, I guess. But cross my heart, every one of them is true."

After a quick stop for fish and chips on the boardwalk, with Zach finishing at least half of her order as well as his own, they drove across town and he parked the jeep in front of the Chinese Food Restaurant. Lisa-Marie's eyebrows went up, "You can't still be hungry?"

He shook his head as he smiled and chugged from a can of Coke. "No, but it was in this very parking lot that Bobby Chou tried to stab his wife." As Lisa-Marie's eyes widened, Zach went on. "Yup, almost on this very spot. He caught her by the walk-in freezer kissing one of the cooks and he chased her right through the restaurant and out to the parking lot. She was running for her life because he was waving a cleaver and screaming a mile a minute in Chinese."

"What happened?"

"She ran right up to a police car and climbed in. That was the end of the whole business."

Zach started the vehicle, drove up to the high school and parked near the back door to the gym. Lisa-Marie smiled over at him, "Don't tell me ... another attempted murder?"

"Worse than that, some might say. All of us kids were as grossed out as if it had been a gruesome murder. We had four gym teachers: Mr. and Mrs. Grimes and Mr. and Mrs. Grits."

Lisa-Marie narrowed her eyes, "Those couldn't have been their real names. You have to be making them up."

Zach bobbed his head up and down, "Ask anyone. We called them Grits and Grimes. Between the four of them they taught all the boys and girls gym classes and coached all the teams. Anyway, it turned out that Mrs. Grits was doing the dirty with Mr. Grimes and Mr. Grits was all over Mrs. Grimes. Neither couple knew what the other one was doing until one day Mrs. Grits and Mr. Grimes walked into the equipment room with their hands all over each other only to find that Mr. Grits and Mrs. Grimes had gotten there first."

Lisa-Marie doubled over in the passenger seat laughing. Zach leaned over to kiss her and said, "We didn't have one winning sports team that year. Teachers can really mess things up for students sometimes."

Zach put the jeep in gear, drove further up the hill to the medical clinic and parked along the road. "One time, Dr. Rosemary got a fill-in doctor while she was away in Africa doing her Doctors Without Borders work. It turned out the guy had faked his medical license and he wasn't a real doctor at all. I guess a few people queried his methods and he got investigated. He got wind of what was happening and he killed himself." To her shocked stare, he said, "Yup ... hung himself right in the back of the clinic."

As Zach pulled onto the road, he said, "I remember it was the year I needed ten stitches in my leg," he pointed to the scar that ran from his knee down the outside of his leg. "I fell out of a tree onto an old fence at the back of our yard. That doctor stitched my leg up as good as anyone could have and he even remembered to give me a tetanus shot." He grinned over at her, "At least, I hope it was a tetanus shot."

They drove up to the local elementary school and got out of the jeep near the playground equipment. While they swung on the kid's swings, Lisa-Marie broached Wynter's idea. "Do you think you could ask Mike if he wants to double date with you and me this weekend? I have this friend at the Camp who's super nice. We could all go out for dinner and maybe head up to the Legion to dance afterward."

Zach stared at her and rolled his eyes, "No way. I know exactly what super nice means. He'd never go for it."

"Come on, why not? It would be fun."

"I'm going to tell you something but don't ever tell anyone else, okay?" Lisa-Marie nodded solemnly and Zach went on, swinging back and forth and dragging his running shoes through the gravel at his feet as he talked. "Mike's never been one for dating. I'm not saying he's queer or anything, he just isn't an operator."

"Like you?" Lisa-Marie laughed and reached out to punch Zach in the arm.

He grabbed the chain of her swing, pulled her close then leaned in to kiss her. As he swung away, he grinned and said, "Where was I? Oh ya. He's sort of shy around girls. Anyway, he only had a date for grad because I set him up with someone. I was trying to get this really hot girl to go with me and she said she would, on one condition. I had to get her friend a date. She and her friend were like polar opposites on the hotness scale, if you follow me. But I was desperate. So, I got Mom on board and together we convinced Mike. It was mostly Mom. She really went to town on him. He was totally stuck with that chick through pictures at our house then later on at her house. He had to be with her through the entire dry grad night and the big pancake breakfast the next morning. She clung to him like a chunk of Velcro. On the way home, Mike pulled the truck over. He hauled me out and punched me right in the gut. While I spewed pancakes all over the gravel, he told me never to try and fix him up again, under any circumstances."

Lisa-Marie choked on a giggle and Zach looked bemused as he said, "Well, I was at a bit of a disadvantage since I was drunk but there's no way Mike will ever agree to go on a blind date that I set up."

Later, as they sat and watched the sun set over the ocean waves, Lisa-Marie asked, "Did you know Izzy's first husband, Caleb?"

"Ya, sure. He was a great guy. He hired me, the first summer I worked up at the sawmill. He was one hell of a ball player." Staring out at the pink and orange streaked sky, Zach said, "There was this kid that lived next door to us. A nice enough guy, a few years older than Mike and I ... he really had a hard time in school ... got left back a couple of times. When we hit high school, he started getting into trouble ...going down the wrong road. My dad talked to Caleb about him and the next thing I knew this guy was working up at the sawmill and really getting himself together. It was like that being around Caleb. He could show you possibilities without making you feel like he was lecturing you."

"Everyone says he died up on the woodlot. Do you know what happened?"

"It was windy and a snag came down and dislodged a big rock that flattened the guy up against a tree. Liam and Beulah were right there. He never even made it out of the woods." Zach let out a sigh, "It must have been horrible for his friends to be there and see something like that."

❦❦❦❦

Cynthia leaned forward in her chair, "I loved the book. The details the author gave on the preparation of traditional native foods were fascinating and the West Coast setting made me think of being right here the whole time I read it."

Izzy held up a copy of *Monkey Beach* by Eden Robinson. The novel had been Liam's choice. She nodded her head in agreement as she caught Cynthia's eye, "Her writing style is so eclectic. On one page she's detailing a recipe for making ooligan grease and on the next she takes mysticism to a new level. I felt like I couldn't put the book down."

Liam laughed, "The way she describes the ravens is priceless." He proceeded to launch into a number of funny raven stories of his own.

Alexander relaxed on the sofa and said, "If my turn ever comes to pick a book, I'll get you all reading Joseph Boyden's *Three Day Road*. Robinson is great on the Sasquatch stuff but you have to read what Boyden does with the

Windigo. The guy's writing will chill you to the bone and break your heart wide open."

Izzy interrupted him to ask, "In *Monkey Beach*, the character, Mick ... in your opinion, is he for real?"

Alex laughed, "Very. Could be any one of a few guys I know."

Bethany shivered as she said, "I couldn't believe what happened to him. I burst out crying. All the scenes on the water, the boats and the drowning ... that stuff really shook me up." She cuddled in closer to Beulah, "Too close to home, I suppose."

Nick sat forward on the couch, "I think what Jimmy did in the end, enacting his own form of justice with Josh, was ... well, noble. I don't know how else to put it."

Fiona had been quiet throughout the entire discussion, drinking her tea and listening, but she couldn't stay that way another moment. Social politeness had its limits and she had just hit the wall. She stared at Nick, "Did you seriously use the word noble?" She shook her head in disbelief, "Native people aren't noble; we aren't a frigging parody of something you've seen on TV. Should we all get up, put on feathered headdresses and do a pow-wow?" She narrowed her eyes, "You missed the whole point of the book. You all have." Looking around the room, her voice dripped with derision, "You're sitting here talking about Pacific Coastal landscapes so artfully painted with words and native traditions you don't know a frigging thing about –"

"That's enough, Fiona." She flashed Alex a defiant look to which he replied, "I mean it. I'm all for a spirited discussion, but we're among friends. I'm sure it wasn't Nick's or anyone else's intention to miss the point, as you put it."

Fiona almost vibrated where she sat cross-legged on the floor. "I don't give a shit if that was the intention or not. Have you been listening to some of the things these people have been saying? What difference do intentions make when people are not getting it?"

"Intentions matter, Fi."

Alex's tone was final and indicated so completely that the subject was closed, Fiona glared at him, "Oh, shit ... forget it. I wouldn't expect you to understand." She jumped up from the floor, walked out of the room and slammed the back door behind her.

Alex made a move to follow her but Liam stood up first, "I'll go, Dad."

Beulah stretched in her chair and said, "Whose turn is it to pick the next book? Isn't it about time for a Western? *The Englishman's Boy* is supposed to be a good read. Can't see how a Western would ruffle anyone's feathers."

Liam spotted Fiona out on the cliff deck, sitting on the swing chair. He walked over and sat beside her. She was staring out at the water with her arms wrapped around her body. She crossed one leg over the other and bounced her raised foot in agitation. He spoke softly. "I know you need to talk. Go ahead, get it out. Tell me."

Fiona stared straight ahead. "Jimmy wasn't noble. Nobility had nothing to do with anything. He killed Josh because he was pissed off about how Josh had sexually abused his own niece, Karaoke. She was Jimmy's girlfriend and because he loved her, he got the incredibly stupid and misguided idea that he should avenge her. Josh was an abusive pedophile because he got sent to a residential school where a pervert priest abused him. Believe me, there is nothing noble about any of those stories.

With her voice ramping up, Fiona continued, "Not one of you had the guts to say a word about the young girls in that book. The stuff Eden Robinson wrote about is not fiction. The scene with the white guys screaming from their cars at the Indian girls – *let us show you how to fuck a white guy, squaw* – that's real. That kind of stuff happens all the time, Liam, and like the girl's aunt told her, it's the girl that has to be careful because she could end up dead. Girls get abused and raped, then they turn to partying hard and drinking and doing drugs to kill the pain. Before long they're on the streets selling their bodies and they end up dead in a ditch somewhere and no one gives a shit."

Liam sat very still and stared down at his hands as Fiona spoke. When she said the word *squaw*, he cringed at the way it ripped out of her ... like the core of her being was being mired in the mud. Her words went deep inside him and he let it all in. He knew now that each time he opened himself to another's pain, his heart could take more. The quieter he became, the more he listened, the huger his heart became. Some days he wasn't sure how he kept it inside his chest. When her words ran out he reached for her hand and held it in his. She rested her head against his shoulder and he said, "I know."

Fiona took a deep breath, "I think I'll go home, Liam. I'm not in the mood to be social."

Later, she was sitting out on the deck of the guest cabin, with her knees drawn up to her chest, staring at the stars when Nick walked up the steps and sat down in the chair beside her. He looking up at the sky and said, "I'm sorry."

She glanced over at him, "You don't even know what you're apologizing for."

Nick shrugged, "Does it matter?"

Fiona got up and began to pace back and forth across the deck. "That's a stupid question. Of course it matters."

"Tell me, then. I'm a good listener."

She threw her hands up in exasperation, "You wouldn't understand. It's ... it's so much more than I can make you see." Her voice choked, "Go away. I don't want you here." She turned to walk towards the door.

Nick was on his feet in front of her. "I don't think that's true."

She stared at him and the moments passed. His eyes locked onto hers and the attraction flared up between them like the jolt of some powerful drug. She knew he wouldn't make the first move, wouldn't be the one to start this fire. When it came down to it, she would have to own up to lighting the match. And suddenly she didn't care. She was in his arms before she could stop herself and desire drove them inside the darkened cabin and up the stairs to her bed.

THIRTY

Irritation had been like a buzzing mosquito just out of Izzy's reach throughout the meal at the A-Frame. It had been ages since she and Liam had sat down alone with Bethany and Beulah and she had been looking forward to the evening. But the talk around the table had circled back again and again to the upcoming ball tournament. Every time Caleb's name came up, she'd had to force herself not to react and to remain calm. All she really wanted to do was get up, swat the irritation away with all her might and knock all the Caleb talk right out of the ball park.

Beulah's innocent request was the last straw. "Izzy, I'd like you to give out the tournament trophy and say a few words about Caleb." The self-congratulatory smile on Beulah's face revealed how pleased she was with her own idea.

Izzy jumped up from the table like she'd been scalded. Ignoring the stunned looks on Beulah and Bethany's faces, she began to pace the small living room of the A-Frame. She rounded suddenly and raised her voice, "No, absolutely not. I refuse to participate in this whole ridiculous charade."

She shook her head so wildly that she could feel her hair flying around her face but she couldn't stop and her voice rose even more as she pointed her finger at Beulah, "You obviously took the baseball-playing ghosts in *Shoeless Joe* too literally. You've been going around acting like you can bring Caleb back with a ball game. Caleb this and Caleb that. Get this through your thick head – Caleb's gone – he's dead – he isn't coming back. Not on the ball field or in any of our lives. This whole tournament idea is –" For a moment words escaped her. "Pathetic, that's what it is."

Beulah's face turned a dangerous shade of red as anger replaced her surprise at Izzy's sudden theatrics. She started to get up. Bethany's arm blocked her. She pushed Beulah back into her chair and whispered, "Don't say a single word. I mean it. Let Liam handle this."

Liam had stood up the minute Izzy left the table. When she turned her pent-up anger on him, he seemed braced for the storm. "You're just as bad, Liam ... pouring over Caleb's journals like you've found the Holy Grail. You can't bring him back through them either." She shifted her gaze from Liam to Beulah who sat with her arms folded over her chest, and back to Liam. "It's all a wonderful trip down memory lane for the two of you, isn't it?" She began to pace again, "Did either of you ever stop to think that not all of us want to wax eloquent about the past? Neither of you have any idea what it was like to be married to Caleb, to be in love –" Her mouth snapped shut. She looked shocked at what she had been about to say.

The frustration and anger in Izzy's voice were quickly replaced by sorrow, "I'm sorry Liam. I don't want to be saying any of these things. I don't want to hurt you." Tears shone in her eyes.

Liam reached out and took hold of her arms, "You won't hurt me with whatever you're feeling right now, Iz. Go ahead and say it."

She leaned her head against his chest and whispered, "I loved him, Liam. I still love him and I still miss him." She pulled away suddenly and stared over at Beulah before she looked back at Liam; tears tracked down her face. "All this talk about Caleb is making me crazy."

Liam leaned close to her and whispered, "I know you still miss him. We both do." He led her over to the couch and sat down beside her, holding her tightly.

Bethany got up from the table and said, "I'm going to get the coffee and bring out the dessert. Come on Beulah, give me a hand."

When they returned to the living room with the tray, they could see that Izzy was once more in control of herself. Beulah sat down and said, "I know nothing can bring Caleb back. But I don't ever want to forget him or what he meant to all of us. The ball tournament is my way of making sure that doesn't happen."

Izzy reached for a coffee. She stared down into the cup as she spoke, "I understand that all of this feels right to you, Beulah." She turned to Liam, "And that reading Caleb's journals has been meaningful for you. I'm just not ready to be so public with my own memories or with facing the fact that he's gone."

Liam's arm tightened around Izzy as he looked over at Beulah, "I'd be honoured if you would let me give out the trophy and say something about Caleb."

Later, when Izzy and Bethany rose to clean up the dishes, Liam headed out with Beulah to help her stoke down the bread oven for the night. As Beulah reached for a chunk of wood from Liam, she said, "Here I was thinking you had landed feet first in a bed of roses – spending Caleb's money and sleeping with his wife." She shook her head, "Well, your wife, now. I never thought about how hard it would be to fill Caleb's shoes."

Liam stared at the stream that flowed down behind the A-Frame, "I never considered filling Caleb's shoes."

Beulah straightened up, stripped off her gloves and knocked them against her leg. "It doesn't get to you ... that she still loves him that much?"

Liam shook his head, "I only want what Izzy is able to give me. I don't need all of her."

Beulah stared at him for a moment before she said, "Doesn't work both ways though, does it? She sure as hell has all of you." Liam nodded his head to acknowledge the truth of that statement. Beulah stoked down the dial on the front of the oven as she spoke. "Don't get me wrong here, Liam. I'm not saying Caleb didn't love, Izzy. You and I know he met his match on that logging road the day he came upon her and that flat tire." They both laughed. "But he didn't love her the way you do. Caleb never needed anyone like that. And if there's one thing I know about Izzy, it's that she cares about being needed."

Beulah grinned suddenly, "Did you see how fast she turned on you, in there? Seriously, Liam, my friend ... don't ever get on the wrong side of that woman, she's liable to knock you into tomorrow before you even know it's time to duck."

Liam let out a quiet chuckle, "She already has, Beulah. Believe me, she already has."

❧❧❧❧❧

As Izzy walked along the trail to Nick's cabin, her thoughts were on the conversation she'd had with Liam in bed the night before. She had lain snug in his arms and tried to find words adequate to explain what she was feeling. "There's this puzzle that was my life ... before ... all the pieces fit together – me, Caleb, my work, this place. It seemed like a finished picture. Then there's this puzzle that is my life today – pieces for you and me, Sophie, Robbie and Lisa-Marie, your father and Cynthia, my work, this place. Then there are the jagged pieces of learning to accept Caleb's death and grieving for my father and the trauma of the shooting. I have way more to deal with now and whenever I think I've got those pieces all fitting together nice and snug, one or two slip out of place. I've found out the hard way that I can't take the piece that was my work from the first puzzle and cram it into the new one we're creating together. It won't fit. I tried to create a new piece for my work when I took on the director's role but I don't think that's fitting so well either. I need more time to think about all of this and I need to talk to Nick."

Liam stroked the hair back from her face and whispered, "Why Nick?"

"He understands how unresolved personal trauma can get in the way of a counsellor's efforts to help others. He's been there."

When Nick opened the door to her knock, Izzy could tell he had come straight from shaving. A forest smell that reminded her of her father wafted out and he dabbed at his neck with a hand towel. "Am I catching you at a bad time?" she asked.

Nick shook his head as he stood back from the door, "Come on in. I was just going to grab a coffee and take it out to the deck."

When they were both seated outside, Izzy said, "I'm not going to waste your time by waffling around. I need to talk to someone about being afraid to go back to counselling."

Nick settled back in the deck chair and waited. Izzy stared at the morning light making its way down the mountainside as she spoke, "Before Liam, I was married to a man named Caleb. He died suddenly and it was a shock. I realize now that I still have a ways to go before I get over that shock, if I ever do. Obviously, that is an issue in my personal life I need to address."

Izzy paused, as if to let that reality sink in before going on. "Anyway, there was something about Caleb and our relationship that gave me a lot of confidence as a counsellor. At least that's the story I told myself ... being with him made me trust my instincts implicitly. Overall, the kids I worked with did really well. Then Caleb died. When I came back to work, I never felt the same kind of confidence again. I started screwing up. A young guy who had been a client developed feelings for me and I did nothing to address the situation." Izzy shoulders slumped slightly as she frowned and raised her eyes to Nick's, "The truth is, I craved the attention. I let a girl who really needed my help slide right under my radar. Another client I worked with almost succeeded in killing herself and I didn't see it coming. Then there was the shooting." Izzy paused to catch her breath before she asked, "You've heard about the shooting?"

Nick nodded. "Jim told me what he knew of it one afternoon when we were golfing together. Would it help you to tell me yourself?"

"The girl involved was a resident here, a client of mine. I was distracted. God, it seemed like my personal life had gone into emotional overdrive with people everywhere – Liam, a baby, Robbie – and everyone needing my time and attention. I missed something. There's no way that her crazed ex-boyfriend should have tracked that girl to the Camp." Izzy's voice rose, "Part of me believes I brought what happened – that violence – down on the people I love because I lost my instincts for this work." She held out hands that were shaking, "It still scares me to think about what could have happened that day and I'm not over it ... not even close. My father was shot and killed right in front of me."

She folded her hands tightly in her lap and went on, "I took the director's position when it came up because I was afraid to go one-on-one with clients. I knew that was the reason, but I wasn't ready to face up to it." Izzy sat back in the chair. "It feels good to say all of that."

Nick took his time responding. Finally, he said, "Fear is a common reaction to trauma and it can be debilitating if not dealt with properly. But you know that." Izzy nodded and he went on, "Even if you had been right on your game, instincts tuned to the max, there's no guarantee that you could have stopped anything that happened. You do realize that, right?"

"Of course, no guarantee, but no chance at all when I was going into counselling sessions so distracted I wouldn't have seen a freight train coming at me."

"I seriously doubt you were that distracted." He narrowed his eyes, "I don't buy the idea that not having a crystal ball has anything to do with your instincts for counselling. We've all had clients who attempted suicide or succeeded in killing themselves. We don't go home with them every night and hold their hands; that's not what counselling is about. We've all been distracted, unprofessional and even unethical at times. So, you are human, like every other counsellor. Is that what's bothering you?"

Izzy gave Nick's question serious consideration. "No, I don't think it's anything like that. I got used to attributing my counselling ability to something outside of myself, to Caleb. I was lucky for a long time and I think I grew overconfident. Maybe I became unrealistic about what I am truly capable of."

They were both quiet for a few minutes, mulling over this idea. Resolve rang through Izzy's words as she said, "I'm thinking of taking some time off. I got an email from Roland yesterday. He and Jillian are coming back early. It seems like a year of travelling together isn't suiting them. He'd like to resume his job as director when he returns if we can work something out and I'm inclined to make sure we can. I need to figure out some things before I decide what comes next for me. I've found administration to be a major pain but I have been challenged in some good ways, too. I have discovered that supervision is quite rewarding. I could see myself going in that direction but if I choose that because I'm afraid to sit down with a client, then it's all wrong. I might as well pack in my career totally. There are enough demands on my attention at home and I don't need to work."

Nick laughed, "Must be nice, that not needing to work thing." He looked steadily at Izzy, "For you to stop trauma counselling completely would be a waste. The fact that you attributed your skills to your relationship with your first husband doesn't mean those skills aren't real."

Izzy crossed her arms over her body and stared ahead of her. "It would be hard for me to sit down in the chair across from someone without that sense of confidence I once had." Her tone was rueful as she added, "Illusion though it may have been." She got up, "Thanks, Nick. I mean that. It helps to talk to someone who already has the context down. I may want to do this again."

Nick got up as well and walked with her through his cabin, "No problem."

As she reached for the door knob, Izzy turned and said, "I reviewed your notes on your last session with Ethan. You were right to turn off the video and confront him the way you did. I'm going to recommend to the Board that there is no need for me to be reviewing any more of your sessions. Of course, you know my door is always open if you want to talk about any aspect of a case and though Roland has a different approach, he can be a good sounding board as well."

Nick reached out to shake her hand, "Peers it is, then. That sounds good to me."

THIRTY-ONE

D arlene Evans stepped up to the mike on the stage of the Dearborn Community Hall and surveyed the crowd. The space was filled to capacity with chairs jammed together in row after row. People were lined up against the walls two or three deep in spots. If the Fire Marshal were to make an appearance, they'd be in trouble. Out-of-town ball players, many of them still in their team uniforms, packed the stairs up to the building, lined the doorway and spilled into the hall. Marathon runners, obvious in their track pants, jockeyed for position. Most of the front rows of chairs were filled with kids from the high school. Darlene bet that the organizing members were kicking themselves now for not charging more than five bucks a ticket.

The words – *beauty pageant* – had raced around the town like wildfire ever since the program had appeared in the local paper. Darlene wasn't sure what people were expecting but from the looks of this crowd, no one had come out to see anything like what Helen Sampson had informed the town council the event would entail – young women being showcased as the professionals of tomorrow.

She took a deep breath and tapped the microphone only to get a glare from Jeremy as he waved his hands at her to stop. She cleared her throat and began to speak. "Welcome, everyone. Wow ... this is some turnout. Okay, to kick off our Dipsy-Doodle Days this year we have a special treat. *The Young Women Shine Cooperative Competition* will feature eight of our local high school girls under the very talented direction of Wynter Snow with musical numbers choreographed by Ethan Black."

She gestured down at a table off to the right of the stage, "Our esteemed judges for tonight's event are ... local business woman and owner of the

Fashion Shop, Julianna Best." A number of whistles erupted around the hall as Julianna stood up in her short dress and spike heels to stroll back and forth behind the judge's table. She had her hands raised over her head in a gesture best suited to a mud wrestling event.

Lisa-Marie stood by the wall setting up her camera. Arianna gave her a nudge, "Remember when she sold you that hot bathing suit last year?" Lisa-Marie looked over at Julianna prancing back and forth and smiled.

Standing at Lisa's other side, Zach leaned over to add, "Dearborn's one and only cougar." She shoved him and he moved up the aisle to find his seat in a row close to the front where Mike and his parents were sitting. Arianna made her way to a seat near Dylan and Rachel. Lisa-Marie had driven all of them in with her so they could root for Ethan and Wynter.

When the whistling for Julianna died down, Darlene's voice rang through the hall. " ... Izzy Montgomery, Director of Micah Camp." Izzy got up and waved while Dylan, Arianna and Rachel clapped and shouted. " ... And last but not least, Catherine Harper, Principal at Dearborn Senior Secondary." The high school kids stamped their feet. "I would like to take this opportunity to thank Josh Benson, the editor of the Cedar Falls Forum for coming out tonight." A short man got up and waved his notebook in the air. " ... And finally, many thanks to Jeremy Lewis of *Mad Man Computers* for putting his expertise and sound system at our disposal." Jeremy stepped out from behind his sound board and waved.

Darlene stared at her notes. She looked out at the crowd and her voice boomed, "So, let's get this show on the road. For your enjoyment tonight, we have three parts to the competition. We'll have a brief intermission between each event; so make sure you check out the dessert table. All proceeds will go to the Women's Hospital Auxiliary." A woman at the back of the hall near a long table held up a plate of doughnuts and several people headed her way as Darlene continued. "The first event will be the parade of contestants which will wrap up with a dance number. Next will come the talent section of the event and finally, each girl will present a three-minute talk on a current affairs topic of her choice." She raised her hands and started to clap and the crowd joined in with raucous enthusiasm. The curtains closed and Darlene disappeared from sight.

Mayhem ruled backstage as people moved in every direction to set up props. Ethan had the girls lined up so he could do a last minute check on the costumes. Wynter held a clipboard and tapped a pencil against the edge. She smiled nervously. Darlene's eyebrows skyrocketed up her forehead as she got a glimpse of the girls. She whistled and hoped she wasn't soon going to be presiding over a riot.

Ethan ran across the stage and peeked through the curtain to give Jeremy the thumbs up. The thumping beat of a hip-hop tune filled the hall. He ran back and slapped Hannah on the butt, "Get ready. As soon as the curtains open you move towards your spot. Break a leg, kid."

Hannah smiled broadly and began to dance her way to center stage. The spotlight picked her up as she emerged from the dark and kept track of her all the way over to the step ladder that shone a dull silver in the stage lights. She wore a pair of brown, Mike Holmes style overalls. The strap hung down off one shoulder to reveal a bright-yellow bikini top that matched the construction hat on her head. The crowd erupted with screams, whistles and shouts. She flipped her long hair to the side and danced around the base and up one side of the ladder, arching her back as she twirled her work gloves over her head.

The spotlight left Hannah in the dark as it picked up a girl in a long, grey Stanfield's wool shirt, black fishnet stockings and spiked heels. She hefted a chain saw over her shoulder and danced around a stack of logs. She stopped, planted her dainty foot firmly on one of the logs and leaned forward to make a cut. Jeremy had worked in the sound of a chainsaw coming to life over the music.

A chambermaid in a short, black dress and flouncy, white apron, feather duster in hand, came into view and danced around the other two girls, flicking imaginary specks of dust away and pouting over her shoulder at the crowd. Near the front of the stage, the lights showed a girl wearing an open raincoat over a string bikini. She pulled up a heavy fish net from the ground at the base of the stage and peered out at the crowd from under her rain hat. The spotlight swung to the side to light up another bikini-clad girl wearing a green grocer's apron and waving a sheaf of invoices in her hand.

Beside Hannah at center stage, the spotlight shone down on a girl in an RCMP officer's red serge jacket. She slid the jacket off, draped it over her shoulder and smacked a baton against her hand. Her matching red mini skirt and tight, cropped T-shirt had the crowd screaming themselves hoarse.

In the second row, Corporal Casey Donavon's wife leaned over to him and hissed, "Where the hell did she get that uniform jacket. You could get into serious trouble for letting her use a uniform like that."

The Corporal slid down an inch or two in his seat and whispered back, "She asked if she could use it for a prop."

His wife punched him, "That's our daughter up there acting like a red-serge stripper."

The spotlight went dark and reappeared at the back of the stage on a waitress in a short skirt and clingy T-shirt with a fish design on the front. She held an order pad in her hand and tapped a pencil against her beehive hairdo. She waited on the table of a girl in a daring, black one-piece who had a wide sash wrapped around her to identify her as the Mayor of Dearborn. She stood up and hammered a gavel on the table as she raised the Town Seal over her head and waved it back and forth.

The spotlights began to flash and spin wildly over the stage from girl to girl. The music got louder. Then everything went silent and black. There was a scuttling, rushing sound as the props were pulled away. When the lights came back up, the eight girls were center stage, lined up and waiting. The music came back on and they began to dance.

Ethan stood behind the curtain counting off each beat and step, turn, spin and twirl. Wynter stood beside him, eyeing the crowd. The ball players and guys that lined the back wall were clapping wildly and yelling. The high school kids were standing, stamping their feet and waving their hands in the air. She tried to make out the look on some of the parents' faces – she knew they had to be parents because they'd been given seats in the front rows. But the stage lights were too bright for her to see much of anything.

When the curtain came down, the girls rushed backstage to change and get ready for the next part of the show. The audience took its first short break and kept the ladies at the dessert table busy.

Wynter smoothed out the creases of her strapless silver gown. She wet her lips and got ready to walk over to the mike that was set up on the far side of the stage. Ethan rushed up and stood in front of her, "Let me look at you." He ran his eyes up and down her dress. He frowned and tugged at the sides of the top, "Get that cleavage happening, girl."

Wynter brushed his hands away, "Stop it, Ethan." When the curtains went up, she counted out the three beats Ethan had told her to wait. She pushed her shoulders back and walked onto the stage.

Smiling out into the blackness, she said, "My name is Wynter Snow and I'm here to introduce the talent portion of our presentation. The contestants have elected to work in pairs and to demonstrate the various types of activities they have been involved in while growing up in the town of Dearborn."

A voice from the back of the hall shouted out, "If you're wearing a bikini under that dress, I'd sure love to see your talent." Laughter erupted and Wynter hesitated as some sort of scuffle broke out. When the crowd settled, she leaned into the microphone and said, "Seriously, what girl doesn't love that kind of a line?" There were bursts of laughter throughout the hall and she continued, "First up will be our Ukrainian dancers."

Amid the polite clapping, mostly coming from the parents at the front, Wynter stood back in the shadows and watched as Hannah and one of the other girls came out in traditional costumes and did five minutes of a staid but energetic dance. They stepped back and Wynter moved forward, "Please welcome our Highland dancers." Two more of the girls came out in bright blue and green tartan outfits and did a lively few minutes of a high-stepping fling. As they moved back into the shadows, Wynter introduced the tap dancers and after them, two girls in ballet costumes who spun and twirled about on their ballerina toes. The stage went dark and when the crash of the music came on signalling another hip-hop number, the girls moved into their next dance routine. Their traditional costumes had been radically altered - hems had come up, necklines had come down and there was enough skin showing to get everyone shouting again.

During the second break, the dessert table got emptier. The judges moved up to the stage to preside over the public speaking portion of the night.

As each girl was called out, she appeared dressed in the classic uniform of the professional woman - tailored black jacket and pencil skirt, white blouse and black heels. Maryanne and Ethan had scoured the community soliciting these items from the women who had such things. Izzy, whose closet had proved to be the most promising, had loaned out three jackets, two crisp, white blouses and a pair of Ralph Lauren pumps.

Wynter hugged herself with pleasure as each of the girls nailed her three minutes in the limelight. They handled questions about economic diversity, growth through tourism versus resource-based industry, Aboriginal fishing rights, climate change, gun control, Canada's involvement in Afghanistan, and two of her favourites - the reality of the glass ceiling and the need for universal childcare to stimulate the Canadian economy.

As the judges gathered to make their decisions and the last of the desserts went for half-price, the girls grouped around Ethan and Wynter backstage. They tried to keep their voices down as they skittered about in high excitement, covering their mouths to smother giggles. Hannah grabbed Wynter's arm and whispered, "We have a surprise for you."

The judges called the girls onto the stage and the eight of them made a striking row of up-and-coming business executives. Hannah stepped forward and commandeered the microphone from Catherine Harper before she could start to talk. Hannah smiled at the three judges and spoke to them and the people in the hall, "We appreciate the work the judges have done in choosing a winner but we have decided that we are going to pick who will be crowned Queen." The girls started to clap and Hannah grabbed the crown from Julianna Best's hand. She strode to the middle of the stage and Corporal Donavon's daughter joined her, waving wildly to her parents in the second row. The two girls took turns reading a prepared speech.

"We were raised to believe we can do anything we set our minds to. We are as strong as our mothers want us to be in all the traditional ways that matter to them. But because we're strong in our own ways, how we present ourselves might not fit your image of us. Don't make the mistake of thinking that you know who we are by the clothes we wear or the music we listen to. Our parents brought us up to express ourselves. If you must judge us, then judge us by our words and actions." They held hands, bowed and raised their free fists in the air to shout, "Girl power" and the other contestants took up the anthem. Hannah gestured offstage, "Without further ado, I would like to introduce this year's Dipsy-Doodle Days Queen, Wynter Snow."

Wynter's eyes widened as she looked over at Ethan. He grinned and pushed her onto the stage. As Wynter came out, amid loud cheers and clapping, she caught sight of Arianna, Rachel and Dylan standing on their chairs with their hands over their heads. She searched everywhere for Mike but she couldn't see him. As she let Hannah put the crown on her head and turned to take a bow, tears glistened in her eyes. She looked offstage and saw Ethan struggling under multiple bouquets of roses. He walked out hidden behind the flowers and whispered, "Hurry up. Present these flowers to your princesses so we can get them into their costumes for the final number."

Wynter gave each girl a bouquet of roses and a hug. After another round of thunderous applause she shooed them offstage and stood front and center with the mike. "Don't move from your seats. If you liked the dance numbers so far, you're going to love our finale."

The curtain came up to reveal Ethan perched on the top of the piano in a gambling parlour. The scene was created by using Vegas Night supplies that belonged to the local Figure Skating Club. Gaming tables were set with cards and chips and a large roulette wheel stood off to the side.

Ethan lip-synched to the Boy George song *Karma Chameleon*. He wore a flashy coat of many colours and a black hat that streamed multi-coloured silk ribbons whenever he moved. When he jumped down from the piano and began to dance, the crowd wasn't sure how to react. The number built, the tune caught on and as the girls came out in their red dresses and black fish-net stockings, the shouts of encouragement began. Wynter appeared decked out in a flashy suit. Her long hair was slicked back under a black fedora and she had a pencil-thin mustache. She moved between the tables, dealing cards, spinning the roulette wheel and leering as she leaned in behind and around the girls to steal and pocket their necklaces and earrings. Between passionate stage embraces, Ethan and Wynter shared the spoils. As they swung into their dance steps, they were joined by the girls who fell in behind them. The end of the number had them all kicking up their legs in can-can fashion.

After numerous curtain calls and multiple bows, the show ended and the girls spilled out into the crowd. Wynter was still in her gambler's costume when Hannah grabbed her by the hand and dragged her over to talk to the Sampsons. As Hannah hugged her father, her mother glanced at Wynter and let out a deep sigh. "It wasn't what I expected. Of course, the costumes were far too skimpy and I'm glad my mother's in the grave because if she had seen what Hannah did to that Ukrainian dance costume, she'd have keeled over." She shook her head and smiled, "But, really dear, you did an amazing job."

Wynter turned and Mike stood at her elbow. She tried to read the odd look on his face as she scrambled to think of something witty to say. Then the way he was staring at her sank in and her hand went self-consciously to the narrow mustache attached to her upper lip. As a blush covered Wynter's face, Arianna and Rachel rushed over and surrounded her, jumping up and down with excitement. She was drawn away to have her picture taken.

Ethan strolled up to Dylan and stood beside him in the crowded hall. "Well, what did you think?"

Dylan shook his head, "You are one brave guy, Ethan. I've got to hand it to you. I don't think half the men in here had any idea you were a guy until it was too late to back out of clapping."

Ethan smirked, "Ya, I hoped it would work out that way. What did you think about the girls' dance numbers?"

"I don't know shit about girls' dance numbers but the whole show looked like something you'd see on TV." Dylan smacked Ethan on the back, "Congratulations, man."

Lisa-Marie walked by and Ethan reached out to grab her arm, "Did you get any good shots of me?"

She laughed, "Dozens. There were more than a few people shooting video. See that girl over there," she pointed to a girl standing beside Hannah. "She was taping pretty steadily and she looked like she knew what she was doing." Ethan took off in that direction.

The small man from the Cedar Falls paper strode up to Lisa-Marie. He stuck out his hand, "Josh Benson. I see you have a fine camera and I noticed you were taking lots of photos. My photographer didn't show up. He and his wife had a baby on the way and it decided to make an appearance tonight. Would you be willing to let us have a look at your pictures?"

"Ya, sure. Give me your email address and I'll send along some of the good ones."

Arianna hugged Wynter, "Oh my God ... you as a cross-dresser. I could date you myself, you look so hot in that suit." She pointed over to Rachel who stood by the wall chatting with a guy. She nudged Wynter, "What do you think? He's a friend of Zach's and he couldn't take his eyes off her through the whole show. I got Lisa-Marie to get Zach to introduce them."

Wynter stamped her foot, "That's my dress she's wearing. If Rachel ends up with a date or a kiss before I do, I swear to God, I'll pull my hair right out of my head with my bare hands."

Arianna burst out laughing, "A bald head might go well with that moustache and suit."

Ethan, still done up in his Boy George outfit, walked up to the Sampson family and draped his arm around Mike, "Well, buddy ... did you like the show? Your little sister is quite the dancer. Makes me wonder what kind of moves you might have."

Mike gave him a shove as his mother turned and said, "Mike ... introduce us to your friend."

He groaned under his breath and said, "Ethan, this is my mother, Helen Sampson."

Ethan did an elaborate bow and kissed Mrs. Sampson's hand. "Now I see where Hannah gets her poise and style." Mike rolled his eyes as Ethan chatted to his mother and Hannah hung on the guy's arm. He looked around for Wynter. She was talking to Lisa-Marie. When Wynter had come on the stage that first time, in that dress, he had thought his heart would hammer right out of his chest. He had actually felt short of breath. Zach had to stop him from jumping up and pushing his way to the back of the hall to punch the guy who had shouted the bikini remark.

As Ethan wandered off to have his photo taken with each of the girls, Mike's mom turned to him and asked, "Would you like to ask Ethan over to the house sometime?"

Hannah stared at her mother for a moment and her mouth formed a perfect O. "She thinks you're gay, Mike." She doubled over laughing like she might choke. Mike turned an outraged face to his mother.

Helen shrugged, "I just want all of you kids to know that both your father and I accept each of you, no matter what."

Mike narrowed his eyes, "I'm not gay." He stomped off.

Helen snapped at her daughter, "Stop that ridiculous cackling, Hannah."

Hannah caught her breath and said, "He's got this massive crush on Wynter. Every time he sees her, he blushes and clams up like a mute. It's hilarious."

Helen looked around the hall until she spotted Wynter posing for a photo. "Oh dear, I think he might have a better chance with Ethan," she sighed

THIRTY-TWO

Nick leaned against the wall of the darkened hall; the music pounded around him. The Dipsy-Doodle Days Dance had been in full swing for a couple of hours and the place was packed. He stared at the woman who stood outlined in the light of the hall's open doors. Days had gone by since he'd seen Fiona. She hadn't responded to his messages and when she didn't show up today for any of the ball games he had concluded that she must be avoiding him. Her behaviour got to him because he'd fallen into some kind of stunned fog after their night together. He couldn't stop thinking about her. His only hope of seeing her had been to run into her at this dance and after the first hour he'd begun to think it wasn't going to happen.

He watched her come into the hall and move towards the bar. She wore a short, brightly-flowered dress. Her long, bare legs ended in strappy sandals that tapped as she walked across the floor. A jean jacket, rolled up past her elbows completed the look. Her dark hair hung down around her face in spiral curls. As far as he was concerned, everything about the way she looked worked – how her dress flounced against her curves and her white teeth flashed when she smiled at the guy behind the bar, how her dangling earrings swung against her face and her silver bracelets slithered up and down her arm when she moved.

As she turned away from the bar, he was beside her, taking her by the elbow and steering her over to a table. He took the drink from her hand and set it down. "Let's dance." Out on the crowded dance floor, he pulled her close and enjoyed the feel of her in his arms. After a couple of minutes, he whispered in her ear, "Why are you avoiding me?"

She looked up at him with a frown on her face, "I'm busy. I thought you understood that."

"Too busy to answer a text?"

She shrugged and remained silent. When the music stopped, she moved away from him. She strolled across the floor, picked up her drink and walked over to sit down at the table where Beulah was sitting. He followed, unsure what else to do.

⚜ ⚜ ⚜ ⚜

Justin stood beside Mike with his back to the bar and did a slow burn as he watched Zach and Lisa-Marie on the dance floor. The guy's hand snaked its way dangerously close to her ass and if he had held her any closer or worked his face any further along her neck he would be crawling right down the top of her dress.

Justin knew he'd had about all he could take of Zach and he now completely shared Mike's opinion of the guy. They'd played four ball games over the last two days and Zach had been a showboat of the highest order. He'd hit the ball out of the park a number of times, caught everything Justin sent zinging his way to first base and had energy to spare for putting his hands all over Lisa-Marie every chance he got.

They'd lost the last game that afternoon and in doing so missed the cut for the playoffs the next day because of Lisa-Marie's useless batting and catching. She'd missed more than a couple of balls that were literally destined to land in her glove – all she had to do was stand there and let them come to her. It pissed Justin off the way she'd laughed and said sorry, like losing was no big deal. It was even more irritating that she'd looked so cute when she apologized and that Zach had rushed up to her and told her it didn't matter at all.

Tonight she wore the same dress she'd worn when they went to the Sea Shed together and the pearls that Zach wanted her to wear all the time because they made her look sexy. Well, the guy was right about that. She was hands down one of the sexiest girls in the hall. Most of the guys couldn't take their eyes off Wynter with her fashion-model figure and a dress that looked like it came straight from the pages of a magazine, but he'd take Lisa-Marie any day.

Justin walked away from the bar, ignoring Mike's question, "Hey, where are you going? I thought you wanted a beer."

As one song ended and the music ramped into the next, he took Lisa-Marie's arm and shoved Zach out of the way with his shoulder, "This is my dance."

She smiled up at him, "Geez, Justin ... you're acting positively possessive."

He tightened his arm around her, pulled her up against him and maneuvered her into a darkened corner as he asked, "Are you sleeping with that guy? I thought I told you to slow down with him." Her eyes widened as she stared up at his face and their movements slowed to a halt in the midst of the gyrating bodies all around them. He didn't loosen his grip on her. "Well, are you?" His tone demanded an answer.

She struggled against the arm that held her and he moved his head down to brush his lips along her exposed neck, breathing in her scent and running his hand down her back. She stopped fighting him and moved closer. He whispered in her ear, "If you need a guy so bad, why don't you come and see me?"

He heard her say his name and her voice trembled. Her sudden surrender snapped him out of the mood he was in. He let her go and she stumbled against him. Shocked at how turned on he felt, he backed up. "Leez, I'm sorry. Shit ...." He stared at her in the dim light. He could see her lips were parted and her breath came fast. He spun around and hurried out of the hall, digging in his pocket for the keys to Liam's old Dodge.

He got in the truck and pounded his fists against the steering wheel. This was fucking insane. He tried to picture Lauren's face and he couldn't bring it into focus. He had to do something. He'd take a few days off and go down to Vancouver – pay Lauren a surprise visit. Things would go back to the way they were supposed to be. With his mind made up, he started the truck and headed back to the lake.

⚜⚜⚜⚜

The beat of a slow song filled the room. Mike swallowed the last of the beer in his plastic glass and stood up. The fact that his own mother thought he might be gay because he didn't have the guts to ask a girl out had forced him to act. It was now or never. He skirted his way along the wall and up to the table where Wynter sat beside Lisa-Marie. He forced himself to put his hand out as he said, "Would you like to dance?"

Wynter blushed right up to the roots of her hair. So many times, she had wished for him to come and ask her to dance; now she was in shock that her wish had come true. She felt Lisa's elbow in her side and she stood up. Her mouth was so dry she couldn't make a sound. She reached out and took Mike's hand. They stood there staring into each other's eyes.

Lisa-Marie broke the spell by getting up with a snorting laugh and pushing them both towards the dance floor, "Get going, the pair of you. I feel like I'm in some teen movie or something."

Suddenly they were moving and her hand was in his. She felt his arms around her as they swayed to the slow beat of the music and the dance was perfect. She leaned forward to rest her head against Mike's shoulder and she felt his arm tighten around her. His breath was warm on her bare shoulder as she snuggled close to him, breathing him in – a clean shampoo smell with a hint of something woodsy.

Wynter had been partnered with dozens of guys over the years of dance classes but this was totally new – heart-stoppingly new. She had no idea if Mike was a good dancer or not and she didn't care. All too soon, the song ended and she held her breath, praying he would say something – invite her to dance again, or ask her out, or hold her closer and kiss her. But he simply stepped back, murmured something she thought might have been *thank you* and walked away.

She left the dance floor on her own and sat down. Lisa-Marie returned to the table and nudged Wynter's arm, "Well, was it everything you dreamed?"

She sniffed, "The dance was perfect but he didn't ask me out or try to kiss me or anything."

Lisa-Marie shrugged, "He's chronically shy or certifiably insane. No other explanation."

✻✻✻✻

Nick watched Fiona pass right by his chair like he wasn't there and he'd suddenly had enough. He got up and grabbed her arm to slow her down. She twisted away from him, "What are you doing?"

He moved in front of her, "What am I doing? That's rich. What are you doing?" He leaned close, "You can't sleep with me and pretend it never happened."

Fiona backed up, "Watch me." She turned to walk away and he grabbed at her arm again.

She spun around and threw her drink in his face. He dropped her arm in shock and watched her walk straight out of the hall.

Fiona stood on the steps of the community hall trying to get her breath. She was filled with a dangerous mixture of emotions and she couldn't sort one from the other. She watched as a native guy she remembered seeing at the addiction center ran stumbling up the stairs towards her. Gary, that's right, his name was Gary.

Stopping two stairs down, Gary gestured back towards the baseball dugout, "A guy's hurt down in the dugout. You gotta come help."

Fiona reacted on instinct and followed as Gary side-stepped down the stairs and across the gravel parking lot toward the dark dugout. As she rounded the corner of the wood structure, another man came out of the shadows. Fiona stopped short. She recognized this guy, too. She'd seen him at the ball field a few times. One night at the Legion he'd leered at her and when she'd turned away in disgust, she had heard him say the words – *stuck-up Indian bitch.*

He walked toward her. "Hand over the clinic keys."

Fiona backed up, "You think I'm stupid enough to go to a dance with the frigging clinic keys in my pocket?" She kept her voice as strong as she could. "You're out of luck." She spun around to see that Gary had blocked her exit. She raised her voice and shouted at him, "Get out of the way before I drop-kick your sorry ass."

"Grab the squaw bitch. Let's have a bit of fun before we get the keys from her."

Gary's voice came out in a high-pitched whine, "Ahh, come on ... let's get the keys. I need a fix bad. You said we'd just get the keys."

The white guy's hand closed on her arm from behind and she fully realized the danger she was in. She let out one loud scream as she pivoted and tried to kick him. He smashed her in the face and Fiona literally saw stars as she staggered backwards. She was completely disoriented as he pushed her towards Gary.

"Grab her fucking arms." She shook her head to clear the fog, everything was happening so fast. They already had her facedown and spread-eagled over the dugout bench. She could feel Gary's hand's shaking as he held her arms in front of her. The other guy tugged up her dress from behind and ripped at her panties.

"Do you know the way Indian bitches like it best, Gary?" Fiona began to struggle wildly and scream as she felt the rush of cold air over her body and heard the rattle of his belt buckle. His body pressed against her as he leaned in close and said, "I'd love nothing better than to hear you scream but that might ruin the fun." He looked up at Gary, "Get your hand over her mouth and keep it there." Instead of reaching to cover Fiona's mouth, Gary let go of her arms as if they were on fire. He slid back along the dugout bench mumbling wildly incoherent sounds.

Nick grabbed the white guy from behind, spun him around and punched him in the face.

The second Gary's grasp faltered, Fiona pulled away, scrambled off the bench and stumbled backwards. She watched as Gary disappeared out of the door at the opposite side of the dugout, running for his life. Her first impulse was to run in that direction as well but she turned back to watch as Nick's fist smashed into the other guy's face for a second time. Her attacker fell over the bench and into the narrow space between it and the back of the dugout wall. She stood frozen as Nick leaned over, with his fist raised yet again. A switch flipped in her head. She was a doctor. She found her voice and screamed, "Stop it! Stop hitting him. You're going to really hurt him. Stop it."

As the sound of Fiona's voice echoed off the rough wood walls, Liam and Alex came running around the corner. They had been with Izzy and Cynthia at the far side of the parking lot when they saw Nick sprinting towards the dugout. Liam moved quickly to grab Nick's arm and pull him back. Alex had his hand on the hilt of his knife and Liam made a cutting gesture with his own hand, "No need for that, Dad."

Liam leaned over the bench and studied the guy who slumped down on the ground. His face was a mess but he was breathing. The dangling belt and open pants told a story of their own.

Liam turned to his father, "We need an ambulance and the police."

Alex walked over to Fiona. She had her arms wrapped tightly around her body as she stared at Nick. Blood ran down the side of her face from a cut above her eyebrow. Alex didn't try to touch her. He stood in front of her and spoke quietly, "Fi ... give me your phone."

Izzy entered the dugout right behind Cynthia. She watched Cynthia scan the scene like a professional, taking in everything around her with a quick turn of her head. Alex talked on the phone and Liam held Nick by the arm that hung down to a bloodied mess of knuckles.

Cynthia gestured towards Fiona, "Izzy, take her out of here." As Izzy walked Fiona away, Cynthia turned back to the men around her. "The police might want Fiona up at the hospital in Cedar Falls." She watched Nick's face as she stumbled over her next words. "They may need to do a rape kit and that should happen right away."

The question mark and hesitation in Cynthia's voice had Nick shaking his head, "It was way too close but I got here in time. What the hell was she thinking following those guys out to a dark dugout?" Nick cradled his hand against his chest. The adrenalin rush of the attack had clearly worn off and his face registered pain and anger.

A dangerous edge sharpened Alex's voice. "Let's not blame the victim here, okay? Fiona had to have had a damn good reason for coming out here." Alex cocked his head to one side and held Nick's gaze, "Don't get me wrong, Nick ... I thank you for your timing and your heroics. You don't want to go and say anything stupid that will make me change my mind on that score."

Cynthia pushed Liam and said, "Take Nick out to your dad's truck. There's a first aid kit behind the seat. Alex and I will wait with this guy until the ambulance gets here."

By the time Liam had gotten Nick over to the truck, Izzy had half pushed and half dragged Fiona away from the dugout to the parking lot beyond. The sirens were loud and a police cruiser pulled up. Corporal Casey Donavan got out and watched as Alex walked from the dugout towards him. The Mountie raised his eyebrows, "You again, Alex? You're a man who always happens to be around when there's a problem. Let's see what's up, here." He called back over his shoulder, "No one leaves ... everyone got that?"

Liam held Nick's arm and tried to get him to sit down on the tail gate of the truck. "Take it easy, Nick. I think you've broken your hand."

Nick brushed him off. He looked around until he spotted Fiona standing by Izzy who had tried, unsuccessfully, to assess the damage to the young woman's face. He headed over to them, calling out Fiona's name.

Fiona's head shot up at the sound of Nick's voice and she pushed Izzy away as she ran at him, slamming her hands against his chest. He staggered back with a stunned look on his face as she screamed, "Did you think I'd thank you for beating the shit out of the guy?" Another shove emphasized her next words. "I guess you feel really noble now, right?" Her hands smashed into him again. "Did you think that because I had sex with you, I wanted you to be my knight in shining armour?" She turned back to Izzy, "Come with me. Turns out I do need something from you."

Fiona walked over to the far side of a nearby truck. She spoke quickly, "Give me your panties. Mine are bagged for evidence by now and I can't walk around in this dress with my ass practically sticking out."

Izzy reached up under her long dress. As she leaned on the side of the truck to balance on one foot and then the other, she slipped the silky bit of cloth over her heels and asked, "Are you okay?"

Fiona grabbed the panties from Izzy's hand and tugged them on, wiggling her dress down in place as she answered. "That white trash bastard planned to cram his cock up my ass to teach me not to be a stuck-up Indian bitch. He didn't get the chance to finish the job, if that's what you want to know."

Fiona walked away towards the police cruiser where she met Casey Donavan. He gently slipped an arm around her and tipped up her chin to touch her face. Izzy watched as the police corporal pulled out a first aid kit and attended to the cut above the young woman's eye while they talked. Izzy took a few breaths to compose herself and returned to the others. Liam gave her a questioning look. She shook her head and said, "Don't ask."

He pulled her close and whispered, "Nick got there in time."

"I know ... thank God for that."

THIRTY-THREE

Mike ran all twenty-one kilometers of the half marathon with thoughts of how badly he'd blown his chance with Wynter pounding the road right beside him. She must think he's a nut case. He'd managed to get out on the dance floor with her and then he hadn't said a word. He didn't even walk her back to her table after the dance and that was something a cave man would have done. He'd been so overwhelmed holding her in his arms that he hadn't been able to think straight. All he remembered was leaving the hall in somewhat of a stupor.

He covered the twisting back-and-forth circuit set up around the town of Dearborn with his mind miles away from the distance he was running, hardly conscious of how he was doing until he came down the last stretch and saw his father jumping in the air. Mike heard shouts of congratulations as he crossed the finish line and realized he had achieved his personal best time. He leaned over to catch his breath and when he stood up he saw Wynter standing on the sidelines looking at him. She was grinning and clapping. He couldn't believe his eyes. What was she doing here? He looked behind him to see if she was cheering for someone else but no one else was there.

He reached for a bottle of water from one of the workers and poured it over his head. Shaking the drenched hair out of his face, he walked up to Wynter, snaked his arm around her waist, pulled her close and kissed her. The moment seemed to go on forever and he never thought about how exhausted he felt. When he backed up, he saw the stunned, happy look on her face and he said, "I should have done that last night. What are you doing here?"

Wynter laughed as she pointed down at the sash that proclaimed her Dearborn's Dipsy-Doodle Days Queen. Her voice shook slightly as she said, "Part of my official duties. I have to give out the trophy and the medals to the winners of the half marathon."

Mike gave her a serious look, "But they don't all get a kiss do they?" She grinned and shook her head. He looked around and asked, "Who came first, anyway?"

"The German guy."

He smiled, realizing he still had his arm around the most beautiful girl in the crowd. She didn't seem to mind at all and several people were taking notice, including his butt-head brother. He looked into her stunning eyes. "Would you go out on a date with me, Wynter?"

✂✂✂✂

Fiona got up from the chair on the deck of the guest cabin when she saw Alex round the corner of the trail. She called out to him, "I don't have any time to talk to you. I'm about to leave."

Alex kept walking and was soon on the deck in front of her. "I'm not going anywhere until you listen to me."

She shook her head, "What could you possibly have to say? This isn't a big deal. Don't turn it into one. It's what happens to native women all the time ... just like what happened to Poppy over and over every frigging day of the week. Native women's bodies are the literal landscape of colonialism for white men."

The power in Alex's voice caught her and stopped her next words. He pointed to the chair and said, "Sit down, Fi." She glared at him but returned to the chair. He hunkered down in front of her, "You can't hide from what happened to you by working it into a lecture on colonialism. I know as well as you do the number of disappeared women. I know about all the things white guys do. And I know about the number of native girls and women who've been violated or had the shit beaten out of them on the reserve by native guys. You've been there and have seen it the same way I have. So drop the crap. This is personal. It's about what happened to you and how you were vulnerable and scared. It's about how you took all of that out on the guy who got there in time to stop the worst of what could have happened." Alex's voice dropped down and his obvious compassion for her was disarming. "And you feel guilty because you know I'm right."

In an attempt to block out his words, Fiona shook her head and whispered, "No, no, no." It didn't work. Tears poured down her face.

He pulled her to her feet and into his arms as he stroked her hair and said, "There, there."

She sobbed out words against his shoulder, "I've never been so scared in my life. I thought I would die if he, if he ... now I can't sleep and I keep having nightmares. That bastard's voice is in my head and I can't get it out."

Alex continued to stroke her hair. After she'd had a good cry, he backed up a bit and said, "Better?" She nodded. He sat her back down in her chair and said, "Aboriginal women's struggle for justice is going to be the issue that brings our people together in the next few years. I feel that in my bones. And women like you are going to be in the forefront, leading the fight. But you won't make it through if you don't come to grips with the anger and the hate in here." He pointed towards his own heart.

She stared at her father and slowly nodded her head. He was brisk with her as he gave orders, "Here's what you're going to do. Call your mother and tell her what happened. Give her a chance to cry with you. When you're finished doing that, you go and find Nick and apologize for going after him the way you did. Then you go and talk to Izzy. She has years of experience working with women who have gone through exactly what you're going through and she knows how to help."

❦❦❦❦

Fiona knocked on the door of Izzy's office and asked, "Do you have a minute?"

Izzy stepped out from behind her desk and waved Fiona to a chair. Fiona sat down and twisted the silver rings on her finger around and around as she spoke, "I keep waking up in a cold sweat feeling that guy's hands on me. And I keep hearing these sounds ... it's his belt jangling and the sound of him pulling down his zipper." She shivered and held her arms tight around herself, "It's ridiculous. Nothing happened."

Izzy waited until Fiona looked up, "Something certainly happened. What you're experiencing now is normal. I'm going to teach you a couple of quick things that will help right away with the flashbacks and dreams. I suggest we also meet a couple of times and talk." Fiona looked doubtful but finally gave a shrug of resignation. Izzy gazed at her thoughtfully for a moment before she said, "I want to ask you a question." When Fiona nodded her permission, Izzy asked, "Is this the first time that anything like this has happened to you?"

"Yes and I can't believe that I was stupid enough to believe that guy's lame story. I responded as a doctor. It never occurred to me that anyone would trick me that way. He wanted the keys to the clinic ... desperate enough to think we keep drugs there for the taking. When it was obvious what the other guy had in mind, and that the two of them were way stronger than me, I couldn't believe it. I remember thinking – this can't happen to me. How ignorant is that?"

"It's not ignorant at all. Thinking that violent attacks only happen to other women gives us the confidence we need to get out and live. I asked you that question because most women who have a first-time incident like this at a point in their lives when they've already developed healthy coping mechanisms and a good support network, usually recover quickly and completely with minimal help from a professional."

"What happens to the rest of the women?"

Izzy shrugged, "The earlier the first trauma occurs the longer the recovery process will be. It makes perfect sense when you think about it. A person can respond in one of three ways when threatened – fight, flight or freeze. A child can't fight or run away, so the only choice is to freeze – maybe dissociate, go somewhere else in her head to escape what is happening to her body. If that type of a response gets repeated over time, other coping mechanisms aren't learned or practiced. That's not a good scenario. There is also research to suggest that having been victimized at a young age makes one more vulnerable to victimization later. Every subsequent trauma reawakens the memories, going all the way back to the beginning."

Fiona had been listening carefully to Izzy's words. "Thanks for telling me that. It helps me feel stronger about my own ability to deal with this. I wasn't going to talk to you because I didn't want you to make me think of myself as a victim. I can see you aren't going to do that. I can't help but think like a doctor. I want to fix things ... surgically remove the problem, stitch something up, prescribe myself a pill and get over it."

Izzy shrugged, "You know the value of having patients talk. They tell you what hurts and you heal them. What I try to do is the same thing ... only no scalpels or sutures."

Fiona got up to pace the room. Finally she looked at Izzy and said, "If we're going to spend any amount of time together, I'll have to put my cards on the table. I resented Liam marrying you because you're a white woman who has everything. Liam's one of the best of our men. It's the same with Alex. A lot of native guys are so wounded by what's been done to them. When good ones come along – like Liam and Alex – well, shit ... there are so many native women who need those guys way more than you or Cynthia. It seems like the best of our men choose to fall in love with white women."

Izzy shrugged, "I'm not going to pick your argument apart, Fiona. I get your point, but as you say, they chose. Shouldn't all of us get to make our own choice when it comes to love?"

Fiona frowned as she stared at the woman who had married her brother. "I'm working at making peace with that but honestly, I have to say, I'm still resentful."

※◦※◦※◦※◦

Nick cradled his bandaged hand in his lap and stared at the woman who stood by the railing of his deck. Fiona's eyes were on the rays of the afternoon sun glinting off the dancing waves. He studied her profile and tried not to think about the two neat stitches that marred her eyebrow.

She turned and leaned against the railing as she met his gaze, "I'm here to apologize for the way I acted the other night and to say thank you for coming to my rescue."

Nick shook his head as he got up and walked over to stand beside her, "I should be thanking you for screaming at me to stop. If Liam and Alex hadn't come along, I think I would have killed the guy." Nick's face was a landscape of naked emotion. "All that crap I've spouted at the anger-management groups ... I'm nothing but a fucking phony. As Corporal Casey Donavan was at pains to point out to me this morning, one punch was justified considering what I walked in on, but three would have been way over the top. I'll be lucky if that bastard who attacked you doesn't charge me with assault."

The silence between them grew as they both considered each other's words. Fiona put her hand on Nick's arm, "I know what that kind of anger is like. I understand."

Nick reached up to touch her face gently. "All of this would be so much easier if your name was Jennifer." To her confused look, he said, "It's a long story. I'm not looking to get involved, Fiona. I did mean that. I came up here to try to straighten out the mess I'm in because of the last relationship I rushed into."

Fiona smiled and he saw that a hint of her wry sense of humour had returned. "It's a tough old life, isn't it?"

"There's some kind of fireworks between us. You have to admit that."

She nodded her agreement. "It's why I didn't respond to any of your texts or messages. I couldn't make our night together feel like a one-off no matter how hard I tried. I wanted to see you again and like I said from the start, I'm not looking to get emotionally involved with a white guy." She shrugged and added, "Or any guy, for that matter."

Nick laughed. "Quite the problem we have here, hey? We're like a couple

275

of kids – wanting all the fun without any of the responsibility or commitment."

"It does seem that way, alright." They were both silent for a moment then Fiona said, "Let's be friends, Nick. I think I'd like to try being friends with you and see where we go from there."

He stared at the beautiful woman who stood beside him. "I can't promise that I won't be a rather demanding friend at times."

Fiona smiled, "I can't promise I won't be meeting you halfway on those demands."

THIRTY-FOUR

Lisa-Marie crouched in the garden trying to get a clear shot of Sophie toddling in between the sunflowers. She saw Justin coming around the corner of the greenhouse and heading down the path. He walked quickly, with his packsack flung over his shoulder and a bag clutched in the hand that swung at his side. She got up and lifted Sophie into her arms. She shielded her eyes from the early afternoon sun that poked hot fingers through the tall evergreens on the edge of the garden. "I thought you were going to be in Vancouver until day after tomorrow?" she called out.

Justin kept walking as he looked back over his shoulder. He held the bottle-shaped bag up in the air, "Come over later and have a drink with me. I'll tell you everything."

Sophie pulled at the camera strap around her mother's neck and squirmed to get down. Lisa-Marie turned to walk back to the cabin. It was past the baby's nap time. She stroked Sophie's sweaty curls away from her face as she said, "What the heck is going on with Justin? Maybe his time with *you-know-who* didn't go according to plan."

She came out of Sophie's room a half hour later. She had given the baby a cool bath and settling her down for her nap. Robbie was draped over the recliner chair reading a book. "Where's Liam?" she asked him.

"Up at Cedar Falls." He glanced quickly at the clock on the wall. "He should be back in a half an hour. Why?"

"I need a big favour." Lisa-Marie fidgeted before the boy. He had his head turned at that strange angle as he stared at her. "Stop looking at me like that. Can you stay here and keep an eye on Sophie until Liam gets back? Tell him or Izzy that I'm staying over at the A-Frame with Auntie Beth and Beulah tonight."

"Why are you lying?"

"What makes you think I'm lying?'

Robbie shrugged, "You are. Where are you really going?"

Lisa-Marie tried to keep her impatience in check, "I don't want to tell you that. Will you give Izzy and Liam the message or not?"

Robbie nodded and as Lisa-Marie turned to head to the bathroom for a shower, he said, "I know Justin is back. I saw him walk by. He's angry and really sad. Are you going to see him?"

She whirled back around, "I said I don't want to tell you. Can't you leave it alone?"

Robbie's large, dark eyes stared into hers and they reminded her so much of Sophie she felt guilty for snapping at him. He looked sad, like he had the burden of the world on his shoulders. She walked over and bent to hug him. "Thanks. I owe you one."

Robbie smiled up at her, "Will you bake a pie just for me?"

Lisa-Marie laughed and stuck her hand out, "Deal. Let's shake on it."

Later, as she crossed the bridge near Justin's cabin, Lisa-Marie smoothed her tight shirt down over her breasts, adjusted her bra and patted the back pocket of her shorts. The condoms that Fiona had brought to Micah Camp and given out to one and all, like a clown at a local parade throwing candy to the kids, were right where she had tucked them.

She knocked on the cabin door and went in. Nestled in the thick trees, the place was cool and dim. Here, the heat of the afternoon sun was never a problem. Justin sat in the rocker. He had an open twenty-sixer of Southern Comfort tucked between his legs. His pack was tossed in the corner. It looked as though he had come in, sat down, cracked the bottle and started drinking.

Lisa-Marie walked over to his chair and leaned down to kiss him on the cheek. She straightened a bit and reached for the bottle. He passed it to her, never taking his eyes from the plunging neckline of her shirt. She stood up straight and took a gulp; the exposed skin of her stomach was at his eye level. She passed the bottle back to him and sat down on the sofa. "Tell me what happened."

Justin took another drink and stared out the window as he spoke. "I got there late and went right to Lauren's apartment. She wasn't home. I have a key so I went in to wait. At about two, I heard her come in but she wasn't alone. She had a guy with her. His arm was around her and they were laughing." He stopped talking and took another drink.

Lisa-Marie frowned, "Then what?"

He narrowed his eyes at her, "I got up and left. Drove to Horseshoe Bay and waited to get the first ferry out in the morning."

"You never said anything to her?"

"Like what? It was all pretty fucking obvious, don't you think?"

She reached across for the bottle, "I suppose." The second drink made her head spin.

Justin stared at her for a moment before he asked, "Are you sleeping with Zach?" She met his gaze and shook her head. He got up suddenly and pulled his iPod out of his pocket. He docked it and spun the dial. Music flooded the cabin. "I plan to get really drunk, Leez. Just giving you fair warning." She watched him take another drink. He plonked the bottle in the middle of the table and grabbed a deck of cards from the shelf. "Let's play poker."

She laughed, "I didn't bring any money with me."

He slowly raked his eyes over her as he took another drink, "You can owe me."

The late afternoon hours sped by with card playing, manic laughter and drinking. When Lisa-Marie was down twenty dollars, Justin rose and crooked his finger at her, "Come on, I want to dance."

The sun set and the cabin darkened as they gyrated around the small floor. He and Lauren had obviously done more than a bit of club dancing because the guy had moves – even as loaded as he was. Lisa-Marie finally collapsed onto the couch. "Whew ... enough." She fanned out the top of her shirt a few times, "Is it hot in here, or is it just me?"

Justin laughed as he sat down close to her. "I don't know if it's hot in here, Leez, but you are definitely hot."

The moment stretched out. Waves of heat pulsed through her body as his eyes caressed her. She slid up onto her knees. Turning his face towards her with both hands, she leaned close and kissed him. The moment her lips touched his, her heart started hammering so fast she thought he might hear it. The kiss went on and on. Then Justin suddenly moved away from her. He stood up and shook his head, "Not a good idea, Leez." But there was no conviction in his words and they both knew it.

She got off the sofa, went into his arms and pressed herself against his body, feeling his arousal at her touch. She wrapped her arms around his neck and pulled his face down to hers. Kisses deepened, hands moved of their own accord, garments dropped to the floor. Soon they were fumbling their way up the stairs to the loft and Lisa-Marie couldn't catch her breath. Suddenly what she had long wanted to share with Justin was all new to her. She was ready, nervous and scared.

They dropped naked onto the bed and now nothing could get in the way of their need for each other. Lisa-Marie stopped thinking and gave in as her body rushed in unison with Justin to a frantic, unrestrained finish. He rolled away gasping and pulled her close to him just before he conked out. She watched the rise and fall of his chest as he fell deeper and deeper into sleep. Her face was wet with tears. She loved him so much she thought she might burst into a million pieces with the force of it. Finally, she fell asleep spooning her body against his.

Justin woke up as the early, dawn light flooded the loft. The bed was warm and he reached out and hooked an arm around Lisa-Marie. He didn't remember everything about the night before but there was one thing he did recall – her voice saying over and over – *I love you, I love you.* Lauren had never said those words to him. To be fair, he'd never said them to her either, or to any girl, for that matter. Last night he had badly needed someone and the girl warm in the bed beside him had been there for him.

He pulled himself up on one elbow and leaned over to brush the hair from Lisa-Marie's neck, nestled against the pillow. He began to kiss her, slowly, running his lips along her skin. He stroked his hand lightly over her breast, letting his fingers tickle and play. He knew she was awake. He could feel her breath quicken and her body tremble. As she turned toward him, her eyes were wide with desire and something else unspoken that made his blood pound. He stretched out each caress until she whimpered with needing him. He knew that after this morning, she would never want anyone but him and the thought of being the only one in her life stoked his bruised ego and turned him on.

Later, as he manoeuvred her body on top of his, he watched as she raised her hands to push her hair away from her face. She arched her back and moaned with pleasure. Right before he lost total control, he heard his own voice saying the words, "I love you, too, Leez. I've always loved you."

Lisa-Marie dozed off and woke with a start to look at her watch. She jumped out of the bed and groped around for her clothes. She found her panties and stepped into them. Justin slept, lying on his back like a corpse except for the regular, quiet, snoring sounds he made. She stared at him for a moment before leaning over to kiss him on the cheek and whisper in his ear, "I've got to go. I promised I'd take Sophie into Dearborn this morning for her shots." Justin groaned and rolled over. She laughed as she grabbed his T-shirt from the floor and pulled it over her head. Her shirt and bra were downstairs.

The memory of how they'd been removed from her body made her catch her breath; a wave of desire washed over her. Crazy - she hadn't had sex forever and now she felt as though she couldn't get enough.

She stared back at the loft bed. This morning made everything she had gone through worthwhile - waiting for and wanting Justin for the last two years. He had said he loved her. Humming a tune, she walked down the loft steps feeling happier than she had ever imagined she could be.

THIRTY-FIVE

L isa-Marie pulled off the gravel logging road and jammed Izzy's Highlander into low gear to make the trip down the steep driveway. Sophie slept in her car seat in the back and Lisa-Marie was so focused on the tight turn she almost missed seeing the small car parked off to the edge of the pullout. She slammed on the brakes and reversed a few feet to get a better look. Icy fingers of dread crept up her spine. Her head started to spin in an odd way and her sight narrowed to pinpricks of light as everything rushed away from her.

Out of concern for Sophie, she shook her head violently. She gulped in deep breaths of air and gripped the steering wheel with hands like claws. The spinning stopped and her vision cleared. She jerked her head around to see Sophie still sleeping peacefully and clutching her pink bunny under her arm.

Lisa-Marie put the vehicle in park and turned off the ignition. She stared at Lauren's car. The next thing that registered was a knock on the driver's side window. Reg stood beside the car jawing on a toothpick and staring in at her.

She opened the window in time to hear him say, "Shit girl ... are you okay? How come you're just sitting here? I saw you drive up a good ten minutes ago."

Lisa-Marie plastered a shaky smile on her face and said, "I took the Highlander because I didn't want to move Sophie's car seat but I've never driven it down the driveway before and all of a sudden, I got nervous. I was trying to get my courage up to give it a try."

Reg drew the toothpick from his mouth and jammed it into his shirt pocket as he waved her out of the driver's seat. "Sure, I get it .... precious cargo. I'll drive you guys down and you can pick up a few pointers along the way."

The day dragged on – each moment an agony of praying that Justin would show up and explain everything. She spent most of the time with Sophie who was feverish and out of sorts from her shot. When Lisa-Marie passed Robbie, he stared at her and she gave him a look that told him in no uncertain terms that he should not to ask her any questions. She saw him swallow hard and look away.

She was helping Izzy with dinner when Liam walked in and said, "I think Lauren's car is at the top of the driveway. Did anyone know she was coming up?"

Lisa-Marie tightened her grip on the potato in her hand and forced herself to concentrate on the squiggly brown parings that whisked from the peeler onto the piece of newspaper in front of her. She had a strange feeling, like she was hanging from the ceiling looking down at a girl who methodically peeled potatoes as if removing every single spot was the most important thing in her world.

"Didn't he just come back from visiting her?" Liam asked that question as he moved over to the counter where Izzy was chopping onions. He nuzzled her neck from behind, "Hi, you," he said.

Izzy smiled over her shoulder at him, "I've no idea why she might be here."

Lisa-Marie made it through dinner by feeding Sophie and feigning a headache as an excuse for not eating much of anything herself. Every bite stuck so badly in her throat she felt as though she might gag or puke or both. She could have hugged Izzy when she said, "I'll bathe Sophie and put her to bed tonight, Lisa. I know you've had a long afternoon with her being crabby from the shots."

Without meeting Izzy's glance, Lisa-Marie said, "Great. I feel like going for a long walk. That should clear my head."

Robbie jumped up from the table, "I'll go with you, Leez."

"No, that's okay. I'd rather be alone." There was a wild look in Robbie's eyes; the kid almost bounced off his chair. He opened his mouth to object but a look from Izzy brought him up short.

Liam cleared the table as he glanced from Izzy to Robbie and over to Lisa-Marie. Frowning, he said, "Take Pearl with you, Lisa. She could use the exercise. And make sure you grab the air horn." Izzy raised her eyebrows but Liam saw Robbie relax and sit back down. "You never know," he said. "Better safe than sorry."

With Pearl at her side, Lisa-Marie walked out along the path that wound towards Micah Camp. From there she headed back down the logging road towards Izzy's driveway. Pearl trotted close to her leg. Disjointed lines kept running through her mind like a song on repeat. *Let her be gone. Please, God, let her be gone.*

She rounded a corner and the sawmill yard came into view. She glanced slowly to the left and her steps faltered. She stopped. Pearl kept walking a few paces then turned to look at her with questioning eyes. Lisa-Marie spun around and began to run wildly back down the road towards the Camp. Pearl caught up and ran beside her. Tears welled up in her eyes but the running and the wind dried them to her face before they could fall. She cut across the Camp driveway and entered the tree-lined path that would take her behind the A-Frame and past Alex and Cynthia's building site. She kept running until she came out in the orchard of apple trees near Izzy and Liam's. She cut along the path and down the stairs to the beach where she collapsed on a log near the water. She leaned over and clapped her hands over her mouth as great heaving sobs racked her body. She could hardly get her breath, she was crying so hard.

Registering the weight of Pearl's body pressed into her side, she reached her arms around the dog's neck and buried her face in the soft fur. Finally, her tears slowed to hitching moans. She sat up and noticed that the sun was setting like a great ball of fire sinking down behind the mountain. She walked over to the lake and knelt down to splash cold water on her face. Lauren's car still parked at the top of the driveway could mean only one thing. Justin hadn't sent her away.

❧❧❧❧

Standing vigil on the porch of the garden house the next morning, Lisa-Marie watched as Justin walked along the path near the greenhouse. He had his arm wrapped around Lauren and his head bent towards her. She knew he had seen her standing there.

It started to rain and she moved inside the garden house to wait. She sat in a chair facing the path; her legs were drawn up and her chin rested on her knee. After about fifteen minutes, Justin came around the corner and walked over to the building. He slid open the door and entered. Closing the door, he pulled up a chair, sat down and stared at the floor.

She looked at him with eyes already bright with the tears she was determined not to shed. "Say it; go ahead and say it."

He spoke without looking up, "Lauren explained everything. I was wrong about what I thought I saw. Her cousin was in town for the weekend and they were out together. She hasn't been cheating on me. She said she loves me and is committed to our relationship. I should have stayed and let her explain instead of running out on her the way I did."

Lisa-Marie bit down hard on her lip to hold back a sob. Then bitter, gut-wrenching anger hit her like a tidal wave. She jumped up from the chair, "What about you and me?"

"I drank too much and you pushed things, Leez. You know you did." Justin stood up to face her. "I wasn't thinking straight. It shouldn't have happened."

She choked on her words as she jabbed her finger at him, "Even if you were drunk and I came on to you that first time, what about the next morning? You said you loved me. I heard you say you'd always loved me."

Justin stared up at the rough-hewn boards of the ceiling for a moment. "Sex makes guys say things they shouldn't say. I'm sorry."

She stared at him in disbelief, "Oh that's great. You're sorry. You cheat on your girlfriend, you use me and that's all you have to say for yourself? You're sorry."

"I did not use you." An edge had come into Justin's voice and his eyes narrowed, "I seem to recall that you were more than willing."

Lisa-Marie voice rose dangerously, "I didn't force you to do anything you haven't wanted to do for a long time."

Justin shouted back, "You've been coming onto me the whole summer," He slammed his fist against the wall. "... the skimpy clothes, the flirting and the obvious attempts to make me jealous by throwing Zach in my face every fucking day. What did you think would happen if you kept on acting like that?"

A note of triumph crept into Lisa-Marie's voice as she said, "If you cared so much about Lauren, you wouldn't have been looking at me and you wouldn't have cared what I was doing with Zach."

Justin backed up a step, his face twisted with an emotion Lisa-Marie couldn't even name. Blood ran down from the knuckles of his hand. He practically spit at her, "You knew damn well I had a girlfriend. You've been trying to screw that up for me from the moment you got here. And the other night ... you could have told me to talk to Lauren, but no. You saw that I was all fucked up and you had to go after the only thing you've ever wanted from me. You don't have a clue how to be anyone's friend."

Those last words knocked the anger out of her. She saw Justin turn away and take a step towards the door. This was it. If he left now, it would be for good. She ran after him and tugged at his arm so he had to turn and face her. "Don't do this, Justin. I'm begging you; don't choose her instead of me. I love you and I know you love me. What happened between us meant something. I matter to you way more than she does.

"It's already done, Leez."

Sobbing, she looked up at him and choked out the words, "I'll hate you forever for doing this to me and someday when you find out she's not the girl for you, you'll want me back, but I won't forgive you and I won't ever love you again."

Justin's shoulders slumped, "I'm sorry. I've never wanted to hurt you and it ends up, that's all I've ever done."

She pushed past him and ran out of the garden house.

⚜⚜⚜⚜

Izzy was ushering Liam and Sophie out the door. Robbie and Tabby were already over at the Camp for a cooking lesson with Brigit. Liam planned to drop Sophie off with Cynthia at the camper while he helped his dad and Reg install the large front window of the new cabin. The back door from the garden slammed and Lisa-Marie ran through the living room, sobbing all the way up the stairs to her room. Izzy turned to stare as the door to Lisa's room banged shut; the sound echoed through the cabin. With her hand on her beating heart, she took a deep breath and hoped that someday soon she would get a handle on her startle reactions.

The look of alarm on Liam's face matched her own. Sophie's lip started to tremble. Izzy stroked the baby's face with one hand as she held on to Liam's with the other. "You guys better scoot along. I'll find out what's going on, though I have a pretty good idea."

Compassion filled Liam's eyes as he glanced up the stairs. He bent to kiss Izzy goodbye.

Izzy knocked on the door and went into the room where Lisa lay face down on her bed, crying. She sat down and rubbed the girl's back in slow circles. After a few minutes, Lisa curled into a fetal position and wrapped her arms tightly around herself. She looked up in misery through her tangled hair. Her face was a red, blotchy mess and her breathing hitched. Izzy brushed the hair from the girl's face, "What happened?"

"Justin and I had sex. But he doesn't love me and he chose Lauren and I can't stand it ... it hurts so much ... I can't stand it." She started to cry again and the sobs were quieter but more desperate. Izzy sat beside her and waited. She didn't say anything because there was nothing to say.

Finally Lisa-Marie choked out the words, "He says I pushed him into it, and I did. I felt like I'd do anything to have him. I didn't know it would hurt so much to get what I wanted. I don't matter to him and he'll never love me." She took a shaky breath and continued, "It's like I haven't learned a single thing these past two years. I'm still that desperate girl who thinks having sex will make someone love me."

Izzy held her hand up to stop the words, "Hey ... you aren't that girl anymore because you're talking to me and you've got family and friends and Sophie and a future."

Lisa-Marie's voice was muffled as she buried her face in the bed, "He says I'm not his friend and he's right. I knew what I was going to do when I went to his place. I wanted him and Lauren to break up."

"Enough of that ... I mean it." Izzy's no-nonsense voice got Lisa's attention and she raised her tear-stained face to look at the woman beside her. "No more dumping on yourself. You've loved Justin for a long time. I understand what you did, I get it. Love makes us take chances ... it makes us do things that don't always turn out the way we'd like. Raking yourself over the coals won't change that. Believe me; I know what I'm talking about."

Lisa-Marie sat up on the bed with her back to the wall. Izzy slid over beside her. In the silence that followed, Izzy thought about Justin. He had not been the best of friends either. She'd seen the way he looked at Lisa and it wasn't like a guy who was in a committed relationship with someone else. They had both played a dangerous game and, of course, he landed on his feet and Lisa ended up with a broken heart. Typical.

"I was desperate and I forced Justin and now we'll never be friends again."

Izzy stared hard at Lisa-Marie, "Justin needn't have gone along with whatever you tried to put in motion. Remember that. It takes two. What you've discovered about your own behaviour is important – not so you can dump on yourself but because it lets you know what matters to you. You're not likely to let this happen to you again; you've learned what you had to learn."

Izzy watched as her words sank in. Then the tears started again and Lisa buried her face in her hands as she sobbed. "It hurts so much; I can't stand how much it hurts to lose Justin for good. What am I going to do?"

Izzy pulled her close, "You're going to let the people who love you take care of you. I'm going to get you a pot of tea and a cool cloth and I'll bring you up a tray of lunch later. No one is going to bother you or make you talk until you're ready. Rest now ... this kind of thing is exhausting."

❧❧❧❧

Lisa-Marie's door was firmly closed and Robbie was asleep. Liam passed Izzy the baby monitor, "Let's go out on the cliff deck and talk."

They sat on the swing watching the water sparkle in the moonlight. Liam reached out for Izzy's hand and voiced what had been on his mind all day. "Is Lisa going to be alright?"

"Yes ... in time."

"Can you tell me what happened?"

"Her side ... that's all I know and I have to try hard not to take sides." Izzy gave the bare-bones version of Lisa's story.

It was quiet on the deck. Only the sound of the gently lapping water interrupted their thoughts. Then Liam noticed that tears were running down Izzy's face. "Hey, are you okay?"

She wore a hopeless expression. "She's says it's all her fault, that she went after him, that she ruined their friendship. For her, that's the worst part of all."

Liam reached a hand out to tip up Izzy's chin so their eyes met. He shook his head, "That's not true. It could not have been all her doing. He should have been strong enough to stop her."

Izzy knew Liam was talking about himself, too. A solemn look passed between them before she said, "Yes, that's what I think, too."

Her tears continued to fall. Liam asked, "Can you tell me what's got you so sad?"

"Oh, it's stupid, really." Izzy drew a shaky breath and wiped her face. "I know how she feels to lose someone so completely, with no hope of ever going back. I know how that hurts. And I remember what it was like to be her age and in love. It feels like the end of the world when things don't work out." She reached into her pocket, pulled out a Kleenex, blew her nose and sat up straight. "She'll get over it ... it just takes time."

Liam pulled Izzy's hand up to his lips. He kissed her fingers. "She might not. Some people never get over their first love."

A sad smile turned up the corners of her lips, "Is this personal experience speaking?" Liam nodded and Izzy's eyes widened in surprise, "Oh, really?"

He pulled her close and kissed her, long and slow. He raised his eyes to hers and said, "You are my first and only love, Isabella Montgomery, and I'll never get over that."

❧❧❧❧

On the second night of Lisa-Marie's self-imposed exile, Robbie knocked on her door. When she opened it, he said, "Izzy says I'm not supposed to bug you but I can't stand it if the jagged light that came out from under your door last night starts coming out again. I can feel it right through the walls."

Lisa-Marie shrugged and waved the boy in, "I'm sick of crying anyway."

Robbie plunked onto the floor and sat cross-legged with his head down. Lisa-Marie slid over beside him, "Hey, what's wrong."

"I don't know. I feel scared all the time and my stomach hurts and something strange is happening but I don't know what it is." He raised dark eyes to hers, "Do you ever think about the guy with the gun?"

She sucked in her breath at the memories Robbie's question brought cascading down on her. After a moment, she said, "I had a few nightmares right after it happened and I worry about Sophie when I haven't been with her for a while, but mostly that day seems like something that happened to someone else. Why? Do you still think about it?"

"At first, I thought about it all the time. I didn't want Izzy to die like my mom did. But then I felt okay. Now, I feel scared and I don't know why." He looked up at Lisa-Marie, "Why does everyone have to die?"

"Hey," Lisa-Marie slipped her arm around him, "Come on. Have you talked to Izzy and Liam about how you're feeling?"

"They look at me weird sometimes. I don't want them to worry." He glanced up at Lisa-Marie, "I want everyone to be alright."

She dropped an arm around him and hugged him close, "Ya, I know. Look, I'm going to be alright. I promise. See ... no more tears. That's a start, right? Want to play cards? I'll teach you how to play Gin Rummy if you like."

Robbie nodded as he got up to go to his room for the cards.

❧❧❧❧

Dear Emma:

Justin will never love me. It's over. It still hurts so much I feel like I can't breathe sometimes but it isn't as bad as it was a couple of days ago. The worst part is that I knew all along that what I was doing was a mistake and I did it anyway. I went back to work today and tonight, I broke up with Zach. He picked me up after work and we went for a drive down to the end of the lake. He seemed okay with it. Since I wouldn't sleep with him all this time, he must have realized I wasn't really serious about him as a boyfriend. I thought about being honest and telling him I was sorry for using him and that he deserves a girl who isn't with him to make another guy jealous. But I changed my mind. I'm ashamed of myself enough without giving Zach a reason to think badly of me. *And I did enjoy going out with him – it wasn't all about making Justin squirm.*

Izzy says things will get easier and I believe her most of the time. It's hard at night but I force myself to breathe and relax and not cry. It broke my heart the way my being so upset affected Robbie. The poor kid.

I've been spending a lot of time with Sophie and it has to be any day now that I'll hear about the internship.

Oh my god, oh my God, Emma – I just checked my email and I GOT THE INTERNSHIP AT VOGUE. I can't believe it. It says I should be there in two weeks and a letter is on its way with all kinds of information. I've got to tell Izzy. OH MY GOD.

THIRTY-SIX

Dylan shuffled the cards while Ethan regaled the table with the story of how one of Hannah's friends had videotaped his *Karma Chameleon* dance at the beauty pageant and posted it to YouTube. The post had gone viral and he was getting tweets and texts from all over the world. Justin swigged deeply from a bottle of Southern Comfort and reached over to thump Ethan on the back.

As he started to deal, Dylan said, "I want to tell you guys something –" He pointed the slim cigarillo in his finger at Ethan, "If you lay a fucking finger on those cards before I'm finished dealing, I'll thump you."

Ethan threw his hands up in the air, "Ya, ya, ya ... if I had a dollar for every time you said you'd thump me, I wouldn't even need to get rich and famous from being such a great dancer with a video that has gone viral. Did I mention that?"

Mike stared at Ethan, "Like two minutes ago. Geez, can you get off your own bandwagon for one second." He looked over at Dylan, "I know what you're going to tell us before you go off to your fancy cooking school in Montreal."

Dylan kept dealing, "I seriously doubt that, Mike."

"No, listen ... chefs really do spit in the food of people they don't like. I knew it."

Dylan slapped the deck on the table and squinted like Clint Eastwood as he drew on the cigarillo clamped between his teeth. He placed it in the ashtray to smoulder and exhaled slowly. "Not true, but if I ever see you in a restaurant where I work, I'll make an exception." As they all picked up their cards he said, "What I wanted to say," he stopped to glare at Ethan for a moment

291

before going on, "is really no one's business but my own. When I get to Montreal, I'll be making a new start. I wouldn't want you guys to hear anything about me later and think I was an asshole for not being up front with you."

As the guys sorted their cards, Justin took another drink before he said, "It might be because I'm fucking blasted here, but what the hell are you trying to say? Or did I miss it?"

Dylan took a deep breath and continued to stare at his cards. He threw two of them face down on the table. He picked up the deck and without looking up said, "I'm gay. There, I've said it. I'm out of the closet at a drunken poker party. I must need my head examined."

Mike choked on a chug of beer and Ethan burst out laughing. "If you could see your face right now, Mike. Did you think all gay guys act like me?"

Mike spluttered and turned beet red. "No, of course not. It's a shock, that's all."

Justin put the bottle down and leaned forward to slap Dylan on the back. "Thanks ... I mean that ... for trusting us. It's a fucking courageous admission and I salute you." Justin grabbed the bottle that hadn't been out of his hands most of the night and took another drink.

Dylan looked around the table, "Okay, okay ... true confession time is over. Are we going to play this hand or not? Who wants a card?"

Mike signalled one and said, "I've got some news, if anyone's interested."

Dylan dealt him the card, "Trying to steal my thunder, there Mike?"

Justin started to laugh, "Don't tell me you're gay, too? I don't know if I can handle being the only straight guy in the room."

Mike examined his cards and frowned, "Ha, ha but this could be about as shocking. I kissed Wynter and asked her to go out with me and," he paused for effect before saying, "she said yes."

The table erupted in a series of hoots, whistles and catcalls. Justin raised the bottle and said, "That calls for a drink, Mike. Congratulations."

Mike smirked and said, "Everything's giving you a reason to drink tonight." He picked up the card Dylan dealt him and added, "I'm glad to get some enthusiasm out of you guys. I told Zach earlier and he almost took my head off. I can't blame him ... bad timing. Lisa-Marie dumped him and he's all bummed out. Not that I feel sorry for him. He'll bounce back and have another girlfriend by next week."

The hand was played out and Mike passed Justin the deck. He attempted a shuffle but the cards flew across the table. He grabbed the bottle for another drink and stared over at Mike, "Lisa-Marie broke up with Zach, hey?

"Ya, that's what I said. Are you going to shuffle those cards or not?

Justin lurched up from the table and staggered slightly, "I can't even see the fucking cards anymore. I think I'm going to have to call it a night." He lurched off to the bathroom then up the stairs to the loft above.

After Mike saw Dylan and Ethan out, he flopped down onto the sofa, pulling the old afghan over himself. He smiled as he thought of the shocked look on Zach's face when he'd told him he had a date with Wynter. It was damn sweet to see that egotistical show-off speechless for once.

On the road, walking back towards Micah Camp, Ethan pushed Dylan in the arm, "You really shocked the hell out of me back there. I didn't think you had the guts. So, you'll go to Montreal and be out of the closet."

"I'm not sure what difference that will make for me. I'm not like you. I don't want to spew out my personal life on Facebook. But it will feel good to be honest. I don't like hiding things."

"What if Mike and Justin are already talking about how you can't keep your hands off me since I'm so hot?"

Dylan shook his head in pained resignation, "I really thought I might manage to get all the way back to the Camp without wanting to thump you."

Ethan danced out in front on the gravel road and turned back to wiggle his hips and laugh as he said, "Never going to happen."

❧❧❧❧

Hearing the grunted words, "Come in," Liam walked into his old cabin. Justin sat at the table with his head clutched in his hands. He looked hung-over and wrung-out.

Liam pulled up a chair. "Mike covered for you. He said you had some important school registration stuff to take care of but if I were you, I wouldn't wait too long to get up there. Reg might come looking for you."

Justin cleared his throat and grimaced, "I'm surprised to see you here. I thought you'd have all banded together against me.

"We're concerned about Lisa but Izzy and I have been worried about you, too."

Hunched forward, Justin seemed lost in thought. He finally looked up at Liam and asked, "Did you ever break a girl's heart? I mean look her right in the eye and stomp on her heart?"

Liam shook his head, "No, I haven't done that. But I spent a good number of years making sure no one got close to me, so I didn't exactly have the opportunity."

"You know that pink bunny that Sophie loves so much?" Liam nodded. "It's like I looked for something that mattered that much to Leez and ripped

293

it apart with my bare hands so I could throw it right in her face."

Liam frowned, "Except Lisa's not a child. She's going to be okay. I'm not saying she isn't broken up over what happened, but she's going to be okay. She's stronger than you think. She's not the same mixed-up kid who came here to stay with her Aunt Bethany two summers ago. She's been accepted to an internship in London. She's got people around her who love her and she has her whole life in front of her."

Justin stared at Liam for a moment. "Maybe that's the thing that has screwed me up the most."

"I don't understand."

"She'll be okay and she'll walk away from me forever."

Liam looked confused, "But you're the one walking away. You chose Lauren."

"Yes, I chose Lauren." He paused for a moment. "I made a commitment to being in a relationship with her and that means something to me. I almost messed that up because I didn't trust her. I went off the deep end thinking she was cheating on me. I saw everything through my own fucked-up lens of guilt because I haven't been able to think of anyone but Leez the whole summer. But it's more than that. I can't seem to get beyond my own past of nothing but lies, manipulation and hurt. Even when I acted like a total bastard, walking out on Lauren and not letting her explain, she came after me. She went out on a limb for me. She said she loved me before I ever said anything like that to her." Justin took a shaky breath, "She's normal, Liam. Can you understand how bad I want normal? She's not screwed up like the other girls who've said they love me – girls I've been scared to have anything to do with because the next thing I knew they'd be slitting their wrists or swimming out into a lake and drowning. Lauren grew up in a home with two parents who love her. She could have any guy she wanted but she picked me. She loves me. I want to be the guy who walks away from all the messed up things in my past and gets to be normal."

"I'm not sure normal exists."

Justin ignored Liam's comment. "And the most fucked-up part of all of this is having you sit here and tell me that Leez is strong ... that she's not messed up anymore. Maybe I could have chosen her and it would have been okay because maybe two people with screwed up pasts can make it to normal together."

"It's not too late, Justin. You could talk to Lauren. Tell her the truth ... tell her that you love someone else."

Justin shook his head, "No ... take my word for it, it is way too late. You didn't see Leez's face. What I did to her ... I can't ever go back on that. I can't make things right by hurting Lauren as well."

Liam let out a deep breath, "Can I do anything?"

"Nah. I better get my ass up to the sawmill. But I do appreciate having you come down here to talk to me. If all of you had turned against me, I'm not sure how I could have stood it. This place feels like home to me. You guys are as close to being family as I'm ever going to get." The raw emotion on Justin's face made Liam look away. "I want to come back next year. I'm serious about changing my major to Forestry. I know I could have a real future working up here."

"You'll come to the big barbecue tomorrow at Dad and Cynthia's place – right?"

Justin shrugged, "I think I'll give it a pass. I don't want to make things awkward."

"Here's the thing about awkward, Justin. You've got to do something so regret and anger don't take hold and it's better done sooner than later." Liam looked slowly around his old cabin. "Otherwise you could end up old like me with years of your life gone because you didn't know how the hell to move forward."

A bitter look crossed Justin's face, "Things seem to have worked out well enough for you."

Liam tipped his head to the side thoughtfully, "True enough. But that's a fairy tale ending, right? I'm not sure there are any more of those floating around. But you never know."

THIRTY-SEVEN

In front of the mirror in Nick's bedroom, Fiona tucked her white shirt into her jeans. She smiled over her shoulder at him as he tugged on his pants. "Better hurry up or we'll be late for the barbecue."

Nick moved behind her to lift her hair and kiss her neck. "I could get used to this friendship."

She pushed him away, "Well, don't get greedy. I'm going into an eighty-hour week so I won't see you for a while."

Nick pulled open the closet and grabbed a shirt, "I might have to show up at the emergency room or something." He clutched at his chest, "I think I feel heart palpitations coming on."

⚜⚜⚜⚜

Beulah and Bethany headed down the trail from the A-Frame to Alex and Cynthia's building site. They were each carrying a bag of buns. Beulah kicked a branch to the side of the trail as she spoke, "I'm finding it hard to get used to working in the bakery without Arianna. Never thought I'd be saying something like that. I'm really going to miss that kid."

"I'll be finishing up work on the research job as soon as Jillian gets back." Bethany hefted up her bag to get a better grip. "Let's take a couple of days off in the middle of September and go down to Vancouver to find out how she's settling in. She might be ready to see some familiar faces by then."

"I like the sound of that." Beulah smiled over at Bethany, "I've been thinking that maybe we should take on another kid for work experience."

"Good idea. I've got a heavy course load for the fall and I'll have to be in Victoria for a week in October and one in November to do on-campus work."

296

With a grin, Bethany changed the subject, "You took the loss of the ball tournament well."

Beulah shrugged with resignation, "I couldn't have expected much ... not with the team I had. There were some serious holes in the line-up. Anyway, it wouldn't have looked good for the local team to have won *The First Annual Caleb Jenkins Memorial Ball Tournament.* But don't hold me to that sentiment next year."

"So the resurrection of baseball in our lives is an ongoing thing?"

Beulah's face took on a comical look as she said, "I might have to change the name of the team, though. Some guy came up to me in town the other day and gave me an earful. Seems the Crater Lake Timber Wolves is a misnomer. Apparently, there are no Timber Wolves on the Island."

"A wolf is a wolf. What's the difference?"

"That's just what I said. Apparently, Timber Wolves live on the mainland and they're big, mean animals. They go up against bears for their food. The Island variety of wolf is smaller and more laid-back. They live out on the coastal stretches, eat salmon and dig for clams." Her mouth twisted to the side as she frowned, "When it comes to being laid-back, this year's team certainly fit the Island wolf profile. Not what I'm looking for next year." She shrugged, "I'll have to consider my options."

✻ ✻ ✻ ✻ ✻

Cynthia stood with Alex in the middle of the newly-framed cabin and looked around. "It's really coming along, isn't it," she said as she grabbed Alex and hugged him.

He chuckled, "I suppose it is shaping up to be a better space than the camper but no matter how great this place turns out to be, I'll always have a soft spot for that camper bed where I first put the steamy sex scenes from your books to the test." He ran his hands down her back and leaned close to kiss her.

She shoved him away, "Behave, you. People will be here any minute." She looked at him seriously for a moment, "Are you feeling okay about settling down?"

"My place is here ... with you and everyone else." He stared out at the majestic view from the front window, "With no effort on my part, I've somehow managed to end up in a place where I'm surrounded by family. I like the feeling. I want to be here to see my granddaughter grow up. Fiona needs me around and I'm interested in seeing where Liam eventually takes his own brand of activism." He looked back at Cynthia, "And I'm worried about Robbie. My gut tells me he needs all of us to stay close."

∗∗∗∗∗

In the kitchen at Micah Camp, Brigit helped Dylan put the finishing touches on a large tray of fancy, dessert squares. "I feel bad going off to this barbecue and leaving you here on your own."

Dylan waved away her words, "I've got only a few days left to have a whole kitchen to myself. Don't worry about me. Ethan said he'd help out. I'm not sure if that will be more of a pain than doing everything myself but I couldn't look a gift horse in the mouth. Take Tabby and have fun enjoying someone else's cooking for a change."

She smiled up at him, "I don't know how to thank you ... you know that, right? I could never have got the hang of things around here without you." She grabbed his arm. "Give me a hug."

She held onto him tightly and only stopped hugging when Tabby tugged on her leg, "Hurry up, Mom. Robbie will already be there." With huge eyes, she looked at the tray of desserts, "Can I have one of those now," she pleaded.

Brigit shook her head, "No way. Come on, let's get going. We don't want to keep Robbie Collins waiting, that's for sure."

∗∗∗∗∗

Izzy stood in the kitchen of her and Liam's cabin and made a face at him when he whistled for the dogs. "Oh good grief, there's going to be at least a dozen people over there and it's the middle of the day. We don't need the dogs getting underfoot, do we?" She dug through the drawer in search of a lid for the large plastic bowl of potato salad. Glancing over at Robbie who was tossing his soccer ball up and down in the air, she added, "Better not do that inside."

Robbie headed for the door as Izzy snapped the lid on the bowl and passed it to Liam, "Let's walk down their new driveway instead of going through the orchard. I haven't seen it since it's been finished."

Robbie stopped, turned back and shook his head, "I don't want to go that way."

"Get moving, Robbie. Don't stop right in the doorway." Lisa-Marie stood behind him with Sophie in her arms and a heavy diaper bag over her shoulder. "What difference does it make which way we go? Can you take this for me?" She let the bag slide down her arm and thrust it toward him.

Robbie grabbed the bag as he said, "It's longer that way." He made the choice for everyone by walking towards the trail through the apple trees.

Izzy gave Liam a searching look as she followed him out the door. They'd talked for a while the night before about Rosemary's inability to find anything physically wrong with Robbie and her suggestion that perhaps he should see a child psychologist. Things weren't getting better. Izzy had to admit Robbie wasn't himself – sadder and more irritable than she'd ever known him to be. She had heard him up more than a few times the previous night and he'd had dark circles around his eyes in the morning.

✻✻✻✻✻

The site of Alex and Cynthia's cabin was a hive of a colour and activity. Wide strips of pink and yellow marker tape had been strung up to show where the grass would be planted. The deck in front of the cabin had been decorated with more tape where the railings would eventually be. Several lengths of bright cloth had been hung from the clothes line where they swayed and wafted in the breeze. Most of the guests had arrived and the sounds of their voices and laughter competed with the musical notes from the many sets of chimes that dangled along the edges of the deck roof and in the nearby trees.

Lisa-Marie jostled Sophie on her knee and fed the child chunks of cheese from a nearby snack tray as she chatted with Josie, Brigit and her Aunt Bethany. The women were seated at a picnic table close to Cynthia and Alex's framed-in cabin. Beyond them stretched a newly cleared section of wilderness that dropped off into layers of salal sloping down to the shore of the lake. Behind the cabin, thick trees marched their way up the hill.

"Hey, munchkin," Lisa-Marie pulled Sophie's hand back from the tray, "You already have a piece in your mouth and one in your hand."

Josie laughed, "Just be happy she has a good appetite. Both my kids were the pickiest eaters on the planet. It drove me crazy."

Brigit took a sip of wine from her plastic glass as she nudged Lisa-Marie, "When did you hear about the internship?"

"Just a couple of days ago. They emailed me last week and asked me to send a set of three more photos. I've been in contact with a girl who got the internship last year. She had told me that if I got an email like that, it would mean they were deciding between two or three applicants."

"What did you send them? It must have been hard to choose with so much on the line." Brigit popped a chunk of smoked salmon into her mouth and her eyebrows went up, "Oh my goodness, this is delicious. I have to know how to make this."

Bethany pointed to the old, battered fridge that stood at the edge of the clearing near the trees. "You'll have to talk to Alexander. According to Cynthia, he's like some sort of alchemist with his secret, smoked salmon recipes." She grabbed a piece for herself and pointed it at Lisa-Marie, "What photos did you end up with? Last time I heard, you were down to about five."

Lisa-Marie held onto Sophie as the baby pointed to Tabby and Robbie and tried to wriggle off her lap. The two other kids had a soccer ball they were kicking around in the clearing. She got up from the table and called out to Robbie, "Can you bring the ball away from the slope and let Sophie play, too."

Robbie shook his head, "Liam said not to play close to the trees. Keep her with you or put her in the playpen." His young voice rose, "She'll wreck the game."

"Come on, don't be like that. She's driving me nuts trying to get down. She'll just scream if I put her in the playpen. All she wants is to be with you guys." Lisa set Sophie down on the ground and crouched beside the child. "You don't have to go all the way to the trees, there's lots of room between them and the hillside. I just don't want her toppling down that slope."

Tabby ran over and held her arms out for Sophie. She called back to Robbie, "We can let her play for a while, right Robbie?" The boy made a face at Tabby as he moved to the middle of the cleared space.

Lisa-Marie turned back to the women gathered at the table and reached for her wine as she sat down. She filled a cracker with a thin slice of cheese and smoked salmon. "Where was I? Oh, right – picking the three photos I would send. It was hard to choose. In the end, I went with one of Wynter's tasteful nudes. We were down by the beach and I got the best look on her face – a sort of wide-eyed, startled thing. I picked a black and white of Beulah – that one where she's pulling a batch of bread from the outdoor oven." She smiled knowingly at her aunt. "And one of Sophie out in the garden."

Josie whistled, "I'm sure you couldn't go wrong with anything of Wynter. That girl seems to have everything going for her. Sounds like you choose a nice mix. When do you leave for London?"

Crunching around the cracker, Lisa-Marie said, "I have to be there right after Labour Day."

Brigit kept her eyes on the kids as she spoke, "Wow ... that doesn't give you much time."

"Ya, don't I know it." Lisa-Marie sighed. "But they expected all the applicants to be ready just in case."

Josie asked, "Do you know where you'll be living when you get there?"

"I haven't got a clue. I emailed the family I lived with last fall when I stayed in London, but they've recently sold their house to move out to the country." She shrugged, "I suppose I'll just have to find a cheap hotel for the first bit until I get a lead on an apartment. I've been searching on the internet ever since I heard."

Bethany reached past Lisa-Marie to grab the last piece of smoked salmon. She stood up with the empty tray. "I better get Alex to refill this before everyone else notices we've chowed down an entire fish."

Brigit got up as well. "Let me go with you. Maybe I'll be able to get his secret recipe." She glanced from the kids to Lisa-Marie, "You'll keep an eye on them, right?" She looked over to where Reg stood guzzling a beer with Beulah, "Ever since Reg showed up on my front porch, I keep getting this prickly feeling down my back."

Josie burst out laughing, "Ya, Reg will do that to a person alright."

Brigit pushed Josie's arm, "About the cougar, silly."

Lisa-Marie swung around to face the kids and sipped her wine. Sophie was hilarious as she toddled on her short, stocky legs between Robbie and Tabby. Her face lit up with a wide smile as she grabbed onto the ball and plopped backwards into the dirt on her bum.

※◇※◇※◇※◇

Inside the framed cabin, Cynthia pointed to a space in front of low windows that backed onto a view of the trees behind the cabin. "This is where the bathtub will be. We've got plans for ceramic tiles in blues and greens for around the whole thing." She glanced back at Izzy, Nick and Fiona. She'd spent the last fifteen minutes expounding on the simplicity of the saltbox roof design, the orientation of the cabin and placement of windows to take best advantage of natural lighting, and her vision of the entire place finished and ready to live in.

But, truth be told, she'd been hard-pressed to take her eyes from Fiona who stood close to Nick and let her hand linger on his arm. She had also noticed the looks that passed between the two of them on a regular basis. She found herself grinning as she turned away. She'd been fairly certain since the night of the book club when Nick jumped up to walk Fiona home, that something had to be up with the pair of them. The strange way they behaved towards one another following the attack on Fiona only confirmed her ideas.

301

❧❧❧❧

Stepping onto the wide, covered deck that ran the entire front length of the cabin, Fiona stared out at the view. The tree-covered hills overlapped each other as they framed the edge of the lake and drew the eye to the mountains beyond. She could picture her father and Cynthia sitting in the wood rockers that already graced the deck and taking in this view. She could hear Cynthia off to one side talking to Nick about the plot for her next novel. Maybe it wasn't so bad, her father and this white woman. She glanced at Nick and a lazy, bedroom smile greeted her when their eyes met. She was hardly one to set standards.

"Fiona, can I talk to you for a minute?" Izzy stood beside her at the railing. "How are you?"

"I'm good. Going into a few long days of work but I'm hoping to free up some time next week to meet with you again."

Izzy's gaze went to Robbie kicking at the soccer ball out in the cleared patch of dirt. "We're thinking of following up on Rosemary's referral of Robbie to a child psychologist."

Without conscious thought, Fiona looked around for her father. He stood by the fish smoker talking to Bethany and Brigit. "What does dad say?"

"We haven't told him. I hoped you'd be on side in case he didn't like the idea."

Fiona shook her head, "I'm afraid that all the influencing between my father and me flows in one direction and that consists of him telling me what to do."

❧❧❧❧

Justin took the cut-off from Izzy and Liam's road and walked down the newly cleared driveway towards Alex and Cynthia's place. The late afternoon shade of the trees was welcome. He was fashionably late, having argued himself into and out of going to the barbecue about a dozen times.

The sun filtered down through the canopy of evergreen branches in shafts alternately darkening and lighting the path at his feet. The quick snap of a branch somewhere off to his right caught his attention. He swung around to stare into the bush. Moments passed and a deep quiet settled around him again. He shrugged his shoulders and carried on. It had probably been a squirrel. For small animals, squirrels could make a lot of racket.

Passing first Reg's truck then Alex's, Justin skirted his way around the camper and almost ran into Cynthia coming down the narrow metal steps with a tray of burger patties balanced in her hands. She laughed as he took the tray from her so she could latch the camper door. "Glad you could make it, Justin. Help yourself to snacks and a cold drink." She waved her hand to the bowls of chips and the platters of food on the nearby picnic table.

He nodded, trying to avoid staring at Lisa-Marie as he walked over to Reg and Beulah. She slapped him on the back. "Let me grab you a cold one, kid." After passing him a beer, she said, "I've been talking to Reg about next year's baseball team line-up. He says you'll be back here working, so I take it that means you're in. We're going to have a damned hard time filling Arianna's spot. And while I'm on the subject of Arianna," Beulah nudged Justin with her arm. "Will you keep an eye out for her when you get back to school?"

"You're about the fourth person who's already asked me. I will definitely check up on her."

Beulah gave Justin a searching look and lowered her voice, "You look like shit. What's up?"

He shook his head and took another drink. As hard as he tried to focus on Reg and Beulah's banter, his eyes and attention kept going to the nearby picnic table and the girl with the long, honey-coloured hair. He couldn't help it and he couldn't stop – not even when he glanced over and saw Izzy staring at him from the front porch of the cabin. He expected her to glare at him but she only gazed at him with what he thought might be compassion before turning back to her conversation with Fiona and Nick.

He told himself over and over that he'd made the right decision. Lauren was the girl for him. But the last two nights in a row he'd woken up in a cold sweat with Lisa's words running through his head – *I'll hate you forever if you choose her instead of me.* Eventually, she looked over at him and the dull nothingness on her face forced him to turn his eyes away.

⚜⚜⚜⚜

Robbie rolled his shoulders as he watched the soccer ball arc through the air towards Tabby and Sophie. He called out to Lisa-Marie, "Come and get Sophie. She's just in the way." A blur of movement through the trees caught his attention. He peered into the shadows but could see nothing but underbrush and darkness. Sweat ran down his side and his skin prickled. All he had wanted to do since arriving at the new cabin site was run back to Izzy and Liam's to huddle in his bed with the blankets pulled over his head. His stomach hurt and he rubbed at the ache in his hip.

Tabby caught the ball and threw it to the ground, gesturing for Sophie to follow her, making kicking motions with her foot as she hop-stepped beside the child. "Let her have one more kick, okay?" she called.

Robbie watched as Liam walked away from the barbecue, calling out something to their father as he waved to where Sophie tried to kick the ball. Smoke rose into the air and he could smell the seared meat. His stomach rolled over with hunger causing an odd, sick feeling that made him think he might have to throw up. The prickling sensation got worse and he scratched wildly at his back as Sophie's little foot connected with the ball and made it roll easily towards him.

He moved forward and gave the ball a solid kick that sent its spinning white and black patches soaring just past the side of Liam's head. Robbie wanted to shout out that he was sorry but a blinding pain hit him between the eyes and he choked on the words that caught suddenly in his throat. A shiver ran up his spine and his heart started to thud like he'd just ran a mile. The hot pins-and-needles sensation on his skin was replaced with a sudden, clammy chill. He spun around and stared into the dark shadows under the trees. He heard Sophie chortling away and clapping. Tabby called his name but it seemed as though their voices were coming from a great distance. Time stood still as he felt the presence of the animal that lurked in the shadows. Pain and fear and longing hit him in successive waves. The cougar was moving, coming out, coming to him. The desire, finally, to answer the intensity of the animal's call overwhelmed him.

Lisa-Marie looked up as Tabby hoisted Sophie into her arms. Her gaze swivelled over to Robbie as he moved towards the tree line. Her piercing scream got everyone's attention. She stood up and swung her leg over the bench of the picnic table. Liam looked past Robbie at the cougar that crouched as still as a statue with its large paws planted firmly in the dirt. The animal's yellowed teeth were visible around the tongue that lolled from its mouth. Its emaciated body was skeletal with ribs standing out in stark contrast along the sides of its golden coat. A vivid, nasty wound snaked over its haunch. The cat's tail began to move hypnotically.

Justin covered the distance that lay between him and Lisa-Marie in an instant. He grabbed her from behind, holding her tight as she struggled to get free. Leaning close to her ear, he whispered, "Don't move. You could spook it. Liam's closest."

Liam moved with slow measured steps. His quiet voice ordered, "Tabby, you hold Sophie tight and stay still. I'm coming for you." The girl turned large, frightened eyes towards him. She clutched onto the squirming baby for dear life and stayed rooted in her spot as if her tiny feet were encased in concrete.

The moment that Reg heard Lisa-Marie's scream, his eyes followed the direction of hers to the tawny animal that stood in the shadow of the trees. He sprinted for his truck, wrenched open the door and grabbed his rifle from behind the seat. He ran back towards the clearing in front of the cabin pumping a cartridge into the breach of the gun as he went.

Liam's heart did a flip in his chest as he got within a few steps of Tabby only to see Robbie tilt his head to one side, look at the cat and move towards the animal. He heard Izzy's strangled gasp in the quiet of the clearing as he grabbed Tabby around the waist, clutched his other arm protectively around Sophie and began to back them all up. He called out, "Robbie, stop. Don't move another step."

Robbie heard Liam's command but he couldn't stop. The animal's call was too strong. A cascade of images flitted in front of his eyes – the cougar as a kitten nestled in his arms, the nights spent with the animal beside him in bed, the hours by the cage scratching the large cat behind the ears, the emptiness he had felt when he went out one morning and the cage was unoccupied. On one level, Robbie knew that none of those things had actually happened to him, but he had become the boy the cat sought. Nothing could change that. He kept moving forward and the cat moved now, too – it was coming to him, its heart wide-open, with recognition in its sunken eyes. It would stretch out on the ground and Robbie would lie beside it and he would scratch the animal behind the ears. Everything else ceased to exist but that one thought.

Reg rounded the corner of the trail near the cabin. He stopped for a moment to register where everyone stood. "Don't anyone move," he shouted. He cursed under his breath as Robbie stepped forward. Reg dropped down on one knee, flicked off the gun's safety, confidently took aim and shot. The bullet struck the cougar broadside going straight through its heart and dropping it where it stood.

The echo of the shot reverberated around and around the clearing in stereo with Robbie's screams. The boy fell onto his knees and began to crawl towards the fallen animal, whimpering a single word – no – over and over. A sudden gust of wind from the lake set all the chimes ringing wildly and items on the clothes line billowed out in a riot of swirling colour.

Alex pulled Robbie up from the ground. Lisa-Marie took Sophie from Liam. The little girl screamed in outrage at having been pulled away from the game. Brigit held her arms out to Tabby. Izzy ran to Robbie and Alex who gently turned the sobbing boy into her arms.

Robbie choked out words against her shoulder, "That cougar didn't want to hurt anyone. He was scared and hungry. He wanted to be close to me. Why does everyone have to die? Why does everyone leave me?" He pulled away from Izzy suddenly and shouted at Reg, "You didn't have to kill him. I hate you."

THIRTY-EIGHT

R obbie walked across the sawmill yard, hanging his head and muttering, "I don't want to hear anything that stupid asshole, Reg, has to say. You can drag me up here but you can't make me listen to him."

Liam dropped his arm around his brother's shoulder, "Come on. Don't talk like that. What he has to tell you could be important."

Reg got up from his desk when they came into the office, "Let's head up to the lunch room. It's more comfortable there."

Once up the narrow stairs, Robbie slumped onto the old couch and folded his arms defiantly across his chest. Reg poured a coffee and sat down at the table. Liam stood near the window looking down into the yard. Reg cleared his throat, chugged the dark brew and said, "I have a friend who's a conservation officer down Island. He called me this morning with the results of the necropsy on the cougar's body. The animal was starving and riddled with infection from the wound on his haunch." He looked over at Robbie, "If I hadn't shot him someone else would have had to. No one would want an animal to suffer like that."

Robbie didn't meet Reg's gaze and Liam didn't interfere. Reg frowned before he said, "Listen, kid, there's more. My friend thinks he knows something about this particular cat. About four months ago, the conservation people got a report from an undercover cop that a cougar was penned up in an old house outside of Campbell River and that it was being used to guard a grow-op. When the cops busted up the operation, the animal was nowhere around. Looking into the whole thing a bit further, they found out that the guy who was running the show had raised the cat from a cub, let it hang out with his dogs, allowed his kid to feed it with a baby bottle, for Christ's sake.

Anyway, the goddamned fool admitted to driving the cat up here and letting it go on the road out to Crater Lake." Reg shifted in his chair, "If it was the same cat, that explains a lot ... why it wasn't afraid of dogs and why it was starving. Cougars are territorial. A young male has trouble at the best of times establishing its own hunting area but with no experience in the wild ... well, the thing was doomed from the get go."

As Reg spoke, Liam watched Robbie. The boy's face had gone pale and though he pretended he didn't give a shit what Reg was saying, Liam could see that wasn't true. The story Reg told had the boy riveted to his spot on the couch.

Before they left, Liam gave Robbie a long look and the boy made a face. He turned to Reg and said, "I'm sorry for saying I hate you." Taking a deep breath, he looked disdainfully at the man sitting at the small table and raised his voice, "I hate what you did. I hate your guns and your dogs. That cougar wasn't going to hurt anyone. He was sick because a bear mauled him. He was coming out to me because he was mixed up. He thought I was the boy who fed him from a baby bottle. He thought I visited him when he was stuck in a cage in a dark garage. He thought it was me who lay outside by his pen and scratched him behind the ear –" Robbie's voice choked with emotion and he stared down at his feet.

Reg frowned and said, "How the hell do you know the cougar was injured by a bear or kept in any cage in a garage, or penned up in some yard?"

"What do you care? The only good cougar is a dead cougar, right Reg?" Robbie turned and walked out of the lunchroom; the thump of his feet on the stairs echoed after him.

As the door slammed shut, Liam turned to Reg and said, "It was all I could do to get him to come up here and listen to you. He'll come around."

Reg shrugged, "Sticks and stones. I had to do what I thought was right. I don't take chances when kids are involved."

After Liam left, Reg took a sip of his cold coffee and shook his head. He hadn't shared with anyone all the details he'd learned about the necropsy, including the speculation that the young, male cougar had been injured by a bear taking a swipe at him with a huge paw. And he certainly hadn't mentioned the fact that his friend, the conservation officer, had told him about going to the home of the man who was suspected of keeping a cougar. His friend had seen the cage in the garage and the pen was still sitting in the backyard. He had even talked to the boy and Reg was betting the kid was probably about Robbie's age. Reg's old man had always told him – *there's a helluva a lot more to this old world than meets the eye, boyo.* Reg supposed that must be true because there was sure as shit no logical way for Robbie to know what he seemed to know. The kid was a strange one, no denying the fact, with an odd, silent way of looking at people.

Reg put his cup down and his mind replayed the moment before he had shot and killed the cat. He saw again, Robbie stepping forward with confidence and he recalled the way the cougar's body had relaxed in that split second before his finger applied the right amount of pressure to the trigger. He knew now that in that moment, there had been no aggression in the animal.

Robbie was quiet on the walk back down the trail to the cabin. Without a word, he wandered off into the garden. Liam watched as the boy made his way out to the cliff deck to sit on the swinging chair and stare out at the lake.

He was working in the shop about an hour later when Robbie came in and sat down on the old couch in the corner. His voice was choked as he said, "I knew everything Reg said before he said it. It seemed like he was telling me about a movie I'd already seen."

Liam moved away from the workbench and the mess of nails and screws he'd been trying to sort and sat down beside Robbie. The boy stared over at him for a second before he said, "I must have dreamed a lot of it but some of it wasn't a dream."

Liam listened while Robbie told him, in fits and starts, everything that had happened since the cougar had been released on the road to the lake a few months ago. He forced himself to remain calm when Robbie admitted, "I took the roast out to him. I remember crawling inside the hollowed out log. When I woke up later that morning my bed and pajamas were a mess."

After that Robbie was quiet and Liam asked, "Why didn't you come and tell us something was wrong?"

Tears filled Robbie's eyes, "I didn't want Izzy to worry. I saw how upset she was when Dr. Rosemary said I should maybe see a shrink."

Liam nodded thoughtfully, "How do you feel now?"

The boy shrugged his thin shoulders, "Better, I guess. My stomach doesn't hurt anymore and I don't feel so weird all the time." He looked over at Liam, "Reg didn't have to kill him. Maybe we could have fed him and made him better."

"Maybe ... but then what? What would life be like for a wild animal that had been so badly treated? He couldn't ever have become anyone's pet. You know that, Robbie. He would have ended up in a cage for the rest of his life."

Robbie looked sad and miserable when he said, "But he would have had me. He loved me."

Liam didn't know what else to say. He looked at his watch and hoped that diversion might be the appropriate strategy. "Lisa will be taking Sophie down for a swim as soon as she wakes up. Want to walk over to the Camp and get Tabby?" They left the workshop together.

When Robbie was down at the beach, Liam went in search of his father. Alex was taking a break, sitting in one of the rockers on his cabin porch. Liam sat down beside him. Alex tugged a letter out of his pocket, waving it in the air as he spoke, "You're just the person I wanted to see. I got this letter in the mail from the granddaughter of that Elder Robbie talked with down on the waterfront in Victoria." Liam's father pulled a piece of paper from the envelope. "Her grandmother says Robbie needs to talk to someone about his animal guide and his gift. Apparently there's an Elder in Cedar Falls who has some experience with this type of thing."

Liam frowned, "I wish she had said something sooner."

"They've a hard time tracking me down. This letter's got more miles on it than my old truck. It went to the university in Victoria, then back east and finally, somehow, it managed to make its way to your post box."

"I came over here to talk to you about Robbie." Liam laid his hands flat on the thighs of his worn jeans and stared at them. "I'm worried about him. His connection to that cougar goes way deeper than we thought. It's behind all the sleepwalking and he says that he not only dreamed about it but he actually went out to the thing when it was sick. It had holed up in a hollowed log up the trail from here. I went and had a look and the log was exactly the way Robbie described it. What he remembers of the dreams matches completely with Reg's information from the conservation officer down Island." Looking over at his father, Liam added, "Robbie could have been seriously hurt."

Alex nodded thoughtfully, "Well, let's take him up to Cedar Falls to see what the Elder has to say."

The next day, Alex and Liam sat out on the steps of a house on the reserve in Cedar Falls while Robbie talked with the old man inside. When they came out Robbie was smiling and showing off the twisted braid of cedar he had made. "I'm going to give it to Tabby," he said. He turned to Liam, "Can I play soccer for a while?"

"Come back to the truck in about an hour, okay. I've got a couple of people I want to check in on but then we have to get back." Liam waved to his father who had taken out a pouch of tobacco which he carried with him into the small house.

THIRTY-NINE

J ustin spotted Lisa-Marie as she came out of Izzy and Liam's cabin. He had
been waiting up near the koi pond for almost twenty minutes hoping to get
a chance to talk to her alone. He stood up and walked down to the kitchen
deck, calling out as he went, "Leez, can we talk?" She halted, turning her
head. The look on her face told him she was going to say no. He held up his
hand, "Just for a minute. Please."

She hesitated and shrugged, "I've got to pick up some things at the Camp.
You can walk with me if you want."

He fell into step beside her as she headed along the path that led through
the apple trees. "I heard from Liam that you got the internship at Vogue. I
wanted to tell you, I knew you would. How could they not pick someone as
talented as you?" When she didn't answer or look at him, he let out a shaky
breath, "I don't want you to leave here hating me."

"I shouldn't have said that. I'll never hate you." She kept her eyes on the
trail ahead. Her voice was controlled and the words she spoke sounded
rehearsed, "I need to get over you. It's been three summers now with me
chasing after you, wanting you to want me. But you never have." He opened
his mouth to answer but she kept talking. "I can't take it anymore ... not after
being with you the way we were. It hurts too much. I need to walk away and
not look back."

Justin kept pace with her as her footsteps sped up. The silence stretched
out as he tried to figure out how to respond. He wanted to bridge the distance
between them but he didn't want to go so far over that bridge that he might
hurt her any more than he already had. He tried to buy some time when he
said, "It's not like we'll never see each other again. I'm coming back next

summer and I want to look for work here when I finish school. And there's Sophie. I'm not going to stop seeing her."

Lisa-Marie turned to face him. As she spoke, her eyes flashed something so cold he shivered in the warmth of the August morning. "No worries. You'll be living happily ever after with Lauren and play-acting daddy with my daughter." She took a deep breath and drew her arms around herself, "I know I sound bitter and right now, I guess I am. But I'll get past it. And when I do," she paused to stare at him, "I'll feel like the singer of that sappy song Izzy likes and you'll be – *only someone that I used to love.*"

She turned to walk away. He couldn't let her go, not like this. He grabbed her arm, "You don't know how everything in the future is going to be. No one does."

She shook her head violently, "You've made your choice, Justin. Let me go."

He dropped her arm and stepped back. "Okay, okay, I made my choice. But that doesn't mean I never wanted you. I did and what happened the other night was as real for me as it was for you. I was a total asshole to try to make you believe anything else. I needed you. I was hurting so bad. Then I felt guilty about what I had done and I didn't want to own up to my part in all of this."

Looking away towards the lake, he tried to find the words to explain, "There are so many things holding us together, Leez. Shit, it's this place and it's Sophie. It's you knowing how I made a fool of myself over Izzy and me knowing about what happened between you and Liam. It's the things we talked about the night Maddy tried to kill herself. It's what happened to Edward and it's me being scared shitless that something could have happened to you or Sophie. We can't ever go back from being with each other through things like that."

Tears had sprung up in Lisa-Marie's eyes as Justin spoke but he saw her swipe them away as a cold look settled on her features. "You chose Lauren."

She backed up and Justin stepped towards her, "Leez, wait, I –"

Lisa-Marie held up her hands to stop him, "No ... don't say anything else. I need only one thing from you. Let me go." She turned quickly to walk down the path and out of his life.

ᑊᑐᑊᑐᑊᑐᑊᑐ

With a loud hoot of triumph, Robbie slapped down his last card in the game of Crazy Eights. He looked around Tabby's cabin and asked, "Where is Mr. Jangles? I haven't seen him once since I got here."

Tabby's head went down and her lip came out, "He's gone. My mom said we had to give him to Jim and let him live in Dearborn where it's safer. He was always trying to get out and even though that cougar is dead now, something else might get him." Tabby picked up the cards and tried to shuffle the way Robbie had taught her but she made a mess of it. He reached out to take the deck from her.

"It's like this." He showed her how to do the shuffle again and passed the cards back. "You'll probably be able to go and visit Mr. Jangles at Jim's house."

Tabby smiled as she managed to shuffle the deck without dropping it. She started to deal and asked, "Why were you so sad that Reg killed the cougar? My mom said it was very dangerous."

"The cougar didn't do anything wrong. He was hungry and hurting and he didn't belong here." Robbie picked up his cards.

"Not like us, right, Robbie? We belong here, right?"

He looked thoughtfully at Tabby and saw the flashing light of need that surrounded her. He nodded as he said, "Yes, we do."

Tabby sorted her cards and frowned, "What do you call those black shovel things again?"

"I've told you a hundred times, spades."

She grinned and dropped a two of spades on the pile, "Pick up two. Do you think we should get married when we grow up?"

Robbie snorted and picked through his hand, gathering cards, "Not if it means wearing a stupid suit and kissing and dancing and making dumb speeches." He slapped down three twos and said, "Pick up eight."

Tabby moaned, "But Izzy was beautiful and Liam didn't mind." She started picking up cards.

"Ya, well, I would."

Arranging her hand, Tabby said, "We could still get married."

Robbie shrugged, "I suppose."

⚜⚜⚜⚜

The noon sun caught in the draping fronds of the wisteria, dotting the kitchen deck with wisps of shade. Cynthia and Alex sat with Izzy and Liam drinking glasses of iced tea. Alex leaned forward in his chair as he said, "I've been reading up on the special significance cougars once had for First Nations people on the coast ... they're feared and revered in equal measure. Shamans made use of cougar teeth, paws, claws and hides to guard against illness and other misfortunes." Alex looked over at Izzy. "The Elder says we need to keep a closer eye on Robbie. The strength of his gift is intensifying and with a volatile and unpredictable spirit guide like a cougar, he's vulnerable."

Izzy frowned as a look of concern washed over her face, "How are we supposed to know what to watch for, Alex? None of us recognized the sleepwalking as a sign of any of this."

"The Elder will keep working with him but he says it's you that Robbie needs the most." Izzy's eyes widened as Alex continued to speak. "This is what I got from what the old man said. Robbie is not over his mom's death and he's afraid of losing you. He's happy here and he feels like he's found his place but there's a part of him that believes it will all fall apart if anything happens to you ... like it did when he lost his mother. And he still isn't over the trauma of the shooting."

Tears came into Izzy's eyes as she stared from Alex to Liam. "Well, to be honest, neither am I. What should I do?"

Liam reached out and squeezed her hand, "More of what you've already been doing all along. When the time is right, I think you need to make him understand that he can come and tell you if he starts to feel anything like what he just went through. He kept way too much of it to himself, mostly because he didn't want you to worry."

Izzy sat up straight in her chair, "I'm going to take some time off work."

Liam frowned, "Hold it ... I wasn't trying to say you needed to make a major lifestyle change. Your work matters."

"I'd already decided. Roland's coming back early and I need some time to think about a bunch of things. And what you're both telling me makes me surer than ever that this is the right decision. If Robbie's going to be able to come to me, I have to be around." She looked into Liam's eyes, "If we're going to do this family thing right, we've only got one shot. It will be over before we know it.

⁓⁓⁓⁓

Lisa-Marie watched as Sophie sucked avidly at her afternoon bottle. The child gazed up at her with heavy-lidded eyes. Comfortable on the swing chair out on the cliff deck, she pulled the top of the large stroller down to shade the child's face and pushed the wheeled contraption back and forth with her foot as Sophie finished her bottle and dozed off.

Gazing at the slight ripple on the lake that made it look like a gleaming sheet of plastic wrap, she let her daughter sleep while a combination of pain and excitement whirled around inside her own chest. Thoughts of leaving Sophie made her throat ache with unshed tears. Knowing she was moving on without even the dream of Justin put a cold, aching chill around her heart. But weaving in and out of those emotions she felt breath-catching anticipation for what the coming year in London would hold. No matter how much information she gathered beforehand, she knew that the internship was more than she could wrap her head around and that it would only be understood as it unfolded. Along with all the excitement came fear. There were so many things to do and arrange.

"Hey, Leez." She turned her head and saw Robbie coming towards the deck. He plopped down on the swing chair beside her.

She nudged him with her elbow and said, "Hey, yourself. How are you doing?" There was concern in her light-hearted tone. For all the fear she had felt when she spotted the cougar, the time between her first scream and the end of the incident had been short. Before she'd had a chance to go over the edge of panic, Sophie was in her arms and the cougar was dead. It was Robbie's sobbing over the animal's downed body that stayed with her.

Robbie pulled a braided piece of cedar out of his pocket, "I made this for Tabby up at the reserve the other day."

Lisa-Marie took the soft, brown bark and smoothed it out in her hand. "If you get Liam to help you put this on a piece of leather, you could make her a really neat hairband."

Taking the braid back and stuffing it in his pocket, Robbie said, "Cool." He kicked the toes of his runners against the deck as he said, "Justin still loves you."

Lisa-Marie shook her head, "Maybe he does. I love him, too. But love isn't enough when he wants to be with someone else."

"It won't last. Justin and Lauren, I mean." Lisa-Marie frowned at him and he added, "Just saying."

"Okay, enough about other peoples' business."

✸✸✸✸

Izzy walked with Liam, hand in hand out to the cliff deck. They stood with their backs against the railing and watched as Robbie and Lisa-Marie swayed back and forth on the swing chair engrossed in their card game. Izzy leaned forward to peek inside the stroller. Sophie was fast asleep. Lisa swept her hand down on the bench, smiled at Robbie and said, "Gin."

Glancing over at Liam, Izzy smiled warmly and turned to Lisa who was gathering up the cards. "We have some news." Lisa and Robbie both looked up quickly and waited for Izzy to continue. She said, "I've decided to take some time off work. Liam and I would like to bring Robbie and Sophie and come to London with you for at least the first month of your internship." Robbie had moved forward on the chair; his face was covered by a bright smile. The look of relief that flooded over Lisa's features was confirmation enough for Izzy that they were doing the right thing. "We can help you get set up with a place of your own; then we're going to explore a bit of Scotland."

Robbie jumped up, "Would I be able to see a real castle?"

"More than one I'm sure," Liam smiled as he looked at Robbie.

Izzy laughed, "You should see how excited Cynthia is to move from the camper into our place to look after the dogs and everything else. Hopefully, by the time we come back they'll have most of their cabin done."

Robbie frowned suddenly, "I'll miss Tabby. I guess she couldn't come, too, hey?"

Liam shook his head, "We'll be gone a couple of months. That's too long for her to be away from her mom. We'll send her postcards and get her some presents."

Robbie kicked the toe of his shoe against the deck, "I used to want to search for the Loch Ness monster but I don't want to do that now."

Izzy pulled the boy close and hugged him, "That's fine." She stepped back so she could tip his chin up towards her. Robbie's face was filled with a seriousness that brought a lump to her throat. She blinked back quick tears and glanced at Liam. In his eyes, so like his brother's, she saw the type of love he offered her and for a moment it was as if she truly had the power he had invested in the fairy tale Queen. She looked into his heart and knew he was healed.

She shivered as she felt a familiar presence. It was a feeling that had come back to her over the years – the knowledge that she stood shoulder-to-shoulder with Caleb and they faced the same direction. She was now convinced he would always be beside her. She would know he was close whenever she admired the home he built or walked in the garden they had brought to life. It would be fine to move on with her life. It was what Caleb would want.

Sophie began to cry and Izzy's attention was caught by the flood of emotion that such a plaintive sound could evoke in her. A smile tugged at the corners of Lisa-Marie's mouth as she rose to lift the baby from the stroller, stroked the child's dark curls and murmured words of reassurance. The bond between mother and child that had been strengthened over the past summer would continue to grow.

Izzy understood, finally, what Robbie had known from the start. What held her to this group gathered on the deck was the reality of family. Far into the future, this man and these young people would fill her days and wrench her emotions to and fro with their messy, often inconvenient, sometimes hilarious and always overwhelmingly important needs. She leaned close to Liam as he dropped his arm around her shoulder. Izzy was sure of one thing – she was setting out on a fascinating journey and she intended to give as much as she got.

⚜⚜⚜⚜

That night Robbie dreamed about running through the dense brush beside the other cat, the one that had beaten his cougar to the deer months earlier. The strength and size of the animal took his breath away. This was the type of cat the Elder had spoken of – a strong hunter, an animal spirit guide to be respected for its physical strength and power. The Elder had given Robbie a cougar claw which he had hidden deep in his pocket and about which he had said nothing to anyone else. It was special, only for him and it would help him to protect those he loved.

He chased down the night beside the cougar as it cleared fallen logs and padded along a stretch of deserted logging road. Robbie was far from anything he recognized, except the long length of Crater Lake far beneath him. He found himself suddenly alone near a hollowed out crevice under a fallen log. He crouched down and peered inside. Deep within the den, a female cougar nursed two furry shapes.

He understood now that to have a cougar as his animal guide was not to be tied to any one animal but to the spirit that moved within the big cats. Being guided by this spirit was his great gift and one for which he must have a healthy respect. He would always carry this combination of fear and wonder, knowledge and danger within him. He heard the Elder's voice explaining that those who are given access to special knowledge must pay the price. Even at such a young age, Robbie already knew what that meant. He would have to learn how to honour his gift without being overwhelmed by it.

In the early hours, in the first moment of waking, he remembered every detail of the dream but then he dozed off and it faded away.

ACKNOWLEDGMENTS

Many thanks to the following:

As always, my husband, Bruce – for support, technical advice and yet another brilliant cover design. It is no easy feat to live with a writer and I admire your tenacity.

Kids and grandkids – your pride in having an author in the family warms my heart.

Friends, both near and far – your accolades are very much appreciated.

Louise – as we complete our fourth collaboration, I have an even finer understanding of what your talented editorial eyes and ears bring to my work.

Hermit-priest and well-known ecologist, Father Charles Brandt – I am humbled by your generosity in sharing your archive of stunning cougar photos. Ask and you shall receive was never more true.

I send sincere thanks from *The Far Side* to my wildlife consultant over at *The Perch*.

Paula Wild's book, *The Cougar: Beautiful, Wild and Dangerous* was an invaluable resource in helping me come to respect and understand these wonderful animals.

Richard Watson who gifted me a copy of *Treed Beyond the River* by Karl Granlund. This author's work gave me a felt sense of what hoofing it through the bush terrain of northern Vancouver Island would be like.

For my local community – the store owners who take a chance on selling my books and those who buy, read and come back for more. This type of support makes worthwhile the long and sometimes lonely process of producing a novel.

ABOUT THE AUTHOR

Francis Guenette has spent all of her life on the west coast of British Columbia. She lives with her husband and finds inspiration for writing in the beauty and drama of their off-grid, lakeshore cabin and garden. She has a graduate degree in Counselling Psychology and has worked as an educator, trauma counsellor and researcher. *Chasing Down the Night* is her third novel in the Crater Lake Series. Her most recent work is the stand-alone novel, Maelstrom. Francis blogs at http://disappearinginplainsight.com. Please stop by and say hello.

ABOUT THE AUTHOR

Francis Guenette has spent all of her life on the west coast of British Columbia. She lives with her husband and finds inspiration for writing in the beauty and drama of their off-grid, lakeshore cabin and garden. She has a graduate degree in Counselling Psychology and has worked as an educator, trauma counsellor and researcher. *Chasing Down the Night* is her third novel in the Crater Lake Series. Her most recent work is the stand-alone novel, Maelstrom. Francis blogs at http://disappearinginplainsight.com. Please stop by and say hello.

DISAPPEARING IN PLAIN SIGHT
First book in the Crater Lake Series

Sixteen-year-old Lisa-Marie has been packed off to spend the summer with her aunt on the isolated shores of Crater Lake. She is drawn to Izzy Montgomery, a gifted trauma counsellor who is struggling through personal and professional challenges. Lisa-Marie also befriends Liam Collins, a man who goes quietly about his life trying to deal with his own secrets and guilt. The arrival of a summer renter for Izzy's guest cabin is the catalyst for change amongst Crater Lake's tight knit community. People are forced to grapple with the realities of grief and desire to discover that there are no easy choices – only shades of grey.

WHAT THE REVIEWERS HAVE TO SAY ABOUT DISAPPEARING IN PLAIN SIGHT:

I devoured this story, felt attached to the characters, and was sorry when it was over.

I couldn't put this down!! I was drawn into the lives of the complex characters.

Disappearing in Plain Sight is a stellar accomplishment for Francis Guenette.

I found it a touching read, at times bringing tears to my eyes.

A story of real life problems and the often unforeseen consequences of the choices we make.

Written with tenderness, you will find yourself feeling personally involved and wanting to delve deeper and deeper.

Disappearing in Plain Sight is one of the best novels I have read in years: the writing is beautiful; the characters are believable and all are people I would love to have a chance to know; the plot is complex and compelling and kept me turning pages well beyond when I should have been asleep on more than one night. I certainly will be looking for more work by this author

I highly recommend this to everyone, especially for those who can use a little bit of healing and compassion

This was a thought-provoking book and healing. I also enjoyed the writer's celebration of the beauty of people, nature, friendships and so much more. I read it in three sittings as I didn't want to leave the setting or characters for long.

The beautiful prose made me yearn for the rugged west coast of Vancouver Island, BC, Canada.

THE LIGHT NEVER LIES
Second Book in the Crater Lake Series

As circumstances spiral out of control, Lisa-Marie is desperate to return to Crater Lake. The young girl's resolve is strengthened when she learns that Justin Roberts is headed there for a summer job at the local sawmill. Her sudden appearance causes turmoil. The mere sight of Lisa-Marie upsets the relationship Liam Collins has with trauma counsellor, Izzy Montgomery. All he wants to do is love Izzy, putter in the garden and mind the chickens. Bethany struggles with her own issues as Beulah hits a brick wall in her efforts to keep the organic bakery and her own life running smoothly. A native elder and a young boy who possesses a rare gift show up seeking family. A mystery writer arrives to rent the guest cabin and a former client returns looking for Izzy's help. Life is never dull for those who live on the secluded shores of Crater Lake. Set against the backdrop of Northern Vancouver Island, *The Light Never Lies* is a story of heartbreaking need and desperate measures. People grapple with the loss of cherished ideals to discover that love comes through the unique family ties they create as they go.

WHAT THE REVIEWERS HAVE TO SAY ABOUT THE LIGHT NEVER LIES:

Holy patoly, what a read!

Guenette is a craftswoman who lets her work see the light of day only when she is sure it is as good as she can make it. Another five stars and I'm pleased that there's a further work in the Crater Lake series in the pipeline.

Far from falling into the pitfall of a second installment not being as good as the first, this book is marvelous and emotional, well-crafted and populated with characters that could be friends, family or neighbors.

What an amazing read, I couldn't put it down. I laughed out loud. I cried. The author does an amazing job of bringing the reader into the story.

Having recently read and very much enjoyed Francis Guenette's debut novel, "Disappearing in Plain Sight", and having been sad to leave the feisty characters behind, I was delighted to discover that the author had a sequel up her sleeve, though I was a little nervous as to whether it could match the first book. I needn't have worried – it was every bit as good, broadening the cast of characters to include all ages and stages of life, from the newborn to the dying. A satisfying, moving and memorable book which, like its predecessor, I'll be recommending far and wide.

Guenette tests the limits of her characters personalities, none of whom are saints. Kudos, that her characters behave realistically, both the adults and the teens. This is a worthy book and a great series thus far. I am looking forward to book three.

The writing is wonderful, particularly in terms of settling the reader into the landscape of Crater Lake and the secluded area of Northern Vancouver Island, Canada. Guenette also has a talent with characterisation, storytelling ability and complex relationship conflicts which are the real backbone of this novel.

MAELSTROM

A shot is fired into the still night air and a young woman dies on Suicide Ridge. A dangerous game has begun. Over the course of one blistering, hot week, winds of change sweep through an isolated valley in small town America.

Sheriff Bert Calder, with the help of Mayor Amos Thatcher, has held the town of Haddon under his thumb for twenty-five years. As things spin out of control, Calder works the angles, ensuring he can make the most of the upheaval that is to come.

Rafael Destino, facing his own mortality, races against time to gain control of the railroad – a lifeline essential to the town's survival. His goal – to financially destroy Thatcher, the man he believes responsible for the death of his beloved sister. His tool – adopted son Myhetta. But how far down the road of revenge will Rafael push the young man who owes him everything?

Myhetta is poised on the edge of controlling Destino Enterprises, the job he has been groomed for. While money, power and influence are his to command, the past continues to torment him.

In a clash of powerful men, with fathers pitted against sons, no one will be left unscathed. *Maelstrom* is a page turner that speeds along like a runaway train.

WHAT REVIEWERS HAVE TO SAY ABOUT MAELSTROM

A wonderfully diverse cast of characters make this story memorable. Good and bad, they are all well-portrayed and realistic.

This is one of those novels that sucks you into the whirlwind of events from page one onward! I literally could not put this book down. The characters got into my head!

With Maelstrom, Francis Guenette has created a thrilling suspense story with local flair. I was drawn into the story immediately and thankfully invisibly! It is up to the reader who to trust and who to fear; don't be afraid of changing your take on things along the way! A thrilling suspense with twists seemingly too real for comfort.

The title of this thriller is appropriate on several levels. The plot is a maelstrom of conflicts. The characters are embroiled in a maelstrom of emotions. The events could be described as nothing else besides a maelstrom.

If you are looking for a book that will take your breath away and leave you on the edge of your seat, look no further! Maelstrom will propel you into a vortex filled with hate and prejudices where the only way out is to find trust and love within your own family.

Recommended for the reader who prefers a study of how it is to be human in an isolated township and an arid setting. This is hard lives, hard survival, in an 'unforgiving' landscape.

www.ingramcontent.com/pod-product-compliance
Lightning Source LLC
Chambersburg PA
CBHW022210010726
47493CB00002B/500